He had made her cry. Cold tears flooded her eyes and ran cold down her cheeks. Susan was crying openly now, and Harry knew it. . . .

He held her head against his shoulder and stroked her hair. "Are you going to be all right?"

"Sure, if you hold me," she said softly.

He pulled her to her feet and put his arms around her again. But some of the urgency had left his embrace. "Susie, I get the feeling we oughta delay this . . . collision a little while . . ."

"Why?"

"I feel like I'm taking advantage of your memories, Miss Susie. Haunted folks getting together, searching for the past. . . ."

"You've given me absolution, Harry. I'm clean as a whistle—and I need you. Here . . . now . . . shameless in the high-noon blaze of the moon."

He'd never been able to resist giving her what she wanted. Not then. Not now. . . .

Barney Leason

Richer Than Sin

BANTAM BOOKS
NEW YORK · TORONTO · LONDON · SYDNEY · AUCKLAND

RICHER THAN SIN
A Bantam Book / January 1991

ISBN 0-553-28940-3

Published simultaneously in the United States and Canada

*Bantam Books are published by Bantam Books, a division of Bantam Doubleday
Dell Publishing Group, Inc. Its trademark, consisting of the words "Bantam
Books" and the portrayal of a rooster, is Registered in U.S. Patent and Trademark
Office and in other countries. Marca Registrada. Bantam Books, 666 Fifth Avenue,
New York, New York 10103.*

PRINTED IN THE UNITED STATES OF AMERICA

RAD   0 9 8 7 6 5 4 3 2 1

For Maurice Harwick

1

"How about you marryin' me?"

"That's a bit sudden," Susan Channing said.

Jasper Gates laughed abruptly. His smooth, soft voice indicated more challenge than genuine proposal. August Hugo Blick had warned her, had he not, that Gates was not a man to be lightly dismissed. Never turn your back on such a man as Jasper Gates, AHB had said.

Gates eyed her unrelentingly, with little tolerance in his expression. Susan would have hated the assignment of plumbing the depths of his feeling about women. But, she thought, he was too cunning, too intelligent, to allow himself to be written off as a mere male chauvinist. The fault might be there, true, but it would be deeply buried.

"I know you're bound hand and foot to Augie Blick."

"No, not at all. Mr. Blick is merely a great and good friend—August and his wife too: Mignon."

"You were married to his son... once upon a time."

"That's true, and even though Roger and I split, my good relationship with the elder Blicks has never faltered."

1

Gates stared benignly and even less than before could Susan read his expressionless face. Jasper Gates was supposedly the epitome of a heartless capitalist, the arrogant corporate raider—and more: a man who took his women for granted, if he gave them even that much. Okay, too many people had attested to Gates's sharp edges for Susan to deny them. But at the same time, people must agree that his appearance, his outward look, the flag under which he sailed, was extremely deceptive. Gates was a short man—you realized that when he stood up—and, again, it had been August Blick who had expounded on the Napoleonic characteristics of men of abbreviated stature. In so many words, never trust a short man—how many times had Susan heard that one? The fascinating thing about Jasper Gates was that his physical brevity absolutely complemented the choirboy innocence of his face, though the latter was obviously older, more worldly than that of the usual boy soprano. Still, there was something, call it a saving gracefulness, about him, only now and then riven by crudeness or vulgarity of expression. And Jasper Gates took no care to hide his social shortcomings, in speech pattern or height.

As far as Susan was concerned, that was in his favor.

August Blick had asked pointedly that she be nice to Jasper. Not so very difficult, she thought, if she kept her distance. And he his.

Jasper did not pursue the matter of her close alliance to AHB, as he might have. Rather, as if embarrassed by the thought, he averted his hard blue eyes, at the same time gesturing grandly, his hand encompassing the sitting room, her suite, the entire complex of the Big Sea Spa Hotel and the acres and acres of great outdoors which lay beyond the panoramic windows: the intensely black night, wet meadow, precipitous cliff and the whole wide Pacific Ocean.

"So, what do you think of all this, sweetie?"

Susan accepted the caress of the plush, velvet-covered sofa, relaxing a little as Jasper perched alertly on the very edge of a smooth glove-leather easy chair. He picked up an outsized glass of bourbon and water and absently drank from it.

"What do I think of it? I don't think I've ever been in a more luxurious place—hotel, spa, French chateau . . . you name it. Anywhere . . ."

"I hope," he rasped, "that August H. Blick is going to be

pleased with the investment . . . though he's never completely happy about anything to do with his money.''

''He couldn't be otherwise. Big Sea is one of a kind. I doubt there's anything like it on the whole Pacific Coast. Including . . .''

Jasper leaned forward, intently.

''Including?''

Susan drew a breath, feeling pressured.

''Including places like La Costa . . . the Golden Door . . .''

''We *are* the Golden Door . . . north!''

''I've been there, Jasper. This is something different, special.''

''Hey, hey! That's what I like to hear!''

''Of course, being in the north of California, it's colder and rainier.''

''Two hundred and fifty thousand a room, Sue, that's what it cost us.''

''So much?''

He grinned explosively, white teeth popping in his tanned face.

''You think Carrara marble grows on trees? What about the fixtures in your bathroom—you have been in your bathroom, haven't you?'' he asked slyly, suggestively. ''The fixtures are gold-plated! There's a Jacuzzi in every tub, bidets, double sinks. Very European—did you notice?''

''The tub is as big as a swimming pool . . .''

''You *have* been in the tub? Big enough for an orgy, they say. Everything has got to be larger than life, that's our policy at *SunSpots*. . . .''

SunSpots was the Jasper Gates International cruise line and hotel chain, called simply Jasper International.

What could she say, should she say? Was she very impressed? Moderately.

''Every room has its own golf cart, Sue, how 'bout that?''

''I've been to places where the golf carts are chauffeured, Jasper.''

He grinned more broadly and winked.

''Kidding . . . I know you've been around, don't worry.''

Susan shrugged. For all he could really know, it might be true.

''Yes, I spend as much time roaming the world as I do in New York City. Too much time on the road, if the truth be told.''

Jasper winked again, skeptically.

"Come on, Sue, you love it. You love traveling around just as much as I do."

"Not necessarily."

"No, no," Jasper Gates cried, great affection warming his voice, "you like the same things I do, I know it. That's why..."

He stopped, pulled back, dropped his chin.

"*Why?*"

She should not have insisted.

"Why I wanted to see you, privately," Jasper muttered, uneasily. "To ask you—"

"Which you did," she reminded him.

"Yes...yes, but not all of it. To ask you, can we be close, involved?"

"What you're asking is..." She stopped, suddenly embarrassed herself. "Jasper, you don't know me...at all!"

"Oh, for crissakes! What the hell does that matter?" He frowned ferociously. "I'm saying we're alike, Sue, and I haven't even touched on the rest of it—the tennis club, racquetball courts, the beautiful golf course, stables, the spa layout. What do you think of the spa, Sue?" he demanded, not giving her a chance to answer, as excited as if this were the first piece of real estate he'd ever developed. "The restaurant...bar...the conference rooms." Jasper ticked off the amenities. "Did Augie give you *any* idea how much we've sunk into this place, Sue? Did you take note of the bridge we built across that tidal area to the island? Did Augie recite you a price tag, Sue?"

"Only vaguely." Susan replied cautiously, for August would surely not be happy if she reported his words too freely. "He mentioned something like fifty million dollars..."

Laughing derisively, Jasper exclaimed, "If a penny, Sue, if a penny. So...?" He clapped his hands smartly. "So, we've got to charge at least two hundred fifty a night, that's the economics of the hotel business. Not peanuts."

"Not exorbitant either."

"Right! A drop in the bucket for the rich Europeans!"

"A captive audience at that."

"Right again! No place within miles for them to go out for a meal...that Wild West hotel in Petertown and coupla more joints farther up the coast. We could jack up the price to five hundred per person per day...."

"Still a bargain." Susan studied Gates carefully. "It'd cost them double that in Southern France or Sardinia."

"Yeah, yeah." He nodded violently. "And on top of that we fly 'em right in to our own airstrip or limo 'em from San Francisco Airport. Once they're here, they got everything the human heart could desire—except maybe hookers."

"I'm not sure the ambiance lends itself—"

"Have I forgotten anything?"

"Not that I can think of."

"Aha! There *is* another thing! We're going to do a line of beauty products with a Big Sea label. What about that?"

"What about it?"

"You've been in every capital city in your job. You've been to all the best places, true?"

Susan nodded. But just because she was personally acquainted with luxury didn't mean she was necessarily qualified to pass judgment on bidets and Carrara marble.

"You've met the best people and interviewed practically everybody, Sue."

She shrugged, wanting to say "So what?"

"Now, Jasper, don't go overboard."

He chuckled hoarsely: too many late nights, too much bourbon. The choirboy face was beginning to sag.

"I've seen all your programs, sweetie. You're a personality, Sue. Famous. A media star... You were in *People* magazine."

"No big deal, Jasper. You could be too, any time you wanted, if you weren't so reclusive."

"Though I can't stand that partner of yours!"

"Jack Godfrey."

Men tended not to like Jack Godfrey or to include him in the flattery which, despite her disclaimers, Susan did not tire of hearing. True to form, Jasper immediately detected he had pleased her and he smiled.

"Not to get the idea that Big Sea amounts to all that much. It's a pimple, a blip on the corporate graph, a little fish in the vast aquarium of Jasper International. You understand that, don't you?" he said, thrusting with a heavy blade. "I don't want to get into total worth, Sue. Shit! I don't even know what my total worth is! If you can count it up, you're not worth much, that's what I say!"

In a way that should have flattened his ego, Susan said,

"August Blick always tells people that if you *can* count it, that just proves you haven't gotten there yet."

Jasper grimaced.

"Sayings of Chairman August? What's he mean by *there*?"

"The point of vast wealth."

"For once, Augie is right," Jasper acknowledged sourly. "You absolutely cannot count it up. The amount changes constantly, everyday, every hour! One minute, a billion-nine and the next two billion-three . . . or even three billion, depending on . . ." His voice rose and fell, monotonously, as if he were not much interested in the subject either.

"Such a problem . . . I've always felt so sorry for men like you and August Blick."

"As well you should, Sue." Unblinkingly, deliberately, he ignored the sarcasm. "We *do* have problems which dwarf those of other mortals . . . for instance, but on a small scale, right *here*. Management of a place like this, Sue, is a bitch. What did you think of the food tonight?"

"Good, I thought." Food had never been important to her either and Susan failed to understand why people always got off on new restaurants. "This is still the shakedown cruise."

"Trouble is," Jasper complained, "in such a godforsaken place it's hard to find good help. A bunch of reformed dopeheads and out-of-work fishermen, not exactly the greatest possible labor pool."

"You seem to have a very good manager—"

"Teller?" He didn't sound convinced. "I dunno. He's a little new at the hotel trade. I know he's a damn good golfer . . . or was anyway."

"Nice guy."

It seemed the kind thing to say, particularly as she'd known another Teller, a Teller named Harry. But Jasper nodded indifferently. Ralph Teller was not what interested him at the moment.

"We got together a good party, wouldn't you say, Sue?"

Yes, they had. With a plane from New York full of what the gossip columnists called movers and shakers—rich, well-placed jet-setters, and/or freeloaders who would talk the place up—another out of southern California carrying midrange movie magnates and the usual available social butterflies, a half-dozen limoloads of San Francisco's leading lights, the grand opening of Big Sea could, Susan supposed, be termed a success, at least in that the party had gone off without a hitch and all two hundred and whatever rooms were occupied over the weekend. Of course, there was no money in it—everything was free. It had to be if you wanted this crowd to show up. But Susan was not about to spoil Jasper's evening by saying so.

"I think," he continued, with great satisfaction, "it was a good idea to bring Skippy Bache and his band in from Chicago. It cost a pile..." He winked at her yet another time, cockily, "...but Skippy is Numero Uno for dancing, or so I'm told. I saw you dancing, Sue."

"Jasper, I would've danced with you if you'd asked me." And she meant it.

"I was too busy glad-handing," he dodged, "but you looked...what can I say? Wonderful. I was watching you at all times. That's why I asked if I could join you here in your suite—gorgeous, isn't it? I mean all the detail-work and accoutrements. A little nightcap, so we could talk. I want to get to know you and I didn't get a chance during the party, it being noisy and you chatting the whole night with von Drasal."

"*Your* German friend...*my* table partner."

"Well," he objected good-humoredly, "you didn't have to spend the whole night with him."

Susan smiled back, for the first time, feeling comfortable with Jasper Gates, that she had some control over the situation.

"I didn't spend the whole night with him, Jasper—just part of the evening."

"Sure, sure! I know."

He rubbed his smooth face, his unblemished babyish face, and looked at his empty glass. Did he expect she'd invite him to help himself again from the bourbon bottle which, together with just about every other known kind of booze, had been laid on in the suite before her arrival? Susan glanced at her watch, not surreptitiously either. It was two A.M., certainly time for a little choirboy to be in bed, and not with Susan Channing.

But Jasper was not particularly interested in another drink or in what time it was. Sighing deeply, he sank back in the leather chair and pulled at his black tie.

"Sweetie, mind if I take this goddamn thing off?"

"Go ahead."

"Formal is not a comfy kind of uniform," he complained, stripping his neck and then whirling the piece of black silk on his forefinger, "although you would not know that by the way Chairman August dresses."

"Chairman August wears a bow tie all day long..."

"And probably with his nightshirt," he agreed jovially.

The surprising thing, Susan might have reported in different circumstances, was that Jasper Gates's black bow tie was self-made, whereas one might have guessed he'd wear a tie with a permanent knot or maybe, judging by what August had said about him, one of the clip-on variety.

"You can go slip into something more comfortable... *comfy*... yourself, if you want, Sue."

"No. I'm fine, thank you, very comfy, just as is."

"Good, good."

Jasper's calculating smile warmed to a pleasant grin and, for a moment, he sat quite still, watching her so intently she'd have been embarrassed if she was any less of a woman. No, she was not close to getting to the bottom of Jasper Gates. He was full of surprises.

"I like your getup very much, sweetie."

"I take no credit. I don't spend much time on clothes. It's Geoffrey Beene. I like his things. Scaasi too."

"You don't wear a lot of jewelry."

"No, I don't care much for jewelry."

"Little earrings."

"Diamond studs. And the bracelet." She held up her right arm; the silk paisley print fell back at the wrist. "This was my grandmother's, emerald and diamonds."

"Beautiful, Sue, beautiful," he said softly. "Tell me, where do you go in New York?"

"Lots of places. For dinner, you mean? Lunch? What about you, Jasper?"

"I don't have much fun, Sue. In and out of New York, y'know? Power breakfasts, they call 'em, at the Regency. Then I'm on my way again."

"Elaine's?"

"I know about it. Never been there. Would you take me?"

"Sure. Next time you're in New York. We'll go somewhere new for dinner, then to Elaine's."

"What about Mortimer's or Le Cirque?" he asked wistfully.

"We could go there, either place, both, whatever you'd like, Jasper," she said, feeling sorry for him.

"And your hair? Did you try *our* beauty parlor?"

"Miss Irene? I was there this afternoon. She's fine."

"Not New York though."

Should she tell him that she was very blasé about hairdressers? Even bored with them? Given the nature of Susan's business, she was constantly being brushed and combed out for the camera's eye. Once in a while, she went to Kenneth, just to put herself in hands she trusted.

"Be that as it may, however," Jasper went on, absently waggling his glass, "you know how much the whole weekend cost us, Sue? I'll tell you, if you promise not to spill the beans to Augie before I get a chance to."

"How much then?"

Not that Susan really cared to know. She'd rather get Jasper talking about his manager, Ralph Teller. The name rang bells. Could there be a connection between Ralph Teller and her old friend Harry? Friend? Well, whatever, Harry had come from this part of the country.

"Teller's wife is charming too," she said.

"I guess, yeah," he agreed, maybe just as pleased not to tell her about the money. "She's that all-American type, also a golfer. I think that's how she met him. *Muffy* . . . is that a name?"

"*Buffy*, not Muffy."

"They were both champion golfers. Then they apparently saw the light and went into hotel management. Cornell . . ."

"And here they are."

"Yep! And here *we* are, Sue." Jasper's eyes were scheming again. "How 'bout another drink? More champagne? I need another one of these."

He didn't wait for a yea or nay, merely scooted forward out of his chair and headed for the wet bar, another opulent feature of the Big Sea layout. Each room had its own wet bar, with refrigerator, sink, and stock of crystal.

"A little more champagne then," Susan sighed, thinking she'd never get rid of him now, "if you're having another."

When she'd just casually mentioned at the table that Dom Ruinart was her favorite champagne, Jasper had had three bottles sent up. So . . . might as well have another, she thought, see where it led her.

Piling fresh ice in his glass, he glanced at her over his shoulder.

"We had two ex-ambassadors, a former governor, and a couple of ex–cabinet officers . . ."

"I can tell you the governor came in handy, Jasper," Susan

purred. "The very man I'm due to interview in San Francisco next week—"

"That's the way I planned it, sweetie," Jasper said with satisfaction. "Never let it be said that Jasper Gates . . . You're gonna talk to him about comparative oil-spills, and thank God I'm out of *that* business, elsewise you'd be pursuing me and we wouldn't want that, would we?" He sloshed bourbon in his glass, then darted back for an instant to grab her champagne glass. "And don't forget about Bunky Harrigan. But he had to come. He owes me money." Jasper grimaced. "Too bad Augie refused the invite. Awkward, since he's one of the owners."

"AHB hardly ever travels. Just once a year, to Wade's Reef . . ."

Jasper made a face. "Yeah! His private island in the Caribbean! You'd think he'd be ashamed. That's what you call him, is it, AHB? Well, call me J.G. or Gatesie, whatever you want, but not late for din-din!" Jasper choked on a chuckle turned cough. "I didn't really expect to see John and Esme Randolph," he said, delivering her freshly rinsed and refilled glass. "Now, there's a pair of old-timers for you. I remember seeing their movies when I was just a little kid in Arkansas."

"I hate to disillusion you, Jasper, but those who know, say that Esme and John will go to the opening of envelopes."

"Sue, Jesus! That's an unkind thing to say."

Placing his glass on the coffee table, a cutdown antique rectory table, Jasper flopped beside Susan on the sofa, then jumped up again to slide out of his dinner jacket.

"Can't stand it! Goddamn uncomfortable, I don't care who tailors 'em, like wearing a piece of armor."

Hurling the coat at his empty chair, he came down again, all swiftness and ease in motion, too late for Susan to jump the other way.

"*Did* you enjoy my pal, Heinie von Drasal?" Once more he went on without giving her a chance to reply. "He liked you, sweetie."

"We just chitchatted about nothing in particular."

"Europeans love small talk," Jasper said, as if he really knew. "He thought you were beautiful . . . *are* beautiful." He held up his glass. "Mud in your eye, sweetie."

Sweetie? Again he was acting too familiar for the short

time they'd been acquainted. Jasper slid closer. Susan did her best to edge away, without being as obvious about it as he.

"Sue..." There was a cracked spot in the back of his throat. "I guess Augie—AHB—told you I'm a recent widower."

"Yes, he did."

Jasper's wife, the second or third, August Blick had not been sure which, had only recently passed away, perhaps not under totally happy circumstances either. According to AHB, none of Jasper's wives had lived very long, or blissfully. Of course, such comments often arose when a man of his reputation was involved.

"It's left me a very lonely man, Sue. I wasn't exactly whistling 'Dixie' when I made that remark about you marrying me."

Susan drew a steadying breath. So? A remark, not a serious proposal after all.

"Now, now, Jasper," she cautioned, "remember, the first time we set eyes on each other was yesterday afternoon."

"No, no, wrong, Sue! I've seen you on the tube thousands of times."

"And *that* doesn't really count."

"I know: that's what you tell all the lads, ain't it? But it *does* count. I feel like I've know you years, sweetie. Ten years... more! Twenty years... more than that!" Agitated, he put his glass to his mouth, grabbed ice in his lips, and chewed it noisily. "You're such a photogenic woman. Blondes like you are meant to be... but I swear you're even better in person! There's a *quality*, I don't know what it is, about your face... your body! Your beautiful blonde hair. You have perfect features."

Some people said too perfect. People who didn't like Susan Channing said her face was *boringly* exquisite, her eyes too blue, though one was gray and one was blue, that she looked like she hadn't a serious or intelligent thought in her head, though she did. And so on...

"It's a face," she said, shrugging, "and I hate to disillusion you, but if it weren't for contact lenses, I'd be wearing big, thick glasses."

"No! I don't believe it!"

Didn't it occur to Jasper Gates that he was that much older than she? Or would he say that by all appearances Susan liked older men... old men? Yes, of course she had to assume he'd

heard the nasty stories about her and August Hugo Blick. She
was sure he had. She could tell by the way he looked at her.

"Sue, I pull no punches," Jasper stated forthrightly. "You're
a desirable woman." Okay, she knew that; let's hear something new. "Christ, Sue, you're utterly beautiful!" He thumped
his glass back down on the table and said loudly, "I'm a
billionaire! I'm just as rich as Augie Blick."

Susan looked at him with deadly calm.

"Why would you tell me that? Why should you?"

"Are you insulted?"

"I don't doubt for a moment that you're a billionaire. And
so what?"

Jasper Gates laid his right hand on hers, a tiny right hand,
it seemed, against her wrist, but there was power in those
fingers.

"C'mon, Sue, for crissakes, you're not tied to Augie
Blick. He's old, Sue!"

Coolly, using her best acting technique, that which people
might say she'd inherited from her mother, well-known but
long-retired actress Margaret Channing, expert in How to Put
a Man Off, Susan murmured, "I'm not tied to any man,
Jasper, believe me."

"Blick talks like he owns you," he muttered angrily.
"'Sue Channing's a big network star and she belongs to
me.'"

Jasper's cheeks glowed with indignation and he'd begun to
perspire across his forehead. What had her father, Dr. Kenneth
Osborne, eminent practitioner of tropical medicine, always
warned? Never trust a man, especially a short man, who
breaks out in a sweat.

"I won't tell you what else he said."

But it didn't matter what August had or had not said. Could
Susan Channing-Osborne trust Jasper Gates's word? That was
the question. Or should she be more inclined to count on
August's lasting good will?

Jasper gently removed the champagne glass from Susan's
hand and set it on the table beside his bourbon. He squeezed
her hands in his, as if in the grip of an emotional spasm. The
small but compact man was possessive like all billionaires
short or tall, Susan thought. But he should not forget that tall
slim, slightly stooped August Hugo Blick was possessive too.
Very much so.

"Don't think Augie put as much money into Big Sea as

he's making out, Sue. Augie likes to talk big but he's not big at all." Dark thoughts of bank drafts, money swaps, exchange ates carried him away for a moment, then Jasper said, "Von Drasal put in a good bit too."

"So?"

"Well, so, there's a total of one hundred and some million committed. Of course, we had to buy the whole goddamn ndian Island. About twenty-five hundred acres. Not a bad nvestment if you consider that whatever happens, the land vill be here."

"Jasper," Susan interrupted sharply, "you need *not* tell me all this."

Besides which, it was time for him to get his little ass out of her room.

Flushed, squirming with irritation, Jasper blurted, "Augie hould know, if you feel like telling him, that we may be in or trouble from the Indians."

"Indians?"

"Right! The fuckin' Indians," he said coarsely, underlining he words. "People are sayin' we didn't buy clear title to ndian Island. *Now* they tell us!"

He was right. August would be tremendously interested.

"But surely—"

"Surely, what, Sue? The aborigines always cause trouble, oon as they see a lot of money involved. Same thing happened to us in Brazil when we were developing the rain orest. Augie'll remember that."

Oh, for God's sake, of course, how could she have forgot-en? AHB had been in on that one too, the destruction of vhole rain forests, as if it didn't matter that the entire planet's veather system could be short-circuited. August never talked bout Brazil, among other things he didn't discuss.

"Our position," Jasper said, "is that we got Indian Island ree and clear from the Oporto family. Portuguese-Irish. They ought the island about a hundred years ago, from a bunch of ussians."

"Fur traders."

"Right! This was big Russian territory back then. Certain asket Indians claim the Russians originally stole the island rom them and that's supposedly when they got shoved into eir garden spot up there on the ridge. They've been bitching bout it ever since."

"Well," Susan said slowly, "I didn't realize there was such an *interesting* complication."

He got the message, right enough.

"Sue! Holy Christ! You wouldn't want to mention any of that on television!"

Susan smiled craftily, as always relishing her leverage. Jasper Gates was not dense—he must realize that she was honor bound, professionally bound, to consider *all* story possibilities. August had made it clear that he expected Susan to squeeze something about Big Sea into the Channing-Godfrey program *Hindsight*. Yes, somehow she would invent a segment to cover this new, luxury resort into which AHB had sunk so many millions. How she managed it, that was something else; that was her problem.

"It would be murder if you reported an Indian problem, Sue—it'd blow sky-high in Washington, that goddamn Bureau of Indian Affairs!"

"What were you counting on," she shot back, "some kind of a bland travel piece? They'd skin me alive."

Too true. Arthur Fineman, her producer—neurotic and suspicious—had been unenthusiastic about the trip from the beginning. Fineman said the country already had enough goddamn resorts and nobody gave a shit about a new one being opened out in California. But Susan had made him see the larger possibilities—the Jasper Gates connection.

"I'll want to interview you, Jasper," she said, giving him no out, "about Big Sea . . . your other endeavors . . . the cruise line, for instance. What about the huge ship you're building in . . . where is it?"

His eyes narrowed.

"In Bulgaria. But I'm *never* interviewed, you know that. I'm the mystery financier. An enigma, a black cat in a darkened room. Didn't Augie tell you about me?" Yes, but obviously not the whole story. "People don't even know what I look like."

"Not so. We've got plenty of pictures of you in the . . . files."

She'd been about to say morgue.

"Bull, you do!"

"Let me explain something to you, Jasper," Susan said very, very patiently. "AHB suggested I do something for Big Sea and I said I'd think about it. He is a friend, after all. And now?" She frowned. "Seems, as a matter of fact, there might be a legitimate piece abuilding."

Bitterly, he owned up, "I admit we had hoped—"

"I repeat: we don't do travelogues on *Hindsight*."

"So? I understand that," Jasper said with a pout. "Jesus, you can get off your hind legs, sweetie! I'm not asking you to piss on your integrity—"

"So to speak—"

Was she being too severe? No, Susan had learned very early to establish the ground rules right away. Otherwise, guys like Jasper Gates would . . . so to speak . . . piss all over her.

Grinning suggestively, Jasper muttered. "*Hindsight*—I like that name for a program. Like looking at somebody's . . . No, no! Never mind, I take it back! I'm just a country boy from down in Arkansas. What I mean to say is that it's nice for a change to have a news program that spends a little time on what's already happened . . . instead of predicting all over hell what's *going* to happen. Bunch of smartasses if you ask me, the pretty boys of the news world."

Susan had heard all this before.

"You people like it well enough when they say something nice about you."

"Speaking of which," he pressed on, "I wonder what Augie Blick had to say about me. Nothing *nice,* I'll wager. Just remember, I'm not as old as that old fart and he hates me for it."

"I doubt that very much, Jasper."

She had to try to be polite, didn't she? What else was she going to do, order him to leave? He owned the place.

"I'm telling you the God's honest truth, Sue," he pledged. "I'm fifty-nine and a half going on forty. . . . And I know Augie is—I'll pay you a million dollars for every year he's less than seventy-four."

Actually, he had it dead right. As Susan had understood at the time, deciphering Mignon's befuddled toast, August had turned seventy-four on his last birthday. And it should not surprise her that Jasper Gates had access to the fact. He'd probably taken out life insurance policies on his beloved partner.

"Sue," he suggested hopefully, "how 'bout loosening up? I'm a very loving kind of fella and I know you aren't anything like the cool cucumber you're impersonating right now."

She regarded him just as coolly as that same cucumber as he held out the champagne bottle. More to drink was the last thing she wanted and it was not going to loosen her up *that* *way*. Jasper put down the bottle and irritably tasted his bourbon.

"Kee-rist! Warm as . . ."

But he made no move to go for more ice. No, he sat stone-still, alert to her every move, the look in her eye, the stern manner in which she folded her hands in her lap . . . and waited. But really, did he think he could somehow intimidate her with all the rough talk and repeated insinuation that she liked older men? What if she did like older men? And young ones too? Though he couldn't know about that.

He was too nervous a man to sit so quietly for so long.

"You are one hell of a good-looking blonde lady, Susan," he said finally.

"Thank you."

He chuckled. "Imperial is the word that comes to mind."

"What you mean is icy."

"No. Imperial," he drawled, probing with suddenly brilliant blue eyes. "Imperial . . . *and sexy*. Imperially sexy."

Susan lifted her champagne flute. She could always throw it at him. After all, as she'd told herself before, she was not a schoolgirl or pathetic drudge out of the Jasper International secretarial pool to be charmed insensible by the likes of Jasper Gates.

"Now look, sir," she said, "doesn't that about do it? It's been a long day and I'm pretty tired. You must be too. Why don't we call it a day . . . or . . . night . . . or morning?" She glanced at her watch again, very openly. "It's going on three—"

"I speak nothing but the truth and the whole truth, darlin'." Jasper took her hand again and lifted it gallantly to kiss her fingertips. "Sue, tell me true—are you a real blonde?"

Susan sighed, more weary than surprised or shocked. She'd been asked that question before and had a ready answer.

"I refuse to answer on grounds of self-incrimination."

Such a reply worked once in a while, not always. Jasper gurgled with delight, his voice pitching toward a giggle.

"You're not being very nice," she murmured.

"Sorry, darlin'," he chuckled, "just a polite question."

"Harassment, Jasper."

"How can it be if you've got the upper hand?"

"Do I? *How*?"

"Because you know that I'll do anything you want in order to win your favor. Isn't that a fact, Sue?"

"Not especially."

Steadily, he asked, "Is it your wish to interview me?" When Susan nodded, he asked, "Why me? Why not Augie? You could do *him* blindfolded."

She paused for a split second. "AHB is no Jasper Gates."

"You said it! Finally!" Eyes watering, still gripping her hand, Jasper cried softly, "Darlin', do you know what I adore about your fingers? It's where they've—"

"Jasper Gates!" Susan tore her hand away. "I'm not putting up with any more of this."

"You want an interview, sweetie," he retorted, "you'll have to put up with it . . . and me. You know how it works, Sue."

"I don't play that kind of game!"

"Trade-off!"

Susan laughed distantly. She felt like patting the poor man's cheek: his naïveté was positively touching. Yes, Susan Channing had been around the block quite a few times. Despite all that, even the fact she'd been through a few wars and had lived with grubby men in the most intimate circumstances, and knew them as well as she knew herself, despite all that, she was touched by his innocence. The little man was trying to barter!

"My dear, I don't have to do that anymore," she said breezily. "Besides, if it's a story I want, I've already got it. You've told me about the Indians."

Jasper didn't take this very well. He dropped one hand on her shoulder and stared in a way that might be considered threatening. Susan stifled a laugh.

"Susan! I don't appreciate being teased!"

"Jasper," she said, "I assure you, I am not teasing."

His eyes changed color, seemed to glaze over, or even turn slightly mad. Then they dropped from her own impassive gaze to her throat where she was wearing a thin gold necklace, a gift from August Blick on her own most recent birthday, the thirty-eighth, one of the few gifts she'd ever received from him.

Next, Jasper's attention went to the silk blouse, with its green and gold pattern, low-cut, with full sleeves tapering to tight cuffs, and black silk evening pants. Very appropriate for

a casual evening party by the ocean in California, but which
now made her feel very vulnerable.

The costume had obviously pleased Jasper's associate, th
baron, and fascinated Gates as well, or so Susan assume
from the look on his face.

But Jasper was not thinking fashion. His manicured fore
finger plucked at the front scoop of her bodice. The eye
came up at her again, blindingly, lustfully blue.

"I'm from Missouri! Show me!"

Susan pushed the hand away. "You said you were from
Arkansas."

His reply to that challenge was to hook the same finger int
the V of her blouse, brush against her bare skin, invade he
cleavage.

Again, Susan removed the hand, holding it in the neutral
space between them.

"That's enough, Jasper. Taps. Beddy-byes..."

"Sweetie..."

Susan felt herself flush, and she was a little rattled. But sh
didn't fear him. He was not the ruffian he pretended to be
His face paled, miserably. There was something he wanted t
say, more than do, but he didn't know how. Susan smile
understandingly, encouragingly. Jasper was not a bad man
nothing like the brutish force of nature August Blick had le
her to expect.

"Sue, sweetie!" Jasper gulped and gasped for breath, lik
a grounded fish. "Isn't there anything I can do for you
When you go down to the city, I'll send a plane for you—"

"You're leaving, Jasper?"

"Worse luck," he groaned. "I've gotta leave earl
tomorrow...today...this A.M. Goddamnit! The worst luc
of all! But I gotta."

He looked positively stricken.

"But—"

"Yes, you're gonna see me again, sweetie! You shall hav
your interview! I can make you that promise!"

Susan laughed like a young girl. "You make me gasp."

"I'll send you one of my fleet. Say the word!"

"I wouldn't think of it. I have a car coming for m
anyway."

"Sue, you're my kind of woman! How 'bout marryin
me?"

"Jasper!" Her control faltered. "Isn't this where I came in?"

"Can I kiss you, sweetie, just once?"

"Well..." She hesitated. "All right, once. Then you've got to go. I'm exhausted." ·

"I promise."

Tentatively, worshipfully, he squirmed forward, placing his dry lips against her cheek. His eyes closed tightly and Susan heard a kind of vibration in his throat, like a hummingbird. Then, without warning, his head dropped. His mouth wet her bare chest, slavered into the cleavage and Susan felt his tongue on the downward curve of her breasts, his fingers striving to push her blouse out of the way. He had realized she wasn't wearing a bra and that, with one bold move—

It was no more, no less, than she should have expected.

"Sue, Sue, sweetie...how 'bout it?"

"I'm looking at my watch, Jasper," she said calmly, "and I see it's after three...."

"And nobody's here 'cept us chickens."

He spoke to her skin, his mouth hard on her collarbone.

"Jasper, I don't want you ripping my blouse, if you please."

"Sue...Sue..." Jasper suspected Susan was toying with him, for she didn't particularly object to the soft lips or the scent of his desire. But she was not going to bed with him. He knew it, and it drove him crazy. "I'll...I'm warning you, I'll rip it off!"

"No, you won't."

He wouldn't and he knew that too. She did have the upper hand.

"Sue, I'll buy you a new one. Just tell me how much it cost."

"Plenty, Jasper," Susan said patiently. "You'd be surprised how much."

2

Susan pulled the softer of her two pillows over her head and tried to go back to sleep.

But it was no use. She had never been able to resist morning. Fog? The previous day had been sunny, almost too warm. Now, a sticky mist licked right up to the windowsill, seemed to infiltrate the room.

Susan moved her left arm to eyeball her watch. Nine A.M. Sleep was gone. And so, it would seem, unless he had changed his plans, was Jasper Gates, en route to God knew where with his pal the baron. To be absolutely sure she hadn't made a big mistake, Susan poked one foot at the other side of the bed. No, nobody there.

But in the cold logic of morning there seemed no doubt she'd be seeing him again, whether she wanted to or not. Best not to think about it. Jasper Gates was gone now, and, later, thank God, most of the other corporate jets and charters would also fly away, leaving Susan Channing alone and unhustled. Nine A.M. Time for breakfast, time to face the new day. Whatever the weather, weekend or not, she would be hearing

from New York about next week's schedule of interviews—
Jasper had had it precisely right. She would be buried in the
business of coastal oil drilling, ecology concerns, the political
footballing; Susan had brought a thick folder of background info
to study so she'd sound like she actually knew what she was
talking about in San Francisco and Sacramento.

So it was stupid and time-wasting to stay in bed, as
pleasant as bed might be. Susan Channing had spent so much
of her life in hotel rooms, so many years getting up at all
hours that she had lost all physical memory of what it meant
to "sleep in." The only satisfaction now would be in knowing
she did not have to get up if she didn't want to.

Faintly, on the other side of the tight windows, a few
hundred yards down the wet green-brown meadow, the sea
thundered against the rocks.

The bed linen smelled perfumed—perhaps an expensive
soap or the Rigaud candles that burned in the room before
bedtime. Nasty thought: Given the money that had been spent
on the place, it was perhaps peculiar Big Sea did not reek of
dollar bills. Of AHB's money, to be precise.

There were plenty of places like Big Sea and *Hindsight*
received more invitations to events such as this one than they
knew what to do with—the fact was Susan probably wouldn't
be here at all if it were not for August Blick.

Seventy-four-year-old August Hugo Blick, her friend, had
indeed asked her on no account to miss the Big Sea opening,
to discover how "that little scoundrel Jasper Gates" had spent
his money. And, by the by, if at all convenient—August had
smiled—why not give the place a plug on *Hindsight*? What
would the god of ethics say? Susan had thought. Well, just
because August was her dear friend—Susan admitted to no
more—a story wasn't automatically ruled out. If nobody
outside of a very small circle of people knew of their
relationship, then it would be difficult to accuse her of conflict
of interest. As a matter of fact, neither Arthur Fineman nor
Jack Godfrey had ever hinted that her closeness to Blick
amounted to anything more compromising than a relationship
of sponsor to protégé, what with AHB's large minority stake
in North American Network. Big Daddy to them all. Certainly, nobody was going to mention *that*.

Susan rolled over on her back—her favorite position—to
stare bleakly at the bleached-wood ceiling. Beams! If one

thought in terms of northern California, what came to mind was wood fires, hot tubs, and *beams*.

Sending her on her merry way, August had complained bitterly about Jasper's profligate ways. Was Jasper Gates mad? What was so special about northern California that the Taj Mahal had to be recreated there? To what end, squandering money in the redwoods?

But why, if AHB was so suspicious and scornful of Jasper Gates, had he invested so much in the Big Sea development? Was money thicker than . . . what?

Why then, ever jealous, always possessive, had August been so concerned that Susan be *nice* to Gates? Wary herself, skeptical, she wondered what he'd had in mind. The explanation for AHB's absence was simple, undevious: his routine didn't allow for trips to California. Except for an annual midwinter expedition to the West Indies, August was bound to New York. Day-in, day-out, he rose early, breakfasted on the *Times* and *Wall Street Journal*, worked with his faithful secretary Emily Eliot the rest of the morning, and then, without fail, was driven to lunch by retired hood Sidney Wilmer, chauffeur, bodyguard, and confidant, always to the same restaurant: an obscure Italian joint on 3rd Avenue. And always ate the same food: grilled fish, three small boiled potatoes, green beans or spinach with a vinegar-oil dressing, and a glass of Moselle, not too cold.

Besides Emily Eliot and Sidney, August and Mignon Blick kept two maids, a cook, and their veteran butler, Konrad. Dinner was invariably, quietly, at home, on Park Avenue, featuring the same sort of training menu, leavened by a glass of Bordeaux for August and three or four Manhattans for Mignon.

Yes, unfortunately, Mignon did have a bit of a drinking problem.

If she happened to be in town. Susan often visited the Blicks in the late afternoon or early evening: she did live next door, for heaven's sake! But there was usually an excuse to say a quick good-bye, something else to do: cocktail parties, business dinners. The NAN network chief, Simon Hayford, was *always* giving parties and Susan was expected to be there, on her own or paired with one of the high and mighty; her availability was taken for granted. After all, she wasn't married, didn't have kids to put to bed. If she was really pressed, there was always catching-up at the office to be done, or something else for her to do from dinnertime until midnight. Susan did try to be in bed by midnight. Sometimes, sometimes not—she never knew in advance—August visited her for an hour or so. Not to disturb her. Susan was always half asleep; she could never had said when he came and went.

Yes, it was all very routine. August had tamed time and made himself a creature of splendid habit.

Now, Susan advised herself calmly, she would have to tell AHB that he had had his money's worth at Big Sea. And then, too, she would report that Jasper Gates was, *au contraire,* a very likable billionaire who promised to give as much as he took.

And she would get him to do so. He had agreed to an interview, and it would be his first ever. Susan began to jot down the names of all the people she'd recognized the night before, the kind of people Jasper Gates could pull together for an "event." You could read a man by his friends.

Jasper prided himself in his association with Baron von Drasal from Zurich—why, Susan wasn't quite sure. Heinie had seemed so stiff and stuck-up, surely. not Jasper's type. It was just as difficult to explain his association with August Blick. Then, out of New York, Irv Flannigan, collector of skyscrapers and wives; George Hilliger, court jeweler, Palm Beach; Flo Slingsby, one-time Wimbledon mixed-doubles champion, and husband; triple-chinned Senator Al St. Stefan, who'd gotten bombed long before the speeches and had had to cancel his own. And the governor, mustn't forget him . . .

Susan's own network competition had not been present. And Jasper had explained that he'd decided to leave out newspaper people. Nonetheless, the notorious gossip, Woodrow Malachy, had finagled entry by the simple device of acting as escort to aging Hollywood star Joanie Apple.

Who else? St. Stefan had been the biggest name from Washington—something to do with election-year caution. Was Jasper Gates somehow a bad smell in D.C.? Susan hadn't heard. If it meant anything to the contrary, she had spotted Dunning Nathan, foreign affairs and terrorist specialist. But he owed Jasper—reportedly for Jasper International's help in a recent Middle East hostage situation. Not surprisingly, Jasper had pulled in international banker Wallace Burner, very big in Third World finances; a particle physicist named J. Lansing Joralemaine from Princeton . . . Really, the people Gates knew!

Ironically, Susan had not seen a single guest whose presence could be credited to friendship or business dealings with August Hugo Blick.

Enjoying the thought of two more full days of... well, almost total relaxation, Susan recalled one chore: she had promised Arthur Fineman she'd try to get in touch with her old friend Jenny Driver, the actress, who lived part of the year somewhere within range of Big Sea. Maybe this afternoon, she thought. Not right now.

The folder marked Big Oil lay on the table by the window... also, not right now. Susan stretched her legs, pushing herself back against the headboard, pulling first the left, then right knee toward her chest; then again lay flat, tensed her buttocks, and hiked her pelvis. Good for the skiing muscles, an instructor had told her once.

The grayness, the wet window made her feel glum, even though it was a pleasure to be alone, left alone, lonely. On the bright side, she *did* have work to do; she didn't *have* to go for a walk; she should not feel guilty about *not* going down to the cliff to stare at the seals and be stared back at by creatures more curious about life than most human beings.

Jasper Gates had assured her that one of the seal family, perhaps the paterfamilias, looked exactly like Augie Blick: long upper lip, bushy eyebrows, and all. But don't tell Augie, he'd warned.

Why would she want to tell him? She *was* August's friend, after all. Jasper seemed to know that. He seemed to know all about her.

One might have been forgiven for asking how in the world Susan Channing had ever landed in such a spot. And why she hadn't extricated herself. *If* they were interested enough to ask, Susan would simply say she'd been married once upon a time to August's son Roger and she'd... well, just drifted into the thing. And, well... you know how it is: inertia can be just as sticky as the predicament itself.

How bittersweet and touching, this alliance of aged moneybags and young blonde TV personality... not so young as all that anymore either.

In pursuit of her career, Susan could have done better, and worse. She might regret it now, but there *had* been a time when Susan had not been above playing the game, as Jasper had suggested, sleeping with unique subject matter, if it seemed the inescapably intelligent and unavoidable thing to do. She was a journalist of the old school, she would have argued, no holds barred: *that broad will do anything, well almost anything, to get a story.*

Susan became aware of noise at the door. She jumped out of bed, grateful to be shaken loose of herself.

"Yes, what is it?"

The response was an unintelligible mutter. Surely not Jasper Gates, back from the airport. No, it was young and male.

"I'm here to do your fire!"

Fire? Susan remembered the fireplace. Along with the beamed ceiling and hot tub went the fireplace. As a matter of fact, it had still been faintly glowing when Jasper had finally left.

"Just a sec."

Susan returned to the bedroom and slipped a red silk robe over her nakedness; tying it at the waist, she headed back to the door. Yes, he *was* young and male . . . and embarrassed. Tall and skinny and red in the face.

He said, "I got fresh wood, Miss Channing, and I've got to haul your ashes . . . I don't want to disturb . . ."

"Come on in."

Susan stepped to the side and he slid past her, swivel-hipped, carrying a pail with a top for the ashes, she assumed.

"I won't take a minute, don't want to disturb you on Sunday morning." His voice was reedy and young and, no, he was not disturbing her, not at all. Susan Channing's got nothing to do, young feller, but sit here and watch your moves. "Not a very nice day," he mumbled, not looking at her, dropping to his knees in front of the fireplace.

"The weather *is* very changeable, isn't it?" she said.

"Yes, it really is! Bear says this is what they call a sea climate."

Susan placed herself primly in Jasper's leather chair by the window, holding the slippery robe closely to her chest and legs.

"You live around here?"

Come on, laddy, loosen up.

"I live ashore."

By that, he must mean the mainland, on the other side of Jasper's ten-million-dollar Indian Island Bridge. He pivoted on one heel, pointing at the pocket of his gray work shirt where a name was embroidered in crimson thread.

"I'm Ted."

"*Ted* . . . what?"

"Ted Jay," he said, then dared to add, "I know you're Susan Channing from the TV program." He smiled eagerly, then turned quickly to the pail and shovel, like a little kid at the beach scooping up powdery ash. "Bear told told me to watch for you. He saw you last night at the party."

"Bear?"

"Oh . . . my dad."

The lad was of some local importance then, if his father had been invited to the grand opening of Big Sea.

"Well, I'm flattered! Did he enjoy the party? I don't think I met any Mister Jay—"

"*Doctor* Jay."

"The local doctor? No, for sure I didn't meet him."

"He's a psychiatrist. A social psychologist. He works in social anthropology . . . and archaeology."

"Well! What, may I ask is a psychiatrist doing here . . . at Big Sea?"

"Not Big Sea, Miss Channing. We live in Petertown," Ted said. "But he's done work over here. You know . . . did they tell you they found an old burial ground when they were digging at the stables?"

Susan shook her head. Oh yes, Jasper, there was a story here after all.

"No, they didn't tell me that, Ted. What sort of burial ground? Not Indian, by any chance?"

"Bear thinks so, but they're not absolutely sure . . . bones, old pots, buttons, pieces of rotting leather. . . ."

"Fascinating."

Ted grinned and nodded and would have said aw shucks, if she'd let him. He was a dear young kid, freckled face, tousled hair, and all, plus, of course, the young behind, presented in such a way that Susan was sorely tempted to pinch—but didn't dare.

"What's your father's name?"

"Bertram. But his nickname is Bear. That's from college. He played football and people said he was built like a bear."

"Really!"

She watched as he swept the fireplace clean, then swept it again, stalling for more time with her. Susan could practically hear his brain ticking over, searching his skull for something else to say. She could help him: there were questions, about Jenny, about Ralph Teller. . . .

"Ted, do you know a woman named Jenny Driver married to a man named Dick Lyons? They've got a ranch around here."

He spun again and cried out enthusiastically, "Jenny? Sure!

She and Mr. Lyons live in Rancho Mondo up on the ridge. Bear is a good friend of theirs. And Jenny is at our house a lot. . . . My mother's dead," he added quickly.

"Oh, I'm sorry!"

"That's okay." Confused, maybe because tears had come to his eyes, Ted covered his pail and jumped up. Then, surprisingly, he faced her again to announce, "Bear is absolutely crazy about Jenny Driver. I think he's in love with her."

"What?"

"Yeah. Who wouldn't be? he says. Trouble is, she's married to Mr. Lyons."

"When you say *in love*, what you mean is, like, they're very good friends, am I right?"

"Well, they are good friends, yes." That seemed to do it. "I'll go get the wood now."

He left the door open and Susan didn't get up to close it, not trusting herself to move. When Ted Jay came back, he was carrying kindling and split wood. Crouching again, he piled the kindling on a crush of newspaper, moving so agilely that it made her weak in the knees just watching.

"You want me to light it now, Miss Channing?"

"Call me Susan . . . please. No, not now." She smiled. "Can you come back later?" Well, it was an attempt, though halfhearted, to communicate. "Ted, Jenny's an old friend of mine."

He looked at her and waited.

Susan tried again, "You remind me very much of . . . somebody. How old are you, Ted?"

"Just eighteen."

"I suppose you're going off to college." He nodded warily. "The boy I'm thinking of is your age," Susan continued. "Are you going to study science, like your father?"

"I wish I knew."

"The boy I'm thinking of . . ."

"Your brother?" he asked politely.

"Sort of. He's going to study English. The amazing thing is, he's already written his first novel and it's going to be published."

This did not seem to amaze Ted at all—or interest him very much either.

"What's it about?"

"I'm not sure. About going to high school in Beverly Hills, I think." Susan had been told a title, something absolutely awful which she'd put out of her mind. "His name is Scott Blake."

"I'll watch for it," he said politely.

Suddenly, shatteringly, Susan realized Ted Jay, with his unruly, devilish grin, did not remind her of Scott Blake, but of somebody else entirely.

Nate Carleton.

Nate Carleton, photographer, who had never ceased advising people to seize the moment. Don't wait! There might never be another chance . . . *or a tomorrow*! And then, in fact, there wasn't any tomorrow for Nate. Susan remembered him as if he'd left the room five minutes before, and somehow returned as Ted Jay. Her thoughts jumped back in time, to when they'd made love so terminally, as if Nate had already known about the land mine that would stop him for good.

For a second, Susan nearly lost control. She wanted this young man between her legs, wanted to be taken, seized like the moment. Entrapped, entwined . . .

Maybe Ted felt something too for, very quietly, with a flat fatalism of tone which went beyond his years, he said, "Got to continue on my rounds . . . Susan."

"Your appointed rounds." Her voice was stretched to a whisper. "Okay. Thanks. Will I see you again?"

"I'll come back just before I leave . . . if the weather stays like this."

He shuffled toward the door, as if he could hear the silent weeping, and waved awkwardly.

"So long then."

"So long, Ted."

She had not seized the moment and Nate Carleton would know that, wherever he was. Outside, Ted was whistling. He sounded happy; he'd already forgotten her. Why not? What about *her* was so memorable? Susan sat for a while longer, staring at the closed door. Really, what could a small-town kid know? In particular, what would he know about Jenny Driver and her passions? Was it in character for Jenny to fall for a man named, of all things, "Bear" Jay, a backwoods psychiatrist? Well, Jenny had fallen for Dick Lyons, no man of the mainstream either. Whatever weirdness Jenny committed would be in character: she was unpredictable, headstrong, and, at her worse, self-indulgent.

Jenny's marriage to Richard Lyons had been stormy from the beginning. Dick Lyons was not an easy man in any sense:

as friend, as lover, as consumer advocate. More people hated Lyons than liked him. Dick Lyons: consumerist, peacenik, troubleshooter, troublemaker, whatever his enemies happened to be calling him that week. He boasted to distraction how many times he'd been arrested, in how many states, cities, on how many campuses, at how many different demonstrations, in aid of how many different causes.

When Susan and Jenny had first met, several thousand years ago, Susan had just dumped or was about to dump her first and thus-far only husband, Roger Blake, who during his own rebellious years had taken the liberty of changing his name from Blick, thus antagonizing his father, changing his residence from the East to the Coast, his theory being that if you can make it in New York as a Blick, then L.A. should be a piece of cake as a Blake.

The little somebody Ted Jay had reminded her of was none other than her former stepson, Scott Blake, Roger's boy from a marriage even earlier than theirs. It was true Scott had written a gruesome novel about teenage sex and drugs between bouts of algebra. More awful than that, he was being paid for it . . . and, devastatingly, going on the interview circuit. The media pump was being primed by hot talk of a new generation of teenage novelists, the mere mention of which was enough to give a person heartburn. On a more personal level, sooner or later, Scott was going to be on one of the national shows and they were going to twist his arm and force him to acknowledge his former stepmother, thus shooting down any claims Susan might have to eternal youth.

Scott had been a precocious child, and a brief exchange with his editor, a Ms. Mandrake, had dashed all hope he had changed. On first read of Scott Blake's novel, Ms. Mandrake had confided, she'd just naturally concluded it was the work of a ruined fifty-year-old.

But never mind about the book or its author. Critical was the fact the publisher intended to exploit Scott's family connection. This boy was Susan Channing's ex-stepson, son of Hollywood producer Roger Blake, and grandson of the aging titan August Hugo Blick! Yes, the same man, once known to the movie-going public as matinee idol Hugo August!

It had been years since anybody had even mentioned the Golden Profile. Most people thought Hugo August was dead. Which, in a way, he was.

Therefore, how infuriated August was going to be, how

awful would be his vengeance when his tycoon cover was blown.

Roused by the thought, Susan strolled into the luxuriously appointed bath and, laughing to herself, prepared once more to face the day. Yes, the water knobs were gold-plated, if indeed that was not some clever alloy. Water gushed, real water; Susan was in the act of slipping out of her robe and into the shower when she heard the door again.

Groaning, not forgetting the robe, she went back outside. It was Ted Jay. He was more nervous than before, his Adam's apple working frantically.

"I'm sorry, Miss . . . *Susan*."

"Well, that's okay." She spread the door, so he could step inside, so she could close it behind him. "I was just getting ready for a bath."

It was as if she'd ambushed his imagination. The image tied him in knots. He cracked his knuckles loudly enough to scare people in the next room. He was such a boy, so ungainly, so tongue-tied, that Susan wanted to put her arms around him.

"I . . . *Susan*, I'm sorry I said that about Bear and Miss Driver. Please, just forget it . . . huh?"

"Consider it forgotten."

"It came to me you might use something like that in one of your programs."

Susan smiled. "Everybody is so afraid I'm going to quote them. Don't worry. I wouldn't do that, Ted."

Which, strictly speaking, wasn't true, but he looked relieved.

"*Susan* . . . if you're going up to Jenny's, I can drive you this afternoon. I'm done here at two. I'd be happy. I can borrow Bear's car or the pickup."

"Oh, no, Ted, not necessary, really. I've been promised a car anytime I need one."

He looked so disappointed she almost took it back.

"No problem," he pressed earnestly, "and you'd have more fun with me!"

"Oh, I'm *sure* of that." Susan smiled. "But better not—I don't know exactly when I'll be going . . . *if* I go at all. I don't even know whether Jenny and Dick are here."

"They're here! See, I forgot to tell you. That's how Bear found out you'd be at the party. From Jenny. Ralph's brother, Harry Teller—"

"Ah! I meant to ask you about the Tellers."

"Harry Teller is also a good friend of the Lyons's, so he told Jenny that he'd heard from Ralph that you—"

"I get the picture, Ted." Curiouser and curiouser. "You're really plugged in, aren't you?" she flattered him. "So, Harry's also a good friend of Jenny's, is he?" No surprise, she told herself. Harry had been noted for it in the old days. "I wonder why he didn't come to the party."

Ted looked at her blankly, not knowing the answer, but surely it wouldn't have been because Harry didn't want to see her.

"You knew him in Vietnam."

"Yes," she said with a nod, "when we were both very young. I was a young girl TV reporter and he worked for the U.P."

"Now he's the editor of the paper."

"He left New York, I didn't know for where." Susan regarded Ted absently. "I'll have to check him out. You're a dear for remembering to tell me."

Susan put her hands on his shoulders and rose on her tiptoes to kiss his smooth, flaming face, right cheek, then left cheek. He was tall and it wasn't easy to reach him, especially as his body jerked back. She had frightened him, she knew, as he felt her breasts against him and dared to glance down, as he did, into the shady glade running into the top of the robe.

"Thanks again, Ted." Steeling herself, Susan stepped away, leaving him quivering, his body suddenly too big for the tight jeans. She had to get him out of there. "You're a love."

Susan practically pushed him outside, slammed the door, and caught her breath. What kind of a place was this indeed? It must have something to do with the sea air: Big Sea air!

Ted Jay had obviously never heard that older women were charged with the initiation of eighteen-year-olds.

If only it were so!

Finally in the shower, humming to herself happily—was it because of having unearthed Harry Teller?—Susan thrust her face into the spray, not caring that she was getting her hair wet.

She considered the disillusioning proposition that Harry was playing around with Jenny Driver. Would he be so anxious, in that case, to see Susan Channing again? She caught herself envying Jenny. *Was* Jenny involved with Harry? Or with Ted's Dad? Or both? Susan tried to remember, had Jenny ever been known to be a great swinger? And what had happened between her and Lyons?

Never mind about Jenny though. She, Susan Channing, was fine. The young Jay-bird had ogled her with reverence, had he not? There was no reason for Susan to feel distressed or worried about seeing Harry again. No, let Harry do the worrying.

Susan stepped out of the shower and grabbed for the huge, fluffy bath towel, printed, so nobody could miss it, with the legend BIG SEA SPA.

She did know what she wanted. She knew, very precisely.

Susan wanted somebody to be standing there holding the towel for her.

The label said *Made in the USA*. Except that she hadn't been made in recent days within the territorial limits of the USA. Or anywhere else.

You could only make do with what you had.

Dutifully, Susan muscled her hair, then did two minutes with her toothbrush. Next, eye inspection: bright blue, bluer than Jasper Gates's baby-blues. Robin's-egg blue, somebody had told her—not Nate Carleton, because he'd never been generous with compliments. Lines? A few visible webs around her eyes. That's what happened to you after age thirty when you had paper-thin, aristocratic, blonde skin.

Susan rinsed her contacts and popped them in place. Now she could see her face a bit more clearly and wondered about a bit of discreet nipping and tucking. Perhaps a peel, Miss Channing? Like hell! Forget it! No lifts of any kind for her. She might be a bit of a phony, which would surprise no one, knowing her business. But Susan knew where to stop, where to draw the line, thanks to the realists she had known, starting with her father, then Nate, and guys like Jack Godfrey and Fineman. She was slim, like a filly, said Jack Godfrey. Thank God, not yet a mare.

Lunch, Miss Channing-Osborne?

It was inevitable. No sooner had Susan taken a seat by the window, prepared to celebrate with a bloody Mary, than Ralph Teller appeared. There wasn't the smallest doubt he was Harry's brother. He had the same tall, loping grace, the same physical self-confidence—more of it, in fact, as befit a professional athlete. Ralph was laid-back, a lot more than Harry.

"I was just going to ask you about him," Susan said, skipping the preliminaries.

"He said you'd remember him."

"Remember him? Of course I remember him—we did hard time together. *Where is Harry Teller?*"

"In Rio Tinto." He paused. "Rio Tinto is the capital city... town... hamlet of Hispaniola County. Harry's got the weekly paper. Actually, it belongs to the family. My father started it up in the twenties."

"And *that's* why Harry left New York."

Smiling easily, Ralph murmured, "But you're alone. If you'd care to join us... my wife and I are with some people."

"Oh, no, please. I'm fine. I've got the Sunday paper to read... then a lot of work to do."

"I'm to tell you, Harry's going to be here later this afternoon. He said to say, if you're not doing anything..."

"I'm not. Wonderful! I can't *wait* to see him!"

Really? Was she so sure it'd be so wonderful? She wouldn't know until she actually saw him.

"Miss Channing... Susan... I... um..." Susan should have been prepared. "Jasper Gates got out so early this morning I didn't get to see him. I hope he was... uh... satisfied with the way everything went."

"He seemed to be having a good time the last time I looked at him."

Meaning exactly what it was meant to mean, that she had been at Jasper's table and that was that. If anybody said any different, that was his problem.

"I hope so." Ralph shook his head, reminding Susan that Jasper hadn't been wildly enthusiastic about the Teller team. "Still..." He grinned, a little recklessly, like Harry. "Wouldn't want it to be easy, would we?"

"I don't know about Jasper Gates," Susan reassured him, "but I'm sold on this place. I had a *very* good time at the party, and didn't everything go off well?"

He studied her briefly.

"Buffy says she just read something about you, in some magazine. You were talking about interviewing the President, or somebody."

"*Vogue*," Susan said. "Something about career women."

"Right. That's it." He laughed easily. "But tell me, now, really—is everything okay? Room all right? Service?"

"Ralph, Ralph—"

"Gotta keep the customers happy, Susan. What are you up to today? I mean after brunch. Golf? Tennis . . . I can arrange a partner if—"

"No, no, just blessed *nothing* and wait for Harry. I don't favor physical exertion."

"Listen then," Ralph suggested, "the most relaxing thing ever—take a turn at the spa. Have a massage. Our head masseur, his name is Mister Max, believe it or not, and he's terrific. I'll arrange it."

"I *could* go for that."

Susan sipped her drink, looked at the paper, and thought more about Harry Teller. *Was* it good fortune or bad to meet again? If she'd had the power, would she have willed Harry back into the shadows? She thought not. There was unfinished business between them, a tangle of past misunderstanding, the memory of which made Susan stare long and hard at the black ocean. Would the sun ever break through?

The trouble with Harry was that he had never liked her very much in Saigon, or later, when they'd bumped into each other from time to time in New York. That was because of Nate Carleton, who else? If Harry was determined not to like her, he especially would not like her if he blamed her for what had happened to Nate.

Everybody had loved Nate. Not only Susan Channing.

And so, therefore, it was imperative for her to take the waters that afternoon, as much to clear her mind in preparation for Harry as for her health.

Later, stroking lazily beyond where the indoor pool joined the great outdoors, she kept to herself at the far end where troubled sky and pool melded with the downward slope of meadow, facing the southwestern quadrant of the Pacific. Indian Island lay like a dislodged cork across the marshy Ross Lagoon, at the mouth of the Tinto River, so named for the red mud carried in great quantities out to the sea during the heaviest rainy seasons.

Chin resting on hands on the side of the pool, Susan kicked lazily behind her and watched the bombastic clouds, hanging over the roiling sea like big green-black bruises. The Pacific looked hard as steel. Mister Max said everybody was mad at the weatherman. But Susan didn't mind. What the hell, she said, if you wanted continual, infernal sunshine, then go to southern California.

Or Wade's Reef, to escape the worst of the beastly New York winter. For the past few years, though Susan didn't admit it to anybody, she'd been allowed two weeks in February at the Reef—in the company of August and Mignon, though transportation of Mignon these days was a logistical nightmare, what with private nurses and major medical equipment. One wondered whether Mignon was aware of the change in venue from Park Avenue to the Blick seaside palace, one hundred yards of sparkling white stucco, a quarter-mile of terraces, billowing yards of mosquito netting, overhanging balconies, all groaning with tropical greenery, such lush decor and marbled baths as to make even the Romans— and Jasper Gates, if he but knew—drool with envy. It was said old Captain Morgan, famed pirate, had also wintered there; gorgeous irony if one agreed with some critics that August Blick was a swashbuckling capitalist buccaneer, Morgan's twin from another age.

People sometimes asked how Ms. Channing managed to escape for so long in the middle of *Hindsight*'s busy winter season. One reason was that she worked hard just so she and Jack, come February, could take a breather. The other, never mentioned, was that the president and CEO of NAN, Simon Hayford, saw no reason why Susan Channing should not recharge the old batteries in the company of her dearest friends, the charming August Blicks. August, of course, being the major minor-shareholder in NAN, and a quiet but effective supporter of Hayford's causes on the NAN board of directors.

Would she have traded time in the Caribbean for two weeks of February in Big Sea? That was a question. But it didn't have an answer. The resorts were so utterly different, one sybaritic, a lotus-land of warm winds, waving palms, and luxury which far outdid Big Sea. The other a beautiful but harsh place of heath and bluff and gale, even in the middle of the summer.

Mister Max would *not* be staying, he'd confided, he'd only agreed for the opening weeks; the weather was just too tough.

He was good, as advertised by Ralph, as good as anybody at Susan's health club in New York—though perhaps less expert than the trainer August included in his February entourage. All in all, it was a wonder a body survived such treatment . . . not only survived but thrived. Mister Max pushed Susan out of herself, back where she didn't ever want to be again.

Things had been so confused during those last days in the shell-shocked city. There were a number of stories, all conflicting, about what had finally happened to the indestructible Nate Carleton. Susan had been such a child then, too ready to obey when Roger Blake, sitting safely in Hong Kong, had ordered her out. What if she *had* stayed behind with Nate? Harry Teller had, for another few days, until they'd plucked the last of them off the embassy roof. But Nate had stayed on, even after that.

The thing was that Nate, though indestructible, had fallen in love with Miss Susie. And she with him? Did it seem so in retrospect? Yes, yes, of course she had been in love with Nate.

The trouble was she had gone back to Hong Kong. Blake, at the time, had been her boss, not yet her husband. What the hell had she been doing in Saigon in the first place? Nate had raged. What the hell kind of dumb crap was it sending a young girl into a situation like this? Only later had Susan found out how it had happened and by then, naturally, it had been too late to tell Nate. Roger Blake, ever the showman, had decided having Miss Susie in Saigon at a time when all hell was coming loose would be great promotion for his TV station in L.A.—just recently bought for him by his rich father (and nobody was supposed to know this) August H. Blick.

Nate had known everything about the world of death and violence—people said he sought it out, that many photographers were like that. It had to do with visual sense—partly that and partly death wish—but Susan hadn't really learned about it until years later, in the Middle East, Central America, dark places in Africa.

One way or another, Nate wouldn't have survived to enjoy old age. If it hadn't come to him in Saigon, then it would have in one of a dozen other places since then and none of it would have had anything to do with Susan Channing . . . Miss Susie.

Susan's problem, she realized, was that she still remembered Nate Carleton too well. She had gone to a psychiatrist once, nobody knew about it, and they had agreed her memory of Nate had grown out of all sensible proportion. They agreed it was time to put Nate to sleep. But Nate refused to go to sleep. Even as Mister Max pummeled her, his hands reminded her of Nate and *his hands*. His touch, alas, remained with her, lived with her still.

And now Harry, again.

Later, finally, wanting to postpone it, but on the other hand so eager to see him she could hardly stand it, Susan stepped into the Big Sea Inn lobby. The room was as big as a barn, dramatically lofted, huge stone fireplace blazing fire, even in June. Harry was dead ahead, his back to her, chatting with a young woman behind the front desk whom he'd obviously brought to the verge of meltdown.

Susan had a chance to look him over before he turned. He had not changed, she saw that. He was still a skinny kid, though no longer twenty-five. His hair was trimmed short, and it was gray-tipped now. From this distance and angle, she could not see the gray eyes, dark eyebrows, and eyelashes, but she knew they'd be the same too. He was leaning nonchalantly against the desk, one hand buried in the pocket of baggy corduroys, his tweed jacket pulled up at the shoulder. Harry still looked like a college boy—or at least a freshman English instructor.

Susan might have asked Ralph: Had Harry gotten married yet? Of course he hadn't. She'd have heard, somehow. Though it was about time he did, before some irate husband shot him dead. That was Susan's last coherent thought before he turned and, realizing she'd been watching him, grinned broadly with his eyes and teeth, dimples popping in his smoothly shaven cheeks.

Forgetting the girl, the chick, the child he'd been talking to, he sauntered toward Susan, nodding approvingly.

He was happy to see her! Amazing.

"Miss Susie!"

3

"Is it five years, Harry?"

"Fifty. Five hundred!"

He stood back, holding her hands, staring at her face, into her eyes, without apology, intensely curious, and Susan smiled cautiously, thinking it might not be so bad after all. This *was* Harry, the same old Harry, she reminded herself. He looked the same, talked the same. She kissed him, first on the cheek, then fleetingly, briskly, on the mouth. Real kisses were on the mouth. She'd forgotten about the soft, full lips.

"And you've got a country newspaper, Harry. Is it something you *always wanted?*"

She sounded too bright, too brittle. And this was obviously not the right question.

"Not particularly, Miss Susie."

"What's it called, Harry? Ralph didn't say, except..."

She was rigid, about to break, terrified she'd put him off. Suddenly, she was not so sure of her ground. This was a new Harry Teller; nobody was going to be the same after a five-year break. All sorts of bad things could've happened to him in the meantime. Or good. Don't forget about Jenny Driver.

"*The Corsair*. My father named it. Not my bright idea."

"I like it, Harry! It's original."

"The old man thought it worked." He grunted. "Suggests pirates. Or homage to the Spanish adventurers . . . and an independent *crusading* spirit."

"So you're . . . satisfied . . ." She didn't ask about happy; she wouldn't ever. "I mean, living way out here?"

"Miss Susie, anything's better than New York and working . . . *who* did I work for? I've put it out of my mind."

"Harry!" Susan risked a nervous laugh. "You worked for a great weekly news magazine."

"So I did." He grinned. "What about you, Suze? I know your show is going great." He hesitated. "Married yet . . . again?"

"No. You?"

"Nope."

Susan chuckled uncomfortably. "Well . . . that seems to take care of the preliminaries, Harry."

Laughing brusquely, ill at ease, despite the fact he was Harry Teller and knew it, he dropped her hands and took her arm.

"We're going up to my brother's, Miss Susie. That okay with you?"

"Fine with me, Harry."

Susan was acutely conscious of his touch as he guided her outside.

"Are you going to be warm enough? It gets a little cold here at night, even in the summer."

"It's warmer now than it was this afternoon, Harry."

"Storm clouds all gone, Susie."

"Sun's out again."

And she was dressed for the weather, hadn't he noticed? Susan had been unusually careful choosing this outfit, her Ralph Lauren stuff—pastel-green shirt and over that a big cable-stitch sweater, tailored tan slacks, and a silky green Hermès scarf, subtle against her brushed blonde hair.

"I keep a sheepskin coat in the back of the car."

Jasper Gates, somehow, had failed to mention the marvel of underground parking across from the Inn. The earth had been excavated, replaced atop the garage and replanted. From the air, nobody could have spotted it: in case of war, a perfect place to hide fighter planes or a battery of missiles.

"The Coastal Commission made 'em do it," Harry commented. "Protect the environment. Actually, a damn good idea. Nothing uglier than a parking lot. The country has been turned into one big parking lot as it is."

"Amen," Susan agreed solemnly, reminded of her oil spill assignments. "This must've set Big Sea Development Company back another ten million or so. Jasper Gates explained to me at great length how all their budget items came in ten-million-dollar denominations . . . the bridge, the spa, I forget what else."

"Ah," he said, with a turn of his lip, "the redoubtable Jasper Gates. Do you know him well?"

"Met him the first time this weekend. Do you?"

"Don't know him personally, been watching him the last couple of years." Harry shrugged. "Ralph thinks a lot of him, that's about all I can tell you. He runs an honest operation. The locals haven't found much to scream about . . . and, believe me," he added unkindly, "if there *was* something, they'd scream bloody murder."

"He seems nice enough, for a tycoon."

"Ralph has the idea you're one of Gates's oldest, closest friends."

'Not so, Harry."

"He's brought a lot of money into the area and that's important, though a lot of the locals might not want to admit it."

Harry found his car—there was no way he could've missed it—a low-slung red Mustang of indeterminate years. The matter of Jasper Gates was forgotten as he grandly opened the passenger door for her.

"Hop in, Miss Susie . . ." Harry circled the car and slipped behind the wheel. "You asked if I was married. Yes—to this beauty. Fasten seat belt, please, and prepare for take off."

With a not very modest roar, the engine came to life and Harry yelled something about eight big ones, meaning cylinders obviously.

"I suppose you have a name for the little darling."

"Naturally," he exclaimed, smirking, "Miss Thunder—"

"I know, Harry: Miss Thunderpussy, am I right?"

"Susie, you haven't forgotten!"

"Bite your tongue, Harry!"

Smoothly exiting the half-acre cavern, Harry throttled down the machine to glide past the inn. Inside was beloved anonymity, *whereas* Miss Susie had rashly consented to expose herself to crushing reminders of the past. Well, it was her own doing.

"Harry, how come you didn't make the party last night?" Remembering Heinie von Drasal, she said, "I could've danced with you."

He shrugged, paying little attention, gearing the car up, increasing speed as they entered the long alley of youthful redwoods, carted in and planted at exorbitant cost per tree, according to Jasper Gates.

"Politics. We had somebody there, you probably didn't meet her: my trusty assistant, Ella Salmon." He pursed his lips. "I didn't think it'd be great of me to upstage my little brother."

"How would you have?"

"I dunno. I figured better we didn't give it any special treatment because of Ralph." He glanced at her swiftly. "You know what I'm saying, Miss Susie."

"Do I ever, Harry." She hummed fondly. "The publisher's burden. You're *responsible* now, Harry."

He turned and laughed, and reached out, touching her arm.

"Yeah, Miss Susie, for the first time in my life."

She put her hand on his for just that split second. With a whir of tires, the Mustang hit the metal grid of bridge. Harry commented wryly, "The Jasper Gates Memorial Causeway . . . so named?"

"I have no doubt."

"Did you *like* Gates, Miss Susie?"

Coolly, Susan said, "No reason to like or dislike him, Harry."

"Never know with you, will we?"

"Meaning?"

"You were always noncommittal, Miss Susie." Harry shook his head, not wanting her to take offense. "Very careful, even when you were such a kid."

"Well . . ." She didn't try to argue, whether it was true or not. "Harry, was it you who first called me Miss Susie? I've been trying to remember."

He didn't want to answer. Then he did, reluctantly.

"No, it was Nate." She could barely hear him over the

motor. "Nate said he'd seen some blonde tootsie from California with a teenage camera crew."

"They were not teenaged and neither was I."

"Close enough."

"You guys were so much older? You're only four years older than I am, Harry."

"Three," he corrected her. "But in those days the difference between eighteen and twenty and twenty-two or -three was a lifetime, great lumps of precious years."

"Yes . . . yes, that's true, Harry."

He nodded and didn't say anything for a moment.

"Well, Miss Susie, we got to Nate fast enough. I think about him, you know."

"It'd be disappointing if you didn't, Harry."

He focused on the road, not that the driving had become difficult. The Mustang proceeded easily enough, across the marshy tidal area and off the bridge now to the stop sign at Route One.

"Susie," Harry finally said, laboriously, "you finally understand, don't you, that Nate always did absolutely what he wanted to do."

"I know that," she murmured.

"He would *not* come with us that last day, Susie."

"I know that, Harry . . . but, why?"

"Susie . . . I don't know, except that he was determined to stay. He said the story was just starting, not ending. Then, of course—" he paused, "it did end. I'm sorry for saying it that way, Miss Susie."

"Listen, Harry," she lied, but bravely, "I got over it. Years ago."

For all she knew, he didn't believe her, not that it mattered.

"Still, he did *end* a lot better than some of the others I can think of."

"What do you mean?"

Her tone was harsh and she was thinking, Christ, they were already in forbidden territory, a place angels should avoid like plague. As usual, as it had always been, Nate Carleton intervened. You might think Harry had loved Nate as much as she had. And maybe he had and suffered guilt too. Maybe Harry realized, far too late, that he should've tied Nate up and shanghaied him out of the dying city and brought him to Hong Kong, to Miss Susie who would never have gone home with Roger Blake, would've done everything in her life so much differently.

"Other photographers . . . doing fashion layouts and PR portfolios, for crissakes! I know of a guy who finally killed himself in Paris because some stupid French fascist called him a Jew."

Susan clasped her arms, shuddering.

"Not nice, Harry."

"No, and let's forget it."

"Harry, I didn't bring it up!"

Surprisingly, he reached across, put his hand on her arm and squeezed. A new Harry? He was saying sorry. All right then. She would do her best too.

The front windows of the Ralph and Buffy Teller house faced toward the ocean, but to the south of the sunset. Nevertheless, Buffy had to close one set of blinds as the sun, with a sizzling terminal splash, died again in the horizon. Days were long this time of the year, approaching the summer equinox, but by nine P.M. the coast washed into twilight, dusk, then toward darkness. Dinner finished, they were relaxing at the rustic table over the last of the wine. The natives would be bored by the spectacular view. Not Susan. It was better than anything over the Mediterranean; certainly finer than day's end off August's island in the Caribbean. As if a couple of feet beyond her fingertips, the northward thrust of Indian Island, the hazy slough of Ross Lagoon, disappeared into darkness, lingeringly backlit by the final purple glow of horizon, the phosphorescence of breaking waves, long swells, Ralph pointed out, coming to them courtesy of Japan and Korea.

"Like everything else," Harry murmured laconically.

This new Harry was definitely not the Teller Susan had first known in the Far East: heavy-duty correspondent, combative, competitive, and then in New York, unhappy, so frustrated by the office politics of journalism. His present tone had a broad brushstroke of resignation, a more philosophical acceptance of things as they were.

Coming home, Susan thought critically, had done a job on Harry.

Slyly, Ralph had just asked if Harry's afternoon had been successful. Harry muttered *very* and, though it was none of her business, Susan was annoyed. Ralph was uncleverly talking around her and Buffy, then trying to cover some sort of insinuation by going on about this *particularly fine zinfandel*. And was Susan aware that there had to be six hundred or more different California wines by now, most of them originating in the north?

"You could've fooled me."

Was she too sharp? Maybe. But Ralph was no Harry. Susan had always had difficulty with the athletic type. Harry or no Harry, Ralph didn't take to her New York tone. But Buffy chuckled. Susan approved of Buffy, despite her childish nickname. Buffy was tough-minded and her own woman. And efficient. She'd prepared dinner with the greatest of ease and minimum of commotion. And how did Buffy Teller do on the golf course? Susan would've bet she outplayed her husband.

They'd been chatting casually about Big Sea and perhaps it'd been Buffy who'd set Ralph off by outspokenly offering the opinion to Susan that Jasper Gates and company had worked Ralph's behind to a frazzle over the two years it had taken to transform Big Sea Inn, a sleepy little fishing hotel, into the two- and three-hundred-dollar-per-night health resort.

"I've had a ball," Ralph declared for the record.

"Buffy's right," Harry nailed him. "They've taken advantage of you, buster. And now comes the hard part: promoting this dump! You're going to have to draw plenty of rich tourists . . . because you're sure as hell not going to get any locals in that Westward Ho! bar for three-dollar bottles of Mexican beer."

Eye on Susan, Ralph laughed nonchalantly. Sure, sure, but what the hell, the locals lived here. Nobody expected them to be checking in. Harry was also right that it had been a monster job: materials and trucking and labor problems and negotiations with the California Coastal Commission, as sticky a government body as any in the country.

"I can tell you, Susan," he said, "it's been a real battle royal. When it developed that we had to rebuild that bridge, I thought it was all over."

That reminded her of something else.

"And what about the Indians? I'm told you've stumbled on an old burial ground."

"Oh, Christ!"

Harry laughed joyously.

"You see. Didn't I tell you? You're not going to be able to keep it a secret, buster. Susan's too good a reporter."

"Too good?" she challenged him. "There's no such thing."

"We are *not* talking about the Indians," Ralph muttered.

"Hey, listen," she said, "Gates himself told me there might be a problem with the Indians."

"He did?" Ralph blinked with annoyance. "I was told we're downplaying it."

"Ralph," Harry repeated impatiently, "you know there're no secrets around here." He turned to Susan. "The Baskets are worried as hell about disturbing their ancestors' bones. It's even touchier because a hundred and twenty or thirty years ago there was a massacre on that spot. A unit of the U.S. Cavalry shot up an Indian camp nice and early one morning. Many dead." He nodded. "Yeah, that's about the sum and substance of it, right, Ralphie?"

"It's a minor thing, Harry," Ralph insisted. "I don't mean the massacre, Jesus! I mean the burial spot—we made a detour. It won't interfere with the project."

But she was not going to let him off the hook.

"I didn't know about that part of it. But Gates said there's another problem. Aren't the Indians claiming they were done out of the island?"

"*Did* he tell you that?" Ralph asked despairingly.

Harry laughed again, sharply.

"See? Gates tells *you* to shut up, then the first reporter who comes along, *he* spills the beans."

"He gets excited."

"Jesus, ever the company man!"

"Yeah . . . well, look," Ralph came back angrily, "if we get a problem, it's going to be because of your buddy Dick Lyons. Is that what you were doing up there this afternoon?"

Susan felt envy and despair tear at her gut. So it was true!

"*You* were at Jenny Driver's, Harry?"

"So?" Harry scowled. "I assure you I don't go up there to talk cowboys and Indians with Dick Lyons."

Ralph stared at him but didn't say it. Neither did Buffy, although her face tightened. Nor Susan, even if she'd have liked to.

"Harry. . ." Ralph tried hard to stay on the good side of his big brother. "You know damn well, we, Buffy and me, decided we were going to make a go of this. I'm trying . . ." He at last looked genuine. "Buffy got sick of playing golf for a living."

"True," Buffy confirmed halfheartedly.

"Ah! You two!" Harry softened. "Maniacs! You play every blasted day, don't try to kid us! Rain or shine."

"Not so," Ralph retorted. "Not a single game all weekend."

"I had to play a couple of rounds with Jasper's baron," Buffy admitted, with a sporting grin.

"The charming Heinie von Drasal," Susan said. "I hope he plays golf better than he dances."

"Heinie von Drasal?" Harry repeated.

Susan nodded. "Like I said, if you'd come to the party . . . You do dance, don't you?"

Think of it: if that was *all* she didn't know about him.

"Dance? Like a dream."

But Ralph wasn't allowing the subject to drop.

"There's no shortage of problems. I've been *trying* to say I admire the way Jasper deals with them. And"—he looked at Susan again, very sincerely—"*not* so you'll go tell him, Susan . . . I wouldn't want anybody to think I was trying to kiss his ass."

Buffy interjected, "Never let it be said that either of the Teller boys go around kissing people's asses, heaven forbid!"

"Yeah, don't even suggest it." But, for future reference, Susan took careful note of Ralph's loyalty. "We're thinking about doing a piece on Jasper International. I don't know if it'll come off, but Big Sea would have to be part of it."

"That'd be handy," Harry said.

"Harry . . . I know what you're thinking."

Then, of course, Ralph had to throw gasoline on the fire.

"And Blick? What about August Blick? He's got money in here too."

Susan groaned softly.

Harry blurted, "That prick Blake's old man!"

Ralph, naturally, could not know that his brother hated Roger Blake and that it was a long-standing hate.

"Blick . . . Blake?"

Frowning, aware of Buffy's inquisitiveness, Susan explained cryptically, "I was married to a man named Roger Blake whose father is August Hugo Blick. Roger changed his name. . . ." What else did Harry expect? "I've stayed friendly with his parents . . . that's all there is to it."

"Did you have—"

"No," Susan answered Buffy precipitously, "no children, thank God."

Harry made a noise in his wineglass. No surprise. Nobody

had ever forgiven Roger Blake—for what, Susan wasn't exactly sure. Maybe for having the gall to marry her. Any mention of Blake or Blick was still enough to give half the world indigestion.

"However it is," Ralph blundered on, "Blick has got big bucks in Big Sea. Jasper mentioned to me that you were a good friend of Mr. Blick."

"*And*," Harry said, "you were to take very good care of her—right?"

"Not exactly," Ralph muttered uncomfortably, finally realizing he had tweaked sensitive nerves.

At that moment, Susan remembered every single time she had most definitely *not* cared for Harry Teller. She knew without question what he was thinking: that she had never really broken the repulsive Blake tie.

"So," Harry pressed unforgivingly, "why didn't the Great Blick come out to view his West Coast investment for himself?"

"He hates California," Susan said defensively. "Don't forget he was in Hollywood in the thirties. He was an actor," she added, for Buffy's benefit.

"Third-rate," Harry said, "like Reagan."

"Nobody remembers," Susan persisted. "He went by the name Hugo August. He was a prewar import from the UFA studios in Germany. And all the money he made he invested in California real estate and oil, and after the war, it just rolled in."

"And now he's the tenth richest man in the country. . . and so what?"

Susan knew she couldn't win it but she had to try. Otherwise, Harry was gone again.

"*So,* out of that unlikely background, he's become one of the country's great risk-capitalists! And don't say so what again!"

"*So what!*"

"Harry! Goddammit! I invite you to think about all the *creeps* you've known in your short and miserable life!" Had she gone too far?

Susan thought Harry would surely write her off. For a second he glowered. But then, the new Harry Teller chuckled and grinned at her and, un-Harry-like, let it slide. And Susan realized something awful: she had become as hard-nosed as Harry used to be.

"Shut up, you guys," he said wistfully, "and stop picking on me. You too, Susie."

She wanted to cry, but only for a second.

"What about Jenny? Social call or what? Jenny Driver is *my* territory."

"*Your* territory? How come?"

"I interviewed her a long time ago, before you ever knew she existed."

"You're kidding! She's a resident of *my* county. And she's a terrific woman to boot. Can't blame me for stopping to say hello . . . to her *and* Dick." For Ralph, he added, "But no Basket Indian stuff, I promise." For a second, Harry laid his hand on Susan's and she felt his warmth and urgency. "Actually, Miss Susie, I was up at the ranch on very legitimate business: to find out if that nutty husband of hers was still alive."

"What do you mean? Harry? What's going on? Miserable—"

"Not going to get you anyplace, calling Harry names, Miss Susie," he teased, glancing at Ralph and Buffy. "Didn't I tell you she was tough?"

"I am not *tough*," Susan huffed. "Listen, we're thinking of updating the Driver-Lyons story, one Academy Award and ten lawsuits later. So, therefore, *Mister Editor*, I'd like to know what's happening."

"I'll tell you, *exactly and precisely*, Miss Susie," Harry said. "If Lyons didn't stage it himself, somebody took a shot at him yesterday afternoon."

"You're kidding!"

"Susie, please, *The Corsair* does not kid." Harry paused to swing his body away from the table and cross his legs. "Dick Lyons walked out of the barn carrying a pail—of horseshit, appropriately enough—and somebody shot a big hole in it. Question: Were they shooting at Lyons, the pail, the barn door, or what?"

"And?"

"And, Miss Susie, by the look of that pail, I'd say it was a hollow-nosed slug. Remember those?"

"Yes." She nodded. "So he was lucky . . . or?"

"As I told Jenny, one of those things hits you and you can drive the proverbial truck out the other side," he said. "And right here in sleepy old Hispaniola County, would you believe it?"

"Harry, you know nobody's exempt anymore."

"Yes, Miss Susie, true. Problem is the shot must have

come from about five hundred yards away, a redwood grove, way up by the next property. The shooter would have had to be a hell of a marksman.''

"Sure," Ralph observed, sensibly, for a change, "*if* he was trying to miss. If he was trying to get Lyons, and missed, then we'd say he was a lousy shot."

"Brilliant, Holmes, that's exactly what I've been telling myself." As Ralph reached for a fresh bottle of wine, Harry held up his hand. "*No mas* . . . at least for me. Susie?"

No, they should be leaving, the sooner the better. Susan needed time with Harry. She wanted to ask him about Jenny, if she could figure out how. Maybe it wasn't true—was it her imagination or had Harry somehow moved closer to her? Unlikely, given the fact they were spaced around such a large table. Absently, as if she wouldn't notice, he had placed his hand on her forearm, leaving it there, the hand that never was, what the Italians called the *mano morta*, the dead hand against your leg on a crowded bus . . . She didn't respond, not a muscle, though the shock of the contact jumped through her. And Buffy Teller noticed, bless her.

"And you may ask, Miss Susie, who is it lives next door to Dick Lyons?"

"I'm asking, who lives next door, Harry?"

"Aha . . . next door lives a very colorful English lady—"

"Emma Bristals," Buffy interjected.

"Indeed!"

"You're kidding!" Susan cried happily. "I know all about her!" So comforting once again to realize how few people she did not know about. "Emma, *the Lady* Bristals. She's married to the man they call the Cockney Press Baron, Sir Guy Bristals. But, I have to admit, I did not know . . . I thought she was in New York still. The plot thickens."

"I knew this would please you," Harry murmured.

He stroked her arm, not concerned about Buffy. Buffy wasn't concerned either. Any mention of Emma Bristals agitated her.

"The woman has a *horrible* reputation. She's been at the hotel," Buffy said, her words suggesting all sorts of sordid behavior.

Susan gloated. "The New York stories about her are wonderful."

"Give us a f'rinstance, city-girl," Harry drawled.

"Chauffeurs in the backseats of limos, butlers in their pantries . . . along those lines, Harry."

"She's had a go at half the men in Petertown," Buffy said, sniffing.

Including Ralph? Dare anybody ask? Ralph, as readable as an open book, showed no sign of embarrassment. Maybe Buffy knew something that . . . well, maybe Emma had put the arm on Ralph without him being aware of it. There were men like that.

"My dear," Susan said quietly, "what a piece you could do on this place!"

She was speaking to Harry but he didn't want to know.

"Cost six or seven lawsuits, Miss Susie."

"Would *you* worry about that, Harry?"

Susan snapped her fingers; she wanted to pinch him, to jolt him out of it. *Harry, don't you remember how it was in the old days?*

How he must—should—miss the old days, regret he wasn't a player any longer. No, Susan advised herself sadly, there would be nothing in scandalous Emma Bristals for *The Corsair* of Rio Tinto.

"Do you ever see her husband out here? Sir Guy?" They shook their heads. "You want a ruthless tycoon? Meet Guy Bristals!"

"I've already met my quota of ruthless tycoons," Harry said.

Susan stared at him, nonplussed. The new Harry? Wasn't he interested in anything anymore? Or was he being deliberately dense, just to infuriate her?

"First Murdoch, then Maxwell. Now the Bristals group is beginning to move into this country, Harry. He's bought a paper in Washington."

"Send him to me, Susie. Maybe he'd like a country weekly."

"You'd regret it."

"Who knows?"

"And there's a rumor he's been looking at taking over a network."

"Not yours! *NAN?* Is that possible?"

"Would you fear for me, Harry?" she asked archly.

"With all my might, Miss Susie!"

Buffy, of course, was not at all interested in notorious Emma's raider-husband. The Lady Bristals was more on her mind. She said, "Emma is Dick Lyons's mistress but he's not enough for her. She's got another lover on the side: Saladin Rivers. God, she's such a—"

"Now, Buff . . ." Ralph looked distraught. Maybe there was something to the proposition that Lady Emma had struck near home. "That's all gossip about Moon Rivers."

"*Moon* Rivers?" Susan repeated slowly. "Does Henry Mancini know about this?"

"Yeah, well . . ." Harry owned up, the rascal; of course, if he was so close to Jenny, then he'd know all of it. "There is a rumor about Emma and Moon." He chuckled, almost embarrassedly, for wasn't Harry Teller too big to be involved in such small-town shenanigans? "Moon is one of my advertisers: *Rivers-by-the-Sea service station.* 'Course, it's his old man's business. Moon pumps gas. Once in a while. When he's not . . ."

Pumping Emma, that's what he was about to say.

"Is it possible that Moon Rivers shot at Dick Lyons? Jealousy's always a good motive."

What Susan really needed to know was whether the story was going to get into circulation. Specifically, would it reach *The New York Times,* the perfect lead-in for a *Hindsight* segment?

Susan could remember, once upon a time, having described the Driver-Lyons marriage as made-in-heaven. *And now, dear viewers, what do we discover? Not only that the great people's advocate Richard Lyons is having an affair with Lady Emma Bristals and she with the remarkably named Moon Rivers; but that Jenny Driver is enjoying the favors of a Bear Jay and, very possibly, those of country newspaper publisher Harry Teller.*

"Think about it, Miss Susie. Any number of people would be pleased to see Lyons dead. Not just a bumpkin named Moon Rivers."

"Harry, what are you going to do about the story?"

"What am *I* going to do about it?"

"Well, yes! How are you going to cover it? It's a national story, you realize?"

Maddeningly, he continued to stonewall her.

"My inclination is to use the sheriff's report and not mention any names."

"Not mention names? *Why not?*" Crazy! If you had big

names, you used them. "I know, you're going to say I'm more and more into trash TV. . . .''

Shaking his head reproachfully, he said, "I'd never accuse you of that, Miss Susie. No, my reasoning is, if it were a prank or a stray shot, well . . . just as well not to give people ideas. You know about all the copycats out there."

Ralph's approving nod didn't deter her, rather provoked her all the more.

"Jesus, Harry, that's not what you learned at the U.P.! Lyons asks you not to print names . . . *and you agree*?''

"As a matter of fact, it was the other way around. Dick was fit to be tied when I said his name probably would *not* appear in *The Corsair*.''

"He *wanted* his name used?"

"Well, of course he did, for crissakes! He's hungry for it." Harry relished the moment. "He berated me for not exercising my First Amendment right *and duty* to print the news."

"Harry," she allowed, "you're the most—"

"Yes, I never change, Miss Susie," he agreed, so loftily she could've kicked him. "But tell me why I should help Dick Lyons get publicity? I've never been a fan of his. I know about all the good stuff, don't get me wrong. But . . .''

"You won't forgive him. I understand that. But this happens to be a *news* item, Harry."

"Yeah, *if* he didn't stage it," Harry said sourly. "Not impossible, you know, for a determined man to shoot a hole in a pail." Harry traced fingertips across her knuckles, forcing her to unfold her fist, to relax. "And it's not a matter of forgiving . . .'' He broke off to explain, apologetically, to Buffy. "We're talking about Dick Lyons making that trip to Hanoi all those years ago."

"They ought to've hung the bastard then," Ralph barked.

Susan was pleased to note, finally, that Harry hadn't completely lost it. He lifted his hand and jabbed a finger at his brother.

"No! Wrong, Ralph! Lyons had every right to go to Hanoi, absolutely. It's just . . . I'd never agree he should've. And, whatever the right or wrong of it, it was publicity-seeking, just like right now, a goddamn self-indulgent gesture."

"Harry," Susan remonstrated gently, "he felt strongly about the war."

"So did I! *So did you, Susan!* I'll *never* forgive, you're right, because it was a cheap protest. Nobody was going to line him up and shoot him, though who knows..." He looked thoughtful. "Maybe somebody's gunning for him. Nah! Anyway, I've always thought, whatever his motives, he dishonored all the young guys... getting killed, for what? Nothing! Wiped out in a stinking political war, for the face-saving of a bunch of stinking politicians. Going to Hanoi, the *effect* of Lyons's so-called protest, was to make sure all the kids knew they were fighting for shit... great, huh, just as you step on something and they write a letter home to your mother about God and country? Oh, no, I'll never be a fan of the son of a bitch."

And, Susan was tempted to say, you cuckold him just for starters.

"So," she remarked mildly, "who's asking you to be a fan? I just want you to report the news."

"Fuck Lyons," Harry snarled.

"The force of your argument is overwhelming, Harry."

But she knew all about it. The old arguments went round and round, like the music, and were never any good to all the beautiful young men, the poor, beautiful young men Harry had mentioned. Beautiful Nate Carleton. All of them beautiful and so many of them dead.

"Okay then, put it this way," Harry said heavily, "if somebody did plug him, it'd be a great crime but I know plenty of guys who'd not be crying."

With that, Harry got to his feet and announced they'd better be leaving. He had a long drive and work to do and... whatever.

Neither Ralph nor Buffy objected. Harry had certainly shut them down. And Susan too. "Thanks for everything," she mumbled and kissed Buffy's cheek. Buffy felt like a friend. At least *they* understood each other.

"I'm sorry, I shouldn't have provoked him," she added.

"He needs a good provoking every one in a while... *Miss Susie*."

Walking back to the car, Susan said, "I'm cold now, Harry. Can I borrow your coat?"

"Sure."

He jabbed the key into the lock of the Mustang's trunk and yanked it open. Reaching inside for the sheepskin, he dropped it over her shoulders.

"Thanks, Harry... it's so warm."

"Yep."

Face fixed in an uncompromising scowl, he bundled her

into the car, bending and flinging the sleeve of the sheepskin out of the way of the closing door and, muttering to himself, jumped in the other side, as if Susan were somehow to blame for the outrage of it all.

"Goddamn Lyons! He even had a headline worked out for me: Sniper Fires at People's Advocate . . ."

"And misses."

"Yeah . . . *and* the story is bound to make *Time* and *Newsweek*. Then he mixes another pitcher of martinis. I've never seen a man put away so many martinis without falling on his face. . . . Constitution of a bull. Only the good die young, as we know, Miss Susie . . ." Harry stopped, started again. "And Lyons is built like the proverbial . . . With a full beard these days. He looks like Tolstoy, except the beard is reddish-brown, not white, or crazy old John Brown of Harper's Ferry."

"He'd love to hear himself described like that: the reincarnation of Tolstoy and John Brown."

"My intention is *not* to flatter him."

"I think we shouldn't talk about him anymore, Harry."

Susan buried herself in his coat which smelled of many things, of male, old tobacco—Harry didn't smoke anymore either—slightly of acrid sweat. But it was warm and she huddled gratefully.

Smartly, Harry drove into an uphill driveway and whipped the car around. They were past Ralph's and halfway down the hill before he spoke again.

"Sorry about sounding off. I don't, very often."

"Listen . . ." Susan twisted in the bucket seat as best she could, pulling her left leg up so she faced him squarely. "Doesn't bother me. In fact, I was relieved you let go. I was worried you'd gone soft in the head."

"Sure," he scoffed, "but what the hell good does it do? What the hell do I care about Dick Lyons anyway?"

"But you do and that's wonderful!"

"But I shouldn't, should I?"

"Of course you should! You still *care*, Harry, thank God! That's half the battle. Most people don't give a goddamn about anything anymore. You know," she recalled, troubled, "when we saw each other in New York, we never talked about anything that mattered—the few times I saw you. Why was that?"

"And here we are in Petertown, California, and are we doing any better?"

"Yes!"

A slow grin infused his woeful face.

"In that case, I'll tell you something confidential—I was very jealous of Nate. Did it show?"

"Maybe. I don't know. A little. I wasn't watching. But . . . I always thought you did okay, that way. Not that it mattered much. When I think about it now, it seems to me we were all insane."

"Yeah. It was all *too* exhilarating, Miss Susie. We had such a wonderful time in the midst of hell. And we never got over it. There are military people who claim the only time they're really alive is when they're in the middle of a war. Didn't have time to think, or want to think, beyond the story, the reality we invented new every day. Remember those briefings? The *follies*? Surrealism. Hold the senses at bay, Miss Susie, that's what it was all about . . ." Harry paused, glaring at the down road. "Isn't that awful? The time of our lives, so alive . . . and it was the worst. Exciting . . . *and foul*."

"At least foul," she agreed. "Harry, you're not making me feel good."

"Am I supposed to, Miss Susie? What should I do?"

"I was hoping . . . trouble is, Harry, everything's *still* unreal, as if we're . . . no, me, as if *I'm* waiting and I don't know what for. Like we're . . . no, *I'm* caught in some kind of a holding pattern, waiting to land. Do you ever feel that way?"

"You're doing okay for somebody who's in a spin, Miss Susie."

Harry jammed the Mustang into first gear and swept them expertly into the steepest part of the hill. The motor whined, tires threw gravel, and they were in the final stretch. He braked, skidding up to the main road.

"Christ, Harry! I'd better check my insurance."

He only grinned recklessly.

"*And* here we are back in Petertown, Miss Susie. Have you seen all the local sights?"

"I haven't seen *any* of the local sights. I haven't budged from the Big Sea Inn."

What now? Harry Teller was world-famous for thinking everything over two or three times. He pointed to the right.

"Local shopping center. Dead ahead, the Petertown Hotel, lights ablazing, like an ocean liner passing in the night."

Or two ships, Susan thought.

"On your left, Miss Susie, Rivers-by-the-Sea service station." His voice was flip and irritating. "And so on: pizza parlor, already closed, couple more motels, a medical center . . . and *that* was Petertown—say farewell, Miss Susie."

"Farewell, Petertown."

But he didn't drive out of town. He slowed and stopped the car opposite the hotel.

"Background, Miss Susie. Petertown, California. Named, if you please, for the czar of Old Russia, Peter the Great. Saint Petersburg, now Leningrad, on the Baltic, and here on the California shore, Petertown."

Harry laughed carelessly, adjusted his long legs under the dashboard, wriggling around so he faced her better. But Susan beat him to the punch.

"Harry, what are you up to with Jenny Driver?"

"Up to? What a strange thing to say."

"Are you having an affair with Jenny?"

"Even if I were, I wouldn't tell you, Miss Susie."

"I should be told—I'll be seeing her tomorrow or the next day, before I leave anyway. I wouldn't want to embarrass you."

He seemed amused, or would've liked her to think he was amused.

"Is that *need-to-know*, Miss Susie? She's a terrific woman, I'll tell you that much." Harry put both hands on her forearm and leaned closer. "Did I tell you the Petertown Hotel bar carries beer from eight hundred countries? Wanta have one?"

"Goddamn it, Harry, I hate beer!"

He smiled mildly, as if commiserating.

"Wanta check in then?"

"Harry . . ."

"Please, Miss Susie, not to be grim. Things ain't so bad. We have a life, which is more than a lot of people on this planet can say. And I'm greedy about life. I want more of it."

Susan tucked her chin into the sheepskin.

"You're a beast. Are you going to tell me about Jenny?"

"Jenny . . ." He shrugged. "I *could* be half in love with her, if allowed. But she's married to Lyons, not that I'd care about that. As it so happens, I'm too smart. My instinct for self-preservation is too well developed. I don't really trust Jenny so very much. Right now, she's supposedly crazy about that mad shrink—"

"Bear Jay."

"You know about him?"

"His son works at the inn, odd-jobs. A nice young boy."

"Well..." Harry shook his head. "Bear Jay is madder than his clients, if he's got any, besides Jenny."

"Since when does Jenny need a shrink?"

"I didn't say she needed one. What I'm hinting is, she's off the deep end with him." Harry grunted. "Midlife career crisis? Living with that big fake Lyons? You heard: him knocking off dizzy Lady Emma... who can say."

"You were always so good at saving girls—"

"I was? When?"

"But you never saved me," she murmured sardonically, "not once."

"Very funny."

He touched her arm and she felt the charge of electricity all the way through the sheepskin, remembering Mister Max's hands and then of course Nate's, and once more that evening she felt like crying. She would've pulled away if she could have. But his grip was too strong.

"Harry, I'm jealous of your brother and Buffy, living here like this, no pressure."

"You couldn't take it for a week, Miss Susie."

"That's why I feel weepy. Because I couldn't and I know it. What am I missing, Harry?"

"Nothing important, that's for sure." His eyes were quizzical; the same solicitous smile worked his moist, newborn face. "How *are* you anyway, Susie?"

"You mean, how am I... *really*? I'm doing okay, Harry."

"I read about your new contract at NAN. You're doing a hell of a lot better than simply *okay*."

"You're talking about the money? Moneywise, I'm fine."

"And you're happy? Enough?"

The Question. In various guises, it popped up in every interview. *People* magazine... *Entertainment Tonight*... *Vanity Fair.* Even in *Vogue*, yes, not as a fashion setter but exemplary of Woman of the Nineties, vying with men on a playing field that was at long last somewhat level. Can a Susan Channing be really, truly happy? Oh, yes, Ms. Channing has enough money for two lifetimes. But is she *happy*? Can a person, a woman who should have a husband and many, many children be happy with money and career?

"Drive on," she said. "This'll take a while."

4

The Mustang rolled onto the Jasper Gates Memorial Bridge. Down below, sea marsh glittered metallically. A hazy half-moon was just emerging from behind the ridge of forest.

"Tide's in?"

"Yeah, maybe," Harry allowed, casting her a sidelong look. "Now, I'm going to tell you something else I never forgot about you, Miss Susie."

"Can I handle it, Harry?"

"This is an easy one. It was one of the last nights at the Caravelle and maybe you won't remember it, out of so many." He shifted his grip on the hand-tooled steering wheel, caressing the patinaed wood as if it were flesh. "Not much like the Petertown Hotel. Anyway, toward the end, there was a big rocket attack and all of a sudden we were all running like hell to get downstairs. *What I remember* is you dashing out of your room with Nate on your tail . . . so to speak. . . ."

Yes, it made her shiver, remembering. Susan looked away, out the window, anywhere but at him. Remember? She'd been scared to death, convinced she, they, all of them were going to die. Nate, the fool, had begun to laugh, as some people did when caught at the epicenter of an earthquake.

"All you had on was a sheet, Susie, and you were trying to keep yourself covered, running and tumbling down the stairs. I remember your eyes were—"

"Yes, Harry, and what were *you* doing at the time?"

"Frankly, Susie, along with being scared out of my gourd, I was having a good look at your stuff."

"Harry..." She shook her head. "That is some terrific memory."

"If it hadn't been for ogling you, I'd have gone crazy out of raw, stinking fear. So... you saved my life and I owe you one."

"Nate and I weren't the only ones caught in *dishabille*. What was that girl's name?"

"Shirley Chapple, the girl from the British agency."

"We *were* crazy, weren't we, Harry?"

"More than a little, I think, Miss Susie."

He looked at her searchingly as they entered the darkness of the alley of the redwoods and too soon were at the Big Sea Inn. Delaying the moment, Harry drove slowly into the neat patch of light made by the bank of windows on the lee side of the building.

"Aren't you going to park? You're not taking off right away, are you, Harry?"

Panic? Perhaps.

"It's a two-hour drive, Miss Susie."

"Why drive back tonight? You could stay over, couldn't you? Is there... somebody... waiting?"

"No."

"Then..." She probably shouldn't have said this and perhaps wouldn't have without the protective cover of night. "Do you want to come to bed with me... like we used to?"

She heard his throat catch. Finally, she had managed to surprise him. But, with a shaky laugh, he recovered.

"Susie, we *never* went to bed together!"

"Everything but. We could have. We were that close, Harry. We could've and not given it a second thought. We should have."

"The fact is, though, Susie, we didn't."

"No," she said calmly. "But then was then, like you said, Harry, and now is now. And don't forget—you owe me one."

He was silent. Christ, like everything else he had to think *that* over too?

"I don't feel like being alone, Harry."

"Are you sure?"

"I wouldn't say so otherwise." She touched his face. "You're such an honorable guy."

Saying no more, Harry drove out of the cube of light and back to the parking garage. When he cut the motor and opened the door, the inside light came on. His expression stunned her. He looked so anxious. Then he flashed her the old smile, the one which challenged her to come clean, his cynical been-around smile. Too late, though, for she had spotted the Harry Teller underneath.

Would he at least kiss her, right now? In the parking garage?

"Do you want to go in for a drink?" he asked, so straight-faced as to be comical.

"Absolutely not. If you need a drink, I've got tons in the room."

Was she asking so much really? She couldn't believe herself. How Miss Susie had changed! But she and Harry were old friends. He put his arm around her waist and they walked out of the garage, Susan holding the sheepskin and his arm and hoping that time would cure them of wariness and doubt.

Clumsily, clinging to the coat and to him, Susan managed to get the room key out of her bag and made as if to unlock the door. But, to her satisfaction, he stopped her, turning her to him.

"I always liked blondes, Miss Susie," he whispered, "and you were the most beautiful blonde I ever saw in my life. Then, Nate got to you first."

"Harry, I never knew...I swear. You were always...I never thought you really liked me."

"Liked you?" His eyes flashed. "I was crazy about you. I was in love with you, Miss Susie."

"*Oh.*"

He kissed her forehead. Then one cheek. And pulled back to gaze at her again.

"There's never been a time when I didn't like you, Miss Susie. Sometimes, I was mightily pissed off at you, yes. Then in New York...You did change, you know."

"I know," she admitted, easily enough. "That was my

ruthless period.'' She faced him in the limbo of the doorway, neither in nor out. ''I never really got along with Blake, or anybody else. Because of Nate . . . *and you,* I suppose. So I had my revenge.''

Poor old Susie, is that what he was thinking? If so, he didn't give it away, kissed her again, finally on the mouth. Susan was thrilled all over again at how well-defined his lips were, soft and full . . . strong and yielding. She tipped his tongue with her own, probingly, tentatively; the force of the kiss stopped her breath. Desire bloomed, filled her legs, made her thighs tremble. She pushed up against him, sending the message that didn't require decoding, offering herself. Understanding, accepting, he made a throaty noise and Susan was aware of the rushing of his blood, the tension that rose in him. Harry was as tight-gutted as any of the beautiful young men. Susan opened the sheepskin wide and took him underneath it with her. He could feel the pressure of her breasts against his chest and he ran his hands, under the coat, across her back, down her haunch, up her thighs and belly, circling the breasts with his fingertips.

''My God, Miss Susie, you're fantastic!''

''All right,'' she said. ''Let's get this door open, Harry.''

''Wait.''

''What's wrong?''

''Nothing . . . I don't know. Ghosts. Susie, let's walk down by the ocean. The moon's up. We can talk.''

Ghosts? Odd, she'd been thinking the same.

''Sure, Harry, fine, let's do it!''

Between the main building and the north wing of the inn, the garden path opened to the whole, wide Pacific, all molten, gray-running metal. And, immediately, as they reached the open meadow, the flighty moon began to perform shadow tricks in the soggy, dew-laden grass. Susan tripped and Harry caught her, gripping her at the waist.

''Hang on, Miss Susie.''

''You hang on yourself, Harry.''

He was in for a rough ride, she wanted to say. That was what she was feeling, as well as very short of breath—why, she didn't know, except it was something physical he did to her, and definitely not that she was struck dumb by the view of yet another ocean, though Susan did stop to stare. Burgeoning, undraped, the moon came out of a cloud.

''It's beautiful, Harry.''

"Yep," he said.

"Corny, I know."

"Nope."

Susan was not, never had been, poetic; but she recognized a good moon when she saw one. Breathless, as excited as children, they strolled to where the bluff ran out and teetered at the brink of death and disaster. Down below, the ocean beat against black rock, throwing lashings of white foam into the wind. She was grateful for his coat, for his arm and hands. She held on to him but he stood, unmoving, staring down at the sea on the rocks, so close to her, so far away, unreachable, that she felt uncomfortable, as if she might have to scream, until she pulled him back, away from the edge.

Had *he* ever thought of going over, seriously considered it? There had been a time for her, yes. Well, everybody had *thought* about it. Not immediately after they'd come back but later, some years later. And, of course, nothing had come of it. The burning question had just not been that painful. The question: *Why?* It was all too complicated, that was the trouble. She looked at Harry and saw a dozen other people, things, times, events, related but extraneous. And, she didn't doubt, Harry didn't simply see Susan Channing. He saw Nate and that girl and the hotel and all the sounds and colors of smoke and battle. Was that why he couldn't deal with her? Why he'd draped her in sheepskin and brought her to the ocean's edge?

Her body wobbled, jarred against him, and reminded him that, yes, she was there with him.

"Miss Susie, let's sit down some place, what about right here?"

They did, to her relief, on a flattish slab of black rock, a bench with ocean view, worn comfortable by centuries of rain and spray. Automatically, Harry reached down for a pebble and, finding the right one, tossed it down at the rocks. The insignificant speck by itself stirred the ocean, triggered the briny smell of salt, seaweed, and kelp, a tonic.

"So, Harry," she whispered in his ear, "what have you been doing for the last five years of my life?"

Full-face, up close, eyeball to eyeball, nose to nose, he said, "Five years isn't so long, Miss Susie. It's only a lifetime. I've been working pretty hard, believe it or not."

"I believe."

"And thinking about you."

"Oh . . . come on now, Harry."

They were haunch to haunch on the hard, flat rock. Whatever the problems, he bulged with life. Susan was so aware of him, the strength, the menace. Harry straightened his back and stretched his arms upward, slammed down his feet and, out of the blue, howled at the moon. One time. Then laughed.

"There. My statement."

Susan took his hand from the sky and held it to her mouth, took it back to her breast, moved it against her, put his hand across her belly and swelled against it.

"Harry?"

A puff of wind riled her hair and his other hand gathered it in a knot in his fist. He tugged, lifting her face, kissing her some more.

"There was something else, about Nate . . ."

"*Him* again? Come on, Harry, just when we're doing so well."

"I know you loved him, Susie, and maybe Nate loved you, but I wouldn't swear to it."

"It doesn't matter, Harry. I told you. I was over it years ago. Do we have to—"

"I know you've been worried about this."

"About what, Harry?"

"What you want to hear is that Nate didn't stay behind because he wanted to be dead."

"I never believed he did, Harry! Please!"

"Even if Nate was *desperately* in love with you, Susie, that wouldn't be the reason."

"Harry, you're telling me I'm not to blame for what happened to Nate. I never thought I was." She shook his arm. "But I think *you* blamed me, Harry, and that's why you were always so standoffish in New York."

There. Let him make the most of it. But he didn't react like she'd expected he would. He stared at her for a long moment.

"I think that's true."

"*It is true!*"

"Well, maybe. Anyway, I've thought a lot about it since then. You wouldn't believe how much I've thought about it."

"And?"

"Believe it or not, sooner or later, I was coming to see you in New York. If you hadn't come here first."

"I believe," she said again. "But are you making me feel

better or worse? You're telling me Nate didn't love me. Therefore—"

"No, no, what I'm saying is, Nate was perverse." But he didn't fully believe that. "I think he did love you. And it was his idea for you to leave. He *made* you leave. So it couldn't be that he deliberately got himself killed *because* you left."

"So I didn't break his heart?"

"Maybe . . . maybe in four places, but nonetheless . . ."

"Harry . . ." Susan shook his arm again, gently. "I appreciate it. I've thought about it too, lots. If we'd ever talked about it . . . I did feel guilty and I still do but not just for Nate. And it's not just guilt; it's a kind of a great, all-encompassing, generalized remorse. Because of all of them! I cannot get it out of my head, the vision of all the young boys, so beautiful. It's not even about Nate anymore, Harry."

He had made her cry. Icy tears flooded her eyes and ran down her cheeks. She was crying, openly, and Harry knew it.

"You're cold."

"No. Scared. It scares me to think about it, Harry. You know what scares me most? It could happen again. So easily. We wander into these things."

He held her head against his shoulder and stroked her hair.

"Are you going to be all right?"

"Sure. Let's go back. It's freezing here."

He got up and pulled her to her feet and put his arms around her again. But some of the urgency had left the embrace.

"Susie, I get the feeling it might be best to delay this collision a little while."

"No. Why?"

"I—in a way I feel like I'm taking advantage of your memories, Miss Susie."

"Really? Do *I* get a vote?"

"Haunted folks, Susie, haunted folks getting together, searching for the spooks."

"No, Harry."

That's crap, Harry, she wanted to say, preach me no sermons.

"Do you know what I'm saying?" he asked.

"Of course I know what you're saying." She was swollen inside, ready to burst, that's what she knew. There was an inevitability come to light here and it would be sinful to deny it. And Harry was spouting nonsense! "I know what you're saying and I'm not having any of it, thanks." She pulled away and sat down again on the rock, *her* rock, her hard place. She was about to ask him if this was about Jenny, this sudden reluctance, then didn't because she knew instinctively it was not. "Now that you've given me absolution, which I didn't ask for, Harry, I'm clean as a whistle."

Susan watched him, towering above her, watched his face as she bent over and took off her low-heeled loafers. He would wonder what she was all about.

"Harry, would you please?" He knew damn well what she meant. "I want this very much, Harry. I don't want to drive you away though."

"You're not driving me anywhere, Susie," he said in a low voice.

"I don't want to scare you, Harry."

"Scare me? Are you kidding?"

"Well . . ." She unfastened the tabs of her slacks. The ground was cold against the soles of her feet. Without shame, in the high-noon blaze of the moon, she slipped the slacks down, then her panties. "All right, Harry?"

"All right," he said.

"By the rock on a hard place on your sheepskin coat, Harry."

"And pray nobody comes down to look at the ocean."

"Harry, we just scream and scare them away. This is what I want, Harry.

She took off the coat. The breeze was cold on her nakedness and Harry stood staring. But he couldn't resist this, could he, no matter how introspective or judicious or dignified he might wish to be. Susan laid the coat on the ground and herself down upon it and held out her arms.

"Come, Harry."

He covered her then and she was very ready, accepting him, taking him smoothly, quickly, urgently. She began to cry again because suddenly everything had been settled. She had been very needy, indeed, and his pulse raced. He had hardly touched her when she climaxed the first time and then again as he did himself. And it was over.

"My God," Harry whispered.

"Harry . . . Harry, quite contrary . . . Harry, I'll remember that as long as I live."

"A long time, Miss Susie."

She gave him a moment, then said, "Delicious, but tough on my bones. Can we get up?"

It had happened, unplanned, and was over, and then it was like it had never happened at all. But it had.

Susan had taken his hand and led him up the garden path, intending to bring him inside. Then she changed her mind about that too. It might have been too much.

"Harry?"

"Yes."

"I hope . . ." And she was at his mercy again; it was not fair. "Harry, now that we've found each other again, you won't forget me, will you?"

"No, no, now look, Miss Susie—"

"Harry," she said, taking it easy on him, "what do you want to do? Stay or go?"

She faced him again, outside her door.

"Come in." He hesitated. "Or go. Whatever you want, Harry."

"I want to stay, Susie, Jesus! Believe me. But . . ."

Susan smiled at him.

"You think I'm nuts. A madwoman. You're entitled to think that."

"No, I do not."

"Harry, it was just . . . I couldn't help it. Everything ran in together."

"I know. I know."

"Not very romantic, on a rock like that, Harry. I'm sorry."

"Susie . . ."

"I know," she said, "you want to think it over."

"Susie, you know I never stopped being in love with you, if that's what you're wondering. But, you, I'm not sure—"

"You think it's just a lust in the blood, Harry?"

"Well, tell me."

"It's *everything*, Harry. I won't forget it."

"Well, I won't either, Susie."

He was hurt now. He figured she'd been using him, to answer a sudden desperate need for love and reassurance.

"You're thinking . . . that I'm thinking something like full circle and now we can start the clock again, isn't that it?"

"I'm not sure what I'm thinking, Miss Susie."

Susan put her arms around him and lifted her face and kissed him again. Good-bye kisses.

"Harry, that was wonderful. What can I say? I . . . I feel like being alone too. I . . . well, I don't know."

"Susie . . ."

His voice was strained to breaking. He was hurting. Good.

"Say no more, Harry. On your way! Drive like the wind. Good-bye. Will you call me?"

"Call you? For crissakes, Susie, what the hell do you think?"

"I think you'll call me."

He stared at her, almost angrily.

"You are behaving goddamn strangely, you know?"

"I'm feeling goddamn strange, Harry. I won't tell you what I'm feeling. I might scare you again."

"You did not scare me, Miss Susie!" He scowled. "You surprised me. I'll be back, for sure before you leave!"

"Good."

She didn't necessarily believe it. But what the hell.

Susan kissed him a last time, coolly, a very proper farewell kiss. Then, feeling what, she wasn't quite sure, she backed away. She was feeling a definite, certain kind of love, or deep and sentimental affection.

And picked one hell of a way to show it.

Okay though. Even after all the years, this was just the beginning of something. Not the end of it.

Susan kissed him one more time, rather an extended sort of kiss. Then breathing intently, stepped out of his way.

"Thanks *very much* for the loan of the coat, Harry."

5

Alerted by the roar of the jeep as it negotiated the potholed road, a woman had come out on the veranda of the ranch house, and faced them from across the still considerable distance, one hand at her forehead, shielding her eyes from the sun. Though they were still a couple of hundred yards away, Susan had no doubt it was Jenny. And as her driver steered the black-and-gold Big Sea Range Rover through a scrappy wooden gate and archway bearing the carved and overpainted legend *Rancho Mondo*, she saw that she was right.

The insolent artistry of her stance, her posture, the tilt of her fine head set Jenny Driver apart. As always, however dressed, made up or not, she was playing a role—in this case, that of the brave homesteader, firmly in possession of her land.

Susan tried to imagine Harry Teller's first impression of her. Jenny looked better in person than in any of the riot of publicity pictures from the studios. As they came closer to the house, Susan observed she was dressed in a shapeless, long granny skirt and blue denim shirt, sleeves rolled up to the elbows. Jenny did not move, stood dead-still as if measuring or timing their approach, hands on hips, feet spread widely apart. Harry would have been most aware of her searching eyes, their intent, slightly squinty focus. Concentration, yes, another of the qualities that made her such a hell of an actress.

What a great opening shot, Susan told herself, for a Driver-Lyons *Hindsight* segment.

Susan's driver, an elderly and taciturn man who normally spent his days mowing grass and cleaning drainage ditches round and about the Big Sea property, pulled into a dusty quadrangle of long, low, staunch-chimneyed ranchhouse, a large, new-looking barn and, to the right and left, weathered, ramshackle wooden structures smothered in bougainvillea. These were the main buildings of the ranch; other tilty structures were scattered about the margins.

Jenny came down the steps from the veranda. Susan swung her legs around and dropped into the dust to meet her.

"Hello, Susan."

It was as if they'd seen each other just the day before, that's how casual Jenny sounded. In a second of intense study, Susan absorbed her from head to toe. Jenny was not wearing makeup—God forbid, not if she was playing pioneer queen. Or *was* wearing it, to achieve such a weathered and anxious look? The long auburn hair was undoubtedly gone slightly toward gray; and again, in character, was gathered behind the noble head in a sloppy bun.

Jenny was only a couple of years older than Susan. Today, she looked older than that. She was also a little shorter than Susan's five-eight—and today seemed smaller as well, perhaps because she had broadened in the beam and the tiny waist thickened. Whatever, it was accentuated, if anything, by a large and heavy-looking conch and turquoise-trimmed belt.

She was wearing too much turquoise altogether, a couple of bracelets on each arm and a dangling pendant necklace, all of it Indian-crafted jewelry, and a pair of big silver-hoop earrings. Too much, too much, Susan told herself. A little turquoise went a long way.

But even so, she looked terrific, a blooming, mature woman, gone slightly to seed, or a couple of months pregnant. That *was* possible; Jenny was still, maybe just barely, within childbearing age. She had always talked about having children, but up to now it had not worked out that way. Career, ambition, the time element. Susan knew all about it. Put it off, for the sake of whatever, and suddenly it was too late. It occurred to Susan that if Jenny was so well-stocked with lovers, she might indeed suddenly find herself with child, and thus fulfill her great ambition. And that would be very ironic.

"We're a little early, Jenny. I'm sorry. This is John."

"Hello, John," Jenny said gravely. "Can I get you something, a beer maybe? We're going to be a while."

"Take'er time," said John. "I'm having a day off. I'll just have a little nap in the back of the car."

Harry would've noticed the reluctant curl of Jenny's smile, the intense blue-violet of her eyes, so perfect for the camera, those Paul Newman eyes, like beacons across a room.

"You look wonderful, Susan." Jenny grabbed Susan's arm, butted Susan with her hip and led her toward the house. "Beautiful blonde beast. *Is* it true? *Do* you have more fun? I know you're busy, I watch you, I read about you all the time. You're more of a celebrity now than the people you cover, honey."

"Oh! Don't say that, please! It's the curse, the kiss of death, Jenny."

"But are you having fun?"

Laughing, flattered that Jenny would take such a personal interest, Susan was nevertheless not prepared to cede her Harry Teller, if indeed there was anything to it.

"You're looking pretty fine yourself, Jenny."

"Well . . ." The slow smile lit her full-lipped mouth. "If you'd like to say so, thank you. I'm a woman of the soil now, Susan. Look at my gnarled hands, my blisters. I'm sore from pulling the plough." She raised her hands, pivoted, pirouetted, proving all of . . . nothing. "We're raising Arabians."

"I read about that some place. How's Dick?"

Carefully, she asked the ritual question, for you never knew if what everybody said was true. Despite the great success of her career, the money and fame, Jenny had never had it easy when it came to men. Dick Lyons would've been a trial whatever his calling. But as a card-carrying, crusading do-gooder he was even more heartache, more headache. Lyons was an egomaniac; he had to be in order to survive. He was also a hated man, a hunted man, a deliberately high-profile target for a nation's bigotry and frustration. There was no doubt his career in hell-raising had been detrimental to Jenny's, but Susan had never known her to complain.

"I'm not so sure about me," Jenny said, not fully answering the question, "but *he* loves it up here."

No wonder he would, as he found it increasingly difficult to muster support for his causes. Dick Lyons was Jenny's second husband, the second Susan knew about, at least. One day, when they'd done that first interview, Jenny had shown Susan the unforgettable clipping describing her marriage to now-forgotten pharmaceutical heir Warren Sunshine. According to sad rumor, said that item, Jenny Driver intended to give up her promising acting career to devote herself full-time to Warren and their Palm Beach estate. Which was considerable: Warren owned one thousand feet of ocean front and docked a 350-foot yacht. Or was it the other way around?

As it had turned out, the marriage lasted five minutes. Jenny had not dumped her career and, in due course, met and married Richard Lyons, then at his zenith. Their union had been a PR triumph—or so it had seemed at the time, Susan thought, remembering Harry's tirade.

"I thought I might see you at the Big Sea party, Jenny. Jasper Gates said you'd been invited."

"Not our cup of tea, Susan."

Boisterously, Jenny bumped hips again. Yes, hers were more amply padded than of yesteryear. Susan's old friend seemed so matronly. She smelled powerfully of the land. Susan caught the odor in her nose, the strongly acrid, slightly sweaty scent of fertility. Fecund, was that the proper word?

Waving her hand eloquently, Jenny said, "As you can see, all this is ours: the main house, the horse barn. The bunkhouse, there with the watering trough in front of it. Dick fell in love with the place because of the bunkhouse. Plus about seven hundred acres."

"You could make your next Western right here." Susan murmured, "and not have to change a thing."

Archly smiling, Jenny said, "*I* do not do Westerns. But we have thought of that. If we ever run short of money, we'll rent it out." She started up the steps. "Come in and see Dick."

But Lyons came to them. His tall and burly figure filled the doorway to the veranda, bearded face and uncombed head clearing the opening by only an inch or two. At first sight, he was a threatening presence, or might have seemed so if Susan hadn't known him better. He jammed his hands deeper into the pockets of a pair of tan workpants. When he spoke, his voice was deep and echoing, in a natural pitch close to a bellow.

"I heard strange noises. *What're you drinking?*"

Ah, so that hadn't changed either.

"Dick . . ."

"I know. It's Sue Channing, for God's sake!" A big grin emerged from his beard, like an animal from its lair. "I never forget a *body*!"

It had always been said about Dick Lyons that he was a charismatic figure and a very well-disciplined drunk, whichever came first, *and* that he was a man with an unrelenting, untiring interest in women. He was, somebody had put it, an Olympic-class ass-chaser.

"Well, Sue, what'll it be? Martini, Vodka on the rocks . . . straight up? A beer? What's your pleasure?"

Glancing at Jenny she said, "Coffee, if you have some on."

"For Crissakes!"

Dick had moved out of the way so Jenny could get past him, but he grabbed Susan as she went by, crushed her to him and kissed her violently on both cheeks, then the mouth, smacking lips on lips wetly, sucking and shoving his tongue between her teeth. Susan gasped in confusion, felt herself go pink, but there was nothing to do but let him run his course.

"Like always," Lyons cried triumphantly, "little Sue, scared to death of a good, healthy embrace."

"Ha! You're just a big, brown bear, Dick Lyons!"

Jenny had not even bothered to turn. Well, if she didn't care, why should Susan? Actually, no reason to take it amiss. Susan knew Dick well enough to be considered a family friend.

"You like?" Jenny asked, gesturing broadly.

The enormous room was what they called open-plan, Susan supposed, with an appropriately Western decorating motif. Its one-story ceiling was beamed and hung with immense wagon-wheel chandeliers. At the far end was an outsized walk-in stone fireplace whose chimney Susan had spotted from the road. The space was filled with floor-hugging couches, battered easy chairs heaped with pillows and all covered in fabrics of Indian design. Amid the clutter, a knee-high square of oak was piled with magazines and old newspapers. A rough bookcase covered one whole wall and on the other side of the room, yards away, a long pine dining table, so scarred it must have been used for folk dancing, paralleled the open kitchen. It was into the kitchen that Dick Lyons walked, his voice booming and echoing as he noted again, and again, what sissies they were for not taking a drink.

"Well, goddammit, I'm going to have some beer and I don't care what you say!" He sounded good-natured about it. "And *coffee* for the ladies."

Jenny put Susan on one of the couches and sat down beside her while Lyons blundered around the kitchen. Jenny smiled in that direction, lifting her thick brown eyebrows in . . . what? Resignation? Disdain? Indifference?

Dick put water on to boil and swiftly opened the refrigerator. In one big hand he grabbed a bottle of beer, twisted off the cap and drank . . . and drank, and reached for a second.

In another few days, Susan would've missed her, Jenny said, for she was about to leave for Maine. Her favorite director was remaking an O'Neill. It was as tough as ever to get your hands on good original scripts, and you did the best you could, which was not always so great.

With sardonic attention, Dick Lyons leaned on the bar separating kitchen and living room. "You know, children, this is the second day in a row we've had media visitors. Today, the famous talk-show person Susan Channing. Yesterday, *The Corsair* of Rio Tinto."

"I heard Harry was here," Susan murmured.

She didn't elaborate and didn't feel confusion either, like she'd somehow been discovered. Would this prompt Jenny to reveal herself or Dick to remember that Harry Teller was a friend of hers? No. Jenny said nothing and Dick went on as if she hadn't said a word.

"Teller came over because he had a tip from the sheriff that *somebody* took a shot at *yours truly*."

"Now, Dick," Jenny said, "didn't we decide some idiot was just shooting at the barn door?"

Pointedly ignoring her, Dick said, "See, Sue, I'm exiting the barn, carrying a pail of you know what horses produce a lot of, and *Blam!* the pail goes flying out of my hand. Missed my dog by inches! *You* think somebody is shooting at the barn door? *You* buy that, Sue?"

"Frankly, I wouldn't know, Dick."

"Well, that dumb ass Teller, he buys it! Some goddamn journalist that man is!"

"Dick," she said, "I worked with Harry. He's a *very* good journalist."

"Oh, yeah? And he's not even going to report it?"

Calmly, too patiently, Jenny said, "We *agreed*, Dick, it was probably some kid...or a wild shot. And there's no point calling attention to you."

"Wild shot!" he scoffed, scowling.

Jenny appealed to Susan.

"Local kids, you know, they get their kicks potshotting cans, rocks, trees along the side of the road."

"With *sniper rifles*? Please..."

"Harry," Jenny said, rolling the name on her tongue. "*Harry*, very wisely, I think, decided it was by far best not to publicize—"

Lyons growled, "Since when can't I take the heat, Jenny?"

"Who said it's about taking the heat, Dick?"

Dissatisfied, irritable, he turned to take the kettle off the stove, and slosh boiling water into two cups.

"But Teller told *you* about it, huh, Sue? When'd you see Teller?"

"Last night, after he left here." She had to explain something. "We've known each other a long time, did he tell you?" Jenny nodded, ever so slightly, eyes wary. "Over in...you know, then New York."

"Sure," Lyons complained, "sure, he's going to *tell* everybody about it but not run the story in that pissant paper of his."

Lyons wanted them to know he was about as disgruntled by this state of affairs as a man could be. He slammed a tray down on the kitchen counter, put the coffee cups on it, then a sugar bowl and a container of milk, and carried it around the counter and over to the oak coffee table.

"Move those goddamn magazines, Jenny."

She did and he put down the tray, eyeing Susan with deadly suspicion. Jenny's body was sending messages: shoulders hunched forward, she reached for a cup. If Jenny had given up on him, it was a very sad day for Dick Lyons. Jenny was probably the last person in the world willing to tolerate him.

Moving back to his beer bottle, Dick deliberately turned the talk away from Harry, and Jenny's irritation.

"So, tell me about Big Sea, Sue. Where'd all the money come from? They've spent a fortune on the place."

"I haven't the foggiest . . ."

His jaw cocked in disbelief and he barked at her, with a sarcasm that had an accent all its own.

"Susan . . . *please*. I have my sources, spread far and wide. You know very well I'm talking about Jasper Gates and August Blick."

Susan didn't waste time hedging an answer.

"Then you know August Blick is a good friend of mine."

And, please God, how often was she to be called upon to affirm the honor of her relationship with August Hugo Blick?

"So then, what role does Blick play in this nefarious partnership?"

Jenny managed to look bored and alienated at the same time.

"*Nefarious*, Dick?"

"Of course, honeybunch! It's bound to be if those two are involved."

"You don't *know*!" Jenny charged. "You *assume*! With no proof!"

"August Blick is an investor," Susan said, smiling, "but I didn't come all the way up this mountain in order to talk about Gates and Blick. Not at all," she added, officiously changing the subject. "*When* are we going to update our Driver-Lyons file?"

"And I thought," Jenny pouted sweetly, "that you called because you wanted to see me just for myself. I hope, Susan, this isn't the only reason for the trip to California."

"No, no! I did want to see you!" Susan twisted the absolute truth a couple of degrees. "We've been chasing Jasper Gates . . . the Big Sea opening seemed convenient."

A fresh frown pulled Lyons's lips and he said ominously, "Gates? Talk to me first."

"Why?" Susan asked, "what do you have on *him*, Dick?"

"Play it cool. He can be . . . nasty."

"Now, come on, Dick," Jenny exclaimed. "You don't *know* anything about Jasper Gates."

"Says you, lady!"

Jenny shook her head disgustedly and looked away.

Hoping to flatter him, Susan asked, "Is there any dirt you don't know, Dick?"

He chuckled moistly.

"Very little. People call me with all sorts of stuff . . . out of the blue. Out of the woodwork."

"I'd love to see *your* FBI file."

"A yard of it," Jenny muttered, not happily.

Squirming with pleasure, he exclaimed, "Thicker! My file dates all the way back to the first time I ever got arrested—for throwing stones at the Russian Embassy in nineteen fifty-six. Over the Hungarian Invasion, remember? Nah, who remembers? Everybody accuses me of being a big pinko—but they forget about that, don't they?" Lyons shook the bottle at them. "They forget, the bastards, that I'm strictly nonpartisan. You know the first time I ever met Jenny?" he demanded rhetorically. "At a Save the Whale rally in Beverly Hills, that's where!"

"Very romantic," Jenny muttered.

"Well, *I* thought it was," he said, as if wounded to the quick.

Which, of course, he was not. Nothing touched him. Lyons was immune. His skin was like steel plate. He had never heeded the admonition about people living in glass houses not throwing stones. He was so pristinely pure of motive, wasn't he? Well, people might ask, what did Dick Lyons live on besides Jenny Driver? Whose money had bought the ranch? Not Richard the Lionhearted Lyons's money, you could be sure.

But that was all right. He was Dick Lyons. He was excused.

Once, Jenny *had* loved Dick Lyons deeply. And did she still? Maybe Jenny had finally grown up. And Susan too. She felt little in the way of tolerance for the bulky maverick, as pitiful as he would in due course become, as sad as it was to think that Dick Lyons's best work was behind him, that he was no longer a safe or worthy object of hero-worship.

In that sense, it was doubly sad that somebody had waited so long, too long, to take a shot at Lyons. To be assassinated in the valley and not at the peak, surely that must be the worst of all.

Maybe he sensed what was in Susan's mind, for Lyons, swigging from his beer bottle, flopped in a Windsor chair at one end of the long pine table and petulantly belched. Then he demanded, "Where the hell's my dog, Jenny?"

"Most likely out in the barn, Dick," she said. "She was with Beau. Beau is our Indian horse trainer, Susan."

"You are training them?"

Lyons snorted. "World's most *useless* goddamn horses!"

"They can be a very good investment, Dick," Jenny said.

"Like collecting dolls, for God's sake! And Beau doesn't know what the hell he's doing. He's not qualified."

"He's a smart kid, Dick!"

"I know that, for crissakes," he bellowed. "But he doesn't know anything about these horses and you'll blame him if anything—"

"*I will not,*" Jenny exclaimed, "and please be quiet about it. They're *my* horses . . ."

She didn't finish, merely turned away, shrugging, realizing she should not have said it.

"Sure! I understand that, all right." Lyons chugged mournfully. "Poor goddamn Indians anyway. How they've been *fucked* over. Steal their land, minerals, water . . . dignity. One of the great crimes of history what we've done to these people."

"Dick," Jenny said warmly, "we agree on that. But it's got nothing to do with Beau Custerd taking care of those horses."

Slumping disagreeably, Lyons fixed beadily on Jenny, then Susan. Whoever had tried to describe him as a jolly Saint Nick look-alike had it dead wrong.

"Since we're talking Indians," Susan said boldly, "I hear the local tribe is creating problems for the Big Sea Development Company."

"Maybe so—"

"It's all Dick's doing, Susan," Jenny said sternly. "He's got Beaumont Custerd and his sister Belmont running in circles."

Lyons grinned slyly and hunched over the table, toying with the empty beer bottle.

"I'm just trying to get them to exercise their rights."

Restlessly, Lyons shoved the chair, got up, and prowled back to the kitchen where he leaned on the counter and spoke earnestly to Susan.

"I ask you not to pursue this just yet. The time's not right."

"Why would I anyway?" she demanded. "It's so complicated you'd need the full hour just to background it."

"No," he disagreed, shaking the big head, "it's really not complicated at all, that's where you're wrong, not since they dug up that graveyard anyway...on the site of the *great* massacre.''

Susan shrugged. "Who cares?"

He whirled around from the refrigerator, holding a new beer.

"Say again! *Who cares?* I don't believe it! The place is a hotbed...a volcano ready to erupt and you ask who cares?"

"Right. I'm asking how I could get anybody in New York City to get excited about a bunch of Indians fighting about an old burial ground in California. The only thing they'd care about these days is if they could get the Indians to *take back* Manhattan.''

"Oh yeah?" Lyons laughed loudly, liking the remark. Then, craftily, he muttered, "What if I said that's why some redneck bastard was shooting at old Dick...because he heard I was friendly with the Baskets and *very* disposed to help them in their cause?"

Critically, Jenny said, "Which is *not* what happened, Susan! Believe me, *nobody* cares about this Indian thing. It's been oversold..." She glanced at her husband. "...and exaggerated out of all proportion.''

"Says you, lady!" Lyons exclaimed angrily, aiming his forefinger at her. "I'm here to tell you, Sue, that Jenny is a person who sees no evil!''

"Oh, really?" Jenny said acidly.

"That's right," Lyons maintained stubbornly, argumentatively. "Just don't forget Emma Bristals heard that shot and she also heard a car or motorcycle or something screeching out of there—''

"Emma Bristals, oh yes," Jenny murmured, turning to Susan to ask acidly, "Have you been told about our *lovely* neighbor lady? Of course, you must've, if you spent time with Harry.''

"Her name was mentioned. In passing..."

Defensively chuckling, Lyons said, "For crissakes, *honey-bunch,* we were talking about her yesterday. Teller wanted to know about her hunt." He explained to Susan, "Emma's thought about setting up an English-style hunt or maybe I should say Irish-style, since she's one of those Anglo-Irish half-breeds. Call it the Petertown Blazers or some such.''

"Which," Jenny said, again disparagingly, "isn't happen-ing either. The local sheep farmers won't stand for it. They'd chase all the sheep over the cliffs. As a matter of fact, *beloved*, maybe that was some farmer shooting at your dog."

"A bastardly thing to do . . . *if* so," Lyons grunted.

He'd come out from the kitchen again and was roaming the room, prowling was the best word for it, pacing from the fireplace past them to the open front door and peering into the distance before coming back to do the same thing again.

"Anyway, Emma's pretty much given up on the idea," he mumbled. "Whata they call it? Pursuit of the inedible by the unmentionable? I'd have to come out against it, you see."

"Come now," Jenny protested, "you haven't said a word."

"My darling," he said, "Dick Lyons is pledged to fight blood sports to the bloody death."

But nevertheless, there was no hiding the fact that he was in big trouble about Emma Bristals.

Neutrally, Susan said, "All I know about her is she's the wife of Guy Bristals."

"*Sir* Guy Bristals," Lyons corrected her, "and they're separated. You should know about *him*, Sue. He's very large in the media—*too* large to my way of thinking."

Lyons scowled mightily and the idea occurred to Susan that if Bristals did make a move on NAN, as Arthur Fineman was predicting he would, they might want to call Dick Lyons to the rescue.

"Too much monopoly ownership," Lyons proclaimed. "I don't know what's happened to the antitrust laws in this country. And do we want a British press lord owning and operating *our* media outlets? I think not! I think *most definitely* not!"

"Try to stop him," Susan said. "He's just gone into Washington."

"Well," Lyons said, "how would we stop him, Sue?"

"I don't know." She smiled naively. "I try to keep away from the politics. Intrigue can be a full-time job. I'd rather just do my work."

"Spoken as a loyal *employee. Underling*." Lyons glowered comically. "I'll call you as an expert witness when I bring this outrage to the attention of the United States Senate. That'll fix your wagon, Miss Channing!"

"He's not kidding, Susan," Jenny said.

"I know but I'm not scared. I'll take the Fifth."

She had seen Lyons in action in Washington a time or two on his own, without Jenny on hand as moderating influence.

For reasons of his flamboyance, volatility, and unpredictability, Lyons had never been a favorite in the Capitol, even among those liberal politicians he supported. He was a loose cannon, they complained behind his back, you never knew when or how Lyons would get into trouble, into the papers, and damage everybody within range. Over the years, as a result, he'd lost leverage in Washington too.

Marching toward the door again, smacking his palms together sharply, Lyons sneered at Susan, at the world in general.

"Naturally, wouldn't want to be quoted, would we?" He stopped, grabbing the top of the front doorframe, hanging loosely, laconically reporting, "Somebody's coming, on a horse."

"Two to one, it's the lovely neighbor," Jenny told Susan.

A clattering of hooves confirmed it. Lyons jumped forward, clumping on the porch.

"Emma! It had to be you!"

"Hello there, Lyons!"

At first sight, Lady Emma was no less spectacular than her high-pitched, unmelodious voice. She strode up on the veranda and marched through the door like one of Napoleon's cavalry officers or a boorish country squire. You would note the hair, long, frizzy, fuzzy, raven-black hair. And the mannish face. Emma's forehead was broad and high, the skin very white, her nose long, prominent, slightly hooked in best-bred Roman fashion, flaring and, at the moment, wheezing with rushed, almost erotic breathlessness which stretched and strained a sweat-stained T-shirt she was wearing with tight blue jeans and a black leather vest.

Taking no notice of the guest, or even Jenny, she howled, "Make that a double pink gin, Richard! *And where's that boy?*"

As if anticipating, a slight youth appeared on the steps behind her.

"Here's Beau," Jenny said gently. "Beaumont, come in a second and meet my friend Susan Channing. You know *Missus* Bristals."

Emma yelled, "I want you to walk my horse around a while, Beau!"

"Hello, Beau," Susan said, smiling nicely at him.

What a very handsome young thing he was too, slim and

tall, like a young eagle. Transparently clear, his complexion was shaded, as if slightly tanned; brilliant black hair was caught in a ponytail behind his head, and his brown eyes were bright and wholly intelligent. So this was the Indian lad Lyons was subverting.

Beaumont Custerd was also shy, for when he said hello back to Susan, his voice was like a whisper in the wind. He approached Lady Emma with great care, eyes cast down. But there was bold and honest reproach in his voice.

"The horse is foaming at the mouth, Missus—"

Emma loosed a great blast of mocking laughter.

"So would you be, Beau, if you'd just spent a half-hour between my legs!"

Beau leapt back, shock, shame, and embarrassment dumping white in his tan.

Emma snorted again and only then did she acknowledge Jenny.

"Hello, ducks."

Taking no notice of Emma's not very good manners, Jenny said, "Emma, this is Susan Channing."

"How do . . ."

Emma crashed across the room, her boots thumping the wooden floor. She took Susan's hand for a brief shake.

"Nice to meet *you*," Susan murmured.

Susan did her best to resist Emma's impact which was, to say the least, larger than life. Physically, Emma was just as intimidating as Dick Lyons. She'd be close to six feet tall even out of her boots. Her build across the shoulders and chest was of a Valkyrie, the outlines of a robust bra showing through the wet T-shirt. She did taper athletically to a small waist and firm thighs. Emma's grip was very powerful.

"Susan does the *Hindsight* program on television," Jenny said.

"Never watch the telly, sorry."

"It's not required," Susan rejoined.

"Ha! Good!" Emma sneezed raucously, then turned to bawl at Beaumont Custerd. "Go on, Beau, before he freezes!"

"Yes, Beau," Jenny signaled, "would you, please?"

Beau Custerd wouldn't have moved on Emma's say-so alone. He nodded but not at Emma and went back down the steps. Then, lowing comfortingly to the horse, he led it across the yard.

One would definitely say he had a way with horses, but it

was absolutely obvious Emma Bristals couldn't spot it, not if it hit her in the eye. She was as sensitive as a stone. And Dick Lyons was no better. He came up behind Emma with her drink and must have pinched her bottom or something, for she jumped and cried out merrily.

"Lyons! *Cheeky!* Ah, my gin!" She thanked him with a loud, smacking kiss, exclaiming, "Yuk! Hair-face. Like kissing a..."

Lyons seemed to consider Emma Bristals some sort of precious commodity. Fascinated, he watched her strut across to the long table, watched as she swilled her gin. Lyons thought Emma was wonderful.

"We were just talking about the Petertown Hunt," he said.

Disgustedly, Emma said, "That bloody nonsense! It's hopeless, Lyons, which should please a wimp like you! Saladin Rivers has put in a word at the county, but apparently to no avail." As socked in with Emma as Dick appeared to be, he could not hide a sour grimace at mention of Rivers's name. Emma took no notice. "*Saladin* has influence in Rio Tinto. But not enough, it would seem."

"Because the man is a stupid moron."

"*Not so, Lyons!*" Emma's face flushed and in sudden bad humor she crossed the room again and dropped her bulk into the sofa beside Susan. "Can you imagine riding behind a pack of hounds *on leashes,* for God's sake! And the bloody fox laughing all the way." Emma spit derisively. "I'm not sure there are any fox around here anyway, Lyons-balls. Saladin and I considered importing frozen ones...thaw 'em out and drag 'em around to lay down the scent and plant 'em in a grove for the dogs to find. *Ha!*"

As Emma took another huge gulp of gin, Lyons looked jittery and said, "I think I'll have a real drink myself."

Face set grimly and making no bones about it, Jenny stood up.

"Susan and I are going outside to see how Beaumont is doing with the horse."

"That's a good boy there," Emma grunted. "Hang on to him, he'll be worth his weight in gold."

Bristling, Jenny led the way, not stopping until they were at the end of the front porch closest to a wood-fenced corral at one end of the big barn. Inside there, Beau Custerd was walking Emma's black horse in big, slow circles.

"A nice boy," Jenny muttered. "I just hope Dick doesn't get him all confused and in a lot of trouble."

"What are they up to? I know it's got Jasper Gates worried."

"I don't know. I really don't." Jenny shook her head wearily. "Dick feels he needs something—"

"A cause."

"Naturally."

Quietly, Jenny asked whether Susan was really serious about doing them again on *Hindsight*? Well, yes, Susan had to say, though she was really only reconnoitering. Jenny countered, predictably, that maybe the timing was not just right.

"Dick would use it, you know. Inform the world his life is in danger. You wouldn't want that. I want him to shut up about it. Having that . . . bitch . . . around doesn't help. She just makes it worse. I'm fed up." Jenny took a breath. "Do you see what I mean?"

"Sure I do." It was fairly obvious. "You're not going to be around."

"I'm going away. We'll see what happens. Back-burner it, what do you say?"

Susan nodded hesitantly, not because she disagreed or otherwise. It was merely better form to play reluctant. In all honesty, she could have argued, an assassination attempt, or whatever you called it, would've made a wonderful lead-in for a new *Hindsight* segment—a hook, as such things were described. But you had to weigh the one against the other: her future relationship with Jenny versus present scoop.

"The truth is," Jenny confided, putting her arm around Susan's shoulders, "Dick would like to end up a martyr. Martyrdom would only be just compensation for a lifetime of lighting fires under the Establishment. And it'd be a way out for him. It's not easy being a has-been."

"Is it . . . so bad?"

Jenny nodded.

"On the other hand, maybe I should thank God for Emma— she cheers him up."

But it must be, should be, inconceivable to Jenny Driver that a man like Dick Lyons could find comfort in such a loudmouthed vulgarian.

"Emma doesn't care if Dick is yesterday's news, Susan. Emma's only interested in one thing . . . *correction*, two things.

That, and drinking gin. Whenever I'm gone, she's over here all the time . . . or him over there. Depending on where *Mister* Rivers is."

"I cannot believe this place!"

Remorsefully, Jenny agreed. "It is too bad Dick's so involved. Otherwise, we could have a good laugh. I doubt Moon Rivers has met up with anything like Emma Bristals before. He's in a tailspin." Susan waited, nodding soberly while Jenny deliberated. "I guess you're old enough for the facts of life. It's said by them who knows that Emma devours men—if you get my slant. Emma's moves are not so common in Petertown."

"I see we're talking about a red-meat type of gal."

They got no further, for the gal in question and Dick Lyons strolled outside, both carrying oversized glasses stuffed with ice and clear liquids.

"Hey, you, Beau," Emma shouted, "keep walking him! Good lad." She laughed in a sort of nauseating camaraderie. "That is a very good-looking youth." She leered. "I wouldn't mind—"

"Hands off the help, Emma," Jenny said crossly. "Well, Dick . . . Susan is interested in doing a show but not just now, 'cause I'll be away. What about the fall, Sue?"

"Could be good."

Why not? Leave it that way: nobody was committed. Arthur Fineman would be satisfied. They wouldn't have time to do it before autumn anyway.

"Will you watch me, Emma?" Lyons asked playfully.

"I've already said I never watch telly. And if I see you every day anyway, why should I turn on the stupid telly? Just reminds me of that *berk,* Guy Bristals."

Lyons rumbled with faraway laughter, like thunder. With the hefty drink, his eyes had come unfocused.

"Anyway, Sue," he said with mock bravado, "better do it before somebody shoots a big hole in Dick Lyons's ass!"

"Who'd bother?" Emma spoke scathingly, then turned and pointed. "What now?" In the direction of her finger, a green car was just turning into Rancho Mondo. "I know! It's . . ." Emma glanced at Jenny. ". . . none other than . . ."

"Bert Jay," Jenny said.

"Oh, great!" Lyons exclaimed. "*Jenny's lover.* Isn't that nice?"

Susan wished she was somewhere else.

"Shut up, Dick," Jenny reproved him. "His big joke. *Very* funny, Dick."

"God's truth!"

"God's *untruth*! You don't like Bear because he thinks you're insane."

"No way!" Dick Lyons cried, suddenly in high good humor, "Professor-Doctor Jay is *with me* on insecticides! We both campaigned on the chemical-fertilizer issue. . . ."

As he babbled insincerely, the green Volvo approached, then slowly entered the quad.

Susan had been impressed by the physical look of Emma Bristals. Now, she was simply surprised by Bertram "Bear" Jay. Agilely, he hoped out of the car. He moved well, with grace. He was of medium height but his body, round and bustling, made him seem shorter. You could imagine him playing college football, but not professionally.

This unlikely character was Jenny Driver's boyfriend? He looked more like a scientist than a lover-boy, more an Einstein than a Barrymore, with his disc of sandy hair like a halo fluttering over his near-bald head. A perfect round of face beamed with a smile while the eyes sparkled behind big, dark-framed spectacles.

It was good that Bear Jay was smart. Otherwise, Susan might have felt sorry indeed for her friend. On the other hand, Jenny had always had a very individual taste in men. Jay was not handsome, true, but he was not ugly either. He would never be a worry. Other women were not going to be chasing him—as they might a Harry Teller.

"Hi, everybody!"

His voice was thin, reedy like his son's, also eager, anxious to please, to be liked. From the bottom of the steps, he gazed up at them, grinning.

"Hi, Dick . . . Emma . . . *Jenny,* dear! And *Susan Channing*! I had to meet you! Jenny's oldest friend." Well, that was going some, but Susan let it stand. "Ted told me you'd be here. And so I came right along. I took the liberty—"

"No liberty, Bear!" Dick Lyons had begun to laugh, with such glee and joy you wondered about him. Did a right-minded man make such a noise when confronted by the supposed boyfriend of his wife. "What're you drinking?"

"Nice cold beer would be much appreciated, Dick." Jay came up the steps and took Susan's hand in his small, warm, wet palm. "*You* are Susan Channing. I'm so *pleased* to meet you."

"Well..."

Susan didn't know what to say, but didn't have to say anything, for Dick Lyons started up again.

"Been telling everybody, Bear, that your work is absolutely essential if life is going to continue on the planet and the human race as a recognizable species. Including, *of course*, your work at Big Sea..."

"Dick..." Jay went nasal. "I keep telling you—they are going to get in a proper archaeologist."

"Proper or improper," Lyons cried, "as long as he knows what he's doing."

6

Jenny didn't have to say she was worried about Dick Lyons. Or why. Susan had seen how he behaved with Emma Bristals. But she did, as soon as she and Susan had climbed into Bear Jay's car. Jenny and Dick had been married something like fourteen or fifteen years now, a long time.

Petertown was deep in the quiet of late afternoon when they brought Susan back down the hill. People were going into the market, coming out, and down the road neon beer signs flickered drowsily in the cloudy windows of the hotel bar. What sounded like jukebox music trickled into the dusty street.

"It's late," Susan said from the backseat of the green Volvo. "I didn't mean to stay so long."

"No problem, honey," said Jenny.

They'd sent the Big Sea driver away and so, really against her will, she'd been stranded up there for the rest of the steamy, sunbaked afternoon. Three or four miles back from the ocean, Rancho Mondo missed the cooling, offshore breezes which air-conditioned a place like Big Sea. A couple more hours of heat, and of Dick and Emma and Jenny and Bear, had not been wonderful. In the beginning, for no good reason, Dick Lyons seemed to have been totally charmed by Bear Jay's pixyish humor, his rather high-pitched style, and they'd managed to chat in a semicivilized way, even allowing for Emma's lapses. Then, unfortunately, after a few more strong drinks and Emma's unceasing provocation, Dick began to fuss and fume and, at one frightening moment, responding to one of Bear's more giddy remarks, marched across the room, yanked Bear to his feet and crushed Bear against his chest for a suffocating second, then dumped him down with a roar and announcement that Bear Jay was "nothing but a silly fucking little twerp who ought to have his ass kicked up and down the coastline." And that was about it. Dick and Emma stomped into the kitchen for another drink and with a curse, Emma said she was riding home and commanded Lyons to come with her to the barn to help secure her horse, which she called Black Bastard. Then, to general relief, and Susan's renewed embarrassment, Dick and Emma stayed in the barn and were pretty obviously not looking for her horse. Finally, the moment came at which Jenny, stonily, stood up and announced they'd be bringing Susan back to the inn now. This turn of events, or last turn of the screw, had to be a strong clue as to the real situation in the Driver-Lyons household. Susan didn't know what to say, or if she was expected to say anything.

"And *now*," she muttered uncomfortably, "here we are at Moon Rivers's gas station . . . a stone's throw from the Petertown Hotel, built in nineteen-oh-five or whatever."

Bear Jay chuckled and Jenny turned in her seat to smile wanly.

"A couple more days and we'll make you our official Petertown tour guide," Bear cried fruitily.

"When I flee New York," Susan murmured.

Why, was she thinking of it? Bear's back straightened and he glanced at her swiftly in the rearview mirror.

"*Could* you handle a place like this? I always wonder about career women like you . . . and *dear* Jenny." He smiled ravishingly, looking like a fallen angel—or choirboy, Susan recalled, thinking of Jasper Gates. Then, with an un-Bear-like giggle, he slowed the car. "Speaking of which, there's a coincidence! See the man on the porch, outside the bar? That's Moon Rivers. He looks drunk, *very* drunk."

Tall and skinny and alone, like a scarecrow in the field,

Rivers stood there, facing the street, swaying with the breeze and melodies all his own. His face was shaded by a floppy-brimmed black hat; a thin, pointy chin jutted out underneath, the smoke of a cigarette marking the corner of his mouth. Moon was a truly cadaverous person, narrow in the shoulders and chest.

Then, giving it away, he wobbled, staggered, and grabbed for the porch railing.

Susan felt let down. But what had she been led to expect? Maybe not a goon but definitely a being slightly more attractive than this.

"Lady Emma's paramour?"

"One of them," Jenny said acidly.

"Don't you *love* it?" Bear chortled.

"Not much," Jenny said.

"Now, now, Jen! We agreed," Bear Jay said sharply.

"Quite a place, ain't it?" Jenny laughed scornfully. "Just like the carryings-on of the rich and famous."

"Why should it be any different?" Susan said lightly.

Bear concurred. "Everything is just one big village!" he cried, delighted by the chance to say so. "Dress it up . . . hand it a lot of money . . . educate it . . . and it boils down to the same thing—little people fooling around with the same dynamite."

Yes, and did that include himself and Jenny? Susan wondered how much there was to it. Bertram "Bear" Jay did not aptly fit the suit of lover, comforter of dissatisfied actresses.

Hooking her arm over the seat and turning to Susan, Jenny said, "You see, Dick always carries things too far. Emma . . . the Custerd twins. It's built in. He's always been like that. And now the Indians—like they say, a little education is a danger-ous thing."

Bear Jay commented, "It's you liberals who say the Indians *should* be educated to take control of their own destiny."

All right, Jenny said, that was so and the Custerds did have a point, and Jenny was on their side too, *somewhat*. But Dick was overdoing it. Jenny remembered that when Belmont and her twin had first broached the matter of the Federal govern-ment's malfeasance in the Indian Island affair, Dick had just laughed at them. Then, after a little thought, he'd become interested, then involved . . . and now, where would it lead?

"Bear says Dick needs help," Jenny said, "but I don't see

how we can help him. He won't talk to Bear. You saw how he behaved."

"I don't get it," Susan said. "What's wrong with him anyway? He seems all right to me. The same as always."

Bear said, "I can't go into detail. That wouldn't be ethical."

"Ethical?"

"Yes. Ethical."

Well, was it ethical to carry on with the subject's wife then, to discuss Dick Lyons's case with Jenny, behind Dick's back?

"Dick Lyons," Bear said after a moment, "is not the type to admit he needs or wants any help. He's much too strong."

"So?"

"Well," Bear said acutely, "it's no secret he drinks too much and it's well established that as a person gets older alcohol has a terrible effect. By definition, he's demented, to a greater or lesser degree. Eventually, it becomes a question of knowing right from wrong, making logical and sensible judgments."

"Do you see, Sue?" Jenny asked.

"I guess so." Yes, Lyons was a mess; he was neurotic, slightly manic. But crazy? "I don't see he's delusional just because he has a feeling for the Indians."

"He's stirring them up just to please himself. It's all ego," Jenny said snappily.

As they cleared the Indian Island bridge, Bear said maliciously, "Poor Dick feels he's been forsaken. But who knows? Dick is expert at rabble-rousing. If he adopts the Baskets's case as his own . . . takes up the cudgels against the Big Sea Development Company . . . well, who *does* know?" Bear paused for effect. "And we *do* have to sympathize, don't we? It sometimes seems like the Cambodians get more press in a month than the Indians have in a hundred years."

"Besides which," Susan observed tartly, "a good deal of progress has been due to people other people have been pleased to call delusional."

Bear laughed loudly. "Point taken!"

For a moment, stirred by Susan's remark, he continued volubly, defensively, though insincerely, on the subject of Dick Lyons, how he, Bear, had always admired the man, especially during all those times when Dick had been such a lonely hero. But lately, *lately*, Bear stressed, poor Dick spent himself chasing his own tail; and in certain instances, he had been more than counterproductive. In particular, Bear recalled that when he'd been at Harvard, Dick had gotten his antinuclear power cause tangled up in a research program in the biological setup of cranberry bogs.

"Dick stuck his oar in," Bear related, "to prove a point which, at the time, no one was interested in making: that in due course nuclear power plants were going to mess up the cranberry industry. Finally, Dick became such a nuisance that they shelved the project."

"What you're saying," Jenny said irritably, "is that you don't like him. So how *could* you ever help him?"

"Did I say that, Jen?" His voice pitched up. "I did not say that! Not at all." He sighed negatively. "What I care about, Sue, is that this is an awful cross for Jenny to bear. Face it, Jenny, he does drink too much. He's abusive. And Emma! He just *throws* that little affair in your face. Jenny's an artist! She should not be burdened! I resent it!" Bear stared passionately into the mirror. "But I've worked with her. I've made her see what's happened: the anxieties and the feelings of guilt. They go back, yes, way back. Jenny looks for a father, Sue, do you understand?"

Jenny was staring at Susan, unblinkingly, intently. But seriously? Susan doubted it. She could not be taking this stuff seriously. Bear Jay was a cuckoo.

"Bear's been a help," Jenny acknowledged, committing herself no further than that.'

"And, Jenny! I *do not* dislike him!" Bear Jay said heatedly. "Lyons is a giant of a man and I wouldn't use the word carelessly...*I love him!* But the truth is he seems a lot bigger and stronger than he really is."

Jenny added, sardonically, "And victimized by such tacky people..."

"Exactly!"

"...like Emma Bristals." Jenny tossed her head. "On the other hand, it frees me from...well, compunctions...look how close Dick has brought me to Bear."

Bear Jay touched Jenny's cheek softly.

"We're thick as thieves," Jenny said comfortably, still watching Susan for the smallest reaction. "We go walking in the woods, we meet for coffee...."

"Well, you're very...grown up about it," Susan murmured. Where were they going, by the way? Susan wanted to detour them from discussion of their not very fascinating affair. Bear had gone on past the inn and was headed toward the north end of the island where, as Susan understood it, the golf course was located.

"Just back there," Bear said, pointing past Jenny's nose, "that's the stable area, where they stumbled on the burial plot. But I thought we'd drive down to North Point. The sunset promises to be spectacular. Is that all right, Susan?"

"Fine with me." Which was not true. She yearned to get away from them. "I'm in no rush."

"Then we can have a little dinner," Bear suggested. "What say you, Jen?"

"Wonderful," Jenny said unenthusiastically.

There was something annoying about this. Susan knew, she just *knew,* that Jenny was leading him on; her mockery of him was so fine and sharp—like razor cuts, very deadly and cruel. And Bear Jay didn't even feel it. Was this, by any chance, the real Jenny Driver surfacing? Or was Jenny merely amusing herself in yet another role, that of vengeful wife, having her own back on her mad husband with the unknowing help of this man of science?

Susan had to wonder too about Bear Jay. He was such a star-struck ninny! Could a man so dense amount to anything as a shrink, could such a simp do anybody any good?

"You told Dick the company is getting in a archaeologist," Susan reminded Jay before they were entirely out of range of the dig. "You've been advising them, I gather."

"Oh, yes. Oh, yes. But I am not qualified. That's why . . . By the way," he said gleefully, "I wonder . . . well, I suppose you have heard the other open secret about Big Sea, Sue." He teased her glibly, watching in the mirror. "No? You? A leading journalist?"

"I'm human. Try me."

"Which is that a Japanese trading company is interested in buying Big Sea."

She scowled. "I hadn't heard that." And, if it was true, she could begin justifiably to hate various people for not telling her, starting with Jasper Gates. "Is that a local rumor? Nobody's mentioned it."

"It's rumor," he said jovially, "grounded in circumstantial evidence—a group of Japanese have been coming up from San Francisco for the last month or so and . . . looking around, as best I can make out."

"Pretty circumstantial. I'd need more than that to go on."

"Would it matter to you, Susan?" Jenny asked, twisting around again.

"For a show on Jasper International it certainly would."

"Harry didn't tell you?"

"No, but maybe he's keeping it for himself . . . or it's not true."

"I didn't get a chance to say so," Jenny said generously, "but Harry is a really nice man. Handsome, my God! I like him but haven't seen half-enough of him. We met . . . um . . . once, by accident, in San Francisco, of course. I happened to be alone. Harry's so funny and easy to get along with."

"Yes, he is that," Susan agreed, her heart pumping poison.

"I admire what he does and he does it very well. He talked sense to Dick."

"And," Susan said tersely, "he told me he thought *you* were fabulous."

Bear's light-colored eyebrows leapt.

"I told Jenny! I told her: Jenny, go for it!"

Jenny smiled at Susan, amusedly. "Easy for you to say, Bear!"

"Jenny, tell it the way it is! We agreed. Always tell it the way it is!"

"There's nothing to tell."

"Well . . ." Susan hesitated. It killed her but she had to ask. "Is Bear trying to make you say you had an affair with Harry Teller? *Are* having?"

Jenny looked less amused. "I wouldn't discuss a thing like that, Susan, you know better."

She turned away from Susan, faced front, folded her arms. The profile of her angular face was beautiful in the twilight, but so cold.

"Now, Jen—"

"Bear, *you* tell it like it is! Tell her about Amy . . ."

Jenny had hit a raw nerve. His eyes flicked up in the mirror, hurt this time. But Bear had it coming.

"She died, that's all."

"She jumped out of a window," Jenny declared, voice vindictive, "and you got sent to Siberia for failing to recognize the symptoms—"

"Not so, Jen! Not so! It's purely voluntary, me being here!"

"Tell it like it is, Bear, tell it like it is!"

"It was bound to happen," Bear said in a small voice, "given the genes. But I was surprised, despite my own training. A sudden onslaught of mood changes, tantrums, depression. I thought at first it was a brain tumor." He turned his head but, as Susan didn't respond, continued. "Anyway, to keep it brief, one fine day when Ted was six years old, Amy went downtown, checked into a room and, while the bellhop was still on his way back downstairs, she heaved a chair through the window and jumped after it."

"I'm sorry."

"It was going to happen. There was *nothing* I could do about it."

"You did not have to tell me," Susan said. "That was a long time ago."

"Jenny wanted me to tell you."

But why?

Bear had parked the Volvo, the nose of the car, it seemed to Susan, no more than ten feet from the spot where the crumbly seaside bluff ended and emptiness began. As if in pain, or cramped up, he stretched, clutching and wringing his hands, then briskly massaging his temples.

"Anyway, one way or another, here we are," he said.

The low rim of the red-orange sun was just touching the blue-sea horizon. Slowly, degree by degree, it would slip away, the process speeding as if, toward the end, there was that much less of it for the sea to devour. From this ringside seat on the horizon, Susan supposed, you could be more appreciative of the fact the earth was more round than flat, the universe endless and life infinite. Unfortunately, the human mind was programmed for ends and beginnings.

"Soak in the scene, Susan," Bear Jay muttered. "Illusion. And when will we see you again? There are so many things to talk about, that we haven't talked about."

"I can't think what," Jenny said. "It seems to me we've talked about everything under the sun, *ad infinitum*."

She might have been saying *ad nauseum*, such was the tone of her voice.

". . . though I'd love to stay. . ."

Jenny laughed.

"What! In this booby hatch?"

"I was going to say *paradise*. I want to thank you for such a nice day and for bringing me back."

Bear looked at her tenderly.

"It was more than just a nice day, Susan!"

Maybe she had it all wrong. Bear was not as softheaded as he seemed. Beneath his bitchy surface, he was pure bitch. As if to help Susan with that point, he leaned across the seat and kissed Jenny, and Jenny turned her head and plainly, only a few feet away, Susan could see their faces, the lips touch, their expressions, and clearly hear Jenny's frank intake of air. What was Bear trying to prove? Or Jenny? He giggled and their tongues twined; Jenny laughed huskily.

As if Susan wasn't there.

But she was there, sitting right behind them. And it was damned embarrassing. Susan did her best to concentrate on the declining sun. All along, Susan had thought she understood Jenny Driver. And never had. Actually, they hadn't ever been such great pals as all that, but still Susan had never counted on seeing a Jenny Driver admit, exhibit, even flaunt mad, old lust. Jenny groaned hoarsely, and her turquoise jewelry began to rattle as Bear had at her with his hands.

Why were they doing this? Bear turned slightly and winked at Susan, why, as if trying to include her in the action, whatever, some form of therapy he was practicing on Jenny. The therapy of humiliation?

Susan began to perspire.

Maybe she shouldn't have been surprised. Jenny came from a cockeyed world. Susan had once been told of a movieland couple who got their kicks from calling perfect strangers on the telephone and inviting them to listen in while they made love. Hi, my name is Caesar and we'd like you to listen while I screw Calpurnia.

Even though he was a shrink, this was not what Susan had expected of Bear Jay.

Suddenly, she thought of Harry and remembered that horrible bit of the conversation. Would she ever know the truth about him and Jenny? A cold and clammy loneliness came down on her, the horror of the void.

No longer was Susan surprised by anything, certainly not now, as, with a gesture Susan could not misinterpret, Jenny pulled open her blouse and Bear's head disappeared on the other side of the seat.

The sun dropped over the edge of the world and was gone.

Susan could not stand it any longer.

Perhaps they didn't hear her open the car door or didn't care when she slammed it shut.

She didn't look back.

Bitterly, she walked the way they had come, not turning around. It was not as far back to the inn as she had feared. She found a path off to the side of the road, in case they came after her, and followed it into the twilight, now restful and finally somewhat reassuring.

She thought of Harry again, if there was any point to that.

It was all ridiculous, not worth thinking about, none of it had anything to do with her. She was balanced on her tightrope, walking fearlessly forward and away.

And she *would* survive. She knew that now for absolute certain.

7

How many more arrivals and departures?

Susan smiled wearily at the single red rose so perkily erect in a polished silver bud vase at the partition behind the driver's seat, a few inches from Sidney Wilmer's prickly-haired neck. AHB would have caused Wilmer to place the flower there. She was touched, despite her bad feelings about the trip.

The city was the pits, already muggy and hot, though they were not far into summer. Susan's plane had been late into Newark, all too naturally—there was nothing anybody, including August or traveling first class, could do about that. Fortunately, Sidney had been waiting and within minutes Susan found herself in the backseat of August's long black limousine, cocooned in comfort that made her smile gratefully.

Sid Wilmer drove steadily, a master at the wheel. For years now, he had been AHB's driver and perhaps his friend too, if it could be said that AHB had any friends. If not otherwise in motion, Sid could be counted upon to meet Susan when she came back to the city from her frequent trips. If he was busy with August, then somebody else got the assignment.

And, as Susan was very aware, droopy, hound-dog Sidney would always be on the alert for any tip-off that Susan had strayed off the straight and narrow while on the road. How those know-it-all Times Square eyes would've rolled if Wilmer had had any inkling of the strange goings-on at the edge of the Pacific.

"Trip okay, Miss Channing?" Susan didn't have to answer. Sid went right on. "There's a cold split of champagne in the ice bucket. I took the liberty of removing the cork," he announced over the front-to-rear intercom, "and slipped a fizz-saver over the top . . ."

Okay? If she'd stayed any longer, the trip would have been an absolute disaster. Escaping from Bear and Jenny, she'd hid out in her room, then early the next morning fled to San Francisco and then Sacramento, cramming work into the schedule, trying to put everything at Big Sea out of her mind. And it had not gone all that well. She'd been tired and out of sorts and angry at Harry—and herself. How unprofessional to allow all the personal junk to interfere with her preparation for the interviews. After Jenny and Bear, and being jealous and upset about Harry, she hadn't the gumption to study the file on Big Oil. So, it was more than partly her own fault that things had gotten away from her.

Dramatizing the debate was difficult enough, even when you'd done your homework. It was months now since the Great Alaska Oil Spill and, as usual, people tended to forget. The ex-governor had been decidedly unhelpful, more concerned with pushing the politics of the situation, and the present governor in avoiding any opinion that might seem at odds with the policy set by his political allies in Washington.

Add to that an obstreperous camera crew from the San Francisco affiliate and you had the makings of an ulcer, at least the mild gastritis to which Susan fell victim from time to time.

She'd called him, of course, made excuses to Harry about being suddenly ordered away. On the phone, cool, detached, uncommunicative, she'd probably made him feel miserable, but what did he expect? Susan couldn't figure out his deal with Jenny and he hadn't helped at all. He'd lied to her, hadn't he? She wasn't sure, given the way Jenny had gone into heat with Bear Jay. But Jenny had hinted and broadly

enough to make Susan cautious. And angry anyway, whatever
the truth of it, because he'd caused her to neglect her work,
just by being Harry, himself.

Susan had let herself be destroyed all over again, thinking
of Nate and making hasty love to Harry.

She'd promised that she'd soon be back to Big Sea, but she
lied. Would she ever return? Maybe. It was doubtful. She
couldn't handle it.

"... and a frosty glass, Miss Channing. At your service!"

"Thanks, Sidney, but no thanks."

How to shut him up? On and on, Sid babbled. She
might've told Wilmer she'd had enough to drink over the
weekend to last her a month, but that wouldn't be wise, so
she reached for the glass.

"So how is that place, Miss Channing?"

Pouring a small dose of the champagne, Susan returned to
the depth of the cushion and said, "Truly lovely, Sidney.
Right on the ocean. You can walk down on the bluff at
night...and see all the way to China!"

"All the way? That's good eyesight!"

Wilmer made her tired. On the ground for only a half hour,
she was ready to leave again.

"Everything okay, Sidney? How is Mr. Blick? And Missus
Mignon?"

Susan always made a special point of inquiring after the
health of her former mother-in-law.

"All is well."

AHB never wasted a phone call to let her know everything
was fine. He resented personal calls—Good God, what if the
lines were all busy and one of the banks called, or the stock-
brokers, his precious metals merchant, commodities company,
Mein Gott! What if his people called from Zurich or Tokyo?

Now, Wilmer had to devote his whole attention to negotiating the approach to the Lincoln Tunnel. He couldn't talk and
drive at the same time. Oh no, she shouldn't denigrate him.
Wilmer did his job; he was far more solicitous to the Blicks
than their own son Roger Blake, Hollywood minimogul.

It wasn't exactly unpleasant sipping champagne in such
pampered circumstances: behind tinted glass, air-conditioned,
suspended in velvet cushions as firm yet pliant as a warm
hand.

The limo slid into the garishly lit tunnel. Thank God for

climate control, one-way glass, locked doors. It wasn't even full summer yet and already the natives were restless.

Susan drank the last of the champagne as they crossed Fifth Avenue.

One did not simply arrive at the place on Park Avenue.

Susan swept in, carrying only her pocketbook and the *People* magazine she'd been reading on the plane. Wilmer would see to her luggage. The night concierge, dressed in a decorous black suit with little crossed gold keys on his lapels like that in a London hotel, leapt toward her.

"Good evening, Miss Channing-Osborne. Pleasant journey? Can we look forward to another smashing *"Hindsight"*? Or was it holiday out in California?"

"A little work, a little play, Mr. Pipkin."

The evening was still young, just past seven, and Mr. Pipkin was in his best mood. Later, dealing with doddering matrons and overbearing millionaires who populated this part of town, chasing unavailable taxis, and taking full responsibility for missed appointments, sudden rainstorms, and random muggings, Pipkin's nerves would fray. So, she supposed, one couldn't blame him for behaving like he was wired. Beaming, he held back the elevator door.

"Wonderful to have you back, Miss Channing-Osborne."

Snob that he was, Pipkin had a fondness for double-barreled names. As the concierge and therefore nosy, he would, of course, know all about the arrangements on the seventh floor.

AHB had once been told that the longest New York fire-ladder wouldn't reach beyond seven. So he had bought flats seven, seven-oh-one, seven-oh-two, seven-oh-three, seven-oh . . . God knew how many more and knocked them all together to create an eight-thousand-square-foot home in the heart of Manhattan. Susan's own two-bedroom place, seven-oh-whatever, was separate but contiguous; a discreet connecting door had been installed in her dressing room and absolutely nobody knew about it, except AHB and, perhaps, the butler Konrad. Thus, when the moon was full, AHB was able to slip in and out like Dracula, protected from prying eyes.

Again, *why*? Why did Susan put up with the unusual arrangement? For how many years now . . . was it the money? The reflected power? No, while she respected both these things, the key was her fondness for the elder Blicks, her former in-laws, nothing more and nothing less than that.

Elevator doors sucked back and Susan stepped into the thickly carpeted corridor, proceeding beneath Bohemian crystal chandeliers from AHB's private stock toward her corner flat. There was no need to take special care to tread quietly. An elephant could've danced down the hallway as lightly as a sylph. Yes, of course, you could hear a watch ticking and or the silky sound of thighs kissing underneath a skirt.

As Susan expected, upon the silver tray on the table within her small, square foyer was the note, a piece of stiff white paper folded precisely to exhibit the embossed silver monogram: A.H.B.

Unfolding, she read familiar, spidery handwriting:

> *AHB requests you ring soonest upon arrival.*

Sure. But first she had to go to the bathroom, *if* he didn't mind. The champagne had renewed the queasiness in her gut. And, naturally, though she didn't feel like it, or was afraid of what she might hear, Susan had to check the office for messages. You never knew: she might be booked on a two A.M. flight to Lisbon. This happened often enough. In the early days, it had been such surprises that had made the job so exciting.

Once in the bathroom, Susan invested another five minutes in a shower and then her walk-in closet for a change of clothes. She put aside her cotton traveling dress, from Donna Karan, who helped a woman *not* make a big fuss about her clothes, and got into a baggy sweatsuit, perfect for lolling-around Saturdays—somebody had brought it to her from Baden-Baden—just right for a quick drink with August and Mignon.

Dressed and ready to go, she saw Wilmer had parked her two slim Vuitton bags just inside the front door, next to the neat little study where Susan kept her office-away-from-the-office, complete with a desk for part-time secretary *and* the all-important answering machine. There had not been much weekend action: two calls re: Sunday brunch; a message from a *Vanity Fair* editor and another from *W,* and what would they want? Probably to pick her brain about somebody they were skewering. Her friend Scaasi begged her to get back to him; toward the end there was a cryptic message from her agent, Morty Morton; and finally a garbled outcry from one Chop-

Chop Roberts at Chez Chow, a new Sichuan restaurant much frequented by the in-crowd. Chez Chow was to host a Peking Duck Feast *dansant* to benefit the Metropolitan Museum's American Wing and they so hoped Miss Channing would be a guest.

Well, too late to deal with it now. Vaguely, Susan had half expected, half hoped Harry would've left a message to greet her upon arrival. But no, not a word. It would seem their final conversation in California had done the trick.

Harry? Harry who? How your outlook changed when you got back to the city. You didn't need anybody.

She called the overnight message desk at NAN.

"Miss Channing! Yes, just a moment!"

The voice was well-modulated male and obviously in training for better things.

"Miss Channing! We have Mr. Fineman three times—first, eleven forty-five A.M. on Friday. Two more from Mr. Fineman Friday afternoon . . ."

Though it would not help, she said, "He should have known I wasn't around Friday!"

". . . to remind you about the meeting," the message-giver continued, "and one from Mr. Godfrey in Washington, that's Friday five P.M."

"Yes?"

The mellow voice broke up with embarrassment.

"I'm sorry, Miss Channing. Saying: Hi, babe . . ." Pause. "How's your ass?"

"*For God's sake!* Who did you say that was from?"

"Mr. Godfrey in Washington."

"He'd never leave such a message."

"It's . . . right here, Miss Channing. I can show you—"

"What'd you say your name was?"

The voice dropped about an octave, ready to open the evening news.

"This is Briarly Prescott speaking, Miss Channing."

Susan's lip curled. She might have taken a bite out of the phone.

"Well, look, Briarly, just tear that up. Okay?"

"Done, Miss Channing!"

"You have a beautiful voice, Briarly." Susan whispered to him throatily. He stammered unintelligibly. "Thanks, Briarly Prescott."

After all, she didn't want the interns and lowly message

clerks mouthing it around that Susan Channing was some kind of a ball-buster who received rude messages from the bureaus.

Konrad, August's veteran butler, greeted Susan at the Blick front door, an imposing ton or so of well-hung wood and bulletproof steel. Gray-faced Konrad's eyes bulged at her significantly and Susan said hello as gravely as she could; it was expected. Konrad preferred to think the lights were going out all over the world. Like a funeral parlor attendant, he led her across the few dozen feet of marbled floor to the nearest door of the four which gave off the foyer, then stood aside and made his announcement.

"Miss Susan Channing!"

A gratified *Ach*-sound rumbled out of the tall, spare, but graceful man who was rising creakily from the jumble of furniture in the center of an eighty-foot salon. The lighting was terrible in here, always had been, with blinds pulled and drapes for all practical purposes permanently closed; what light there was emanated from a single large Tiffany lamp in a position of honor atop an Empire table said to have been used by the Empress Josephine for her bibelots. The Blick salon, Susan had always thought and not very originally, was both like a mausoleum and a museum, if the world had known, an art gallery of chaotic dimensions. The furniture collection was best described as eclectic in style; along with Empire, it was heavy carved Victorian, modern, and postmodern. August's own favorite chair, for example, was a leather lounger, easy to get into, hard to get out of. The same mad and often tasteless inventory carried to the walls, these lined with old and new masters, portraits of old and new ancestors, indiscreetly mixed into the company of the real treasures: a small collection of Giottos, a Rubens or two, a corner of Leonardo sketches, too many early Italian landscapes, a Michelangelo and four or five of his school, a dozen or so of the Impressionists, three early Picassos, a handful of Braque, a half-dozen Ignotos . . . and so on.

Susan had wondered aloud, but only once, whether any of the art was "hot"—since no one ever came here, the world would never know. AHB had not taken kindly to the flip remark, saying that for him, a lover of art, provenance was of little consequence. You liked the stuff or you didn't.

August Hugo Blick was a courtly man who seemed much

taller than he actually was. His face was long and lantern-jawed, with a big, bony nose and thin gray hair receding from an outlandishly high forehead. And his eyes! Those of a bird of prey, hawk-keen, eagle-fierce, slanting down a vulturelike beak.

"My dear! Welcome home!"

August's voice was low and powerful. The remnant of accent added to its timbre and reminded one of his theatrical background.

And Mignon. The little old lady stared blankly at Susan from her nest in a brocade-covered couch. Whereas August was old but grand and vital, Mignon was merely old. There was *bird* about her too—but in the plumage, not the eyes. Mignon was dressed in a riotous mismatch of color and style: long greenish Donegal tweed skirt, ruffled orange silk blouse, and yellow shawl clutched around her neck.

"It's Susan, come home, *Schatz*, and just in time for a cocktail!" August said loudly.

Taking Susan by the hand, possessively, AHB gazed into her eyes, interrogating her without words.

"You're tired," he said. "Sit . . . sit."

Holding her hand high, August escorted her to the grandest of his Tudor chairs, tapestry-covered and not comfortable, something, by the feel of it, that one of the Henrys could've parked on.

"Hello, Mignon." Susan spoke sweetly but didn't go to her. Mignon had a bad habit of biting the proffered hand. "Are you well?"

"Never better!" August said, jollity forced. "And, now then Konrad!" Having reseated himself, AHB clasped his big-knuckled hands in front of his jutting chin and stared wickedly at his petite wife. "Konrad, line up the Manhattans for this little lady!"

For as long as Susan had known them, Konrad had been lining up the Manhattans for the little lady. But Mignon already had a Manhattan in front of her on the scarred coffee table—yes, everything in the room needed refinishing, but why bother?

"*And*, dear Susan, what would you like?"

"A Perrier?"

"My dear! Not the usual?"

"No thank you, August. The trip, the plane, you know . . ."

"Well, never mind!" A slight deafness made him speak too loud. "For me, Konrad, brandy-soda."

After Konrad had retreated, Susan went into her spiel, beginning with departure from Park Avenue . . . God, a hundred years ago. Always, when Susan returned from a trip, August called upon her for a detailed report: Where she'd stayed, restaurants visited, people interviewed, etcetera, etcetera. Of course, Susan was often forced to fictionalize and this time was no different. She was not about to tell them about Harry and how she'd mishandled that, or about Jenny and Dick and Bear Jay. He could have no inkling of the things Susan had *not* told him about—how could he, unless he'd been so crude as to have her followed? That was always a possibility, although Susan liked to think August wouldn't so demean himself. Nonetheless, she was always careful on her trips and equally careful upon her return in the editing of her adventures.

No, the flashbulbs popped not in ambush of Susan Channing!

August thought of himself as a man-of-the-world and, in the normal meaning of the term, he was. But was he *man* enough to allow that a woman of Susan's age and temperament might, from time to time, require a bit of the real thing?

"And, my dear?" he asked. "What about our friend Jasper Gates?"

"An interesting man, I thought. Something of a diamond in the rough, I'd say—"

"Perhaps zircon would be more like it."

Question: should Susan attempt to report what was happening at Big Sea? No, better wait, maybe even write it all down in the form of a memo. It was all too complex to go into now, particularly as Mignon was eyeballing her with such rigid suspicion, the hostility of the perfect stranger. If looks could kill, she was a dead woman.

AHB noticed Susan's bemused look and smiled loftily, probably thinking she'd appreciated the crack about Gates. But he let it go for the moment, to watch as Konrad carefully placed the three fresh Manhattans in front of Mignon.

Mignon gestured feebly for Konrad to come closer, then whispered to him behind her hand. Konrad muttered a reply.

"What did you say?" she demanded in an off-key tone. "Speak up, I can't hear you!"

Konrad handled it with weary resignation.

"She is Miss Susan Channing, Madame."

Well, for . . . Mignon didn't recognize her! August flushed irritably.

"Mignon! *Gott!* Susan was married to your son!"

"I don't care who she is," Mignon yelped. "Get her out of here!"

With that, Mignon lunged forward, plucked the first of the trio of fresh Manhattans off the table and with unlikely dexterity shot the contents into her mouth. Seizing the second, she lifted her eyes and for a moment, August dared her unbalanced glare. Then, registering extreme melancholia, he looked away. His thoughts would be unhappy ones; he would be contemplating The End of the Road. And the brandy-soda wouldn't help.

"Well." August sighed. "We have missed you, whatever we say."

Could Mignon know about them? Was that the problem? Maybe a better question was how could she fail to know? They lived in adjoining flats on Park Avenue, breezeway-linked suites at the Wade's Reef villa and, no, it didn't seem possible Mignon didn't know, even in her dotage. To be truthful, of course, August kept her plastered most of the time; he never came to Susan until Mignon was well and truly asleep, read: passed out. So whatever knowledge she had could just as well have come from liverish nightmare.

Konrad hovering, August watched silently as Mignon polished off the second drink, then said calmly, voice flat as still water, "It seems, *Konnie,* that you may prepare another round."

"No." Mignon sneered. "The third will be enough and then I shall go to bed. I know you wish to talk business with this . . . young lady."

"Now . . . *Schatz* . . . before dinner?"

This would never do. Susan had had enough. This, on top of the weekend, and her upset stomach, was too much. Susan finished the Perrier and jumped up.

"Actually, I have to go. I've got a lot of homework and a meeting early tomorrow." She didn't wait for August to protest or for Mignon to realize, if she was capable, that she'd been very insulting. "Good night, Mignon." And to August, she said, "I'm sure in due course you'll want to hear about Big Sea."

August looked shaken, annoyed.

"Yes. Surely."

* * *

More than simply tired from the trip, Susan was groggy with fatigue and despair by the time August arrived at her bedside. As always, he behaved so reticently, as if bearing a message marked Grim and Foreboding. It was a while before he said anything and Susan don't help him out. She waited, drifting along the edge of sleep.

"I am sorry about that, my dear," he finally whispered. "The little lady is *kaput.*"

Kaput? The little lady's problem was too many Manhattans, Susan might have disagreed, but she remained mute, though moaning a bar or two so August would know she was not feeling exceptionally receptive. By and by, he put a hand on her forehead and lightly caressed, as if to induce rest. This was the way he liked her, passive, inert, stroked to lassitude. *Be still, maiden, and let me have my way.* AHB put hot, dry lips to Susan's cheeks and throat and kissed. More than kissed. She felt his jagged teeth.

Eyes tightly closed, Susan willed herself to sleep, to slip away. But abruptly August called her back.

"Tell me about Jasper Gates."

"I already did, August," she murmured.

"He telephoned me."

AHB unbuttoned her pajama top and began to roll her breasts in his fingers, like quicksilver or loose coins, then put his thin lips to the nipples. He was always like this. The caveman noises subsided, giving again to the deceptively serene and civilized tone of voice that so often presaged something awful and in this case did too.

"Jasper thought you a wonderful creature," he hummed, pinching delicately the underside of her left breast, "especially since you let him put it in your bottom."

At first, half-unconscious, Susan didn't hear, or understand, and then couldn't believe she'd heard him right. "He said *what*?"

"That you let—"

"August! That is a goddamn lie!"

"Why would he tell me, August Blick, such a thing, knowing that you and I are special friends?"

Susan pulled her pajamas together, wanting very much to scream loud enough to wake the dead. He could go to hell! And so could Jasper Gates!

"Do *you* believe him?"

August shook his head sadly, but Susan saw his eyes. They glittered, tepidly lascivious.

"I could make him suffer for saying it, darling."

"August, I'm telling you the truth!"

Her face must blaze with shame. Susan couldn't believe Jasper Gates would say such a horrible thing. August was as bad to repeat it! But she had to remember, such a filthy slur would please his Germanic sense of humor.

"*Mädchen*, would I accept that you . . . ,"

Her anger crystalized into something harder, more realistic. Really, what the hell did she care what Jasper Gates said about her? He'd asked her to marry him and she'd turned him down, that's what was behind it. Someday, somehow, she'd use it against him.

"Not that I should be shocked, August," she said bitterly. "I've heard you captains of industry say much worse things than that."

"Not I!"

"Oh yes! I wonder what you've said about me!"

His eyes widened in denial. Resigned to infamy, Susan sank back against the pillow and closed her eyes. Naturally, AHB took this as her signal to reopen the pajamas. Jasper Gates was forgotten.

"I love your golden breasts," he hummed huskily, clearing his throat noisily as desire welled up, "breasts in recline. Lolling like defenseless birds. Fat little pigeons or perhaps ducks. I could bite them."

Susan hissed vindictively. "Your *beloved* partner is going behind your back, August. There's a report he's going to sell Big Sea to the Japanese . . . did you know?"

August pushed his long, cold nose into her bosom, snorting passion. He turned on one cheek to gaze up at her in the dim light.

"Jasper *is* my partner."

"I asked if you knew about the Japanese."

Something that had the feeling of a grin crinkled the skin of her breast.

"But does Jasper know I have been talking to the Hong Kong Chinese?"

"The Chinese? You're dealing with the Chinese . . . and he's dealing with the Japanese . . . and neither of you knows what the other is doing? And you're *partners*, August? Jesus!"

"Perhaps I *should* make him suffer."

"How, August?" she demanded sarcastically. "He's your partner."

He drew his fingernail, like a scalpel, down her middle to the elastic of the pajama bottoms and playfully snapped.

"It is *odd,* Susan, that the American entrepreneur will go to any length to have his way... *almost* any length," he underlined, "then shy away from the ultimate."

"I don't get you."

"Bismarck..."

"One of your heroes..."

"Yes," he whispered, tonguing her navel. "Bismarck said war is an extension of diplomacy. August Hugo Blick says that *Murder One* should be taught at Harvard Business School."

"Are you sure they're not already teaching it?"

Really, though, come now, who would believe AHB was actually capable of plotting and paying for a murder?

"MBA in Business Elimination!"

"Why don't you try for an honorary degree?"

"Susan, my dear, did you miss this old fellow at all?"

"I did, August, yes, against my better judgment."

He never heard what she said. He never listened.

"And I... *you!*" His mouth was afloat on her belly, his tongue rat-tat-tatting her skin. "Rest, my dear... rest now."

August was enormously gentle as he proceeded. As he said himself, a man must treat a woman tenderly, for this in turn kept the meat tender and sweet. The dear creatures must be coddled, kept happy, agreeable, malleable. Elsewise, they were inclined to turn sour and stringy.

She let him go, forcing herself, so to speak, to look the other way. Thus, the effect was general, as in anesthesia, not local. Susan was aware of everything but of no single caress by itself: his mouth, hands, worked in unison, passing her along toward some form of finale, not precisely climax, something perhaps more satisfying, as if tiny fingers were inside her, playing her nerves for harp strings, jostling her along to a fulfillment more far-reaching than the purely sexual kind, to a less shattering orgasm, the difference between someone banging on the door and hitting a set of chimes. Was that *really* possible or just some kind of a stupid conceit? Well, rather possible, yes. August had been at this for some years now; he'd had lots of practice and, as the piano teacher had promised, practice makes perfect.

"Rest, rest, *mädchen* . . ."

AHB had convinced himself of his hypnotic powers, and Susan was willing to go along. Her mind was supposed to shut down, she to descend to purely physical response. He waited for the sound of her steady breathing. And Susan obliged. When, at last, he knew, *thought,* he was in command, he slipped her pajama bottoms off and went for her thighs. August had given it as his expert opinion that the inside thigh was the greatest of all erotic, the most telling of all erogenous, zones, this softest place, he said, in all the world, nothing softer.

With devotion and precision, AHB kissed her at some length up and down this softest place.

She let him go on, turning her head, sighing deeply in her sleep. Don't look. Pretend it's Harry.

8

As it did in the jungle, morning came to the big city. Susan was never fully aware of exactly how AHB managed to make the nocturnal experience so whole and true, the numbing, maddening sensations, building and receding and building again, for hours and hours. Susan should have been exhausted, unable to move. But she was not.

Eight A.M. and she was alive. Very much so as she bounced out of bed.

This was not to suggest Susan Channing was some kind of a nymphomaniac who required that kind of hammering for sanity's sake. *Au contraire*. She could take it or leave it. But being honest, it was part of the answer to the riddle of why she put up with the unusual Park Avenue arrangement, on a long-term basis.

Susan had showered, made coffee, and felt brand new, in body and soul, long before her daily help Meriam O'Rourke was due to arrive. *The New York Times* had been delivered to the apartment door and she went at it with gusto, sipping coffee and nibbling a sesame seed bagel skimpily covered with ricotta cheese.

Nothing to hold her attention in the way of news. Susan's mind kept slipping away, back to California: to Jasper Gates, Big Sea, Harry. The onset of morning, the night's good rest had made her more optimistic about him—just because they'd said good-bye so inconclusively didn't necessarily mean all was lost. Morning was always brighter than the dead of night. After all, nobody could say anything for sure, could they? Pity the *Times* didn't carry a horoscope, for Susan was in the mood to be told, by anybody, that life began right now.

Susan flipped pages. There was no *big* story, merely a lot of little ones. Riot, famine, plague; little wars, civil wars, all-out wars; bank robbery, forgery, counterfeiting, embezzlement, influence peddling, securities fraud; gunrunning, drug smuggling, wife beating, child beating, husband beating; disaster in the air, disaster on the ground. Ozone-layer depletion, sunstroke, cancer, AIDS, poisoning, water pollution, nuclear leakage, nuclear explosion, nuclear waste; assassination, politics, religion, morality . . . And there it was, an item on the social page announcing the upcoming Peking Duck Roast-Dansant at Chez Chow in aid of the Met.

There wasn't much in this smelly potage for Susan Channing and Jack Godfrey. *"Hindsight"* 's purpose was not to worry or depress; *"Hindsight"* was illusion, that *somebody* was in control. *"Hindsight"* was intelligent, thoughtful, and more, but lighthearted in tone, even frothy. Friends said it was a viewer's *Time* magazine; critics said it was superficial. No, *"Hindsight"* was definitely not trash-TV. They would fight that trend to the death, that national urge to cheapen, to lowest-common-denominatorize every last news event and every personality, no matter how exalted. Or at least Arthur Fineman said they would fight it to the death.

Bravely, Susan carried the last of the coffee into her dressing room to prepare for the rest of the day. Despite what had or hadn't happened over the weekend, she didn't have any real complaints. So far, at least, life had been good to her. She had made plenty of money, traveled everywhere, stayed in the best hotels, ate well, talked to and even became friendly with some of the important men and women of the last days of the century. Susan Channing was the envy of many of her generation.

And she wasn't even forty years old yet.

Life did not revolve around AHB, or Harry Teller for that matter, like planet to sun. They were a few, among many. There *had been* others. There *were* others. And there *would be* others.

Sometimes, when she felt emotionally rattled, Susan liked to recall past victories of a personal and professional nature. After Vietnam, *after* Roger Blake, she had covered politics in Washington, been assigned to Europe, visited marginal wars in a number of marginal places, done a stint in Moscow, and interviewed . . . and interviewed . . . and interviewed. At this point, she doubted there was anybody in the world she had not seen in person or in passing. Her list of the fascinating and famous and fabulous was not a short one. According to Susan's count, she had been friendly or, so to speak, very friendly in past years with two European prime ministers, one a socialist and the other a Mediterranean-style Christian-Democrat; with one and a half NATO commanders, the half being commander-designate; *many* press spokesmen; a certain Polish Communist Party bigwig. Not to speak of lesser fry, or taking into account what went on in this country. *And* the Far East; don't forget about the Far East.

This was *not* for quotation, even to close friends.

Of course, that was all in the past, when she'd been young and very enthusiastic. It was different now. One had to be a lot more careful. But, yes, how convenient it was that love and lust and physical integrity were constantly renewing quantities, like energy and gravity.

Every day, she was a virgin all over again.

What a gruesome thought. Susan finished with her lipstick and stared at herself bleakly in the makeup mirror. She never bothered to spend much time on her face in the morning. Not much point in tiring out your skin if you were going to be made up all over again during working hours.

Susan went to the window for a clue to the outside weather. June: it would be warm, not hot, the sun not yet merciless or humidity-drenching. She chose a blue linen suit with bone buttons, a Chanel which she wore with a casual white blouse—best for interviewing, keep it simple, don't compete with your subject-matter—blue Chanel pumps, and simple jewelry, the delicate gold chain at most, nothing anybody would feel driven to tear off her neck.

And met Meriam O'Rourke emerging from the elevator just before nine.

"Hi...and good-bye! I'm off! I'll call you from the office."

Some things never paled—it was always exciting to get back, after even the shortest trip. Susan jumped out of her cab, hustling through the sidewalk traffic and into the soaring atrium of the gleaming white North American Towers. The network operated on four floors of the midsection of the fifty-story edifice, above a hotel, parking lot, brokerage firms, assorted other businesses, and below a dozen floors of very luxurious, and expensive, duplex and triplex condos, New York at its very ritziest. Susan wouldn't have lived at The Towers for anything, preferring the anonymity of Park Avenue. Magazines and scandal sheets didn't send photographers to stake out Park Avenue—but they camped at the North American Towers.

The elevator, as efficient as a bullet, projected Susan onto NAN's executive floor, exquisitely laid out. Who said there was no money in media? Susan kept an office on this floor for prestige purposes, with a window, an oblique view of downtown Manhattan and a secretary to handle her mail. But her battle station was upstairs on the news floor.

Susan said hello to Miss Green, the secretary, and, groaning, knowing what awaited her, walked into her office. Disgusting that a mere three or four days worth of incoming mail would be stacked practically to the ceiling. Miss Green had opened it all and sorted it by content and importance...but Susan didn't bother with it now, not for one second. Fineman's executive secretary, Maybelle Minorr, nabbed her immediately for a meeting.

Fineman never changed either. Susan had used to think of him as rock-solid, like the NAN building; lately the rocks were showing some telltale fissures. Not saying anything, Arthur motioned for Susan to sit down which she did, on one end of his leather couch. Fineman brushed a line of perspiration off his upper lip. Imaginary? It wasn't warm in here, not with the air conditioning going full blast.

"Well," he grieved, "what's new on the Coast?"

Susan adjusted herself in the smooth leather before trying to reply. It occurred to her that if Fineman had had a couch *then*, their five-minute affair might have lasted longer. Certainly, it would've been more comfortable than on his desk, littered with memos, pencils... the heavy stapler which had almost left a permanent mark on her back. Did he even remember? By now, he probably had her confused with somebody else. Fineman was too preoccupied with survival. He thought of Susan as he did Jack Godfrey, in stark terms of ratings. Still, for all Susan ever let on, she didn't remember either.

Actually, he didn't expect her to answer his question. Fineman tilted his chair back, put one foot against the desk and stretched his arms at the ceiling. You could view Art Fineman this way: as a scrawny, four-eyed little neurotic, and you more or less had it. Why had she given in to him in the first place? Well, she still had her job, if that helped answer the question. But then, of course, nasty people said her job security was named August Blick, not Arthur Fineman.

Finally, Arthur explained why they were sitting there at 9:30 A.M. when both of them had better things to do.

"Waiting."

Fineman wiped his brow again. They were waiting for Jack Godfrey, who was up from Washington for the day. That, Susan thought tartly, explained his unpolitic phone message, but didn't excuse it.

Abruptly, Fineman banged down in his chair and jammed a cigarette in his mouth. He lit it as if he were firing a torpedo at the enemy. Death wish was written all over Arthur Fineman. He didn't sleep, no secret about that, or that he worked all hours, ever planning and plotting. If anybody said exercise, he ran the other way and, of course, he smoked nonstop.

"Well, Arthur?"

"Suse," he muttered, studying his smoke, "shit's hitting the fan from about fourteen different directions."

"Tell..."

Studying her keenly, he asked, "Any truth to the rumor CBS offered you a bundle?"

"Arthur," she replied smoothly, "didn't I just do another contract with NAN?"

"No secret we don't pay as much as those guys."

Nodding, she parried. "No secret NAN is run like a Russian whaling ship."

"Not so, then?" He was satisfied for the moment. And, if it had been true? Was she going to tell him? "Simon H. was fit to be tied, Suse. He came charging in here Friday like a wounded deer.''

''That's why you left the messages? You knew I was away.''

''Simon made me do it. He wanted denial, right now.''

''Poor man.''

He paused, then murmured. ''I took advantage of the moment to tell him you signed the new but short-term contract with great reluctance, that you really did want more money, but that I talked you out of it, making a vague and noncommitting promise that next time around, in one year, that is, we'd have a serious salary renegotiation.''

''Okay . . .''

She managed to sound acquiescent and disappointed at the same time.

''Suse, you're making half a million.''

''So? Everything is relative, Artie. Barbara is making double that, not to mention Diane. My agent Morty was very unhappy with me for caving in.''

''Yeah? Well, fuck him,'' Fineman said daintily, ''fucking troublemaker.''

She smiled at him patiently, as he lapsed back into silence, puffing furiously on his cigarette and rounding his lips for a try at a smoke ring. It almost formed, then cracked raggedly; he grunted disgustedly. Susan wondered what else. Mention of the half million was embarrassing, though he'd always known to the nickel how much she made. In comparison to other Big Money, it was not all that much these days, but Susan could remember without thinking hard that a bare five years before she'd been making only a tenth of that figure. How her fortunes had changed. Anyway, after taxes, she was down to something like three hundred. Then, throw in the Park Avenue place: AHB had made sure she'd gotten a terrific deal buying it but he'd never made a move to pay the monthly fees which added up to about a hundred thousand a year, not to mention Christmas, Easter, Fourth of July, Labor Day, and Thanksgiving presents for the pushy concierge, Mr. Pipkin. Of course, her food expenses were negligible—she was always out for dinner or traveling. But then it cost her another twenty thousand a year to buy the loyalty of Meriam O'Rourke. And, in the end, Susan was lucky if she managed to bank five thousand a year.

''Speaking of which,'' Fineman said, glancing at her irritably, "did you do an interview with somebody from *Vanity Fair*?"

"Not an interview. They called with a question about the fashion preferences of the well-dressed TV reporter—"

"And you have to rave about Scaasi."

"I didn't rave," she demurred. "I said I like to wear his stuff when I go out formally."

"Well," Fineman huffed, "whatever . . . half the New York fashion community is drastically pissed off at you. *Why does she always mention Scaasi?*" he mimicked. "Somebody—I won't say who—even accused you of getting free dresses in return for the plugs."

Hotly, Susan exclaimed, "Not so, Artie! I pay full price and I've got the check stubs to prove it. And it leaves me broke! As you know, NAN doesn't come up with any kind of a clothes allowance—even though I'm *always* representing the network, always working . . . half the time helping the Hayfords entertain big advertisers too!"

"I know that. I know that," Fineman said soothingly.

"So, another goddamn lie! I'd like to know who said that. I'd sue their ass!"

"Why, Suse, are we so afflicted by lies these days?"

"Somebody's always making up something about me! Everybody's got some kind of a story to tell." Susan stared at him angrily, now he had got her going. "Goddamn it, Artie, do you know how much I paid for that dress when I went to the White House the last time?" He nodded, then shook his head. "Is it fair? Jack just slipped into his tired-out old black tie and I had to go order a new dress! You can't go to the White House looking like an old ragbag!"

"You love it!"

Fineman always said that. No matter how you bitched and complained or about what, Arthur Fineman always foreclosed the argument by saying, "You love it." Even if you were tortured by the KGB while in pursuit of a story, you'd loved it, he'd say, because wasn't being tortured what made the job so wonderful?

Laughing cynically, Fineman stubbed out his cigarette.

He was about to present her with the third instance of shit-in-the-fan, when he was interrupted by a rich baritone from just outside the open doorway.

"Who says I wear tired-out black ties?"

Fineman jerked around.

"You son of a bitch! You've been listening."

Evenly tanned, or was it makeup, teeth so true and even and stunningly polished: enter Jack Godfrey. He was dressed like a grad student, in tan cotton pants and what real men would call a candy-assed seersucker jacket and bow tie.

"Hello, darlings! Sorry I'm late."

"There must be some mistake." Fineman sneered. "I don't have an appointment with Noel Coward. Fifteen minutes late, Jack, fifteen minutes of my valuable time down the tube, forever!"

Jack winked broadly at Susan.

"You dog! You're complaining about fifteen minutes alone with this gorgeous creature, your own anchorperson and—"

"Sit the fuck down, Jack."

The nice part of it, perhaps the best part of it, was that they were genuinely fond of each other. And, within limits, they understood each other, though Susan sometimes teased herself with the question of whether Jack or Arthur knew about the other making it with Miss Gorgeous. No, they wouldn't know. Arthur wasn't the kind to brag about it, if he did remember, and in that way, if in no other, Jack was probably a gentleman. He was the kind of man anxious mothers would call a likable rascal, a charmer, the man they prayed Daughter would never meet. Fifty, more or less, formerly an athlete, still a sportsman, Jack had started in the business as a baseball announcer. He was a fine golfer, a useful skill within the modern corporate setup, and a favorite at the winter corporate meetings in Hawaii or Arizona or somewhere in the sunny Caribbean. Everybody wanted a game with Jack Godfrey.

What else? Besides being very attractive in person, Jack was very photogenic. And he was quick and smart and glib. Over and above that, and most vitally, he was a happy man and that was what added the final touches to his charisma.

Star Quality they called it and Jack had it in spades, far more than Susan, and she knew it. Whatever she had was learned, not natural. Jack was like the man who played the piano by ear and effortlessly. He was the envy of his fellows and, obviously, Susan liked and admired him. The wonder was that she had never fallen in love with him. Just as well. Everybody else had.

Jack dropped beside her on the couch. Pausing only to straighten the crease in his pants, he grabbed her hand, noisily kissing her knuckles. Susan pulled away, gasping stagily.

"Not now, you fool! *He's* watching!"

Jack laughed loudly and Susan kissed him collegially on the cheek.

"Whenever you're ready, clowns," Fineman muttered.

"Shoot, boss!"

Fineman got up and came around his desk and sat down again in a plaid-covered easy chair opposite the couch, first throwing a disordered pile of magazines on the floor.

Staring at them morosely, he said, "It's confirmed, kids. Bristals is going after us."

Jack spouted scornfully, "Come on, Artie, no way. He's fully occupied in Washington."

"Oh no." Fineman wagged his head. "And I can tell you that Simon's ass is on the line, sweetheart."

The CEO? Bad news, worrying news. Susan wondered why August hadn't mentioned it—if he knew. Certainly, if his friend, Simple Simon Hayford, were in trouble, AHB should've been the first to know.

"Shit!" Jack said.

His reaction wasn't out of any great love for Simon Hayford. No, it was merely that anything, anything at all, which interfered with the status quo set *angst* to rumbling through network corridors.

"They're on to us at last," he joked weakly. "I wondered how long we could last."

"Be serious," Fineman barked. Then, apologetically, he gazed at Susan. "I thought, maybe..."

He was hinting at her Blick connection, but Susan was not about to bite.

"All I know is the rumors," she dodged artfully.

"Rumors been around for months, Artie," Jack scoffed. "Boardroom crap."

"...if you two ever read anything more serious than the *Post*..." Fineman clenched his teeth. "Don't you ever look at the business section in the *Times*, for fuck's sake? Jesus," he grumbled, "the Flying Wallendas of small talk."

"The Nijinskys of babble," Susan murmured.

"Schmucks! Somebody has been buying up NAN stock. And we know who that somebody is and Simon thinks that *somebody's* going to have to declare his intentions pretty soon. Simon's spending his waking hours hustling white knights to rescue us.'' He chuckled sourly. ''Can you believe it, he's even trying to peddle us to General Motors...''

''Why not General Electric?'' Jack's eyebrows lofted quizzically; they were so light-colored, even lighter than his sandy hair, they had to be colored for the camera. ''They already own everything else.''

''Why not General Screw-Up?'' Fineman trumped him, sarcastically, trying to smile.

''God knows GM's got the dough to do it,'' Jack said, his eyes bright. ''Hey, maybe they'd issue us a new Caddy every year.''

''Bristals?'' Susan repeated. ''Are you *really* sure? It was just a rumor before.''

Fineman snarled, ''Yes, for God's sake. *Sir Guy Bristals!* Bristals London Group.''

Jack asked, ''What about the board?''

''Well, what about 'em?'' Fineman demanded. ''They don't want it. Even *they* know better. But they're chickenshit. What if, all of a sudden, Bristals is the biggest single shareholder?'' He glanced at Susan again. ''*Bigger* than August Blick...''

He didn't have to finish. Susan felt herself turning white inside. She didn't know what to say, so she improvised.

''I happened to meet his wife in California. I think they're split.''

''And *she* said?'' Fineman asked.

''Nothing. She refuses to talk about him. But AHB wouldn't let Simon go down, would he?''

That was weak. What Arthur wanted was for her to ask August that same question directly. She already knew the answer. If it suited him, if there was a buck in it, AHB would throw Simon Hayford to the wolves—without blinking twice. Even once.

Angrily, at last angry as well as worried, Jack exclaimed. ''That son of a bitch, Bristals! First Murdoch, then Maxwell, and now Bristals. The scandal-mongering bastard! I've been quoted, you know—about Bristals and his gutter-press. Sensationalist rubbish! Everybody I know in London says so too. Fleet Street agrees absolutely!''

''I'm glad *you* said it and not me, Jack,'' Fineman muttered. ''the point is if he grabbed us, it wouldn't matter a goddamn bit what they think in Fleet Street or anywhere else.''

"And so?" Jack demanded, red-faced. "What do we do? Sit and wait for the shaft?"

"Maybe he's got a short memory, Jack, or is very forgiving," Fineman said insinuatingly. "Maybe he won't cut your nuts off. Look, you guys," he added, more rationally, "he'd be crazy to monkey around with *Hindsight*."

Fineman's phone rang then, catching him off-guard. He thought he'd told Maybelle no calls. The pope was bitching about NAN's coverage of his last trip to Poland. And what did the pope care? It was his PR people, like everywhere else; they were concerned that the American Catholic population would take something he'd said about population control to mean a softening of the line on birth control. All right, all right, Fineman was arguing, tell 'em we didn't mean anything like that and, Jesus, NAN can't be responsible for every time the guy goes to the bathroom.

Jack took Susan's hand again, smiling coyly.

"Receive my message?"

"Yeah, some message. The kid was thrilled to read it to me."

"I'm staying overnight..."

"Sometimes, Jack...It's a good thing we don't see each other very much."

"You mean in the *flesh*," he whispered, "as opposed to the Washington-New York feed." Jack glanced over his shoulder to make sure Fineman was still occupied. "What about a little—"

"*Not* if you were the last man on planet earth."

"Lunch, I was going to say, Sue, lunch!"

Jack was so sure of himself, so convinced that Susan allowed him, even encouraged him to charm the pants right off her.

"I forget," Susan teased, "are you married just now, Jack, or not?"

"Single right now, Suse...Will you marry me? Now's your chance. Is your answer Yes?"

Jack wouldn't ever be serious, if he could help it. Jack's problem: he was a very nice, unserious man, fortunately never a mean or vindictive man. Jack hadn't ever worried about Susan as competition. In the beginning, he hadn't been madly eager to work with a woman coanchor; but magically, for magic was the only explanation, the Channing-Godfrey formula had worked, proving one more time that there was no predicting which chemistry would take, which would be rejected. It was a total crapshoot, as the production boys said. Since way back then, Jack had never begrudged Susan her share of their success. Maybe it was natural enough that in the process of working together so closely, they'd come to know each other very well indeed. Again, magically, they'd been able to extend the relationship from professional to personal, and now and then to intimacy, against all the odds, media authority said, that such a partnership could survive if it slipped from a strictly professional level.

Anyway, it had survived. Susan and Jack liked each other on and off camera. The arrangement had gone as far as it could, however. When Jack joked about marriage, they both knew it was just that: a joke, a pleasantry. Poor Arthur, they took advantage of him. Playfully, so Arthur could see and scowl and turn his back, Jack kissed Susan's cheek, smiling at her temptingly.

"Sue, let's get out of here."

"Our master isn't done with us yet, good sir."

Curtly, Fineman finished with the call and slammed down the phone. For a second, he looked perplexed, as if he couldn't remember what they'd been talking about: to wit, the integrity of the NAN news department in the face of Sir Guy Bristals. Absently, he began muttering about upcoming stories: something about Canada and her new prime minister and the Canadian-American free trade zone; somebody, that is one of the researchers, had a bright idea for a scare-piece on declining investments in the pure sciences; oh yes, Jack and Suse were scheduled for a trip to Atlantic City for a look at the Trump operation. And . . . he looked at Susan dimly. How had it gone in California? What about the Big Oil Slick show?

"It was not great," she admitted. "Both your governors, I don't know, Artie—"

"Boring as batshit, right? I told Simon! Jesus, those two fucking guys, if that's the best the parties can dig up—and I *mean* dig up—might as well vote anarchist. I'm sorry, Suse. Can we salvage anything?"

She was off the hook, sort of. One couldn't be sure with Fineman.

"Oh, sure. I mean, out of two hours apiece, there's got to be something there."

Then, he wanted to know about Jenny Driver and Lyons. Susan was noncommittal. If she started on that they'd be talking the rest of the day. Mention that somebody had shot at Dick Lyons? No, don't talk about Lyons at all, because that would set Jack off, for the same reasons it got Harry Teller agitated. Jack had already warned her, if they had the Driver-Lyons duo on the show again, include him out!

"Listen," she said agilely, "Jasper Gates has got to be it. And I think we can get him. My story, Jack!"

"You got it, honey!"

Fineman at last looked interested.

"I can't remember anybody's ever gotten to Gates. Just because he's a rich bandit, though, doesn't automatically mean he'd make a good show. Look at your two fucking governors, for instance."

"He's fascinating, Arthur. He's building the world's biggest cruise liner—"

"Well?"

"Isn't that interesting to you?"

"Moderately."

Slyly, Jack said, "I think Suse is in love again, Artie."

"Oh yeah?" Fineman studied her solemnly. "Could be, Jack. There's a certain *je ne sais quoi* about her cheekbones . . ."

"You two mother—you two . . ."

Grinning, Fineman said, "So, the trip wasn't a total loss?"

"I never thought it would be, Arthur!"

"Jesus," he groused at Godfrey, "covering the opening of a health spa, can you think of anything more revolting?"

"Good golf course, Jack."

"Suse?" Fineman mused, "Gates runs a big map, doesn't he?"

"Coast to coast and on every continent. You name it and he's there. They're building the ship in Bulgaria."

"Bulgaria?" Fineman joked awkwardly. "I thought the Bulgarians made yogurt."

"Artie, it's a *good* story."

At that moment Maybelle Minorr cracked open the office door and stuck her head inside.

"Sorry. A call for Susan. *Mr. Blick . . .*"

But AHB *never* called her here. Perhaps once, maybe twice. Flushing, Susan glanced at Fineman.

"Speak of the devil," she muttered. "I'll . . ." She was on her way to the door. "Excuse me."

"Suse . . ."

Fineman arched his eyebrows meaningfully. Yes, all right, sure, she was to find out . . . *everything*.

Susan walked back to her office. There was no way in the world she'd be able on the precious telephone to turn AHB to the matter of Guy Bristals. No hope, either, after she heard why August was calling.

"Susan," he announced solemnly, "it is my sad duty to tell you that Mignon died during the night."

This was the last thing she'd expected. In fact, didn't the least expected always happen first? Stunned, instantly worried for herself, she stammered words.

"But Mignon was . . ." Indestructible. Pickled in Manhattans. The next thing to immortal. "August, oh, August. I'm . . . I don't know what to say. I'm so sorry. I know how you loved her."

Well?

"Say nothing," he murmured, voice deep enough to make the phone line vibrate. "We found her this morning. Konrad found her this morning."

Of course, AHB would never give it away that he was devastated. Mignon had of late annoyed and irritated him, at times even maddened him, and from time to time he had probably wished her dead. But although he didn't sound it, he was obviously shattered.

"Is there anything I can do?"

"Nothing! The arrangements are simple enough. Death is far easier than sickness as a management problem. Easier than seating a dinner party, we know that. I have had Emily call Roger Blake." So bad was it between August and his son, that he'd have his secretary, Emily Eliot, call to tell Roger his mother had died. "Roger will be coming to New York tomorrow," August added stonily, "with his son, Scott . . . my grandson.'"

"That's good."

"Yes," August agreed harshly. "It is good that I will see my grandson. As to Roger Blake, formerly Roger Hugo Blick, it is of no consequence whether he comes or not. If he believes there is something to be gained . . ."

AHB said something, probably filthy, in German, as he usually did when he'd run up against the subject of money, inheritance, that kind of thing. Susan didn't say a word. Why should she? She was in no way answerable for Roger Blake.

"August, *should* I come?"

"I would prefer not," he answered swiftly. "We will have all this business finished and done with before evening. As if little Mignon has gone on a long trip... which she has, I suppose, on a long flight into the wilds, as if to Brazil, or Africa, to visit the headwaters of life itself. We will drink her health... or whatever... later... in Manhattans."

Susan didn't like the spiteful sound of that very much.

"But, AHB, so many details—"

"My dear, Susan! I am not bothering with them personally. Sid Wilmer and Emily Eliot are in complete charge."

Of course. Sid and Emily knew all the details of the August and Mignon ménage, so they could handle the final details too. If needed, they could've, in fact, written obituaries for Mignon, and AHB, long enough to fill whole pages of the *Times*. Perhaps even better than Sidney, Emily knew where all the bodies were buried. That being the case, Emily might as well see to Mignon's body too.

"I have only to sit here and sign a few documents to bring to a close the *histoire* of Mignon Guadalupe Rey Gelbvogel."

"That was Mignon's full name? I never knew that, AHB."

"Well... yes. And I am about to have Konrad bring me a brandy-soda for strength."

"August, please don't overdo it."

"My dear," he said grandly, "by the time you arrive this evening, this old man will be completely recovered."

"August..." She started to say something else of a cautionary nature but couldn't remember what. "I'll see you then."

"It will be my pleasure, *Schatz*."

Schatz? Susan repeated the mysterious endearment. The word meant treasure and just about anything else a man might want to say to his good friend. Susan hung up the phone, thinking, What next?

Indeed, the status quo was crumbling, collapsing around their ears like loose bricks.

Susan stood there, for a long moment considering the tenuous grip all of them, any of them, had on life. Then she dialed Maybelle and asked her to get Jack on the line.

"What's cookin', honeybuns?"

"Jack, will you tell Arthur I didn't get a chance to ask AHB about anything important. The reason he called was to tell me that Mrs. AHB died during the night. . . . So, I could scarcely—"

"For crissakes! Does that mean lunch is off?"

Should it mean that? Lunch with Jack Godfrey or no lunch with Jack Godfrey, Mignon Blick was just as dead. And perhaps a cheerful few hours with Jack Godfrey was as good a way as any to celebrate her life.

"Not at all, Jack."

"Thatagirl, Sue!" But he never could leave well enough alone. Voice throttled down to a whisper, he said, "Man! I am *so* hungry! I could *eat* a bear."

"So we'll go to the zoo for lunch, Jack."

9

"Remember you? Sure I do, Susan. You were the best looking of all my mommies."

Like father, like son . . . like grandson. Susan remembered as if it had been yesterday the boy's tenth birthday party and now he was eighteen, finishing high school, and off to Princeton in the fall.

Son was a shade taller than Father but that wasn't saying much; Roger was no Tarzan and neither of them was as tall as AHB. Mignon's tiny genes must have prevailed. Susan automatically measured one against the other as they sidled into the restaurant. Sidled, yes: Roger had always moved as if somebody were tailing him. Susan had chosen the meeting place here at the Plaza. The two Blakes were staying close by at the Pierre and her white tower on Madison, the NAN building, was only a short cab ride away.

The salient fact was that the two Blakes were not staying with August Blick. The kid, Roger explained unconvincingly, had publishing business which might disturb The Old Man and they wouldn't want to be in that gloomy old place anyway, would they?

Since there was nothing Susan needed or wanted from Roger Blake, it was entirely curiosity which had made her agree to lunch. The meeting, though, was turning out to be an educational one, possibly useful background for a segment they could easily call "Jaded Youth." For Scott Blake was impossible. Roger had always been full of himself, but his conceit was Mignon-sized compared to that of his son.

Roger, Susan was happy to note, looked used, like an old Ford, or maybe Chevy, battered around the fenders and dented in obvious places. The first thing he had to say was that he was twenty pounds overweight and his tennis game had gone all to hell. And you knew you were in the presence of greatness: Great Failure. Scott, not so surprisingly, looked and acted more like the younger Roger than the older Roger did. The chunky build was familiar, so too the thick, curly mess of hair. Scott reminded her that once upon a time Roger must have had *something;* Susan hadn't been so brainless as to hook up with a porky nonentity.

"Have you been up to see your father yet?"

"This morning. I had to, didn't I? That's why we're here." Roger grimaced. "Not for any services, that's for sure."

"Oh? I didn't know. I wasn't told. I would've thought . . ."

"She was an atheist," Roger muttered. "The old man says so anyway. And we know he doesn't believe in anything. Cremation and . . . by the wild wind possessed. Remember the movie of the same name?" Roger wagged his head dismally. "So why are we here, you may ask? Like I said, the kid has got business. And I think, at a certain point, you've got to do the right thing."

Well, that'd make for a change.

"It's good you came," Susan observed. "No matter how he acts, or what he says, still—"

"Let's hope so, Sue." Roger tried to laugh. "I'm not his favorite animal. I know I've been bad. I never called and I didn't send flowers. Say, what about ordering a drink? *Not* for you," he cut at Scott.

"So? Who needs it?"

Signaling for the waiter, Roger irately informed Susan, "This *kid* got himself sloshed last night. Ordered up a bottle of vodka *for his father*! Jesus!"

Scott just grinned contemptuously.

"And how did *you* find your grandfather?" Susan asked pleasantly.

"It wasn't easy in that big old room."

Roger aimed his forefinger and warned, "*Nobody* likes a smartass!"

Scott shrugged, then, thinking better of it, said, "Sorry. He's my grandfather and I have to respect him."

Memories of the years with Roger and Scott came swarming back. The boy had always been a trial and tribulation, what people too easily excused as precocious. His spoiled, wanton-looking face took her back. At age eight or nine he'd figured out a way to peek at her when she was half undressed and charged his little friends a nickel a look; another time, they'd discovered him trying to wire their bedroom.

"Besides, he's got the bucks—"

"That's . . ."

She wanted to slap him.

"Just ignore it, Sue," Roger said grimly. "You'll get nowhere with him. Aren't you glad you're not saddled with a punk kid who's written a crummy novel everybody says is going to be a bestseller? His head is as big as a house."

"Well," she said, freezing Scott with a look, or trying to, for she had absolutely no effect on him, "you should just hope he makes a lot of money and leaves home."

Grabbing desperately for the waiter, Roger ordered a scotch and water.

Nastily, Scott said, "And may I have a Shirley Temple, Mommy?"

"Yes, you little *snot*. And another glass of the Chablis for me, please," she told the slightly startled waiter. "I think I need it. And who is your mommy now, little boy?"

Susan was curious to know if Roger was still married to the popsie who'd come in the back door just as she was exiting the front. But she wasn't madly curious. Why should she be? In a couple more years, she wouldn't recognize Roger on the street.

"I don't have a mommy anymore, Mommy."

Roger seemed to fade. For once, he had nothing to say. His lips were sealed, as if he'd stuck them together with Super glue.

When it became apparent he had lost all traction, Susan murmured, "I am sorry about your mother. She was a good friend to me."

He shrugged.

"She was out of it, Sue. That's the reason I quit calling." He studied her shrewdly, then tried the wicked Blick-Blake smile. "I guess we can count on you keeping your eye on The Old Man, right, Sue?"

Was he implying something? If so, she decided to ignore it.

"As best I can, I guess so. AHB has always been nice to me too, very supportive when I came to New York."

"You sure left me in the lurch, Sue," Roger accused, "but what does it matter now? You took the city by storm!" His dead eyes lit up a little. He was trying so hard. "But, why wouldn't you, after all you learned from me?"

Make no mistake, Roger Blake was as full of it as he'd always been. Never mind, it was better this way; she needn't worry about stepping on his ego. Business wasn't great, so what else was new? Only his reserve of Blick-bucks kept Roger Blake afloat.

Expansively, ever the bluffer, he said, "All I have to do is keep a couple of balls in the air, that'll pay the bills. Development money: you know how it is." His drink came and he lifted it nonchalantly. "Cheers, dears!" Then he winked, "'Course, I don't ever show a profit. Taxes, you know."

"Don't worry. I'm not going to ask you for any of it."

That would hurt. He knew she was making plenty. Too late, it occurred to Susan that Roger definitely had the gall to ask *her* for a loan. She almost wished he would ask, so she'd have the pleasure of turning him down, or demanding to see the books.

Indeed, mention of money made him melancholic and with a wistful, faraway look in his eye, swigging scotch, he said, "You know, Sue, Augie never even let my mother have a credit card of her own? She was never allowed to spend a dollar. With all that money... coming out of his kazoo..."

Scott drawled, "Maybe I should try to hit him up for some of it."

"There's the rub! He'll *shower* it on this kid." Roger stared at his fingers, clinging possessively to his glass. "Just when... you know, a very small infusion of some Blick capital... small by *his* standards... like I'm talking four or five mill... I could reach for the stars. But..." He shrugged, without hope, and manfully clinked her glass. "Here's to you, Sue. You're looking wonderful."

She was not fooled, not for an instant. This was typical Roger: he was asking for money . . . and he wasn't. It was so sad and boring. She was well out of it. How wise she'd been to leave.

Skirting Roger, she asked Scott politely, "What exactly is your novel about?" Forget Roger. Perhaps there was some hope for Scott. "Somebody told me the title—"

Loudly enough for the whole room to hear, Scott announced, "The title of my book is *O Savage Youth.*"

Roger rolled his eyes helplessly.

"I'm told it's a little racy."

"*Oh?* Do you mean *sexy*? *Erotic?*" He spoke so superciliously Susan yearned to do something damaging to him. "I prefer to think of *O Savage Youth* as realistic, even naturalistic. Do you understand what I'm saying?"

"*Can* we order lunch?" Scott glared at the interruption and Roger snarled. "If you want to know about our bedrugged youth, read *O Savage Savages.*"

"It's possible *you* wouldn't understand."

"Horseshit!" Roger hissed, not very paternally. "Give us a break, will you, Scotty-boy?" Scott smiled at him so casually that Roger turned red with fury. "My son, the little pain in the ass! Listen! We know you're ruined. And so what? *Kee-rist!* Read his book, Sue, you'd think he was weaned on coke. *I mean*, excuse me for living, but we wouldn't dare mention anything so low class as *grass!*" Scott tapped his fingers slowly. He looked at the ceiling. "These kids! Sue! Their biggest problem is they can't decide whether to turn in their BMWs for Mercedes or for Porsches. You'd think they'd be a little bit grateful."

Scott looked at his father, pityingly.

"Oh, thank you, thank you, dear Dad. You've just proved one more time, *Dad*, that your generation has got its head up its ass."

"How literary," Susan said.

"You asked—"

"Horseshit!" Roger whispered frantically. "Horseshit!"

"Dads is pretty eloquent himself, isn't he?" Scott grinned lopsidedly at Susan and what he said next sounded like a threat. "One of my earliest memories is of an elderly couple, such as yourselves, spaced out on joints."

"*Can* we order?" Susan asked frostily.

* * *

In mid–main course, Scott pushed aside his Shirley Temple.

"I'm being picked up here and I don't want her to see me drinking sissy stuff like this."

They were to be joined, Scott informed them, by a young woman reporter who was going to profile him for the newest of the revived sophisticates magazines, *Fast Set*. Scott said he'd been told to expect a tall, dark, and impossibly beautiful girl whose name was Ivy Eva Smith.

"And also, she gives great head."

Susan felt her insides wither. Even Roger, with Hollywood under his belt, was embarrassed.

"So! Brave new world, isn't it! Don't be disgusting!" she lashed out. "That's a piggish thing to say! You're not old enough to talk like that. *Nobody* is old enough to talk like that. One more word, I'm warning you, and I'm out of here! I do not need this. Most definitely not!"

"It's just something people say...Christ, Susan..."

She was about to fry him, but before she could, the woman in question arrived. Scott cried out softly and leapt to his feet. Next came Roger's wolf whistle. Of course, she was very good-looking—in a coarse and earthy way. Her style was gypsyish, no doubt studied with dedication: heavy black hair brushed straight past padded shoulders, accentuated black eyebrows, and very thick, very red lips that parted in a vampish smile when she recognized the great writer.

"*You* are Scott Blake!"

Scott nodded boyishly. Somebody must have coached him not to act himself.

"I am Ivy Eva Smith."

The information was for all of them, for the whole wide world. Stuttering like a shy schoolboy, Scott introduced Roger Blake and Susan Channing.

"But I feel that I know you already, Miss Channing!"

Susan nodded gracefully and said, "Thanks. It's always nice to hear it. Why don't you...we're about to have coffee. If you two have time..."

Halfway up, on the tight side of the table, Roger exclaimed, "Sit down, Miss Smith."

The young woman, though older than Scott, to be sure, winked at Roger.

"Call me Ivy, please!"

Roger motioned for the waiter, more vigorously than before. Scott watched sullenly as Dad moved in. She was *his*, not Dad's! Ivy Eva Smith popped down in Scott's chair and he had to squeeze into the banquette beside Susan. His leg was warm, trembling with nerves. Meanwhile, reacting so predictably, like Pavlov's dog to the scent of meat—Ivy Eva Smith's scent was heady, a powerful floral fragrance which, of course, would stop an elevator—Roger's face collapsed into a white-toothed California smirk. Ms. Smith was his type. Except for Susan, Roger had always like them cheaplooking and obvious, bosomy and with legs that would crush you to death. Roger needed a full minute of leer to soak her in and while he did so, Ivy Eva gazed at Susan with a supplicant's smile on her face.

Susan knew what was going on in Ivy Eva's mind: Was it too soon to use Susan's connection at NAN?

"Well, Miss Ivy, do I detect an English accent?" Roger asked playfully.

"I am from London."

"I knew it!" he cried, emotionally. "I'm crazy about London. I'm back and forth, I don't know how many times a year. Hell, I'm part Brit. How long have you been in this country?"

"Two years."

Cups and saucers arrived at the table, a pot of coffee, silverware, crisp new napkins. Would they care for anything else, perhaps something off the dessert trolley?

"Many thanks, no, not for me," said Ms. Smith, not waiting for the rest of them, turing her big and intimidating eyes on Scott. "We must have a plan." He nodded, agreeable to anything she'd suggest. "You *do* have the whole afternoon?" Yes, yes! "I thought, if it's all right with you, *Scott*, we'd go for a stroll in the park and chat, get to know each other. *Rapport*, you know."

"Oh, gosh, sure, Ivy."

Jealously, Roger repeated, "Rapport? How much do you need of that?"

"Well, that all depends, Mr. Blake."

"Roger..."

He was ready to cry. How could this be? His own son walking away with such a tasty morsel?

"It all depends how talkative Mister Scott H. Blake is. . . . Or was that H. Scott Blake?"

"H. Scott, actually," Scott whispered. "The H is for Hugo . . . not exactly a popular name these days."

A blatant lie! Roger was floored. His own son deceiving the press so disgracefully! Rather funny, if the truth be told. And Ivy bought it, or didn't care enough to doubt him. Of course, she'd already know the truth if she was any kind of journalist, which she must be if she was British-trained, in the hardest school of all. Closer inspection of the eyes, as always, convinced Susan that Ivy Eva was by no means as youthful a creature as she first appeared. She was in her early thirties at least, which meant that she was not much younger than Susan—but younger nevertheless and that was always a pain.

Ivy Eva must have been aware of Susan's skepticism, for she spoke straight at her.

"My editors believe the phenomenon of this generation of young writers, like Scott . . . the *Lit-Pack,* as we're calling it, harks back to . . ."

She didn't need a lecture from a two-year resident whose makeup was . . . well, frankly, garish. It was possible, Susan let herself think, bitchily, that Ivy Eva Smith's proper place was underneath the lamppost by the barracks' gate.

". . . the nineteen-twenties, writers like F. Scott Fitzgerald." Ivy Eva blinked significantly. "Now, handily . . . H. Scott Blake."

"Hell sakes, Ivy," Scott gushed again, "I'm nowhere near that league."

"*Gee, Scott,*" Roger openly mocked, "it's only your first book . . . Ivy, what led you to New York?"

"Simple, really! I worked in Fleet Street for one of the Bristals papers, you see, and when Sir Guy—"

"Sir Guy Bristals!"

"That's the bloke." Ivy looked to Susan as if she'd like to say more, but settled for less. "Are you acquainted with him? Did you ever—"

"Interview him? No. I've never met the man."

"When Sir Guy bought *Fast Set,* he asked me to come over."

"So many young English women are working in the New York media."

"Yes," Ivy Eva agreed, "and Americans in London. The exchange is brisk." Her voice dipped toward the authoritative. "We offer each other cultural exchange, a fresh outlook."

"Maybe I should do a stint in London," Susan said dryly.

"I know it's been good for me in New York!"

Roger cried out enthusiastically, "You're bored with London, you're bored with life!"

Ivy Eva nodded understandingly. She was not a stupid woman, despite the overdone makeup. Perhaps they should talk a little shop. For instance, what would Ivy Eva know about Sir Guy Bristals taking over NAN? Or, should Susan mention that she'd met Emma, Lady Bristals, in California? She led off with an innocuous question.

"Do you really call Sir Guy the cockney press lord?"

Caution flooded into Ms. Smith's fluid eyes. She looked over her shoulder. Ah, the walls have ears.

"It's true his background is the East End of London. Sir Guy is a self-made man."

Roger rushed into the conversation.

"The kind of guy we admire in this country, up by the bootstraps and all that."

"Like you, *Dads*," Scott murmured.

"That's right, Scotty."

Like hell! If Roger Blake was self-made so were all the Rockefellers, Fords, and Gettys.

Susan resumed, "I guess I forgot that Bristals was reviving *Fast Set*."

"Sir Guy is very low profile," Ivy Eva said earnestly. "I'm sure you're too busy to keep up with *all* the corporate raiders."

"Would you consider him a raider?"

A mite uncomfortably, Ivy Eva said, "He thinks of himself as something of a swashbuckling capitalist."

"At least not *swish*-buckling," Roger tried again, foolishly.

"Oh, no! Not at all! Nothing like that! Far from it!"

And there Susan had it: a first hint of Bristals's human side, aside from the fact that Emma Bristals considered him a big bore. Ivy Eva's tone indicated that Sir Guy might be something of a cocksman. Perhaps Ms. Smith knew this from personal experience. Yes? Well, how else had she gotten to New York?

"I hope to meet *your* Sir Guy Bristals," she said.

"I'm sure you will. He'll be surfacing 'ere long, now that *Fast Set* is on its feet and, wonder of wonders, already in the black."

"Really!" Roger clapped hands. "That's some going!"

Ivy Eva flashed him a brilliant smile.

"By the way," she said, "we're going to be doing a piece

on the Coast pretty soon . . . and I know you're involved in the film business, Roger.''

At last an opening and Roger said wildly, ''I hope you'll be kind to us.''

''Don't count on it, Roger. You know what *Fast Set* is like. No holds barred!'' Ivy Eva went on gleefully to recite some delicious recent Hollywood headlines. ''Cesar Morgan Buys Whopper Studios . . . Boris Whopper Shoots Cesar Morgan in Parking Lot Altercation . . . Morgan Paralyzed From Waist Down . . . Candace Morgan Leaves Cesar Morgan . . . Etcetera.'' Roger looked horrified, even more so as Ms. Smith continued, ''Whopper Sentenced to Three Hundred Hours Community Service . . .''

''I wasn't anywhere in the vicinity, your honor!''

''But you people don't do that kind of sleaze,'' Susan protested.

''We don't?'' Ivy Eva reached for her pocketbook. ''I see you don't know Sir Guy.''

''Jesus Christ,'' Roger said, ''I'm telling you, keep away from that Morgan-Whopper thing, Ivy. Playing with fire, oh boy!''

Ivy Eva was not impressed. Calmly, she finished her coffee.

''Well, H Scott, shall we take a walk?''

After her brief moment of truth, Ivy Eva Smith was very formal. She'd been ever so pleased to meet Susan Channing and to make the acquaintance of Roger Blake of Tinseltown.

Watching them make for the door, Susan murmured, ''What a cute couple.''

''Sure, Sue! You hear what she said? She's gonna do a job on the kid . . . and me. And you too. He'll tell her we were married and you helped bring up the little slimeball!''

''I am not worried,'' she said blithely. ''People have been libeling and slandering me for years.''

Impatiently, as if he'd been waiting a day or two to say so, Roger blurted out, ''I'm divorced again!''

''So I gathered.''

''Second time since you took off.''

''Is that all?''

Susan had already remarked that he had the dog-eared look of the much-divorced man. Used goods, very much so. Ripe for markdown. Roger, of course, had not so much failed at life; it was just that he'd never been successful. Roger was a phony in the classical sense, a cardboard man who lived in never-never land.

"Hard for me to imagine you without a bimbo on your arm."

"Here you see him, Sue, a four-time loser. Christ, I can't *afford* another bimbo. And I'm only fifty... I'm fifty in September."

"You've still got time for a couple more wives."

Miserably, he appealed, "Please don't sneer at me, Sue. I'm trying to tell you, I'm cleaned out."

"I'll get lunch, Roger."

Try as she might, though not very hard, Susan couldn't muster much sympathy. Whatever had happened to Roger Blake was his own invention. How striking the difference between Roger Blake and his father. Blick was a scientific machine; Blake a Rube Goldberg contraption.

Half joking, half seriously, he said, "What about us getting married again, Sue? You were the best of the lot, I've always said so—and did the rest of them ever get burnt up when I told 'em so."

"Please," she said, "don't be stupid! I don't suffer from amnesia, you know. I remember a big-titted redhead whose name I shall never forget."

"Patty Kakes?" Incorrigible, yes, like father, like son, like grandson, he couldn't resist self-congratulation. Yes, he had had a lot of bimbos, now you mention it. "There went a half-mil of my hard-earned," he muttered, almost happily.

"At least you can't say about me that I walked away with a half-mil."

"You're special, Sue. I've always said so."

"Well, you can stop saying so."

He nodded, not really hearing. Susan was about to find out why he had been so eager to see her.

"Sue...I wish..." His eyes turned moist; he cleared his throat nervously. "I wish you'd help me with The Old Man. No kidding." He reached into his shirt pocket, found a loose pill and tossed it in his mouth, then swallowed water. "For my gut. A gift from Number Four, who's at the moment taking me to the cleaners. The way it looks, I'm gonna have to sell the company so she can have her half. You know that goddamn California law! There won't be enough left for me to operate decently. You know what it's like, all that up-front bullshit. You gotta put on a show—"

"I don't know what I can do, Roger."

She sounded like an unforgiving confessor.

"Well, Christ, Susan!" He looked sweaty. "You see enough of him! Even I know that much!"

"*So?*"

"Well," he said pallidly, understanding he must go carefully, "the opportunity must come up, like, once in a while, for you to say something nice about good, old Rog."

"I've never said anything about you that wasn't nice."

He shook his head, as if dazed.

"Jesus, my own father! Doesn't it ever make you feel, like, *uncomfortable*?"

"What are you saying, Roger? Please explain what you're saying."

"I'm saying I need more than *making nice*," he said, at least daring to look her in the eye. "For crissakes, I don't even know what he plans to do. In his will, for God's sake! Yes! Okay! I'm a heel, Sue," he said, not meaning it, "but if I did know, I'd be able to borrow on the strength of it. Augie's got a couple dozen bankers he practically owns. One of them would cough up, I know it. I'm saying, Sue, I'm saying, telling it like it is, and you can say I'm a selfish prick if you want to . . . *but!* But the point is, it wouldn't take much at all, you know, relatively, to put me in the top ten in Hollywood. None of those fakes operate on anything but borrowed money. Do you understand what I'm saying?"

"I'm not dense, Roger."

Giggling a little, slightly mad after all, Susan would've thought, Roger pressed on.

"'Course, I wouldn't want it until *after* Numero Quatro is finished raping me. Yes, think of it as rape, Sue, 'cause that's what it is. Otherwise, she'd claim half of that too." Not thinking straight, he put his hot hand on her arm. "Couldn't you do that much for me? For old time's sake?"

"Old time's sake? You've got to be kidding!" This was the moment: Revenge. But she knew revenge was not really in her. "Roger, I am not, repeat *not,* going to ask August about his will! Make up with your father, that's my advice."

"And how am I going to do that? How . . . when he won't even say hello?"

"Keep trying, that's all I can tell you. Change your name back to Blick. Ever think of doing that?"

"Blake to Blick?" His lips quivered. "You're kidding. Aren't you just playing with me? Have your fun, Sue!"

"Look," she said resignedly, "all I can promise is that if the matter arises, I'll do the best I can. And that's all I can do."

"You're still bitter! I cannot believe it!"

Bitter, yes. Largely because he made her remember the old days. The Blake of old had used her. He'd taken advantage of her youth and energy and trust. If it hadn't been for the Blake of old, Nate Carleton might still be alive. Blame him for that—if anything.

"I could be bitter. But I'm not bitter. You know why? Because I don't care to dwell on it. Or on you."

"That's terrific—I'm written off. A nonperson. Thank you very much."

"You're welcome, I'm sure."

He snapped back in his seat and then, out of desperation, made a huge mistake. He spoke too impulsively, not thinking, showing his colors. And he could've ruined his case completely— could have, that is, if he'd been dealing with a person less tolerant and kind.

"Okay, Susan, so you've been the loving daughter they never had. The old man worships you." His voice dropped and he fixed a look on her which was spiteful, angry, vindictive, even a little threatening. Any less a person might have taken it personally. "So *you're* going to get it all, aren't you? That's the game you're playing, clear enough for a blind man to see."

Despite herself, and she should have seen it coming, Susan began to boil. She could've gotten up then, all very ladylike, and told him in a quiet voice what he could do; she might have slapped him and called him a filthy name and screamed bloody murder. But she did not.

"It's typical of you to say a thing like that, Roger, and I resent it ever so much."

"Oh, yes, oh yes! I just hope you've got enough smarts to share with me. Otherwise—"

"You stupid son of a bitch," she continued, in such a way anyone hearing the voice level would think she was complimenting him on his tie, which she was not because his tie was as garish as Ms. Smith's face, "you're really the dumbest . . . Otherwise, *what*?"

"What? Otherwise..." He faltered, again no surprise. "Otherwise, don't forget I've got lawyers."

"Oh, you've got lawyers? I'll spot you ten lawyers and still come out ahead."

"You *really* never got over it, did you? Your heart is set on making me pay."

Roger rubbed his forehead with his fingertips, then gripped the pressure point at the bridge of his nose, thus appealing to his physical self for calmness.

"When I get *all* the money, Roger..." She stared at him until his eyes dropped away. "When I get all the money, Roger, if..."

"What?"

"I'll give you a couple of bucks, why not? Will you do the same for me?"

"Sue... you *know* I would." He was so sincere, so pathetically sincere, so bedraggled in his sincerity. "You don't have any idea about me, Sue. I'm far from being a happy man. I don't think I've ever been a happy man, Sue, except when you and I... I've always done my best, Sue. Through the years..."

"Roger..."

"Yes, Sue?"

"Shut up."

10

That night AHB asked Susan to become the second Mrs. Blick.

My dear Susan, I invite you to become the second Missus Blick.

The surprise, if there was a surprise in the proposal, was in the fact that Mignon had been the only previous Mrs. Blick. For some reason, Susan had always assumed August was a much-more married man than that.

If Mignon's demise had even temporarily disturbed August, it didn't show. Gravely, he sipped his brandy-soda while waiting for Susan to say something in the way of yea or nay, memorializing the first Missus Blick only in the steady way he stared at her former spot in the sofa. Wondering what to say, Susan took a pull of vodka martini which she'd had Konrad make stronger than usual, having anticipated just such a trying moment.

Truthfully, she was *not* surprised by the proposal, though it might be just a little premature, Mignon having flown the room no more than seventy-two hours before.

"August, I'm flabbergasted. And flattered. I don't know what to say."

His eyes gleamed, for AHB would like to be remembered forever after as a man who "flabbergasted" in both professional and personal life.

"My dear Susan, it is fated. Kismet. What we Germans call *Schicksal!*"

She studied him across the coffee table. Captain of Industry. Robber Baron. Matinee Idol grown old. Former father-in-law. Suitor. Prospective Husband?

Husband? Mrs. August Hugo Blick? TV personality, Madame Susan Channing-Osborne-Blick? How did it sound? A little cumbersome, actually. And was it fated after all? She must have been staring at AHB very hard: he pursed his lips and turned his head away. How did Billionaire Heiress Susan Blick sound? No, there was something about big numbers that embarrassed her.

She thought of Roger Blake and laughed aloud—maybe she should go ahead and do it, for his sake, or to spite him even more.

"So amusing?"

AHB cleared his throat shrilly and Susan saw, as if for the first time, the florid, sagging cheeks, like two skinned animals, the stiff, gray hair, the clerical upper lip and bushy eyebrows. God, what a collection of features; any one of them by itself would have done proud a Roman warrior's bust.

"I admit that I have little left of pulsing passion." Her protesting bleat was meant to reassure him. But she needn't have concerned herself. "On the other hand, Susan, I've always judged you to be an intellectual of the flesh."

"August . . ."

He held up his hand. No, she was not supposed to interrupt until he had solemnly, logically presented the complete argument.

"You see, Susan, I've always believed you to be more dedicated to career and accomplishment than the questionable rewards of male-female intercourse. I mean of course the physical act. . . ."

It was terribly sad. How could August have gotten it so wrong?

"I'm not sure I understand you."

"Bluntly, I am saying that you consider lovemaking more a means than an end. You are, first and foremost, a careerist."

His old eyes challenged her and Susan told herself, okay, fair enough! AHB thought she used sex for career, that she was not capable of love, freely given and taken, no strings attached. Tears welled up in her eyes. AHB didn't understand her any better than ninety-nine percent of the men she knew. Of course, he didn't, couldn't, know about Harry, much less Nate, but he *was* familiar with Roger and that was enough to make him think the worst of her.

"That's not true, August, and it's not nice of you, or fair, to say so." Too sharply, she added, "If one is never given love, August, one is inclined to concentrate on career."

"Ah..." He performed his ancient Mandarin smile. "And what, then, do you call my deepest affection? Is that, as we used to say, chopped liver?"

The effort to contain her tears hurt her face.

"I do like my work and I'd never deny it. But that doesn't mean I sold myself to get where I am."

"*Sold yourself?* That's putting it crudely," he reprimanded.

"No more crudely than you've just put it yourself, August."

She could stare him down, even prevail, for she had something he wanted: herself. He assumed she'd grovel, beg him to accept her acceptance. But she was not his slave. If crunch came to crunch, Susan could move out tomorrow, *tonight*, never see him again and survive very nicely, thank you. Yes, as she'd told Roger, Susan was fond of August but, strangely enough, given the hypocrisy of the three-cornered relationship, she would miss Mignon most, the *old* Mignon, lively, vivacious, flirty Mignon.

But how weird to be thinking in these terms. After all, AHB had just asked her to marry him.

He made a guttural sound in the back of his throat.

"My dear Susan," AHB grumbled, "I respect and admire you for being realistic. Like a fine instrument, my dear, that is what you are. A violin does not make beautiful music on only four strings..."

"August..."

"Beauteous Susanna, the huntress..." Wrong, but she didn't try to correct him. AHB's Mongol eyelids slipped lasciviously; a bemused smile softened his worldly face. "AHB will strum your strings. The long, cool blonde form of the purest... integrity, firmer than a piece of ripe peach. Blue eyes like glacial lakes I knew in the Salzkammergut. An old Aryan soul of appetites most basic... and searching... and daring. The intellect, so keen, like the hardest diamond. The wit... *and,* dear one..."

"Please, August..."

But he only smiled, the more self-assuredly, laughing huskily, coughing.

"And the femaleness, your life-center, the core of existence, furnace of the gods, bubbling cauldron of creation, your sex, yes, the wound that never heals."

She was blushing wildly, like a schoolgirl. "August! Please! Isn't that enough?"

He was in full flight. His nostrils hummed, like a hound's in chase.

"Your *place!*" He choked on his own vehemence. "Opened rosebud, tulip's crimson petals and the flower within the flower, the imperial purple of the night orchid—"

Susan covered her face with her hands. "Is this *all* there is?"

"*All?* It is *everything!* The life-force, sustenance..." Susan wailed and shook her head but he insisted, "You do sustain me, *your* juices: my life's blood!"

"I'd *rather* you did suck my blood, like a vampire!"

The remark didn't faze him.

"Shall I tell you more?"

Peevishly, she said, "I don't find it amusing to hear my privates described like a floral arrangement."

August put one hand in front of his face and snickered behind it. He'd always liked her sense of humor.

"I think I know what is troubling you, Susan, but never fear. Once you are the second Missus Blick, we shall consummate our union in the tried and true and most conventional fashion. I held back, you see, so long as the first Missus Blick was alive. I am a faithful man."

"I'm pleased to hear that, August."

"Well then!" He clucked happily and slapped his hands together, a signal to Konrad that they were ready for a second drink. "What is to be, Susan? Yea or nay?"

"Another vodka martini, please," she said.

"Aha... aha. You are dissembling, dear one."

"Aren't you forgetting something, August?"

"I can hardly fall on my knees."

"I don't mean that," she said swiftly. "What I mean is, aren't people going to be surprised? I was married to your son... you *may* remember."

"I try to forget."

"The former Missus Blake becomes Missus Blick?"

Too late for him to reply. Konrad was at hand.

"Konrad, my old friend, I will accept another brandy-soda and Miss Susan, I believe, is ready for a second vodka martini, light on the vermouth, am I right?"

August didn't speak again until Konrad had tracked back across the long salon.

"You would legally be the second Missus Blick *and* the former Missus Blake, if it was mentioned at all."

How to play him along? Did Susan want this?

"August, I'm not convinced you really mean it," she said haltingly. "My feeling is..." His eyes flickered. "...that you should wait a week, or longer until the fact of...I'm sorry...Mignon's death sinks in. You must absorb that before you move on, August."

"Meaning?"

"Meaning I want to be reasonable. I want *you* to be reasonable."

"I am not an impulsive person, Susan."

"Well, then, for my sake," she argued unconvincingly. "Give *me* the luxury of thinking it over, August. I don't want to seem impulsive either. *Or* like I've been sitting here, waiting. I've never counted on this, August."

"Have no fear! I am aware you are not a fortune hunter." Susan smiled her thanks for that much anyway and he went on powerfully, clipping and firing words like a drill sergeant. "Think about it as long as you like, my dear, but I simply will *not* have no for an answer!"

"Oh? But how can I promise that my answer won't be no?"

She didn't mean to challenge him, but nevertheless his face went rigid. Out came the same kind of remark she'd heard at lunchtime.

"If it is no, *Missy,* then I cannot answer for your future!"

The words, the threat, flew at her like slings and arrows. Her body jerked as if taking a spear full frontally.

"AHB! I'm surprised! You mean that if, out of conviction, I *have* to say no, that you'll—!"

His body caught in a furious spasm of denial, or acknowledgment that yes, her future did depend upon him. His eyes blazed up. Any closer, and they would've set her on fire. God, yes, Susan understood, a little too late, he *was* upset about Mignon. August had never in her memory been so brutal. And, what else? He reminded her, again, forcibly of Roger Blake, né Blick.

"One word dropped into the wrong ear, Missy, and Susan Channing is *verstört*, ruined, destroyed, *verbombt*, bombed out." He stopped himself, rearranged his face. "But we are hypothesizing . . ."

"I can't believe I'm hearing this with my own ears, August."

If he intended to frighten her, it worked. The image of Morty Morton, her agent, swarmed forward.

"Simon Hayford is finished! Don't you know that?"

Giddily, she replied, "I meant to ask you about it, August."

"The *Englander* is moving in," August thundered. "I give you fair warning."

"I was hoping you could tell me what's happening, August."

"Hayford is a dead goose!"

"So you say. But I thought—"

"That I would protect him?" August cracked his loose knuckles, like pistol shots. "I supported him, as he supported me . . . as I support you. But now? We shall see," he said coldly. "If the London *swine* buys control, what worth to AHB to maintain his position in NAN? And, without AHB, where is Hayford? Or you?"

For an old man, AHB certainly kept his knives sharp. But Susan, despite her protestations of shock and surprise, was quite unmoved. AHB was simply not as lethal as he'd once been.

"What you're telling me, in so many words, AHB," she said calmly, "is that you may sell out to Sir Guy Bristals."

"Very possible."

"If the price is right."

"As the business school mavens say, we scratch each other's balls, my dear. I tell you very frankly, Missy, grubby Bristals looms on the horizon." AHB's long jaw wobbled. And then, just as Susan hoped his spite might be subsiding, he lashed out again, more cruelly than before. "You may have to *please* him too—as you *pleased* Jasper Gates."

"And just what do you mean by that?"

"You said it yourself, Missy, five minutes ago—you sell! We buy!" August stared coldly. If he meant to hurt, this was working too. "Career, my dear."

"August—that's horrible! Another awful slander!"

"Another?"

Susan put her glass on the coffee table and jumped up, carelessly sloshing clear liquid over some of his papers. Her heart was pumping like an engine. She couldn't stop the tears, of fury, now; they streamed down her face. He did not know anything.

"Sit down!"

"No, I will not, August! You can't treat me like this. And you expect me to be the second Mrs. Blick?"

She was gone before he could say another word. She swept by Konrad, barely missing his tray. Konrad was startled but he would never be surprised.

From the salon came August's furious cry.

"Come back! At once!"

"Never," Susan exclaimed, saying to Konrad for no good reason, "This is a cruel and unusual man!"

It was none of Konrad's doing that AHB had blown a fuse. Understanding, as how could he not understand, that she was leaving, Konrad balanced the tray on one hand and opened the apartment door with the other. Grandly, with great effect, Susan picked up the second of her vodka martinis as she went by, saying thank you very much, stepped outside and hurried home.

She double-bolted every lock she could find, including the secret closet entrance. August Hugo Blick would not be welcome this night or, considering the depth of her anger, any other. Susan dumped Konrad's pallid martini and made herself a stronger one. Then, she went into the living room and flung herself into one of the easy chairs from which she could see a good thirty degrees of the stone towers of Manhattan, randomly lit like so many spaceships tethered among wet, low-slung clouds. Her town. Her town? Whose? It was beautiful in any case.

But she would be leaving all this. No big deal, as Jack would say. You hired movers and went to the office and went home that night to a different place; he'd been divorced enough to know about it. It wasn't a question of money. Ironically, August's one bit of generosity—calculated, not thoughtless, to be sure—meant Susan had the wherewithal to thumb her nose at him. She'd been able to acquire the flat for next to nothing and now it was worth well over a million. Add a few assets AHB couldn't know of and she'd be fine. Susan Channing would survive! And then some!

Of course, she suddenly realized, if they'd lived in California she might have hit him up for palimony, the very latest thing. How he'd hate that, not merely because of the money either. The publicity would demolish him. All these years of cultivating a low profile blown away. More than low profile: AHB actually preferred the world to think of him as dead. People don't sue the deceased, he said.

But Susan had her own profile to consider. Careerwise, it would be suicide to flaunt such a geriatric romance in front of the public's face. And, of course, since nothing had ever been put on paper, it would be Susan's word against his that the King of Kunnilingus had promised her the moon.

Susan finished the drink and, thinking what the hell, she'd make another, was headed for the kitchen when the doorbell sounded.

August? More likely Konrad, bearing one of AHB's notes. No, she would not answer. She stood silently, pretending nobody was home. The bell buzzed again, more insistently, before she gave up.

"Who is it?"

Not Konrad.

"Susan . . . *please*."

This was Scott Blake's voice, in extremis. What the hell was he doing here? Susan reversed all the latches and yanked open the door before he buzzed again, possibly alerting them next door. Susan was shocked. His clothes dirty and disheveled, Scott faced her anxiously, face dead white, eyes red-rimmed and anxious. On the plus side, whatever had happened, arrogance had taken a holiday.

"Why are you here? What do you want?"

He staggered forward, swayed, reeled back, shaking his head drunkenly. But she didn't think he was drunk. Drugs, more likely.

"*Well?* Say something!"

Whispering, he got out words: "They rang The Old Man. Konrad told 'em to lemme in. But I wanna talk to *you*."

Susan had no choice but to haul him inside. She slammed the door and threw all the locks again and dragged Scott into the living room. He dropped on her long designer sofa, like new, so rarely sat upon. That, too, because she was hardly ever home and never entertained when she was, for fear *August* might object.

"Are you sick or something?"

But he looked more crazy than feverish. The obvious thing was to ask him about the drugs. Talk about profile: she'd simply call the police and have him hauled away.

"No, no, Susan . . ."

He was denying what? Before she could get out of his reach, he grabbed her hand and put it against his cheek. She felt herself give way. Her instinct was to comfort him. He was so young . . . too young.

She stopped herself quickly, rejecting the mothering impulse.

"Susan . . . Sue," he stuttered, "that woman tried to *strangle me*. Look!" He pulled down his tie and opened his collar. "Look! See the fucking . . . see the marks she made?"

Too true! Susan felt sick, seeing the bruises, black and blue marks, and bloody scratches where long red gypsy fingernails had dug in.

"That's ugly!"

Of course, she shouldn't be surprised. Susan had known all about Ivy Eva Smith as soon as she'd walked into the Plaza.

Confused, embarrassed, the poor boy's expression was a tangle and, for the moment, Susan forgot how nasty he'd been at lunchtime.

"I couldn't get away from her, Sue. She . . . like, she went berserk!"

"Why . . . what happened?"

"I dunno. Could it be PMS?"

"Are you crazy? Women don't murder men because of premenstrual syndrome." Suddenly, a more realistic thought dawned. "What did you do to her, Scott?"

Naturally. There was your answer: he'd reverted, forgotten to act nice, or said something foul and the gypsy in poor Ivy Eva had surfaced. Susan could easily imagine it happening.

"I swear," he cried, "we were just talking about my book, like my writing habits . . . you know . . . how imaginative I am with my characters . . . everybody says so. Wait'll you read it, Sue, you'll see—"

"Get to the point." She'd had enough of the Blick-Blakes for one night. "You're disturbing me."

"Gee, I'm sorry. I'm really sorry." He sounded sincere but with a Blick-Blake, how could you be sure? "I have to tell *somebody*. Who'm I gonna tell? The Old Man?"

"Your father?"

"Him! He wouldn't listen. *She tried to kill me*. I was choking to death!" Scott goggled at her, eyes brimming.

Susan wasn't buying it. She didn't trust a Blick-Blake any further than she could throw him. "I had to grab her by the . . . before she'd let go!"

"I'm listening."

God Almighty! Scott *was* just like his grandfather; he was a younger model of AHB. In the old days, August must have looked exactly like him. Susan studied the smooth, almost beardless face: this youth, this child, this awful boy. He smelled of sourish baby sweat and talcum powder. And, for all the world, Susan told herself emotionally, forgetting about his lies and misbehavior, Scott looked exactly like those other boys; he was a perfect composite of all those eighteen-year-olds, all those dead boys; and so lucky, though he couldn't know it or even learn it, he'd been born a few years later.

"Poor boy. . ."

He took Susan's vast compassion, that which shook her violently, to be meant solely for himself. How could he know otherwise? Thinking to ingratiate himself, Scott smiled woefully. It must be so obvious what had happened: predatory Ivy Eva Smith had tried to rape the poor little thing!

The phone rang, startling them both. Scott shook his head violently, yelping that she shouldn't answer and that whatever anybody said, it wasn't true, and he wasn't there anyway.

And Susan would not have answered if she hadn't been confused or if she'd known it was August. He addressed her haughtily, his voice only slightly troubled.

"Are you . . . ? It is August speaking. Is everything in order? Someone rang from downstairs saying he was my grandson. But no one has appeared. Have you . . . Should I send Konrad to your assistance? Can you speak, are you alone?"

"He's here, August."

"Oh, no!" Scott cried out faintly and slid off the couch to the floor. Babbling silently, mewling, he kicked his heels in the air like a spoiled child, then on all fours crawled around the coffee table and grabbed her legs. Susan pushed at him but he held on for dear life, burying his face in her lap and then lifting himself to hiss in her ear, "Don't betray me to The Old Man. Let me stay here . . . *please!*"

He was all over her and, angrily, feeling used again and very warm and embarrassed, Susan shoved at him, frowning and scowling and shaking her head, pointing at the couch. He backed off a little but remained there, crouching at her feet and making a babyface. What was he all about anyway? This Scott was not the maddening but still relatively innocent child she remembered.

"Susan, it's rather late," August muttered. "Will the boy—"

"He and I are having a chat, August. He'll be leaving soon."

"I should not have Konrad—"

"Don't wait up."

He didn't know what to say or how. He'd know his grandson was there, and listening.

AHB murmured petulantly, "Will you ever see me again, dear child?"

Susan shook her head, at August, and at Scott.

"Not tonight, August."

Scott need not worry. Susan had decided she would not turn him over to his grandfather. But, one false move . . . and he was dead meat.

"Be good to him, Susan."

"I will, August."

Not waiting, so as not to disturb the truce, Susan hung up the phone.

Scott's eyes glistened with joy.

"Thanks, Mommy."

"You can cut out calling me Mommy too," Susan told him unhappily. "*Betray* you? To your own grandfather."

Warily, he replied, "Well, you could've made me go when I'd rather stay."

"Come now! Not exactly a betrayal, is it . . . would it be?"

"Everybody betrays everybody else," he said blackly.

Nervously, he fingered his neck, delicately pressing the bruise marks.

Not very compassionately, Susan remarked, "You were always getting in trouble."

"Well, you wouldn't want me to change, would you?"

"You were a really rotten kid, even at the age of eight."

"But you loved me . . . right?"

"It was love-hate. I think I handled you pretty well, given, I mean, you weren't *my* kid."

"I'd run circles around you now, lady," he said boastfully.

"*That's* a laugh."

He nodded, admitting, "You're right. When I said you

were the best of my mommies, I meant it, you know. You were good to me, Sue.''

"Well . . .''

It was difficult to know when to take him seriously.

"Because of you, I really like older women.''

"Older women have more sense.''

"And they're beautiful. *You're* beautiful.''

"Age is relative anyway,'' she went on, self-consciously. "What counts is spirit.''

"Hey! Do I know that? Believe me! I've got girlfriends in California who are even older than you . . . and they're *full* of piss and vinegar.''

Susan crossed her arms slowly, wondering if she should kill him now.

"*Even older?* I'm thirty-eight, for God's sake. You think that's old? I wasn't talking about me! I'm not an older woman.''

Scott grinned deviously, then pointed at the table where she'd put her glass.

"Yours? What is it?''

"A martini.''

"Hey! How 'bout I freshen that and make myself just a teensy-tiny one?''

"No way!'' Susan snapped. "That's one thing about being old. I can drink and you can't.'' He rounded his eyes, mocking her irritation. "What women are you talking about anyway? I didn't raise you to be a gigolo, little man.''

"Do I get a drink?''

Blackmail again! Okay, maybe he deserved something after his run-in with Ms. Smith.

"That's a *vodka* martini. Did *Miss Smith* give you anything to drink?''

Like a lush beyond his years, Scott homed in on the little wet bar which combined with minor butler's pantry in the kitchen entrance. As men do, muttering about ice cubes, he spoke wrathfully over his shoulder.

"A lousy light beer! Like, you know, we don't do a little boozing out on the Coast.''

"Hey! Hold it! You're sounding like a movie producer!''

"Like a producer named Roger Blake, you mean!''

He rattled ice into her glass and, with seeming expertise, added vodka and a dash of vermouth. Then he gave himself a good deal more than a tiny bit of the same thing, on the rocks, and rejoined her, seating himself comfortably on the broad arm of her easy chair.

"Thanks for protecting me from August."

Susan tasted the drink; he'd made it well or maybe she'd merely had too many. Whatever, determinedly, she maintained composure, pretending he wasn't there, where he was, his warm leg against her shoulder.

"I can tell you Miss Smith had herself a joint while I drank my crummy beer."

"And you had one too, no doubt, *with* the beer."

"Nope." He chuckled merrily. "I hate to disillusion you and the old man, but I don't like the stuff."

"But write about it nevertheless," Susan observed.

"Well? It's a part of contemporary . . . you know," he shrugged indifferently, "society, modern times, all that stuff."

She liked Scott better as some of the conceit dropped away and he behaved as he should, like a naive young kid. And liked August that much less. Susan had never thought about it very much but there was definitely a spiritual something or other that was missing in August. Not readily could she or did she want to identify what it was and the vodka, of course, didn't help.

"The joint put her over the top," Scott added, leading Susan on. "She turned on me . . . like a hurricane."

"I want to hear about your women in California."

"Aha!" He winked confidentially, as August might have. "I don't ordinarily mention them—they're married, see, and I wouldn't want to get them in trouble." He sensed her disbelief for he tapped her shoulder fondly, as if to say Susan shouldn't doubt him. "You know, the old man stuck me in that apartment over the garage, so I'm out of the way. His last wife didn't like me. . . ."

"I can imagine! What'd you try on her?"

"Point is my . . . friends can come and go as they like—so to speak!" He laughed loudly. "Get it?"

"Mister Hollywood."

"Sue! Please! Don't say that!" he pleaded, eyes so sincere. "I'm, like, a victim! They're crazy about me, like this maniac Ivy Eva. I don't know why. I mean it, honestly. When I'm back from school in the afternoon, you know, and some Saturday mornings, they'll . . . um . . . park up the street and, like, pay me a little visit. They say . . ." he gazed down at her in fake bewilderment ". . . that I do good work."

"I hope you're not making this up. Or are you . . . like the book?"

"Yeah," he agreed smoothly, "probably."

"If you're so experienced, what went wrong with Ivy Eva?"

"Nothing."

"You're fibbing."

"Fibbing?"

"Don't kid around with *me*."

"Not to say I wouldn't like to kid around with you, lady."

"Stop that! And stop calling me lady." Mood reversed, she wanted very much to slap the daylights out of him. "Look, I've had enough of everything for one night and I'm going to go to bed. What are *your* plans?"

"You're mad because I told you about my mistresses."

"Are you going next door or back to the hotel? Your father must be wondering where you are."

"Nope." Scott shook his head. "And I don't know where he is. That's why I came here."

"How'd you know I'd be home?"

"The Old Man told me I should talk to you, that you'd give good advice on the media."

"I think," she said sardonically, "I can advise you that you screwed it up with *Fast Set*."

"Well, what could I do, give in?" he demanded. "I didn't want to tell you, Sue, you know, to shock you. The truth is she tried to force me to . . . and I . . ."

If she believed him, then she had to believe that Ivy Eva Smith was some kind of a spoiler, a frustrated media hack who, like so many of them, had never gotten it quite right about life. Susan could have warned Scott. No, there were certain things boys had to learn for themselves.

"I would've thought *you* could handle it."

But he brooded at her. "Sometimes I wonder whether it's worth it . . . you know, just for a little piece and what does it all mean? Where are we going?"

"You're leaving. You're going back to the hotel, that's where you're going, little man."

"No kidding, I'm not kidding, Sue. You know, I got a character in the book blows his brains out with his father's skeet-shooting gun. That's after he beats a girl to death with a polo mallet 'cause she pushed him too hard for sex and he's not exactly sure yet whether he's straight or gay."

Susan punched her elbow into his gut.

"Sue! Gosh!" he whined. "That hurt! We *did* have a classmate kill himself. So I'm starting with something realistic, then I take what we call poetic license...."

"Charming."

"It's just fiction."

"You know," Susan said, very slowly, very patiently, "none of you *children* know which end is up!" He smiled weakly, not daring to deny it. "Do me a favor, Scotty. I don't want to hear about suicide. Just...I don't know...just, *please,* think about it a little. You've got everything to live for. You know?"

She nudged him again, harder, more emphatically.

"But he did kill himself. Could you tell me why?"

"No."

Stubbornly, he said, "It did happen. And I put it in the book. Should it be ignored?"

She shook her head, No. But there was something very important for him to understand, although he probably never would.

"Would you like to consider all the eighteen-year-olds who got killed in a war I know about? Shot, blown up, burned? They weren't ready to die. And you want to dwell on stupid teenage suicide!"

"I know that," he cried. "I know all that."

"It could've been you, *idiot!* You're lucky you didn't find out about it firsthand!"

"And maybe I'm sorry I didn't!" That stopped her. Susan squinted at him tearfully. "I mean...at least, then, there was *something*..."

"Something, what?"

Oh, of course, the answer was so obvious, to him anyway. Taking a deep and daring breath, Scott said, "Something versus nothing."

"All that means to me," she muttered bitterly, "is that you don't know what the hell you're talking about."

"No, it means *nothing.* What happens? Nothing. What do we do? Nothing. What interests us? Nothing. What do we believe in? Nothing."

Now she felt guilty for rejecting him. What did he know, really? *Nothing.* Scott dropped down on his knees and stared intently at her face. She was crying and let him see her cry. It might be good for his soul.

"What's wrong?"

"Nothing. I don't know."

It was unlike Susan to let herself go. Why now? The answer was before her, young and dumb, believing like all the young ones that he was immortal. His swollen lower lip quivered; his eyes begged pardon. Incredulously, Susan watched her slim hand, blonde, rather lovely, with its perfect nails, little half-moons of cuticle at each fingertip, watched, fascinated, as the hand patted Scott's curly head. The warmth and hope, despite all his blather, rolled off him. Then she laid the palm of her hand against his flaming cheek and touched her lips fleetingly to his forehead.

"Forget it," she said, "nothing for you to think about."

His face fell to her breast and Scott impulsively flung his arms up and around her.

"Please . . ."

Susan was not able to resist him. Normal caution failed, no reason why. Something deprived her of judgment and she didn't care. Something told her to let it go. Scott pulled her blouse out of her skirt and with trembling hands tugged at the bra straps, so ineffectually that, not thinking straight, Susan undid it for him, freeing her breasts. He went mad, seeking her with frantic lips, suckling, noisy lips which made her groan, then melt with desire, and fear. She was terrified of his body and of herself. Squirming, Scott forced himself between her knees, pulling and blindly pawing. He was wild, possessed . . . beautiful, like all those strong young animals she thought of so often.

"Susan . . . *please!*"

It was, perhaps, disappointing that she would not have him first. Still, he was not as experienced as he pretended. Fumbling, he went too fast, too clumsily, caressing and grabbing, gasping and shaking, quite out of control, and hurting her.

Susan grabbed him by the hair and pulled his head to her, putting her lips to his mouth, kissing him deeply and even instructively, striving to calm him, slow him down a little. He couldn't stop trembling though; his breathing was erratic, uneven.

"Easy does it . . ."

Susan couldn't remember the last time she'd had such an effect on a man. Man? Boy!

His heavy tongue thrust at her, between her teeth, tangling

with her own and Susan felt torment then. He was heavy on her and she shifted, putting a hand to his hip, then, continuing to surprise herself, his crotch, the shivering loins, and his body literally leapt and, at once, she was aware of his rippling, coursing orgasm.

Scott grunted, cried out angrily, cheated.

"Oh, shit, darling, I'm sorry... sorry!" Breathlessly, he scrambled up. "Excuse me. Oh, damn it! I don't want to stain my suit."

"The bathroom is beyond the door, to the right."

Scott hobbled away. Saved by a whisker, breathing a bit tempestuously herself, Susan gulped some of her drink. She needed it now. She gulped and swallowed, inhaling, exhaling, steadying herself. Unbelievable! This would never do. Fair warning. What had happened? No explanation.

She stood up, in confusion, horribly embarrassed, poked at her hair where he'd mussed it, redid the bra and tucked her blouse back where it belonged, primly and properly, then sat down again.

Enough about the brave, young men, bodies all pink and flawless.

Susan sighed deeply and Scott must have heard her as he came back.

"You'd better leave now, Scott."

"Darling..."

That again. He was behind her. Susan turned to stone when he put his hands on her shoulders. She did not react at all, though it killed her, as he ran his fingers downwards, under her blouse, under the bra again, finding her nipples, hardening.

"You have to leave."

"Darling..."

The voice was raw, reedy, choking.

"Scott, please go."

"You really want me to go?" he asked in a low voice, miserably. "Don't you just love it?"

"I want you to go."

Yes, she did want him to go. This cheapened her. He'd be comparing her already to his California mistresses. Try to remember about Madame Butterfly: they always sailed away. Yet the memories and yearning were so powerful.

"No," she said. "You don't have to go. If it's late—is it late?"

"It's eleven, Sue."

"Eleven? Is that all? Let me see your watch."

She pulled his left hand away from her, took his wrist and turned it. The watch reported digitally: Eleven.

Susan held onto his fingers. Supple, pink fingernailed, the back of the hand unblemished, she brought the hand to her mouth and put her lips to it, bit gently on the tips of the fingers, caressed the palm of his hand with her mouth and the inside of the wrist. He drew air sharply.

"It's very late," she said. "Too late for you to go, too late for you to stay."

"Susan."

His voice was really so young when you didn't see him, and she couldn't see him because he was behind her.

"Come around," she said. "I want to look at you when I talk to you."

11

Feeling far from pleased with herself, or very proud, if the truth be told, Susan had to force herself into the day. Dressing, putting a few strokes of makeup over her washed-out face, she had regrets. God, if anything would, a night like that added lines to your face! Had she really, finally blown it now? No wonder Harry had run. She scared him; she scared herself.

Really? How could she be sure? Susan felt so relaxed and, though tired, as loose as a goose.

Or depraved.

Her mood swung between gloom and elation.

What had she proven? That she was unstable, that she couldn't trust herself around children, young men. Yes, yes, no argument—but, on the other hand, once she had given in, the act had been deeply fulfilling; why, she was not exactly sure, certainly not because Scott was a great lover. Perhaps because she had finally achieved her goal, frankly, of making love to all those beautiful young men: through their chosen representative, young Scott Blake.

For shame! Worse yet, once you'd acquired this young lover, what next? It was all too nerve-wracking for words, and unusual, to say the least, when you considered that right next door, the boy's *grandfather* had a mere few hours previously asked her to become the second Mrs. Blick.

Susan had to get out of town, she had to go! But she didn't want to leave. Could one get enough, more than enough, too much, of fresh young flesh, better than yeasty bread?

On the other hand, the whole mad episode could be terminal. One could die, expire of overindulgence, that too was possible. Forsake such lechery! Moderation would be her watchword.

If Susan had ever seriously contemplated killing herself—God, they'd been talking about that the night before, suicide, the thing that had set her off in the first place—seriously, now was the time to do it. A pact: the two of them, gone together, in a fit of satiation, joining the ageless universe where a couple of years made not a whit of difference.

No, all was not lost after all. Nothing was lost. Nobody would ever know. Admit it, wasn't she *happy*? Wasn't this the very thing she'd been fantasizing all these months, years?

The young thug must have been dreaming about that which she was thinking: half-asleep still, he smiled, probably pondering, Susan told herself sadly, whether he could tell his friends about this new conquest and whether they'd believe him. He'd already promised, but Susan knew she could expect to appear in his next book, not that she cared, and provided he ever wrote another after she was finished with him.

Alongside his slim, tanned body, her skin was rosy, rubbed pink and new from the massive collision of flesh. It had been many a moon. . . . But she had to flee before he was properly awake. And he read her mind again, so supremely confident of himself by now, and put one arm lazily across her shoulders and drew her down for a lingering, sticky, morning kiss, sucking her lips, eating her tongue. He tasted of milk, raw and warm and went to her breast, with his slim-fingered hands to the small of her back, her hip, caressed to the thigh, and buried his fingers in the dampness of her loins.

No, she had to get out!

He was ready again, hard and erect. Susan touched and he reacted convulsively, his body straining. Unable to help herself, but knowing this was the last of it, she used him with her mouth.

Gasping, he tried to speak but she put her hand over his lips.

"This never happened," she said.

Meriam would know. Women always knew. Women understood that sometimes you stumbled and fell. Susan, as usual, met Meriam on her way out and by the look of her knew that it had also recently happened to Meriam. Susan had suspected for some time that AHB's man Sidney had a thing going with Meriam during the daytime when Susan was gone. But she'd never said anything.

The young man in the guest room, Meriam, that's young Scott Blake, former stepson, grandson of old Mr. Blick who lives next door, whose wife just died.

Meriam, of course, already knew all about it.

Once in the cab on her way downtown, Susan felt badly, *and* exhilarated. She'd been bad but it had been very good: that was the only way to look at it. She was aware of aching leg muscles, a sure sign of a busy night, and the logy sense of accomplishment. Yes, and what did she expect?

Get out of town, Miss Susie! Before Scott woke up to what had happened, before AHB pressed her on the matter of becoming his second wife. Surely there would be a good reason for her to join Jack Godfrey in Washington for a few days or to go on assignment somewhere halfway around the world.

"Think, Arthur, think."

But Fineman had declined into black despair when Susan reported to him what August Blick had said about the probable, impending demise of Simon Hayford. Sir Guy Bristals was going to gobble up NAN and very soon they would be fighting for their lives, or, if not that, then struggling for every budget penny and fending off Bristals's time-honored habit of turning media-class into sleaze.

"It's been shown time and time again," Fineman sorrowed, "that there's no peace, continuity, or longevity in this business."

"I'll go anywhere, Artie, to get out of town."

"Why? What's wrong? What's happened. Tell Arthur!"

"In due course."

"Where can I send you, Suse?" Fineman's voice thinned

with concern. "There's Toronto—but it's not quite ready. We're still negotiating with his press people. They want more control over the questions."

"Screw them, Arthur," Susan said fiercely. "Weren't we going to do something in South-West Africa? What about Mongolia?"

"Sweetheart—that's too far away right now. What about the State Department, the Defense Department? You can hop down to Washington for a few days, can't you? I want an interview with that schmuck David Holtzenmeister. . . ."

Who happened to be the new secretary of state.

"They'll put us out of business, Artie."

"Because we've found theft and corruption?"

"They'll have us assassinated, Artie. They were ready, a few years ago, remember?"

"Nah!" he chortled, happier thinking about that, "just Jack. They weren't going to kill you, Suse."

Wincing, then, his grin dropped away and Fineman slapped a hand to his stomach. The ulcer, it always kicked in when things got tough. One day, it would kill him, if he didn't kill himself first, he always said.

"You see I'm suffering, Channing! What the hell do you want from me?" Despite his discomfort, however, he intuitively pinpointed half her problem. "What else did Blick have to say?"

Out of despair she'd come up with anything better, Susan invented the story that AHB recommended they beat Guy Bristals to the punch: take their show and sell it lock, stock, and barrel, personnel included, to CBS or ABC.

"Doesn't he understand, for crissakes," Fineman squalled, "you can't just do that overnight? It'd take two, three months of fucking around. You can't just go and say 'Wanta buy a good show, mister?' " Arthur was perspiring heavily. "He's on the NAN board, Suse! Hasn't he got better advice than that? Jesus, I've been at NAN fifteen years now. I ain't gonna just jump ship, goddamn it!"

Yes, Susan had to agree, there should be a better explanation for August's pissy attitude.

"He doesn't know whether to sell or hang in there."

With a sweaty sneer, Fineman demanded, "You're telling me Blick is thinking of *our* best interests?"

Susan stared at him. It was hopeless. She had to divulge. Turning to make sure the door was closed, then looking him in the eye, she confessed, "AHB wants me to marry him."

For a second, his own suffering remissed.

"You marry Blick? That old . . . asshole? Sorry." He burped acidly. "That's ludicrous, Suse. You and Blick? Whatta laugh!"

"Arthur, it happens to be true."

Among other problems.

"Suse, I always figured if you married again, it'd be like . . . in the family." She heard and waited, having no idea what he meant. "What I always thought," he said mournfully, "was that if it came to that, you and Jack—"

"Me and Jack? I thought you were going to say . . . *you!*"

"Me? Oh no, sweetheart. I'm a sick man. Besides . . ." He eyed her shrewdly, ". . . you and Jack, I mean, what the hell, he could make an honest woman of you one of these times."

"Arthur . . ."

Say no more. He knew.

"August Blick . . . Jesus!"

"Arthur, the problem is, if I don't agree, he's going to dump his stock in NAN, throw me to the wolves . . . and you and Jack too. That's why—"

"That's why . . ." Gleefully, he finally got the point. ". . . that's why you better get out of town, Suse! Keep Blick on ice as long as you can, until we figure out a way to head off Bristals!"

"So I reasoned, Arthur."

Staring at her haggardly, perspiration spilling out of the trenches on his forehead and running into his sparse eyebrows, Fineman whispered admiringly, "Sweetheart, believe me, I didn't realize your plight was so desperately touch-and-go. I am going to work on it, with all my heart." He stopped and stared. "But I mean, you *don't* want to marry him, do you?"

They were blessed. *She* was blessed. Rescue came sooner than expected and from a most unexpected quarter.

It came in the form of a phone call from Jasper Gates of Jasper International and directly to Susan's boss Arthur Fineman. Gates was in New York, you see, and damned if he hadn't been thinking about this interview Susan Channing had proposed for *Hindsight* and, having thought about it up, down and sideways, he was now prepared to say yes. The hitch was that Jasper Gates was horrendously busy all day, and had been since his arrival in the city, and in order to arrange this thing conveniently and timewise, Ms. Channing would have to fly off with him to California that very night. Jasper Gates's suggestion was that they could discuss ground to be covered, a line of question and answer, that sort of thing, even go right ahead with some taping when they got to San Francisco. And then, naturally, Ms. Channing and a camera crew would want to accompany him to Bulgaria when Gates went to visit his cruise ship, which would obviously lend color and meat to the whole project.

The thing was, Jasper Gates said, they had to understand there were several supersensitive departments at Jasper International that could not be discussed—but if Ms. Channing and he could agree, he'd give it a go.

Fineman hated anybody trying to instruct him on how to run his business, but in this case he was prepared to be cooperative, although, for the sake of appearances, he had to hedge a little. Fineman was already conscious of Sir Guy Bristals looking over his shoulder.

For example, how long was all this going to take? And it was very much all-of-a-sudden, was it not? But that was their problem, not his, said Jasper Gates. He was presenting them the proposition and if they didn't think enough of him to make an effort of their own, Gates warned, then *that* would be the end of that. NAN and *Hindsight* were being offered Jasper Gates's one-time-only exclusive and in-depth interview. Was that a scoop or what?

His PR people were horrified, Gates maintained.

Fineman, wanting Susan out of town for the reason they'd discussed, would have agreed to almost anything and so it was arranged, virtue once again the child of necessity, Fineman philosophized. They were losing control of their own destiny, he went on, because of pressures of the financial marketplace.

Whatever, Susan was to meet up with Jasper Gates's corporate jet in a private hangar at La Guardia Airport.

"At midnight," Jasper told her, after he'd finished with Fineman. "And don't thank me! The time has come for Jasper Gates to expose himself."

Predictably, August Hugo Blick was immensely put out that she was leaving so unexpectedly and so soon after he became a widower. Had he not, he complained, taken the initiative to smooth over their nasty altercation? And Susan was leaving; leaving, moreover, without answering the question: Would she consent to be the second Missus Blick?

Susan was very sorry and very apologetic. But orders were orders. Assignment Jasper Gates was too good to pass up. And, come to think of it, wasn't AHB curious? Didn't he want to know more about Gates's rumored deal with the Japanese? Wasn't he interested in what might be revealed of the inner workings of Jasper International?

Of course, of course, that went without saying. Long face stretched dismally, his expression like a bad weather front, AHB behaved, nevertheless, as if Susan's departure with Gates was the most disheartening event of the century.

"We've had no time to talk about anything, my dear," AHB groused. "The business with Mignon pushed the Japanese rumor right out of my mind. And now, suddenly, you must race away with this parvenu, this graceless manipulator Jasper Gates! This man with the manners of a Mongolian footsoldier!"

All true, but business called. Hadn't August himself described Gates as one of the foremost moneymen in the country, Susan argued, politically powerful, a man, like AHB himself, who backed presidents and toppled dictators, upon whose whim markets rose and fell? Surely, he was a man they should seek to interview.

Cajoling him into better humor, Susan said, "And when August Blick is ready for his interview, Susan Channing has the exclusive, am I right?"

"There will never, never be such an interview."

"I know," she said sadly, "and the world is the loser."

"Perhaps the world deserves to lose," AHB leered. "And . . . before you go, what is your answer to my proposal? You accept to be the second Missus Blick?"

Susan had had all day to work on her answer.

Smiling brightly, she said, "August, my answer will come in a quiet moment. Not when I'm in such a rush. That wouldn't do you . . . or us . . . justice. Don't you agree?"

He had to admit the logic of it, even if he didn't like it. It would've been churlish of him to make another bad scene.

August nodded halfheartedly, then informed her, "By the way, I lunched today with the young man from California."

"Good . . . Fine. Did you have a good talk?"

"He worships you, my dear."

Susan did her best, muttering, "Well . . . I always thought he . . . I always tried my best with Scott, right back to when—"

He lifted his hand for her to stop right there.

"He doesn't seem a bad sort of young man. I think I may have a plan for him. Of course, I never see boys his age anymore. Therefore, it's *good* that you get along with him *so well*, Susan. When you are the second Missus Blick, you'll be a good, solid grandmotherly haven for him."

"Does he think of me as a grandmother now?" She could well imagine the little man making just such a mocking remark. "I *was* his stepmother."

"What is important is that we two cherish him, if not his third-rate father."

"I suppose."

Surely, the little idiot hadn't given them away. Deny everything. Never explain, never complain. By now, in her mind, Susan advised herself calmly, Scott Blake was yesterday's news. She'd managed already to reduce him in her mind to *very* manageable proportions. He was a man, no different than any of the others. Anything special about him? Through him, perhaps, she had succeeded in raising some of the dead. For certain, Nate had returned, if only for a few seconds. During those wild moments, she had yelled loudly enough to wake him.

"You'll be gone, how long?"

"Just a few days, August. Once I've got it organized, we'll wrap up Jasper Gates in no time at all. Cruise ship, oil, gas, timber . . . you name it . . ." Then, something brilliant occurred to her. "Any good questions for him?"

Ah, this did appeal. AHB grinned reflectively, hiding his long nose behind his fingers.

"Yes! Why *not* ask Jasper from where his seed money came. He has talked often enough about that mysterious bank in Texas that supposedly underwrote his first oil rig. Of course, he sold out of oil, very conveniently, at the high, immediately before the collapse of the first OPEC embargo. But, don't be shy about asking after his dealings with the Mexican national oil cartel." August's memory bank flooded as he called up his Jasper Gates dossier. "Ask him about . . . African metals and diamond mines and his lumber consortium, his enormous deals in China."

"August, I can't approach it with the idea of embarrassing him. . . ."

"Embarrassing?" AHB laughed abrasively. "Jasper Gates has never in his life been embarrassed. Not even when he was indicted."

"Indicted? I hadn't heard that."

Shrugging scornfully, AHB said, "He was caught! The charge was a securities manipulation. Charge dismissed." He paused. "If you don't want to alarm him, do *not* mention the influence-peddling scandal . . . or the dead widow."

"Dead widow?" she repeated. "You're not very encouraging, AHB. I'd prefer a few petty larcenies."

World-weary eyes alert, he said, "But I thought, my dear, you'd be briefed by now on the matter of Jasper Gates."

"You can read and read and never know the truth."

Susan might have pointed out, as a matter of fact, that she didn't know very much about the origins of August Hugo Blick's billions or the workings of *his* investment company. There was the standard explanation—like all good Germans, AHB had worked hard and saved his money. Unlike most actors, he had been very clever financially. Those who thought they knew, talked about his land investments, the hundreds of thousands of acres he'd collected in the West, Southwest, and on foreign shores; but very few people knew about the New York skyscraper properties or the highrises in London, Hong Kong, and Singapore.

Hong Kong—of course, there was AHB's Chinese connection.

"Also, my dear, you might ask him about Latin America. Our Jasper was very important in Cuba before Castro cleaned house. And maybe still is. I would be fascinated to know."

Drugs? Susan's heart thumped. Gambling? Was Gates involved in the arms-for-drugs trade? She hoped not and, in fact, he did not seem the sort. But, apparently, she didn't know much about the real Jasper Gates.

"I wonder, August, why you do business with him?"

"Only the Big Sea Development Company at the moment. In years past, from time to time, our interests were tangential."

"*Why?* You make him sound like such a crook."

How naive! What a dumb question. August grimaced, it was all so obvious.

"Money. Nothing more than that." He was amused. How dare she act the innocent? "Land, Susan, property. In the case of Big Sea, a considerable acreage is involved, three thousand or more acres, I believe, of a choice island. You can never, never lose by investing in land, *Liebling*. You should always remember that."

"But so much money has been put in the hotel. The whole layout, it's totally luxurious."

"Yes." He frowned. "I know. But we will double our money. If the Japanese . . ."

"Or Hong Kong Chinese . . ."

"Yes."

"It seems a shame to sell it, though, after putting in so much work. It's a wonderful place."

"As wonderful as our place at Wade's Reef?"

Susan didn't falter, didn't miss a beat.

"Oh, no."

"Well, Susan, you should always remember you must not sit sentimentally on such an investment as Big Sea if the right offer comes along. You must not tie up your money."

"You're tied up at Wade's Reef," Susan pointed out.

She knew the answer but it pleased AHB to state it.

"But Wade's Reef is ours, my dear, specifically and especially so." He shook his head. "This has nothing whatever to do with California. You must remember when you speak to Gates that the Japanese invested in the neighborhood of fifteen *billion* dollars in American real estate last year alone. Think about that, young lady! *Fifteen billion!* Therefore," he suggested smugly, "*we* would not want to deny their appetite. Not to speak of whether the people in Washington— *our leaders*—will not eventually forbid them from buying any more . . ."

It was not easy to focus on billions. Her attention slipped away.

"As you know, I am not materialistic! I merely *believe* in capital. I *believe* it is in the best interests of peoples everywhere that the world become not only racially but financially intermarried. That is the American way, Susan!"

"Incestuously, August?"

"No, no, the very opposite, but that *is* a clever thing to say, my dear," he said. "Incest will be *verboten* in that future world! Well-policed greed will be our motor. Without healthy, free-market greed, why, the motor would stall."

Very simply, as she made ready to leave, greasing the slope for departure, Susan flattered him flamboyantly.

"You're a genius, AHB. And one of these days, I will interview you!"

August gazed at her approvingly. Would he disagree? Why should he?

"I am a genius, my dear. But tragic." He touched his long, wide forehead. "It has been so easy. Too easy. It would have been better if I had had to work harder for it, the millions and billions. . . ."

12

"Rich boy makes good, Sue, that's me," Jasper Gates said. "Did I tell you I went to Harvard? Take me and you're getting a Harvard man, sweetie."

He couldn't stop. He absolutely would not stop. Susan shook her head groggily. The trouble was they were alone in the cabin of his personal 727 and it would've been impolite to doze off. And the other thing was God knows what he'd get up to if she lapsed into unconsciousness. Jasper had already hinted a half-dozen times that the stateroom in the aft of the plane was available if she was especially tired or if she'd like to continue their "talk" undisturbed.

She might have made a very big mistake. Susan had been prepared to go to almost any length to get out of New York and away from Scott Blake and his grandfather, but now she wasn't so sure she hadn't performed the well-known leap from frying pan to fire.

Scott had called at eight or so, while she was packing, to tell Susan about lunch with Grandpa. He'd "be over" later, he told her confidently, as if there wouldn't be any question about his coming; right then, the junior roué was kind of busy, see, having dinner with . . . *whoever* he was with for dinner. No, as luck would have it, Miss Channing was not available. She was dashing off on assignment, sorry!

"Harvard business school, that is," Jasper chuckled. "I'm an MBA in good standing, sweetie. . . ."

Dutifully, as soon as they'd sat down within the opulence of the 727 lounge, even before takeoff, Susan had begun taking notes. Now, fighting sleep, she scribbled MBA and Harvard, at the same time stifling a yawn. He was fascinating, yes, but the events in her own life, in fact every moment since she'd returned from California barely a week before, had been action-packed, exhausting. Therefore, the plush comfort of the deep leather chair in which she was sitting was, as Peter Rabbit had discovered about cabbage, soporific.

The cabin decor, built around yards and yards of this same soft glove leather, was very restful too. Shades of brown— tan, chocolate, mocha—had been mixed with a soft ivory color. A dozen zebra skins in Plexiglas hung on the walls and were scattered over mud-brown wool carpeting on the cabin floor. The glasses from which they were drinking were of milky white Lalique crystal; and the little bar where Jasper's steward had made the drinks was covered in a shiny white and brown fabric, meant to simulate zebra skin.

". . . not that I ever needed a degree from Harvard for any of my business deals," he was going on. "You can ask Augie about that!"

Should Susan tell him that she had already asked Augie? Her inclination was to close Jasper Gates down for the night by inquiring about his Texas seed money. But no, better judgment told her not to and it was fortunate she didn't, for the simple reason that five minutes later, Jasper dropped a pearl of information that made the whole hurried expedition worthwhile.

It seemed that Jasper Gates was a business acquaintance *and* good personal friend of their British nemesis, Sir Guy Bristals. Jasper had owned the TV station near Detroit which had become the beachhead for Sir Guy's American invasion five years before.

Would Jasper be aware of Sir Guy's further plans, possibly including the takeover of North American Network? A question not for right now either.

If only she had not been so tired. Jasper's soft, droning

voice, added to the high-pitched sound of the jet engines, was better than a sleeping pill. The one repetitive thought jarred Susan's befuddled brain: Were *all* moneymen related, as August had prognosticated?

Tireless windbag Jasper Gates ogled Susan pleasantly, his smooth, bland, tanned face showing no evidence of weariness. He was remarkable, no question of that, for a man of fifty-nine years of age, as he reminded her again, while fondling his drink, a large glass of bourbon and water, very low class in comparison to August's brandy-soda.

Susan had chosen a dry chablis which she reckoned wouldn't be too gassy so late at night. Cautiously, she recrossed her legs, moving them to the side of the low-slung table that she kept between them.

"Jasper, it's three A.M. and I'm pooped. Why is it we always talk in the dead of night?"

"Sweetie," he said quietly, "I'm a creature of the night, like Churchill was. You know Napoleon never got a good night's sleep. He napped, a half-hour, couple of hours, at a time, all the way to Moscow. But, if you'd like to retire for a little nap before we get to . . . well go right ahead."

He didn't go any further, for the padded door behind the flight deck opened and Jasper's steward, Mr. Dudley, stepped out.

"Wish to report we're right on schedule, sir!"

"Good! Good! What time are we landing, Mr. Dudley?"

"Sir, we'll be landing in Shannon at ten A.M. local!"

Susan jerked forward, fatigue driven back.

"*Shannon?* Shannon, Ireland?"

Jasper nodded. His body shook with laughter for a good ten seconds.

"Aye, lassie, Shannon, Ireland. The wrong way, to be sure."

"No, no, we're going to L.A., Jasper. Not funny!"

"Yes, we are going to L.A., but not today."

To Susan's relief, Mr. Dudley looked a little anxious. Kidnapping was no laughing matter.

"Will there be anything else, sir?"

"Not right now, Mr. Dudley."

Dudley retreated, closing the door firmly behind him. He needn't have bothered. Susan was not going to storm the cockpit, or jump.

"You *are* joking, of course," she repeated.

"Nope." Jasper shook his small, perfectly barbered head. "We're going to Ireland, sweetie."

"We *cannot* be going to Ireland! Our business is in California."

"Susan Channing," Jasper declared, so very pleasantly though, "I've decided to keep you captive 'til you agree to be mine."

"In other words . . . I'm hijacked."

His reply was a complacent nod and Susan could only laugh disbelievingly. This strange man, this maverick, this . . . *crook*? Best to play down that part of it if they were en route to the Emerald Isle, though she didn't think she was in any danger. If he was merely having her on, then it should be established right now that she hadn't fallen for it.

"You're very sweet, Jasper, but I don't plan on being yours."

He raised his sandy eyebrows and said equably, "Then you're condemned to a limbo of forever flying hither to thither in my airplane, back and forth across the North Atlantic, from Togo to El Ropo, for I'll never set you free!"

"El Ropo? Where's *that*? Can you really be serious? You can't!"

"Oh, yes I can."

Hand unwavering, Susan picked up her wine. She could throw it at him, or scream, but face facts—who was going to save her? She sipped.

"You can't do this," she said. "It's wrong."

"Wrong?"

"I know what you're going to say: You're a law unto yourself."

"And we're over the high seas. I am commander of this ship!"

"And crazy. Mad! But you're not mad, are you?"

Jasper shook his head, never ceasing to grin at her. Yes, he thought he had her by the tail. But Jasper Gates should not forget the parable about the man mounting the tiger.

He loosened his seat belt and stood up.

"Would you mind if I got a little more comfortable, sweetie? May I remove my jacket?"

"Sure," she said, acidly, "my kidnapper should make himself very comfortable."

Next, she supposed, preparing herself for it, he'd be asking if he could take off his pants.

"Thank you." Jasper slid out of the charcoal-gray, pinstriped double-breasted suit jacket. He was wearing red suspenders. "I have my suits made in Savile Row."

"Really?"

"Yeah, but still like wearing a straitjacket." He sighed. "I prefer a, you know, rough-and-ready style, like when I was a wildcatter."

His well-built figure, although short, said he'd done his share of hard work. Jasper's shoulders were broad and his chest full. There seemed to be no fat upon him.

"So, sweetie," he mused, sitting down again, "here we are. Now, would you like to go in back for a rest?"

"I'm fine."

"Do you mind if I loosen my tie?"

"No, go right ahead." He did so, pulling at a heavy red-black printed silk foulard, then reached again for his drink. Happier, he seemed prepared just to sit and stare at her. Finally, impatiently, and who wouldn't be, Susan blurted, "I don't understand you, Jasper. I mean, what's your method here?"

"You think there's madness in my method, don't you?" he joked.

"I wouldn't know about that, but I do know I won't be yours," she said, matter-of-factly, making her eyes pop with conviction. She knew where *she* was going in life; at least, he should think she did. "I'm very very surprised *you'd* pull a stunt like this, Jasper. It's so . . . untypical."

"But you don't know me well enough yet to say what is typical!"

"You don't fit Mr. Blick's description, not at all."

"Piss on Augie Blick," Jasper blithely replied. "What's he know? Augie is bangin' on senility's door, Sue!"

"I don't care to hear such things."

"Susan Channing," he said, more sharply, "it's not necessary for you to defend him. Augie is quite capable of taking care of himself."

"You said that before, Jasper! *People* keep drawing these conclusions about August Blick and me. And none of you knows what you're talking about, none of you!"

Jasper shrugged, in half apology, and then only made it worse, saying, "I'm sorry, sweetie, but there's nobody doesn't know about Augie. . . . You should excuse the thought."

"Go to hell!" Susan exclaimed impatiently. "God, it just

makes me tired! And I want off this airplane as soon as we get to Ireland. I'll go back commercial. This is false pretenses! You had no intention of—''

"But I did! And I'm sorry, sweetie, but I'm sick and tired of dwelling on you and Blick! Everybody knows what he gets up to and it's really... and if it's not you, then somebody else's, like that—''

Again, she cut him off. "That's a coarse and horrible lie!"

"Yeah?" he retorted, "how can it be coarse and horrible unless you know exactly what I'm talking about?"

"*Jesus* save me!" Susan looked around desperately. If there had been anywhere to go except to the cabin in back, which was where he was trying to get her to go, she'd have gone. But there wasn't. "You're *not* a nice man!"

"And un-American!" Jasper charged, but he was talking about AHB, not himself. "I never claimed to be a *nice* man. The road to hell is paved with *nice men*!"

The trouble was, he looked nice. Looks were so deceptive. She learned that anew everyday. Even saying awful things, he didn't bark or bite. She'd have hated to do business with Jasper Gates—he'd cut your heart out while singing you a lullaby.

"This whole plot... for what? And I fell for it!"

"Sweetie," he said lovingly, "you shouldn't blame yourself. I've been pulling jokes like this for years. I'm state-of-the-art when it comes to practical jokes. I learned it at my fraternity—we were a chapter of Crossed Bones and Eyeballs." His border-state charm dripped like acid on metal. "I just can't help it, sweetie. Shall I confess my secret desire? Yes?"

"You might as well. You've confessed everything else."

"Sweetie, being very frank," he declared feverishly, "I want your body *mucho-much* and I won't quit 'til I get it."

Susan breathed her aerobic best, willing herself to calm.

"Forget it, Jasper! Stand off! And there's no way you can keep me captive indefinitely. My people are going to be looking for me."

"Where?"

"The whistles and alarm bells are going to be going off all over L.A. and New York City." He shrugged, totally unconcerned. "The flight crew," Susan argued. "Your man Dudley saw how surprised I was. They're certainly not going to go to jail as accessories to kidnapping."

"You'd be surprised, sweetie. They're British and I pay them *plenty*!" Such reasoning was foolish and Jasper knew it, for he laughed at her raucously. "We don't fly to major metropolitan areas. We fly the backroads and nobody'll know where to start looking for you. What do you say to that?"

"I say you can't hide an airplane."

"Sweetie, is it smart for you to resist me? Why not trade off a little bit right now?"

She blushed and gasped, deciding to test run a half-dozen pearly tears down her cheeks.

"I'm so tired." She sighed, as if she were truly trapped and at his mercy and at last admitted it. "Surely, you're too civilized to want a trade of sex for freedom."

"Wrong!" he responded happily. "I'm *not* too civilized, thank God!" He studied her fondly. "Besides, you trade it all the time. People know how you land those big-shot interviews."

"Stop!"

"Sorry, sweetie," he soothed, "Augie as much as told me so."

Never! More tears came, uncalculated this time and scalding. August had *never* talked about her in such a way. Jasper was a devil; he made these things up. Yes, she remembered, just as he had when he slandered her to AHB.

Determined to outface him, Susan picked up a magazine and opened it, idly flipping.

"Mr. Blick told *me*," she mentioned casually, "that *you* were on the phone to *him* to say some very *nasty* things about our very *ordinary* and *normal* evening together at Big Sea."

He looked shocked, demanding, "What'd I say about you?"

"Something goddamn nasty that I'm not going to repeat."

"Susan, sweetie, believe me, I never said anything about you. The *other* way around." Jasper was stunned. "I am not the type of man to call a man and tell him about his woman—especially if I got lucky with her. And I sure don't talk about *my* women, sweetie. That's the code of the old West, and new West too."

His argument left her riven. What did he think, that she'd just cave in, take his word for it? Susan had come to trust and believe in AHB. He had failings but he was a gentleman, a man too involved in big things to have time to be petty.

"August Blick would not talk about me like that."

"No? About you being on his payroll, him putting you in an apartment right next door..."

Susan was conscious of the movement of blood, from her head toward her feet. She knew better than most people how difficult, even impossible, it was to refute such slander. And Jasper wasn't finished.

"'Bout you being his mistress?" He grinned joyously. "And him, keeping all the girls happy, being the champion ...you know. He brags about it to anybody who'll listen ...something he learned in Berlin before the war." Not very calmly, he took a long drink of bourbon and water. "He calls himself, what is it?..."

Coldly, Susan interrupted, "I know what you're going to say, so you can skip it. If you'd like to know, I've never been so embarrassed, Jasper. *You* can tell everybody that you *embarrassed* me like nobody ever has."

Was it her imagination, or were the airplane noises becoming more unbearable? Head buzzing, she declined toward total lethargy, not caring anymore. To hell with them all.

Jasper bolted forward, putting his elbows on his knees and looking at her keenly across the table.

"Sweetie, nothing is further from my mind. Hell, I don't want to embarrass you at all. I'm just illustrating the facts—"

"Very luridly, I'd say."

"I know you, Sue," he pledged, "better than you know yourself. I don't hold any of *that* against *you*. All I want is for you to say you'll be my bride."

Was he introducing some kind of nerve gas into the cabin? Susan was losing it.

"Jasper..."

"*Yo!*"

"Make me a drink...a brandy and soda, please," she said faintly.

"I'll call Dudley."

"No, *you* make it for me. I see there's a bottle of Hennessy there."

"Okay."

He didn't question her at all, merely leapt up nimbly and made for the zebra bar. Jasper was more agile than AHB, she'd say that for him. But of the mind? He was very complicated, or was that confused? Rattling on about her supposed sordid activities, just as easily he dropped the subject and asked her to be his *bride*? How did that follow?

"Say when on the soda, sweetie." Susan watched and signaled. "That's all?"

"Long on the brandy, short on the soda..." Like August Blick, her former friend. "You're having another, aren't you?"

Laughing brashly, he said, "Trying to get me sloshed? Would I let you drink alone, sweetie?"

With great care, proudly, even reverently, Jasper brought her the drink. After all that had been said, it should've been difficult to stay in the same room with him. But it was August whom Susan blamed, for everything. And the more bitterly she felt about him, the more she liked Jasper Gates. The only negative thing about Jasper was his height. But think of all the famous short men of history! Jasper had already mentioned the Emperor Napoleon. Who else? Jasper was handsome enough to be a buttondown shirt model or one of the guys who sat so splendidly in new-model cars or slid across the boudoir to place priceless gems around a beautiful woman's neck. And, unlike AHB, there did not seem to Susan to be a whiff of conceit about him.

Wearily, choosing not to fight him any more, Susan thanked him for the drink and said, "You're an interesting man, Jasper."

"Yeah?" Resuming his seat, he braced one foot against the edge of the table and held up his drink. "Here's to one damned interesting woman! And one breathtakingly beautiful one too."

"And one very tired one..."

"I know you're tired," he said, "but not tired enough to go in the back. For the simple reason you don't trust me. You think if you went back there and dropped off, I'd be there like a shot, slipping it to you, isn't that right?"

"Something like that, yes."

"Shows you don't know anything about me and don't understand me either."

"I'm sorry if you're insulted."

"You're better looking than Mona Lisa, you know that? And she was a very puzzling dame."

"No, Jasper. I'm all on the surface. What you see is what you get."

"Bull!"

Shaking her head wanly and not really believing it herself, never mind whether he did, she said, "I'm nothing, a machine, a TV person, that's all. I think you're infatuated, if that's the word, with an electronic signal.''

His eyes rounded with hurt and he leaned forward again, extending his hand across the table in a kind of appeal, but not reaching her.

"Now you really are insulting me, sweetie! Are you kidding? *Nothing?* You got it wrong—there's not a woman alive wouldn't give her left tit to be in your shoes! Traveling. Living high. Friends with all the biggies. Your picture in the magazines, the ads for your show everywhere.''

"They see one dimension of it, Jasper.''

"No, no, you gotta be among the ten best-known women in the country, the world, after Mother Teresa and what's-her-name. Listen, sweetie, it definitely does not sound good you knocking your job . . . and yourself.'' He stared at her closely, analytically. "You just quit flagellatin' yourself, sweetie.''

"So? What then? You tell me.''

Jasper blinked at her, his jaw working in agitation.

"What the hell do you think? I'm in love with you, Susan Channing!''

"Oh, no!''

She felt as though he'd shaken her, like a limp dishrag. Just like that? No hemming or hawing, no qualifications, no strings attached . . . even after all the August Blick smut? And the other stuff he didn't know about but could stumble upon at any time? Was it any wonder she was feeling so discouraged?

"I mean, you couldn't be. You're just—''

"Hallucinating, you're going to say?''

Susan regarded him sadly, engaging his eyes. Was that it, what he figured would do the trick, get her into the aft cabin?

"How many times in Jasper Gates's long life . . .''

"Fifty-nine and a half years of age, sweetie!''

"How many times has Jasper Gates been in love?''

He cleared his throat, staring at his depleted bourbon and water, then chuckled carelessly. He knew what she was getting at.

"Couple hundred times, more or less.''

"And how many times has Jasper Gates actually been married?''

Susan remembered something else August had said, if she could believe any of it—that Gates had been cruel to his women.

"Three times, that's all. The last wife . . . I told you, she . . . Scarlet, she died."

Susan had said she was sorry, that night at Big Sea.

"So why me?" she asked directly.

"Because."

"That's not a very good reason for a woman to marry a man who's a good twenty years older, people would say old enough to be her father."

"Maybe, but, on the other hand, not old enough to be her grandfather."

No answer to that. Susan lifted her glass self-consciously, silently frowning. At that awkward moment, the plane bumped and rocked. Susan shrieked lightly, grateful for the diversion, but Jasper's face registered real alarm.

"Shit! Air pocket. I told Bligh to avoid all air pockets."

"Augie's reach is long," Susan murmured ominously.

"He would too, if he could, don't kid yourself."

An intercom voice broke in: "Sorry about that, Mr. Gates. Seat belts, please!" The pilot? Crisp and British, as Jasper had said, probably with an RAF moustache. "Clipped the edge of a storm front, sir."

Sorry sir! Both engines have fallen off and we're in a steep approach to the North Atlantic.

No, but it was bound to happen some day. You lived in a plane, you died in a plane.

"Are you scared of flying, Jasper?"

"Me?" He nodded. "Sure I am. I'm realistic. Man was not meant to fly."

"I had a hypnotist once," Susan said. "That helps."

Words, however, did not help. Jasper's face twisted with anxiety. He put down his drink and clasped white knuckles in his lap. Susan went on talking, rapidly, with the idea of taking his mind off it.

"Jasper, the reason I've been doubtful about you is that August truly did tell me you'd said that you and I, well, did get up to some unusual antics."

"No, no," he groaned, "like I said, I swear . . ."

"Actually," she muttered, so softly he couldn't possibly hear above the background whine of engines, "I'm very . . . um . . . very usual, that way." Susan gazed at him compassionately, poor airsick man. She might have come out with the most shocking things ever and he couldn't have heard, or cared, his attention fully given to roiling gut. "My people were missionaries from way back."

"Say again! Can't hear you!"

"Nothing."

"Sweetie, listen, I don't feel so well."

"Why don't *you* go lie down, Jasper?"

Though enfeebled, he had to try one more time.

"By myself?"

She didn't bother to answer. The moment had come to be alone, to rethink her situation. If they were going to crash— of course, they were not—Susan needed time for her life to flit before her eyes, to dwell again on all the things she regretted, so few, and the others she wished she'd had more of.

"Jasper?" He was on his feet, nauseously swaying. "You see, Jasper, I've been in love before myself—"

"Sue, listen, I—"

"I'm not what you'd call an innocent."

"Sue!"

He was so anxious to go lie down. Susan hoped he was not going to be sick just as she was explaining the problems— how and why it was impossible for her to entertain a proposal. His getting sick would not be a help. Quickly, she pressed on, for this was her best opportunity.

"Jasper..."

"Please! Say no more!"

"No. Look—you're being totally honest with me, aren't you?"

Very distressed, though certainly not by the question, he stuttered, "Jasper Gates is one of the straightest shooters on the American economic scene, I promise you that, Miss Anchorperson."

"Then *I* have to make a clean breast. My life should be an open book."

What? Did she mean this?

"Sweetie, as far as I'm concerned your breast is one hundred percent clean, A-Okay. Clean and shapely with the best of them and one of the attributes of yours that I admire the most. Now, please..."

"Jasper, that's not what I mean. *What* am I going to tell August Blick?"

His lips shook as he struggled with his malaise.

"Augie? Why do you have to tell the son of a bitch anything?"

"Well, because . . ."

"Because he's your protector, Sue? Because he keeps you?"

"He *does not* keep me! I told you, I pay my way!"

"Well then, *goddamn it*?"

Inhale . . . exhale . . .

"I must tell you, Jasper, that August has just asked me to marry him, to be the second Missus Blick."

But how ridiculous it sounded, as grotesque as a naked truth. Holding on to his belly, Jasper guffawed fraily, but derisively, his voice the sound of a man shuffling through broken glass.

"The second Missus Blick? Holy Jesus!" he whispered. "The man is Methuselah's first cousin. Shitfire! His average age is deceased, sweetie!"

"Be that as it may . . ."

"It *is* as it may!"

"I'm just pointing out to you one of the difficulties . . . an embarrassment."

"*Bullsheets*, sweetie! *Where's* the problem? You just got to tell Augie it's all over."

"*Jasper, I'm used goods!*"

The hair seemed to stand up on his head.

"*Used?* What're we talking about, a garage sale? I know you were married once, I know you been around! Sweetie, will you please, once and for all, quit knocking yourself like this!"

And would nothing put him off?

For effect, Jasper bashed his hand against the top of his chair and gazed at her with huge annoyance. He seemed really put out, even though he was feeling so terrible. Susan cringed before his maleness. He was right! She was overdoing it. She was really not so soiled and ruined as all that.

"I've gotta go inside," he exclaimed.

"Yes."

"And what's the forecast?" He looked optimistic. "I just wish, sweetie . . ."

"Jasper! I'm hopeful I'll be able to suggest a compromise that'll allow me to regain my freedom."

"Sweetie, I count on you."

With that, ashen-faced, miserably, Jasper skirted the huge

briefcase he'd carried on board, containing, he said, the past, present, and future of Jasper International, and shuffled into the aft cabin. He turned briefly, intending to say something else but didn't, and disappeared.

There wasn't any justice, was there? A man reaches the exalted position in life where he can afford to fly about all by himself in a huge airplane and then he gets airsick at the first hint of bad weather.

And so she was alone, alone as she'd ever been.

After a moment, Susan went to the bar and made herself an abridged repeat of the drink, thinking *Down with August Hugo Blick!* It was only hours since he had insulted her, "tested" her, as he'd explained, in the very act of marriage proposal, and gone on, sordidly, about her body, which he'd boasted to Jasper he'd so delighted with his special artistry. In truth, should this skill, like playing the violin, give AHB, decadent Berliner, some extraordinary hold over her?

Tasting irony at its best, Susan laughed to herself bitterly. As the philosopher wrote, You closed one door and another opened. Good-bye, AHB; hello, Jasper Gates! Another marriage proposal. After going for years with nary a nibble, she'd had two of them in two days.

And neither of them interested her in the least. All this and Harry Teller—and he was the toughest nut of all.

Susan Channing, anchorperson, was approaching another moment of truth.

Jasper said he loved her. Harry Teller had too—rather, he said he'd loved her in Saigon. The other night, he hadn't said anything, although in his defense was the proposition that action speaks louder than words.

Someday, Miss Susie, *romantic fool, you are going to get your comeuppance!*

Susan peeked into the stateroom. Jasper lay as still as a corpse, his eyes tightly closed. But he was not dead, for he groaned loudly when he saw her and then once more when the plane lurched again. Susan sat down beside him, the ministering angel.

"Poor Jasper, how you're suffering."

But wasn't everybody?

He moaned faintly when Susan felt his brow.

"I'm miserable, sweetie . . . but not poor."

Haunted by his voice, the vulnerable look on his pretty face, touched too by his profession of love, Susan lay down beside Jasper and held him, sort of cradled him, in her arms, very chastely caressing his belly, reassuring his tumbling solar plexus, soothing him as best she could. Given the circumstances, to her own satisfaction, for Susan was feeling a little queasy too, it went no further than that, it could not go further than that, so fearful was Jasper of the bucking plane.

When she woke up, he was gone, and he had not touched her, so far as she knew.

The weather had cleared and they were flying as smoothly as skidding on ice. With a half hour or so before arrival in Shannon, Susan had a shower, dried on a huge towel marked SunSpots, the banner of the Jasper International cruise line, then dressed again in the heaviest of the clothes she'd brought with her, a long leather skirt, one of the oxford-cloth buttondown shirts, and hip-length wool tunic, green, an Irish outfit if ever there was one.

And with an appetite! She was ready for the continental breakfast Mr. Dudley had laid out in the forward cabin.

European day had dawned, warm sunshine streaking the interior of the plane. Jasper put his freshly shaved, luridly cologned face to hers in greeting, then sat, whistling madly, in an excess of euphoria, and watched Susan devour two warm croissants, coffee and juice.

"You look wonderful! And hungry!"

"Ravenous."

"It's the . . . well, you were sweet to me, sweetie!" He stopped, abashedly. "I . . . And you know what? In memory of this, our first night, I'm going to have a couple of silver pins cast, of twin hearts embraced by a couple dozen angels."

In memory of what? Sleeping together? Literally that. Jasper was too good to be true! A gent of the old school! Susan hadn't heard there were any of them still around.

It was unlike her to be so hungry, particularly in her own precarious state, which she wasn't going to mention. But there was something about Jasper Gates, the plane, the adventure, which had set her juices to running hot and heavy. Never mind the togetherness hadn't amounted to anything like the riptide of passion that had swept over her and young Scott Blake. That wasn't important. Important was that Jasper was pleased. And that he was going to be a reasonable man.

"Well, sweetie, what's the bottom line? Are you having fun so far?"

"Heaven, Jasper."

Forget the funny business. The bottom line was that he liked her. And Susan was sure now that AHB's story about Jasper's brutality was totally false. He had behaved gallantly. Men smacked women, as it had been established, usually out of a pure self-hate, and there was no indication Jasper had anything but the deepest love and respect for himself.

"I don't mean for you to get away so easy," he remarked leadingly, "but I was just too out of it, what the Frenchies call *mal d'air*, or something like that."

Craftily, Susan said, "Can I consider myself a free woman now?"

Looking at her boldly, he said, "Yes, if you agree we're engaged."

"Engaged to do what, Jasper?"

"Well, sweetie, eventually to get hitched! Unless, of course, we change our minds."

"Right," she commented dryly, ready to be just as offhand as he was. "You haven't tested the goods yet, Jasper, whatever you think happened during the night." She grinned, "Y'ever buy a pair of shoes without trying 'em on first, Jasper?"

He grinned uneasily, then whooped, "That's my anchor-person!"

He did not get the point, so Susan said, "If I get engaged to somebody, Jasper, I wouldn't expect to cancel it an hour later."

"Nor would I, sweetie, nor would I! We're just kidding around here, aren't we?" She worried him and he continued swiftly, "When we land, we're gonna drive down to Limerick, to my house."

"I didn't know you had a house in Ireland."

"How could you know, if I didn't tell you?" he demanded. "It's a castle, actually." He watched for her reaction; what should she do, jump up and down? " 'Course, anything with two stories on it is a castle over here. Actually," Jasper said, apologetically, "it's got fifty rooms. So who's counting? Most of them haven't been used for a century or two except by the ghosts and they aren't even furnished. Or heated. One wing's been refurbished, with electricity and plumbing."

Susan was looking for her pad. What had he done with her pad? Better write that down too.

"Fishing rights on the River Radley. You like to fish, Susan?"

"I used to fish with my father on Chesapeake Bay."

"I never asked . . . your dad? He—"

"He's a doctor, he teaches too. At Johns Hopkins."

"When do I get to meet him?"

Susan smiled coolly. After all, they weren't engaged. What was he asking? Her father wouldn't know what to make of Jasper Gates.

"Maybe next time you're in Washington—"

"Good, good!" Jasper preferred to talk about his castle anyway. "It used to belong to one of those Anglo-Irish families. They were given the land back at the time of Queen Elizabeth—the *first,* not second—so they'd come over and colonize the Irish barbarians." Jasper's eyes gleamed. "I'm really anxious for you to see the old joint."

"Which reminds me," Susan said severely, "we should be in California at this very minute! You haven't forgotten the interview? I'm going to look like an awful fool if you change your mind."

Jasper grinned shiftily.

"If I've gotta . . . then I guess I've gotta."

"*Exactly!*"

"You are one hard case, sweetie. One tough little cookie. One—"

"I am *not* known as a pushover, whatever August Blick told you."

Just wait, Susan was thinking, maybe he thought all that would be shelved now that he had won her over to his side. Oh, no. He didn't know it, but she had him against the wall. Surprise again!

For, solemnly, Jasper announced, "My plan, sweetie, if you agree to be Jasper's one and only fiancée . . . my plan is to sign my Irish castle over to you."

Just when she figured she had him at her mercy, because of favors still unextended, ironically, more than of favors roughly taken, he pulled a fast one.

"Over to me? What do you mean? Why would you do that?"

"Well, what did I just now say?" Jasper cried, as if she were already disagreeing or something. "I mean, it's yours! part of the bargain."

"What bargain?"

"Our bargain!"

Susan's mind worked rapidly enough but not very logically.

The first thing which came to mind was that August Blick had never given her anything. The flat on Park Avenue? He'd arranged a very good price for it, but it was not as though he'd given it to her, despite his boast to Jasper. Oh, maybe a cheap necklace and earrings set and the crummy little gold chain, worth altogether maybe five grand and which, if the truth be known, August had probably lifted out of Mignon's jewel box. And, now, thinking fast, what if, after all this, Susan made the mistake of becoming the second Missus Blick? Chances were AHB would treat her just as he had the first, who hadn't had even a credit card to her name, let alone a castle in Ireland.

"Sweetie," Jasper said loudly, boisterously, "I don't like discussing money stuff with the woman I love. I'm signing Greenswards over to you and that's the sum and substance of it."

13

Susan had not quite forgotten where they were: in Ireland, on their way to Greenswards.

And was big, bearded Mr. Sullivan, chauffeur of the ancient black Austin Princess limousine, keeping up with the conversation? He'd adjusted his mirror so he could see them clearly in the backseat.

Jasper must be thinking, as Susan was, that Mr. Sullivan had very big ears, for he moved closer, jostling the leg where she was holding her reporter's notebook. Susan was making a big point here of business-as-usual, never mind about Jasper Gates's grand words and big promises. At least, she was going through the motions. Otherwise, how would it look? Dudley must be suspicious already of hanky-panky.

The problem was that Jasper, like so many big-business-men, viewed the reporting business as play, not a really serious endeavor for a grown person. He'd been going on at great length about his Bulgarian shipyard and how it was not duck soup doing business with the Commies, while Susan madly scribbled.

Amused, Jasper squeezed her knee. Mr. Sullivan would not have missed that.

"*That's* my anchorperson," Jasper crowed. "Ever been in South Yemen, Sue?" No, fortunately, she never had. "Got a camel farm down there."

Susan was getting tired of hearing about all the things he owned. Sooner or later, they were going to have to talk about Jasper Gates, the man. Diligently, however, she wrote down *Yemen Camel Farm*.

"How many camels—or have you counted?"

"Haha! I *thought* you'd never ask! At last count, five hundred twenty-four, with the mares or whatever the hell you call them carrying another fifty or sixty. Camels take a long time about it, mainly because they're very shy. Inhibited, some people say."

"I do *not* believe that."

He laughed. "Anyway, wouldn't that make one hell of a story for you guys?"

"It'll make two and a half minutes of our takeout...."

Interesting enough, yes. The fact of the matter, however, was that she and Jack were never short of color pieces, including such rarities as camel farms in South Yemen. It sounded terrific, but a couple of minutes of camel farm was more than enough for the average low-brow American viewer.

"Tell me how you started your business career, Jasper."

That was the first real question and he looked startled, as if she were invading his privacy.

"My father," he muttered, "man by the name of Sam Gates, they called him Rusty Gates. I tell people I'm a self-made man, but in fact I wouldn't be registered on the *Forbes* scale if it hadn't been for him. Built my first shopping center in nineteen fifty-one and bought my first uranium mine in fifty-five." He struggled to see what she was writing. "This is like background, right?"

"Yes, I need to ask you a lot of questions in order to know what questions to ask." Then she sprang AHB's. "So it's not as though you ... married into your seed money?"

Exasperated, Jasper punched at the seat, again jarring her pen.

"Augie told you that, didn't he?" He shook his head doggedly. "The son of a gun told you I took the money away from a *pore* little old lady, didn't he?"

It wasn't wise or ethical to reveal a source even if he was AHB. Susan didn't answer; her silence confirmed it.

"The man is certifiable, sweetie. Now you know." He murmured confidentially, "Look what he said about *you*."

She glanced quickly at Mr. Sullivan's back.

"Don't talk about that."

Jasper followed.

"You're right, sweetie." He addressed himself toward their chauffeur. "Speaking of camels, it's a farming economy hereabouts, horses wherever you look in Ireland, as far as the eye can see, it's horses." Jasper extended the blarney. "Mr. Sullivan himself told me the Irish race is part horse and part Catholic. Am I telling the truth, then, Mr. Sullivan?"

Mr. Sullivan's eyes rose to the mirror.

"I think it's the matter of which end is the horse and which the Catholic, Mr. Gates," he said, none too happily, "though, if the truth be told, you might say both ends are horse, and the same end of the horse—that is, if it's on our recent history that you judge us. Time has passed us at the starting gate. There's more past in us than there is a future—"

"No, no, Mr. Sullivan!" Susan disagreed vehemently. "Your future *includes* all your history."

Jasper glanced at her sentimentally and softly exclaimed, "I *love it* when you talk like that!" He leaned close. "Talk like that in bed, sweetie, what a thrill!"

Susan laughed for him, huskily, her TV laugh. "Who takes care of Greenswards? Are you ever here, Jasper?"

"I'm never here! Maybe a total of five or six nights since I bought the place, am I right, Mr. Sullivan? Mr. Sullivan and his wife are in charge of the place."

Sullivan nodded companionably.

"Mr. Gates is here less that the Greenswards ghost, Miss Channing."

"A ghost named Tommy," Jasper agreed. "He rattles empty beer bottles, isn't it so, Mr. Sullivan?"

"And what would an old house be without its resident ghost, Miss Channing?"

"Who was Tommy?"

"Ah, Tommy. It's said he was born in the house and killed in a faraway war. . . ."

A chill ran down her spine. Tommy?

Jasper, moving right along, fortunately didn't give Susan

time to dwell on it, very conveniently coming up with another nugget of news.

"You know, sweetie, I acquired the place from Sir Guy Bristals."

"The one and only?" she echoed him. This was deadly serious stuff. Hesitantly, Susan asked, "Did I remember to tell you I met Lady Bristals out in California, after you left?"

"Hi-ho!" Jasper cried. "Hear that, Mr. Sullivan? Mr. Sullivan can tell you all you'll want to know about Emma Bristals, am I right, Mr. Sullivan?"

Sullivan's earlobes turned bright red and he muttered something in Gaelic.

"Guy unloaded the place about the time he left Emma—" Suddenly, Jasper clutched his forehead. "You *have* to remind me about Big Sea?"

"Why?"

"Holy Kee-rist! Talk about Ireland being a confused place! I told you about the goddamn Indians—"

"Not everything." She timed it perfectly. "*Not* about the burial ground, Jasper..."

"No, okay," he admitted, a little sullenly, "or about Lyons being behind it."

"I found out."

"Sure, you did. That's my anchorperson," he said again, not as jubilantly as before. "That goddamn rabble-rouser! I didn't know until too late he lives there, right up the goddamn hill!"

"Next to Emma Bristals."

"Yeah." He nodded bleakly. "Him and his ditzy wife. Friends of *yours*, I am told."

"Casual friends. And I don't think she's a ditz."

Again, Susan lifted her eyebrows in Mr. Sullivan's direction. For all she knew, Sullivan was on the payroll of one of his former employer's scandal sheets. No sooner would they have left than he'd be on the phone to the *London Scumbag* or some such. The elements of the story swirled: Big Sea, Big Money; Jasper Gates versus Redmen; Dick Lyons, Knight in Shining Armor; August Blick, *eminence gris*, and Guy Bristals, barbarian from the Old Country. And the women: the delicate Jenny Driver and the earthy Emma Bristals.

Susan Channing, Observer.

Some Camelot.

* * *

"Aren't we coming to the turnoff, Mr. Sullivan?"

A man who hated direction, Sullivan said, "Yes, Mr. Gates, I do see that. I'm about to turn, sir. I'm turning into the road at this moment, Mr. Gates."

Jasper muttered something about Irish anarchists. Mr. Sullivan swung onto a long, gravelly drive, bordered sparely by fluttering poplars. Several fields away lay an ordered pile of gray stone, more like growing out of the green. Greenswards. House? Castle? A bit of both perhaps. Facing in this direction, shining in the clear sunshine were more white-shuttered windows that you could count and, sure enough, woven into one end of the thick frontal wall was a slotted round tower of flimsy appearance, not much taller than numerous unmatched chimneys stepped erratically across the long sharp peak of slate roof. Coming closer, Susan saw wide stone steps; they led up to a balustraded stone porch and imposing front door, whose brass also shone in the morning sun.

"Well, Susan, what do you think?"

"It's more chateau than castle, Jasper. It's gorgeous!"

And how securely it was attached to Mother Earth. Only fire or flood could take it down.

"We gotta admit that Bruce the Magnificent had a lousy architect," Jasper said whimsically. "But you love it?"

"Jasper, I'm speechless."

He refused to hear, instead raising his voice and pointing at two brown horses that were standing quite still in the middle of the field in front of the house.

"They're waitin' for it to rain, am I right, Mr. Sullivan?"

Thoughtfully, Sullivan agreed. "It is a strong possibility the horses can feel the rain in advance of its arrival."

"That's called horse sense where I come from."

Sullivan glanced at him in the mirror.

" 'Tis a good bet, Mr. Gates, that it'll precipitate five or six times a day, horse sense or not."

Naturally Susan fell in love with the place but she was wise enough not to begin thinking of it as her own. She didn't have the appropriate piece of paper in her hand; and who would care to predict Jasper Gates's true intentions? What happened if she didn't play his game?

"Think of it as an instrument of good faith, a nonrefundable deposit. How's that?"

The Sullivans went with Greenswards. So did the Austin

Princess and the two brown horses waiting for the rain. On the other side of the house, the property ran past a long white barn and assorted other outbuildings to a spring-fed lake and the green banks of the winding River Radley.

Sir Guy, it appeared, had not liked Emma's horses.

"He sold them all, except for these two, within days of Lady Emma's departure." Had Emma broken Sir Guy's heart, or what? Mr. Sullivan laughed scornfully and spit, "Him? No, he happened to hate horses, that's all. It had to do with his childhood. Bitten by a nasty nag or something of the kind. Then the new lady..." New lady? So Bristals's heart had not been broken. "Maybe I should not be talking this way," Sullivan muttered.

"You can't stop now, man," Jasper said.

"Well, sir, a Continental lady, I believe. Perhaps French or from one of those Mediterranean countries."

"Christ man, there *is* a difference!"

"In any case, Mr. Gates," Sullivan said gamely, "they were not long on the premises, as *you* know. And sorry I am to talk about Sir Guy in a way you might consider derogatory."

"Forget it," Jasper growled, "he's no particular friend of mine. We do business together from time to time, that's all." He was reminded of something else, God! Another bit of invaluable news. "You're likely to meet him when we get to California, sweetie."

"In California? Why, what's he doing out there?"

Jasper winked, like he knew something she didn't, which happened to be true, and drawled, "Guy is most likely at Big Sea right now, meeting with my friend Shira Guchi."

"Shira Guchi?" she repeated.

"My pal from Tokyo, sweetie."

"So it *is* true!"

It made her angry to find out like this.

"So what's true?" he responded cagily.

"That you're going to sell to the Japanese."

"Not if our Indian friends have got us tied up in court."

"Honestly!" she huffed. "You and August trying to out-smart each other. Do you know August's plan is to sell his share to the Hong Kong Chinese?"

"I do know."

"How do you know?"

"But thanks for the warning anyway."

* * *

Just as they sat down to tea prepared by the matronly Mrs. Sullivan in the perfectly proportioned Greenswards drawing room, Jasper began to talk about leaving. What about flying on to Paris, for instance? If anything, Susan would've loved to stay right where they were. Why couldn't they check into Hotel Greenswards? A peat fire smoldered peacefully, but Jasper paced to the French doors that framed a harmonious country scene better than any of the half-dozen nondescript landscapes hanging on the walls, back to the table for a sip of tea, then once more to the doors.

"There's a green sward for you," he said expansively, sweeping an arm toward pond and beyond, to the river and across the river, the trees. But it wasn't enough for him, beautiful as it was, and Susan began to understand Jasper couldn't be comfortable unless he was in his plane and on the move. "Dinner at Maxim's, Susan! We can fly back from Paris just as well as from here."

"You're *too* much, Jasper."

"What do you think, Mrs. Sullivan?" he demanded.

Sullivan answered for his wife.

"Mr. Gates, this is a woman who's never been to an airport, much less inside an aircraft."

"Off to Paris with you!" cried Mrs. Sullivan.

Before Susan had caught her breath they were out of time. Jasper allowed ten minutes for a quick tour of the habitable part of the upstairs. The master bedroom suite was as long as the house was broad, with its own expansive view of the green meadows and sluggish river. One might have expected slightly less spartan furnishings, given the exotic nature of Emma Bristals. Nothing was missing in the way of comfort, but there wasn't an excess of it either. Perhaps her mentality was more barracks room than exotic. If she ever had the chance, Susan thought, she would compliment Emma on what she'd done here—or maybe not. It would be cruel to rub her nose in the fact Susan Channing was the new mistress of Greenswards.

Susan said a hurried good-bye to Mrs. Sullivan and promised to come back soon. Jasper packed her into the car. Sullivan, by now part of the whirlwind, spun wheels in the gravel and Greenswards was soon in the distance.

"Well, what do you think?" Jasper settled in beside her. "Tell me the God's honest truth."

"About what? Greenswards?"

"The truth about everything! Do you think you'll be able to learn to put up with me?"

A direct enough question for people who liked frankness. Did Susan feel better about him now, having seen the estate and in light of the undeniable fact that he worshipped her? The arguments raced in her head. Jasper was a man to keep you on your toes. Nobody would ever say he was boring. He might even be lovable in a jumpy sort of way. But could a person keep up with him? Susan still made no commitment.

Tersely, but equivocally, she said, "I seem to have survived the last twenty-four hours."

"And we've been together nonstop, except for time in the toilet. But, it's not twenty-four. More like twelve or maybe fifteen hours." He did have a way of putting things. "That's why I'm hell-bent to take you to Paris."

"Jasper, we've already fit a week of adventure into those few hours."

"Adventure?" He grinned. "I hope you'll remember it that way, Sue! Hey, you know, something I forgot—we could've driven on down to Killarney. We own a hotel down there, on the lake."

Susan sighed, saying how sad they'd missed it. Was that all there would be to Jasper Gates, hurried passage, headlong rush, around the world on a whim? What was he fleeing? Himself? Death? Once back in the car, she noticed, he calmed down. This was telltale.

"From Paris, it's just a short hop to Bulgaria. . . ."

"Jasper, I *cannot* make a trip to Bulgaria."

He'd never take no, or maybe, or perhaps, for an answer. Clearly, he was annoyed. He wanted his way. He seemed so frustrated that she couldn't understand.

"We are not talking Big Sea here, sweetie, a mere pimple on the Jasper International ass. We're talkin' big bucks, the Red Star shipyard, we're talkin' quality control, lemme tell you! Sloppy riveting work, blistered steel, paint that doesn't dry. The Bulgars claim to work cheaper than the Finns but if the goddamn boat sinks on launch, you got a big problem, right?" Susan tried to speak, to reason with him, but he cut her off. "Sweetie, if it's a question of NAN, I'll fix it—"

"No! I wouldn't want that, Jasper!"

"C'mon, sweetie, what does it matter? I'll take it up with old Guy—isn't he about to buy your network?"

"So, you do know about that! And you never said anything. That's not fair, Jasper!"

"So, I'm telling you now. And, as I said, he'll be in California." He winked jovially. "Did you know he's another of your big fans, sweetie?"

"You're stringing me along, Jasper," she said. "I don't like that."

Susan remembered how August had scathingly predicted she'd be forced to sell herself to Bristals. Surely not, not now, now that Jasper was on her side.

"Sorry, sweetie, I kinda forgot, what with . . . you know."

"I would like to meet him," she said cautiously.

"And so you shall, sweetie." Jasper patted her hand. "And soon as we're back at Big Sea, after Paris and Bulgaria—"

"Jasper! I'm not a jet-setter. I have work."

Paying no attention, he continued, "We'll go to a notary in Petertown and have the property turned over to you. I already got my personal attorney to draw the deed—"

"Already? How could you? . . ."

He smiled, a little vainly.

"Don't you think I had it all figured out, sweetie? Listen, I'm way ahead of you."

Once again, Susan was touched, shaken by his belief. Impulsively, she kissed his cheek. Jasper blushed brightly and when Susan glanced his way, she saw that Mr. Sullivan was watching in the mirror.

Jasper International kept an office at Shannon for expediting freight shipments and so forth, and Mr. Dudley was waiting for them there. Corrigan, their agent, had a call for Mr. Gates in his office. The Jasper International legal department was on the line.

"So they did catch up," Susan said.

"What do you mean?"

"It's obvious. They're looking for me."

"Yeah, sure, you're valuable property, sweetie. Maybe it's Augie."

Telling Susan to take a seat outside, Jasper went into the office and slammed the door, just primed to be nasty, she knew it. But it wasn't about Susan Channing. She could hear him clearly through the thin walls. Jasper said hello, listened, began yelling, swore, listened again, swore again vilely, then brawled, "Well? *Fire* the son of a bitch. Isn't that the American way?"

When he emerged, he was shaking his head.

"Didn't I tell you I had trouble in Bulgaria?"

"Serious?"

He didn't answer.

"C'mon, let's go."

Jasper was so preoccupied now, he seemed to have forgotten she was even there. When they were back in the plane, Susan reminded him.

"Who was that you just fired?"

"Hell, I didn't fire him," he said disgustedly. "You can't fire Bulgarians. You can talk about it, but you can't do it. Ever been there, sweetie?"

"Transit, once," she said. "I forget where I was going."

"Well, we can't go now, can we? But soon. To Sofia and then down to the Black Sea coast...."

Again, she was tempted to tell him that if he wanted a constant traveling companion, he should've hooked up with an airline stewardess.

"...*career* permitting," he added meaningfully, ahead of her again. "You know, sweetie, I could help you. What about an exclusive interview with the Commie bigshot who runs that place? I don't think he's ever been interviewed by a Westerner. His name is Todor Zhivkov."

"His name could be Schwartz, and I still have to go by the numbers, Jasper."

Business, business, business.

"I can get you interviews with anybody you want, sweetie, no problem! They love me in these communistic places. I bring in business, dollars which they desperately need to buy Western goods, such as dirty magazines and carbonated drinks."

"Great," she murmured.

Mr. Dudley warned them about seat belts and took orders for after-takeoff drinks, and then the plane went rushing like the wind itself down the runway. Steeply, they climbed, banked, and eventually leveled out; and Dudley announced the heading this time to be New York. On the other side of the cabin, Jasper had begun hauling papers out of his huge briefcase and throwing them on his desk.

"Sweetie, no way we could go to Bulgaria, or Paris, for that matter."

"Not really." But Susan was somewhat taken aback by the cavalier way he proposed Paris, then withdrew. "But I have to say I could've done with dinner at Maxim's."

"Next time, okay?" He waved at his paperwork. "This ole dog has got to put his nose to the grindstone." In exasperation, he slapped his hand on one of the files. "Bulgaria! All the info on Bulgaria is right here, Sue. Somebody said, maybe it was my late wife, if the briefcase goes down, so goes the empire."

"I'd just as soon not go down with the briefcase, thank you very much."

Laughing wickedly, he cried, "Nobody's *going down* anywhere. Give me my drink?"

"I can do it as well as Dudley."

"Yeah, and he's gonna be gettin' dinner. With ginger, sweetie, instead of water," he proposed as she went to the bar.

Sickeningly sweet, definitely low-class. The thought of such a drink, never mind about making it, turned her stomach. Susan didn't know what to have. She was not feeling very stable.

"Yeah, there, like that," Jasper said. "Thanks, sweetie. And you?"

"Nothing right now."

When Susan brought him the drink, he wrapped his arm around her hips, pulling her possessively close, and rubbed his cheek against her belly.

"So soft, sweetie, you are *so* soft and luscious."

Not in the mood just now for romance, Susan reacted passively. She didn't resist as Jasper reached under her skirt and up the back of her leg and under the elastic of her panties. Then, impatiently, she pushed his hand away and stepped away.

"Jasper, Mr. Dudley could walk in any second—"

"Well? So? What's he gonna say?"

"I think you'd better get on with your work." He frowned crookedly, trouble in his eyes. Susan tried to smile. "And I'm going to read the newspapers Mr. Dudley brought on board."

"You do that," he grunted.

He turned quickly enough to his work, ignoring her again. Very well. Susan picked up the London afternoon newspapers. But then Dudley interrupted. Susan had beat him to the drinks, so tartly he asked about food. They'd eat in about an hour, okay, and that should hold them until New York. After refueling, they'd be flying on to California. At least, that was the current plan—it could change without notice, as Susan had learned. And apropos of that, Jasper was reminded he had business in Florida.

"But first things first. Got to get to Big Sea."

"Not L.A.?"

"Why'd you think we were going to L.A.?" he demanded. "No. We're gonna be in bed at Big Sea by midnight, at the latest, if we maintain present airspeed."

When he said in bed, he underlined the words. He meant *in bed*, the two of them, together. Oh? Susan studied him coolly. They'd see about that when the time came. Right now, and there was no use fighting it, she was steadily more preoccupied with her stomach. Nothing to do with airsickness, it was more or less that time of the month, though perhaps a little early. Being realistic, one might conjecture Scott Blake had speeded things up. Still, as they said, better early than late! Also, nice in a way to know you were still fertile.

Jasper glanced at her with another of his calculating frowns.

"You want to know what's the big rush getting to Big Sea? Or maybe you're not interested?"

"Of course I am."

"Got *trouble*," he said ominously, as if he enjoyed it, and maybe he did. "That phone call . . ." He watched her closely. "Teller, my manager? His brother's got a paper in Rio Tinto, that half-pint metropolis."

"Harry, yes, he's a friend of mine."

"Ralph Teller's brother, Harry, yes, terrific! A friend of yours," Jasper repeated sarcastically. "Well, your *friend* has run an item in his rag about that fuckin' rabble-rouser Dick Lyons getting shot at some days ago by person or persons unknown. You knew about that?"

"Sure."

"You did not tell me, sweetie," Jasper said heavily. "Why didn't you tell me?"

Susan shrugged. "I didn't think it'd interest you, I suppose. You didn't have much to tell me about Big Sea, the burial ground and all . . . which I heard from Ralph."

"And from Harry, your friend," he said bitingly. "Ralph spilling our confidential stuff to his brother . . . *and you!* And then it's in the Rio Tinto rag and *now* reprinted in *The New York Times* and just yesterday *Time* magazine: Jasper International locked in death struggle with California Indian Tribe! Jesus!''

"Well? What do you expect?'' she demanded sharply. "Don't you have a PR department, Jasper? You can't keep that kind of stuff secret.''

"Teller said people are saying the attempt on Lyons is connected with the Big Sea thing! Jesus Christ! Sweetie, *sweetie!*'' Jasper exclaimed, as if in awful pain. "Do you know what this does to my standing . . . to my stock price . . . the whole deal with Shira Guchi?''

"Jasper, that's the story, isn't it?''

"For crissakes! We didn't shoot at Lyons.''

"I know that. You don't have to shout at me.''

Agitated, Jasper cracked his knuckles.

"I could sue him, I suppose, but then what?''

"Jasper, Harry didn't say you were behind it. What he said was people were speculating there's some kind of a connection. Harry's careful.''

"The miserable son of a bitch.'' Jasper scowled blackly, then muttered, "Some people I know do take direct measures.''

Susan half nodded. Perhaps she should confide that AHB had made a bad joke about having *him* eliminated?

". . . sort of *extralegal* procedure that's used from time to time to settle very important business disputes.''

Susan pretended she didn't heard.

"If I'd had *any* idea Lyons lived within cannon shot of Big Sea I would've steered us well away, believe you me!''

"It's kind of a pathetic cause for Dick Lyons, wouldn't you say?''

"He's not choosy. Any goddamn cause will do. It's not so much what he can do in court even. I got lawyers on my payroll trained to do battle and win. Sweetie,'' Jasper brooded, "the bitch is that *whatever* Lyons touches, turns into headlines. Soon as he's involved there's a good chance they win on public opinion. Even if we won in court, which we would, he'd ruin my deal with Shira. Y'see what I'm saying?''

"That's always been Dick Lyons's clout. Like Nader.''

"You could help, sweetie.''

Jasper held up one of his small, sun-flecked hands and inspected his fingernails closely, as if he hadn't just made a very indecent proposal.

Susan retorted, "The only way I can help is to advise you to jack up your PR people—''

"*Hindsight* could be *very* useful, sweetie... very."

"We cover both sides, Jasper."

And that was in spite of everything and anything that passed between them on a personal level. He might as well know it, right now. Give him a chance to change his mind. And so, visions of Greenswards began to dim in her head.

"You *could* help me though!" he insisted shamelessly. "With Teller. With Lyons. Don't you have any influence over him?"

"Influence?" Susan laughed negatively. "Over Harry Teller? I should tell Harry Teller how to do a story?"

"Over Lyons?" Jasper demanded. "What do you think he'd say if we offered him something, to lay off?"

"Oh, no, no! That'd be the worst thing you could do. He'd broadcast it everywhere that you tried to bribe him. It'd be like waving a red flag at a bull. And Lyons is a bull."

"How do you *know* he'd turn it down? Has anybody ever tried it on him?"

"I don't know."

Jasper's eyes flicked at her and Susan reminded herself it'd be a huge mistake to take him for a kind and gentle man. Jasper was a killer.

"Does Augie know any of this?"

"Not from me, he doesn't," Susan said, lying mildly. "The only thing I told *Augie* was that Big Sea is a marvelously opulent kind of place and it'd be a shame to sell it... to the Hong Kong Chinese."

Jasper flushed with affection and laughed. He stretched his arms toward her, signaling he'd like to hug her.

"Oh, sweetie... *sweetie!* I still love you, *mucho-much!* I'm not blaming you for any of this, don't get me wrong. It's like you were tossed into a beehive. I could really get on Ralph Teller's case, though, for spilling the beans."

"Oh, no! Please don't! Harry knew more about it than Ralph...."

"Sure he did. He got it all from Ralph!"

"I don't think so, Jasper, really. Harry's such a hell of a good journalist. You know, he didn't even come to the opening party because he wanted to keep his distance."

"Sure! So I wouldn't pick up on the connection."

"No! I'm sure not, Jasper."

"Well!" He fixed his cold eyes on her. "One thing I've discovered is that you really think a lot of Harry Teller."

"Do I?"

Did it show? How ridiculous.

"I'd say so, yes." Jasper grinned thinly. "I hate him!"

"Come on now, Jasper. Harry and I go way back."

"Like they say. . . sure."

Well, he'd given her something to think about, that was certain. Susan turned to the North Atlantic for reassurance. Far below, through scattered white clouds, the blue ocean seemed calm, peaceful, endless. Not a particularly helpful observation, for down at sea level it was windy, cold, and rough. The same with Harry: he was better at long distance. In a strange way, however, it was comforting that Jasper, no dullard when it came to intuition, had noticed something.

He had gone back to work, in earnest, with a vengeance, never a single look out the window on his side of the plane. Totally focused on his desk, Jasper waded through his paperwork, memo after memo; Susan was aware of his writing hand, making corrections, initialing pages. He finished one folder, returned it to the large briefcase, and pulled out another, now and then speaking to a tape recorder he kept at his side.

Yes, she did think a lot of Harry Teller. And a lot about him. And a lot of good it did her!

Giving up, not knowing what she really thought, a headache coming on, Susan finally turned to the newspapers and, as luck would have it, the first she picked up was one of Sir Guy Bristals's scandal sheets, *London Final*, which happened to carry a scabrous "inside USA" column devoted to the most disgusting "typically American" stories available on any given day. And so it was, she came on the following, which made her sit up very straight and forget about a stomachful of butterflies.

The headline read:

Young Writer in Knifing Incident

Scott Blake, 18, whose first novel *O Savage Youth* is to be published in the autumn, was admitted to University Hospital last night suffering a stab wound allegedly administered by his literary agent Prunella Grosz of New York City. Blake, of Beverly Hills, California, is the son of cinema producer Roger Blake. A recent graduate, Blake has been identified with a new literary cult dubbed the "baby lit-pack," whose striving writers are mostly under the age of twenty-one. The altercation was reportedly triggered by a literary disagreement. Ms. Grosz, 43, was booked and released. According to police sources, Blake has refused to press charges. The wound was reportedly superficial, but Mr. Blake was detained for observation.

First, Ivy Eva Smith, attempted strangulation and now this, a knife in the ribs? Susan dropped the newspaper in her lap.

"Jasper, Augie's grandson was stabbed."

He had a gift for tuning out. It was a second before he looked up.

"Say again!"

"Scott Blake, he's August Blick's grandson, he was knifed."

"So?" Was this relevant? "*Blake?* No, don't tell me—Augie's kid changed his name, what a little turd! That's the guy you were married to the first time, am I right?"

"Yes. The boy is Roger Blake's son."

"You were the kid's stepmother," Jasper said. "Poor you!"

"I'll have to call August."

That didn't make him happy.

But what Jasper Gates couldn't know and she was not about to tell him was that if she hadn't come away with him, most likely nothing would have happened to Scott.

"So, who stabbed the little shit?"

"His agent. A *woman* agent. Young Scott's a novelist—"

"A little weird for his agent to knife him, isn't it?" he asked disdainfully. "Like killing the goose, if the little guy is making any money."

Jasper watched her closely. Did he fathom that she was more anxious about the boy than she should have been? After all, the paper said it was a superficial wound. Nevertheless, her stomach churned.

"Jasper, I've got to lie down for a while. I'm . . . tired."

"Sure," he said, hearing but not hearing, his expression contemplative. "I was just thinking, hell, I could write a book. I've had some great experiences, a lot more than some young kid. What about my year on the Amazon?"

Susan stopped at the door.

"I'm making a mental note."

"Yeah, and the Yangtze River in China. I was young,

young, *young* then, sweetie, on the last boat down the river ahead of the Maoists in nineteen hundred and forty-nine.''

"I'll remember that too, my dear."

Good God, just as she was near death and needed to get to the bathroom, Jasper Gates opened the floodgates of memory.

"I had a Chinese mistress, you know. Long before your time, you weren't even born then. . . ."

Susan nodded fixedly, listening, not quite believing.

"She was the daughter of a Kuomintang warlord. Her name was Ching-ching, or something like that, maybe Ching-chang or Chang-ching. Sweetie, aren't you going to write it down?"

"I'll remember." A little spitefully, Susan observed, "She sounds like a giant panda."

His lips tightened but he went on. "She was very beautiful, in an Oriental kind of way. Small, with tiny hands and feet, and well, you know, little tiny breasts—"

"Tits," Susan interrupted, "you're a titman, remember?"

Jasper blushed. ". . . the size of little apples, crab apples, nipples like crisp little stems."

"I get the picture!" Susan murmured, gassily. "But tell me, if you did so well with the Chinese, how come you're in business with the Japanese?"

"You forget, I had to flee to Japan. That's when I became a judo master. Can you remember all this? I break bricks with the heel of my hand and I've got all the belts. And that's when I first met my friend Shira Guchi who's now the CEO of All-Nippon Prosperoso. Say, am I making you nervous?"

"Jasper," she murmured, "I don't feel very well."

He didn't hear.

"Shira is a clever guy. *Prosperoso* could be any nationality of company. Doesn't scare people. Could be Spanish or Italian. One of his ancestors, as a matter of fact, was a Jesuit missionary, believe it or—"

"Clever of a Jesuit to leave some descendants."

"Sicilian, really. Sicilian-Japanese, to be absolutely accurate," Jasper elaborated. "Anyway, Shira has built up one shitfire big company, fifty times bigger than anything allowed in this country. Vertical, Sue, vertical *and* horizontal! From cradle to grave, just like *mucho*-hated socialism. In fact, Prosperoso companies make cradles *and* coffins, how do you like that?"

She could, might, faint, if he continued. Susan stuck it out, hanging on the door, listening to very tall tales.

"So, you see, sweetie, Big Sea could do a lot worse. They've got all the money now."

"We're not completely broke."

"Close enough! A good American-type capitalist is noplace these days, sweetie. Why? Because there's like four hundred billion a year of drug money running through the system, like a laxative. Like a fart through a keg of nails, untaxed. Inflation money. My program is to shoot the coke dealers and take their money, balance the budget overnight!"

"Can I quote you, Jasper?"

"Goddamn right, sweetie!" He shook his finger at her proudly. "What we need is a benevolent despot for a couple of years. Amend the Constitution! Every eight years, we get two years of benevolent despoting to scrub down the country, fire all the fools, hang the crooks and shoot all the bureaucrats. And I'll run for despot."

"I *will* quote you."

Susan rubbed her eyes and Jasper finally noticed.

"You look a little peaked, sweetie."

"End of interview?"

Feeling as she did even after a dash of cold water to the face, Susan knew she was not going to make up her mind about anything now. She felt bad enough to cry. Past was past, yes, but all the same, what would Nate have had to say about Jasper Gates and Scott Blake and Greenswards . . . and Harry Teller? Nate would've stared and shrugged and focused a camera and said, "Big . . ." Beautiful, yes, that went without saying, but nothing to die over, Susie.

Nothing to die over? People talked in opposites. They said: It's to die over. But that was absolutely *not* what they meant. Naturally, nothing was so terrific that it was worth dying over, except maybe love. If anything *was* worth dying over, Susan had argued, then you wouldn't be around to enjoy it, this wonderful thing that you had died over.

Once, back then, Nate *had* said something which had made sense—and no sense at all, since there was no way to prove it: that people paid in the long run for what they did, and so did nations. Take a look around. No, don't. Susan closed her eyes and inspected the inside of her brain. There was not a great deal of hope. She had her work, a few relationships, some possessions, erratic desires . . . erotic desires, was that better?

Nate would have recommended Harry Teller to her tender attentions.

"Hi, sweetie."

Or did Jasper Gates represent the security for which Susan would've been madly chasing if she'd had any sense? It sometimes seemed like a nice idea to be cared for by men with lots of money.

"Asleep?"

"Dozing."

He must have known what was bothering her for he laid his hand across her belly and for a moment gently caressed her. Susan smiled frailly. Would Jasper understand the signal? Susan wondered about all the geisha girls and his Chinese mistress. What had those foreign ladies thought of Jasper Gates, American?

"I know, you've got your period, don't you, sweetie, proving yet again that you're a bountiful, delectable woman! You think I was born yesterday? No apologies necessary. Mother Nature operates her own schedule, come hell or high water."

"Seemingly."

Guardedly, Jasper said, "You know, sweetie, some of the places I been to, they use that stuff in magic potions."

"In voodoo concoctions, like?"

"That type of thing, yes."

Susan was ready for him. She might not be the swiftest person in the world but she *was* learning her Jasper. Fight fire with fire, strong medicine with strong medicine.

"We know, do we not," she intoned pompously, "we children of modern science, that *such* is the stuff of superstition. That sort of thing went out with the Salem witch trials. When you speak of places like Haiti, Jasper, you speak of people and customs that advancing time has left far behind."

Jasper snorted adoration.

"I love it, sweetie! I absolutely *love it* when you talk like that! My dyed-in-the-wool anchorperson!"

He put his cheek to hers, kissed her on the lips with his cherub's mouth. Then, without warning, he grabbed her hand and put it to his crotch.

"*Sweetie . . .*"

He cried out as if she'd taken him by surprise which,

obviously, she had not. Susan smiled, so perceptive now of his wiles. Curiously, her feeling for Jasper had grown to something like affection. A strong affection, though he might not like the moderation of the emotion. Susan certainly didn't worry about him at all; how despicable of AHB to spread the rumor of Jasper's brutality to women. For such a cranky little nutcase, Jasper was amazingly sweet and tender.

He could love her if he wished, Susan supposed. She would treat him as a good friend, and wasn't that a *good* compromise?

Gently, therefore, she inquired, "And what have we here?"

Gasping, gurgling, Jasper bleated, "You have within your grasp Jasper Gates, of Little Cock, Arkansas."

Just then, for a second or two, surprising herself, Susan surged past mere affection. She chuckled fondly, even lovingly. A man who could laugh about sex was quite a man.

14

Once upon a time, Susan had commented snidely to *USA Today* that so-called shuttle diplomacy should be a piece of cake. Look, you didn't have to worry about getting to the airport or about luggage. You even had an aide to carry your briefcase. So why had Henry K. gotten so much credit? Everybody else had come out of it frazzled wrecks and he was fresh as a daisy.

Susan remembered that on this particular day. Carrying only a pocketbook, she flashed her passport, marched through the terminal, caught a cab, and, like that, was on her way to Park Avenue. She'd left her bag with Jasper on the 727, as surety, swearing up, down, and sideways she'd catch up with him in California.

Still, nothing in this world was ever as easy as you liked to think it would be. Jasper argued otherwise, but Susan decided she had no choice. Hearing Susan's voice when she called him from La Guardia, AHB seemed to go completely to pieces. He simply could not cope! Getting into this mess, the boy had used his name, and now people wouldn't stop calling:

newspapers, business friends and rivals, and ambulance-chasing lawyers.

But was Scott badly hurt? August wasn't quite sure.

"Please come home, Susan! This old man needs you!"

Jasper predicted dire consequences if August got his hands on her again.

"Jasper, I owe him that much."

"Sweetie, you owe him *nothing*, but all right, go! I warn you, if you don't keep your word, I'll do something desperate."

"What?"

"I dunno. Maybe send one of my plutonium plants straight to meltdown and destroy the modern world as we know it."

No, no, Susan swore again, on a stack of Bibles—cross my heart and hope to die—she'd come along first thing in the morning and meet Mr. Dudley in Oakland or San Francisco International Airport for the hop across to Big Sea, she promised.

The weather turned cooler as the cab rattled across the East River. To the left, in the twilight, the rosy-golden silhouette of the United Nations complex and all those familiar man-made shapes, sharper but reminiscent of the stone boulders in Stonehenge, opened occult vistas toward the southern tip of the ancient island of Manhattan. Susan Channing was home again.

Funny, when you thought about it, Manhattan had once belonged to the Indians too. The Russians had probably paid the Basket Indians the equivalent of twenty-four dollars in vodka and kewpie dolls for Indian Island on the Pacific.

It didn't matter. Susan was debated to a standstill. Tiredly, through the barely stable haze of smog and static electricity, she gazed at the approaching, ever-, never-changing skyline. The cab was part of the scene, bumping from one pothole to the next, the driver negotiating collapse and disrepair as nonchalantly as if he'd been sitting at home with his six-pack, watching summer reruns.

Things had gone too fast, and Susan needed private think-time. She'd no doubt be seeing Harry again and what was she going to tell him? That this was just a little fling, a flutter, nothing to be taken seriously? How to explain Jasper Gates to Harry Teller? How to explain anything to Harry Teller? Or explain Harry, for that matter?

Why, after all, had he made such a big story of the Lyons incident? Harry intended to spit in somebody's eye.

In just such a perplexed and confused state of mind, Susan arrived at the Park Avenue address. She handed money to the driver, only then noticing his identity card on the front dash. He was some kind of a Ukrainian or Georgian. No wonder he hadn't said anything, only flashed white and gold teeth and spoke numbers and streets.

Susan added another five dollars. Expense account money, and Jasper had offered her a wad when she'd left the plane—was she some kind of a bimbo? In the morning, Jasper said, she was to fly to Oakland, first class, and he'd pick up the tab for that too. Susan hated to tell him, and so didn't, that it was so long since she'd flown anything but first class she couldn't remember when—even from La Guardia to JFK or JFK to Newark. She'd have gone first class on the Fifth Avenue bus if they'd had one.

When and if she ever stepped foot on a bus.

Susan nodded grandly and swept past the doorman, into the lobby, into the elevator, even as the obsequious night concierge hustled to hold the door.

The closing whoosh shushed him, thankfully, and Susan rose toward the deathly quiet of *seven* . . . to face the music. Something she hadn't told Jasper Gates was that August, once he'd finished being hysterical, had turned quite curt, become so rude and insulting that if she hadn't been concerned for the boy, there had been excuse enough not to go into the city at all.

Susan decided to put off the confrontation for a few minutes by going first to her own place to freshen up. The flat was silent, a tomb to the very well-known anchorperson. And, they might have said, the poor thing had been gone only a matter of hours. She did look next door to death, no joke. The bathroom mirror reported back bloodshot eyes and new lines, though who was counting? She had not been treating the body well.

What Channing went through to get a story was not to be believed. She should've been sainted and perhaps would be some day: Saint Susan—*She Gave*.

Finally, as calm and composed as she was likely to be, resigned to looking like a washed-out blonde, Susan trod the familiar carpet down the hall to *seven-oh-oh* and pressed the bell.

Reserve itself, dignity incorporated, his wing collar stiffer than ever, if that was possible, Konrad opened the door.

"Good evening, Miss Susan."

No, she had never been away."

"Hello, Konrad. Mr. Blick is expecting me."

The double doors to the musty salon, proof, if locked and bolted on the inside, from annoying visitor and terrorist attack alike, were tightly closed.

"Miss Emily Eliot is with Mr. Blick," Konrad said, "but I know he wants me to interrupt."

He knocked sharply and, not pausing, swung the door wide.

What came next was remarkable. Afterwards, Susan was not entirely sure what happened, or had been happening, when she and Konrad went into the room. Reality clicked along in curiously staccato fashion, as if one and the same with surrealism, but Susan thought she did not mis-see what passed before her eyes.

August Blick, as quickly as he could, but still in slow motion, jerkily, awkwardly, and with an irritable groan, was rising from a kneeling position in front of his confidential secretary, fortyish Emily Eliot. As AHB pushed upwards, Emily snapped back, frantically rearranging her skirt and bashing her thighs together with the splatting sound of herring hitting the wharf. Smiling crazily, she grabbed up a pen and dictation pad from the table at her elbow.

Face of stone, Konrad announced, "Susan Channing has arrived."

August attained his feet, though swaying. He brushed his hand across his lips and tried to smile. The only question was how he'd handle it.

August said, "I seem to have dropped my lucky talisman on the floor and damned if I can find it. But leave it. . . . No, Konrad, *leave it for later!*" Instinctively, Konrad had lunged forward. "Susan!" AHB followed up with a more confident greeting. "Thank God you're here. You made good time."

"Yes, I did."

August pirouetted toward Emily Eliot.

"We've just finished our correspondence. . . ." The transparent lie didn't help Miss Emily. Her lips trembled and her bright red blush deepened. "Where were we, Emily?"

Where had they been indeed? How un-Augustian of AHB. Oh, Emily Eliot, misused spinster.

Slowly, Emily's eyes resumed focus behind her steel-framed secretarial specs and she gazed at AHB, adoringly enough to launch him into orbit.

"When you dropped the talisman," she said meekly, "you had just been advising Aristotle Suavia of the Hong Kong Mercantile Brothers—"

"*Yes!*" August stopped her. "Just add Sincerely Yours and With Best Regards etcetera, etcetera . . . and that should finish it up, wouldn't you say, Emily?" Never breaking stride and no one could say he was not agile, especially for an older man, August turned to Konrad with the familiar words, "The drinking lamp is lit, Konrad. My usual, if you please, and I venture to say a vodka-tonic—or a martini—"

"*Martini!*"

"And Emily? After a long day's work?"

AHB was all gallantry. Hong Kong, was it? He was still plotting to swindle Jasper Gates? And Emily Eliot was *not* going to do the right thing, namely retreat.

"Just a tiny glass of sherry, if I may."

AHB glanced at Konrad to make sure he'd gotten the orders, then let himself down into his usual place. As irony would have it, Emily Eliot was sitting on the horsehair couch, in the very place Mignon had vacated.

Like old times, Susan told herself, while August repeated how relieved he was she'd arrived, how he couldn't survive all this without her, which, of course, was a big exaggeration, if not a lie.

"I do not know what to do with the boy. Pity his so-called father has returned to Los Angeles. I want Scott to leave as well," August complained, "but his goddamned publishers say he cannot."

Low-keyed Emily Eliot humbly murmured, "I believe he's scheduled to be interviewed by *Time* magazine. They feel such exposure will sell thousands of books."

"*And to my discredit!*"

None of this had anything to do with Susan. She was in town for only a couple of hours. AHB didn't need any help. It was a *farce*, ludicrous at this point even to mention the possibility of her becoming the second Missus Blick. And a *charade*! This awkward incident was not the result of bad timing. No, it was a provocation. August had chosen very deliberately to be surprised as he practiced his famous specialty on Emily Eliot.

And why? It was pretty obvious.

"And how is it going with Jasper Gates?" AHB grabbed his brandy-soda off Konrad's tray. "How *is* the interview shaping up?"

"Well," Susan said. "I hadn't realized Jasper is such a *very* interesting man. I don't think you do him justice."

That hit home. August's eyebrows vaulted.

"Really?" He drank thirstily, and cranked out a supercilious laugh. "If Jasper Gates were done justice, he'd have been *hanged* long ago."

Never again would Susan take seriously anything the man said.

"You never told me, for example, that Jasper prospected along the Amazon River."

August blinked. "I did not because he did not."

"And," Susan went on pointedly, disregarding Emily Eliot's alarm, "you never told me he was in China at the time of the Communist takeover, or that he'd lived in Japan."

Spitefully, August snapped, "Perhaps, because so far as I am aware, in nineteen forty-nine when Mao seized power, Jasper Gates was *in jail* in Arkansas."

"In jail?"

August's turkey gobbler wobbled over the knot of his gray foulard, stained, Susan noticed, around the pearl tiepin. It didn't concern him at all that he was slandering Gates very drastically and in front of potential witnesses, though, of course, Emily Eliot would never go against him.

"You see, my dear," AHB related, "as a youth Jasper was a member of a notorious band of Arkansas bank robbers. They were called the *Dinky Gang*"—his lip curled—"evidently because they were all very small. One of them was actually a midget safecracker whose mother, named Ma Petite, had been a horse thief—rather, Shetland pony thief—and whose grandfather in the old days in the Basquelands of northern Spain or southern France had been a renowned painter of miniatures. I won't go on. But, if Jasper Gates claims to have been in China in the late forties, he is being very sloppy about his geography."

"How can I believe such nonsense?"

"Could I invent it?" Gleefully, August raised his glass. "To the ladies! Long may they wave."

There, just *there*, August had lost it again, had gotten

tangled, uncharacteristically, in a maze of words. AHB was *definitely* losing it.

August had one thing to add: "As for Hugo Limited doing business with Jasper International, as we all know, money follows no flag. I invest for profit. Not for the sake of morality."

"You'd do business with the devil if you could turn a dollar at it," Susan muttered.

August's look was scorching.

"Not necessarily, but I would certainly consider it."

Jasper would never, never have been quite so fiendish on the subject. Susan didn't think he'd so openly, boastfully, even proudly, sell out to the devil. Or Doctor Faust, whatever the old fraud was called. At least, not yet. AHB had, in return for what? Untold riches, of course; and what else? Everlasting youth, ageless lust? Seeing Susan's doubt, possibly reading her mind with another of his devil-given talents, AHB fiddled self-consciously, conceitedly, with his tie. No, he was no Jasper Gates.

Out of this stalemate, Emily Eliot finally decided to exit. Warbling good-bye noises, she rose off the tainted couch.

"No, no, please don't get up, Mr. Blick, please don't!"

And he didn't, settling for an earnest, "Thank you for helping me so very efficiently, Emily."

Smile on her plucky face, Emily Eliot rounded the coffee table and pointed herself at the drawing room doors.

Only then did Susan notice what she was leaving behind.

"Emily, isn't that your handkerchief I see there?..." So suggestively wadded between the cushions? she wanted to add.

Ms. Emily shrieked. Hadn't she felt it was a little drafty? She whirled around, in a frenzy of embarrassment, snatched up the white panties, and crushed them into her pocketbook before you could say August Blick! Not risking another good night, she rushed for the door.

Emily had said it all, so for Susan a tight little smile would suffice. If ever there was an opportune moment for the cancellation of her alliance with August, this was it. And August seemed to dare her to make the first move. He stared at Susan quizzically, then laughed, cackled actually, a very un-Augustian sound, for he certainly didn't have a sense of humor.

"A bagatelle in the grand scheme of things."

"A *mere* bagatelle?"

"Exactly."

August finished his brandy-soda and, as if congratulating himself for managing everything so cleverly, slammed the glass down on the table and clapped his hands, like the pasha he considered himself to be. That was for Konrad, faithful Konrad, the Grand Eunuch of Park Avenue; August didn't speak again until Konrad had been dispatched for another brandy-soda.

Shockingly, his brain obviously in full disintegration, he murmured, "Well, my dear, have you considered my most earnest proposal?"

"We've disposed of Miss Emily Eliot, have we?"

Majestically, August cleared his throat.

"Nothing is what you suppose it to be: the first law of physics."

Handling it rather well, she thought, Susan said, "Tell me about Scott."

She was not jealous, *not* concerned about Emily Eliot? He was disappointed.

Grudgingly, AHB muttered, "A superficial wound, says Doctor Trevor Fleiss, my internist. A goodly distance from the heart."

"The heart?"

"Of course! Would I, otherwise, be in such a state?" Outraged, August exploded, "This woman, whatever her name is, this literary monster—"

"Prunella Grosz, the paper said."

"Whatever! The boy has no accident insurance of any kind. Think of it!"

"Bill Prunella Grosz for the hospital charges, August," Susan suggested.

"Have no fear, we will bill the wretched, perverted swine! And sue, too, for my mental anguish! Prunella whatever stabbed him with a kitchen knife, hit one of the lower ribs, perhaps the floating one, glancing off, close to the heart but far enough so we can say that it was not an affair of the heart after all."

"Odd his own agent would knife him. Something must have happened."

So Jasper Gates had speculated, but she wouldn't mention Jasper.

Waiting for Konrad to come and go again, AHB mused, "It was something to do with passion, I suppose."

"Passion?"

"Yes," he pontificated, "things people do to each other in heat. A Frenchman escapes the guillotine every day by showing his violent act was motivated by jealousy." His eyes fired up. "As I would be excused if I were to cut Jasper Gates's throat—and perhaps *yours* too. Really! Travelling hither and thither, alone with Gates in his plane, not even a chaperon on standby!"

"Tell me about Emily Eliot, August."

"Oh, for heaven's sakes!" AHB was insulted that she'd ask. "Emily Eliot is my most private secretary. She is also a poet . . . more *manqué* than successful. She has a densely poetic mind."

"Really?"

"Now you see it, now you don't! The conjuror pledges: you see, but you don't see," AHB brazenly explained. "Your eyes play tricks on you, particularly in a room that is all lights and shadows, shadow sometimes light, light sometimes shadow . . . No?"

"No."

He began again, his displeasure apparent. "Remember how I described your sweet treasure, your birdhouse, in terms of flowers, marigolds, nasturtiums, carnations entwined in a garland with your silky pubis, do you remember?" Susan shook her head, as if she didn't know what he was talking about. "And, my dear, you rejected my best-intentioned metaphor. I haven't forgotten, believe me. August Hugo Blick doesn't forget! So, how to explain Emily Eliot? Think of Emily as a rose, a wild rose."

"I'd never mistake a rose for Emily . . . or Emily for a rose. Though," she added nastily, "her hair is dyed a rather shocking pink."

"Indeed!" Then you might like to consider the matter in terms of the English poet's advice to gather *rosebuds* while ye may."

"August," Susan finally said, raising her voice, "you can't seriously expect me to be the second Missus Blick."

His vintage, vanishing eyebrows lofted again.

"I can't, for the life of me, think why not. Surely, my dear, you're not prepared to throw millions . . . hundreds of millions of dollars out the window?"

"The matter is closed."

Assertion of independence was tiring. And then he had to mention money.

"My dear, regardless of what you think, I am not going to live forever."

"Can you be sure, AHB?"

His long and wrinkled face stretched downward, grew extremely petulant.

"Joke, if you like. A few hundred million per year. Millions per month. Thousands per hour. Tens of thousands for every instance of my most intimate attention."

"I've never been interested in money, AHB, yours or anybody else's."

"What is more important then?" he jeered. "Don't bother to tell me. Love? I don't buy that, Susan."

"But you do buy love," she countered, "you're trying to buy me. All on the basis of money—I'm to ignore everything else. What sort of loyalty could I expect from you, August?"

"I am too old, my dear, for loyalty."

August Hugo Blick had never said anything so honest, at the same time so depressing. Susan blinked back tears. So much for all the squandered years! But fortunately, they needn't continue the pointless debate. Konrad announced that young Scott and Sidney Wilmer had arrived from the hospital.

August cursed in his first language, then said, "All right, Konrad. Let them come in."

Scott wasn't moving very peppily. His left arm was in a sling, the sling bound fast to his chest, his jacket caught over the shoulder on the wounded side.

"Sit down," August said. "You too, Sidney."

Even in normal times, Scott's complexion testified to excesses of junk food. Now, he was a walking ruin, eyes dark-circled, face drawn, and his pasty skin bleached out, like swollen dough. He looked ten years older than when she'd left him.

"Good evening, Miss Channing," Wilmer muttered guiltily.

"Hi, Sid . . . hello, Scott."

August tapped forefingers on knuckles.

"Sidney, any problems at the hospital? You have kept me out of this, I trust?"

Wilmer was definitely not comfortable with it.

"As best I could, AHB. As far as anybody knows, I'm a friend of his dad's." Wilmer hooked his thumb in Scott's direction and said, ''Scott's got to take it easy, not move the arm, otherwise the thing is liable to open up and start bleeding again. The cut wasn't long, but it was a little deep, like knife wounds—''

''No gruesome details, Sidney.'' August swiveled his eyes to his grandson. ''*Well?* Brave young Turk?''

Squirming, Scott mumbled, ''No story really. She was making spaghetti and just went berserk—''

''Drinking?'' August demanded.

''She opened a bottle of Italian red wine, not very good stuff, some kind of plonk.''

''I wasn't aware you were an expert.''

August's tone with Scott was sardonic but, clearly, he didn't have any idea how to handle the boy. Scott sensed this for he turned cockily toward Susan—in the wrong direction if he was looking for support.

''I've packed in lots of experiences...'' He must be in shock. ''You've only got to read the book, Grandpa, to realize. By the way, you're getting an autographed copy.''

The boast, the promise, seemed not to register on August. His face drooped into its deadly mandarin configuration; eyelids hunkered down, he was the wise and devastating old Buddha. And had not the slightest idea what to say.

''Scott,'' Susan asked distantly, ''what actually happened?''

''Nothing much.''

''Come now,'' she said reasonably, ''I think in light of all the publicity and all, it's as well we ... at least AHB ... know the truth.''

''Yes! Amen!'' August thundered.

Scott returned her look boldly, ready to lie. Yes, he had the old man's eyes, the very same unholy eyes, still hidden in a boyish face, but there, all the same.

''One minute, Prunella was dumping spaghetti in boiling water...'' He looked shaken, what an act! ''I was telling her about my next book, you know, the characters I have in mind and such. I was trying to explain to her. Well, she's not a writer herself, how could *she* know? I thought she was interested.'' Scott drew an unsteady breath; it would hurt him when he talked. ''And she turned around, with this funny look in her eyes...''

''*And?*''

August's own eyes were riveted on his grandson. Either he didn't believe the story or it reminded him of one of his own.

"She bent down and kissed me." August snorted outrage, and Scott hesitated, to make the most of it. "I don't know how to tell you, Grandpa. She grabbed my hand and shoved it up under her skirt and made me touch her pootie."

"Pootie? Sidney, what is a pootie?"

"Dunno, sir."

They knew very well what he was saying, the little liar!

August dropped back and weakly clapped his hands. Yes, he would need another drink.

And Scott went on, unmercifully. "I was so surprised, I leapt to my feet and that's when she grabbed the knife, Grandpa . . . and the rest of it, as we say, is history."

"Stabbed you, the tart!"

In confirmation, Scott nodded and gingerly caressed his sling, under which lay the freshly stitched wound.

Susan didn't believe one word of it. No. What had actually happened was that Scott had made some sort of revolting remark, or worse, actually moved on Prunella and the poor woman, in shock-horror reaction and self-defense, had grabbed the knife and stuck him, the little pig.

August glanced at Susan, his expression pedantic.

"Such things happen. Things happen for which we have no explanation! True, Sidney?"

"True, yeah, too true," Sidney agreed, gloomily.

"Important is that you weren't badly hurt."

Too eagerly, Scott said, "Never mind, Grandpa! It was a great experience! I'll make good use of it." August looked blank. "In my new book, Grandpa."

August winced, "And what is to be the title of your *new* book?"

"I think I'm going to call it *This Side of Oblivion*."

"Whose oblivion?" August said loudly, his deep voice echoing. "*Yours?* Your generation that we hear so much about from our so-called leaders? Drugged and drunk and promiscuous?"

"Yes."

"*Charming,*" August said, with cleansing snideness. "I am sure I have no wish to read about another generation of spoiled . . . soiled brats."

Scott didn't falter. Had he got it wrong? He should know August didn't tease.

"We've had a tough time of it."

"Have you indeed? Has the life been difficult growing up in such a disaster area as Beverly Hills, California?"

"Not easy, Grandpa," Scott said sullenly, then cried out emotionally, "We perish! In a society of plenty, *we perish*."

"*Scheisse!*"

Sid Wilmer then said something not electrifying.

"After the First World War, chief, there was a bunch that called themselves a lost generation."

August studied Wilmer as if he'd declared himself a freak, then, with labored politeness, murmured softly, "Before your time, Sidney. But not mine. I saw the end of that *so-called* lost generation when I was still in Europe. Working, young man! As an actor!"

"It runs in the family, Grandpa.

"What does?"

"The arts."

August allowed himself to be amused. "Judging by your performance, Mister Scott . . . Blake, maybe it does."

"*Blick*, Grandpa, I'm going to change my name back when I get to college."

August was stunned. Of all things, he had not expected this. Mayhem, death, destruction, yes, but not this. His face brightened, the hard line of mouth softened.

"Really?" he whispered. "Is that so? Is that *really* so?"

"Sure. Don't you believe me?" Scott whispered back.

August shrugged delicately, fearfully, thankfully.

"Why not? Why shouldn't I believe you. It costs me nothing." He smiled fraily. "I am touched . . ."

Susan couldn't believe AHB had fallen for it, like a ton of bricks. His grandson, shrewd Scott Blake, soon to become Blick, clever beyond his years, had fooled him, finessed him, where dozens of business rivals had failed. Yes, AHB would grow to love his grandson.

And, now, even more cleverly, Scott compounded the deception.

He hunched over and, fixing admiringly on August, begged, "Tell us more about Europe, Grandpa."

"Oh!" August wilted. "It makes me sad, Paris in the springtime. My friend Gertrude Stein. A rose is a rose is a rose, another sort of rose, Susan? Miss Stein gave me one of her Picassos in nineteen thirty-eight."

"Really?" For a moment, Susan forgot not to believe him. She knew the Braques; but where had the Picasso gotten to?

Lost, perhaps, in the mishmash of the Blick collection, much in need of some good curating. "Where is it, August?"

"I sold it when I first came to New York. Starving actor. I never told Miss Stein, or Alice."

He was lying.

"Well, they sure as hell won't find out now."

"*You* needed the money?" Scott said disbelievingly.

"I was not always enormously wealthy, young man."

No, and August had never had a Picasso from Gertrude Stein. He had never known the two ladies, Stein and Toklas. However, on second thought, AHB had been rather a number in late-thirties Europe.

August lifted his glass gaily, suddenly loving his audience.

"I was working then at the *Comedie Française* . . ." Yes, he had lost it. "All Paris was at my feet. Pay attention to *me*, young man, and you might after all have some good material for your next book."

"I am listening."

And loving it too. They were alike. If somebody didn't stop them, they'd sit there all day telling each other stories.

"We often talked of death, in the afternoon, and of love and tragedy. Now and then the American writer Hemingway was there. You know of him, young man?"

"Well, yeah . . . sure."

Scott flinched and Susan read the doubt in his face. Would *she* recommend that he believe AHB? August spotted her irritation and stopped himself in midsentence.

"Enough for now. This young man needs rest, Sidney, isn't that what the doctor ordered?" August glanced at Susan. "But what to do with him? *Susan!*" he yelped, as if he'd just discovered her, "would it be too much? Could you . . . might he not sleep where he did the other night? Konrad and I are not spry enough and Sidney is no nurse. I think the boy needs a loving hand. . . ."

He left her no out. It wouldn't have entered Susan's mind not to offer the boy refuge, but it was damned annoying for August to take it for granted. She gave August back his bland look with a sour one of her own. And something, a bad spirit, or the spirit of Nate Carleton, made her say what would hurt him most.

"I do not think, by the way, it's such great sport to make up stories out of thin air."

"I beg your pardon!"

Susan was on her feet. She stuck her hand out for Scott.

"*This*," she said, "and *previous* stories." She yanked Scott to his feet, too roughly. He yipped pain, but she ignored it. "Say good night! Good night, *August* . . . Sid."

Susan dragged Scott after her, into the marbled foyer and out the front door, without benefit of Konrad.

"Susan!" Scott began to dig in his heels. "What's wrong?"

She was desperately sorry now she'd bothered to get off Jasper Gates's plane.

"Runs in the family, does it? Fiction runs in your family, you're goddamn right about that! Why am I wasting my time with you?"

Susan unlocked her apartment door, pulled him inside and slammed it violently.

"*Fiction?* What do you mean?"

"I *mean* your whole family is expert at making up stories. I wouldn't go putting it in your book that your grandfather drank pernod with Gertrude Stein or that she gave him a Picasso."

Shrugging meanly, he said, "I wouldn't use a bunch of old shit like that anyway. Who the hell cares about Gertrude Stein? Who *was* Gertrude Stein?"

Susan groaned bitterly. Pretty soon the kids wouldn't know or care about anybody dead. Only alive would count. History itself would be a dead issue.

"American woman writer who lived in Paris. You ought to look her up."

"She must be pretty old by now if The Old Man knew her in the nineteen-thirties."

"Jesus Christ, Scott, she's dead! I mean, look her up in the library."

"Too much to read."

"Not my fault. I don't write books. Come on, I'll put you to bed." Susan ignored his look. "You can't undress by yourself, can you?"

"I don't think so, nursey."

"Are you going to tell me the truth about what happened?"

"I already did."

"Do you have to go to the bathroom? Then go ahead, now . . ."

Obediently, he did what she said, Susan turned down the bed in the guest room, hung Scott's blazer in the closet, then, suddenly seized up, sat down on the edge of the bed, thinking morbidly of pale bodies and red-gash knife wounds. Why did he always remind her of the bad times?

The bathroom door opened and closed again.

"Don't say anything," Susan said over her shoulder, "just shut up."

"You keep telling me to shut up."

"It's got nothing to do with you anyway."

About Nate Carleton, she had never learned how it had really happened, except for the vague report of a landmine. Had the wound been mortal, simultaneous with death, not hurting him beyond that exact, precise, riveting second of death? Or had he lain there suffering half the day?

"Susan, I'm sorry."

"For what?"

"The Old Man, he's such an old fraud."

"Which Old Man?"

"Both of them."

"Right."

Underneath his shirt, on the left side, the heavy bandage packed his lower ribs, enough to make her sick. Scott stared at her self-consciously.

"Well, come on." Susan slipped off his shoes and peeled off his socks. "And don't get any bright ideas."

"I really love you, Sue . . ."

He was already half asleep.

"Sure," she said roughly, "and there will be no fooling around tonight. If you get fresh, I'll cause you great pain, buster. How about a broken arm to add to your roster of physical punishment at the hands of infuriated women?"

"Sue, I love you . . ."

"Me too, as mother to son." Clinically, Susan whipped down his zipper, and grabbed the cuffs of his trousers. "Hike your ass, buster!"

"Would you marry me if I were older?"

"I've already been married to somebody in your family. Are you going to tell me what happened with Prunella?"

"She went wild: the truth!"

Change fell out of one pants pocket and, as Susan held them up to fold along the crease, a package of condoms from the other.

She waved them under his nose.

"One's missing. Was that the one with Prunella's name on

it?'' Scott shook his head dumbly. "You did something to provoke her, didn't you?"

"Just minor.''

"I'm surprised she didn't cut off *your* pootie."

Scott laughed happily. He loved the attention.

"If you don't want to marry me, darling, you could be my mistress," he said shamelessly. "You've got to admit I'm a lot of fun.''

"Do I? Are you?"

"It wouldn't cost you anything," he urged, sounding, though he couldn't know it, very much like August, "and then when I'm out of school, maybe we would get married. Older women like me, they really do, don't ask me why.''

"I'm *not* asking you why. I'm not interested in why.''

"I'm going to make it very big as a novelist, you know.''

"So?'' She laughed caustically, tapping the tip of his nose. "I play the field, buster.''

He grabbed for her, but Susan got out of the way.

"Whatever happens, I hope you'll always like me," he said.

"I guess so. You're one of the prettier Blick-Blakes.''

Susan couldn't resist him. She laid her hand on his chest, where the bandage met skin, feeling the warmth. Scott's eyelids sagged.

"You were the best thing," he whispered. "After you took off, it wasn't ever any good again.''

Well, she'd known that, and if he hadn't grown up totally rotten, she got some of the credit, didn't she?

"I don't know why you don't take better care of yourself . . . getting stabbed, for God's sake!''

"Tell me . . ."

Susan paused, torn. Sorely, was she tempted, but that would never do. She had become the mother again.

"Are you comfortable?''

"I've got a little headache. I think it's from all the drugs. My side is achy and sore.''

"Not surprising. You're lucky, you know that?''

"Tell me." He looked teary and just this once Susan might be prepared to believe him. "I really screwed it up, Susan. I don't blame people for thinking I'm an asshole.''

"That's a step forward.''

"Kiss me?''

Feeling a fool, Susan gave him a motherly peck on the

cheek, then on the cupid lips. Viperously, his tongue darted at her.

Susan slapped him lightly and sat back, breathing tensely. "Sue, do I have to be alone?"

" 'Fraid the nasty woman is going to come and hurt you?" Of course, he was. He was afraid of everything. "I'm going to California in the morning, early."

"Oh, no!" His eyes flicked open. "Why?"

"Work."

"I want to go too, Sue."

"You can't. You've got *Time*. And I hope you survive it, buster."

"Please, Susan, don't laugh at me."

"Who's laughing?"

"You are." Tears did come to his eyes. "You're always laughing."

"I am? I certainly hope so."

And so, well, what about it? She stared down at him and had to smile. He was something else.

And, thinking so, did it really matter so much in the universal scheme of things how she handled the next fifteen minutes?

15

Susan had been scarcely older than Scott when Roger Blake, his father, had sent her to be the youngest, blondest war correspondent in Southeast Asia. And later, when it was over, Roger, never at a loss for immortal words, had shouted at her in the airport in Hong Kong, for everybody to hear:

"Honey! I never thought you'd make it. For sure I figured you'd get blown away."

Any regrets about that, Mr. Blake?

Well, honey, look, if it *had* happened to you, if Fate had thrown you the black card, think what terrific publicity! It'd have *made* our station: K-Rap, talk and rock radio. And it would've *made* Susan Channing too—like *posthumously*: youngest, blondest, deadest war correspondent of the Vietnam War, the late Woman-of-the-Year. Perhaps to Roger Blake's regret, Susan had never really thought it through, Channing had not become a posthumous heroine. Susan didn't intend to cry about it. Things were as they were; and that was not going to be any more so, or less.

Susan was half asleep by the time the plane lifted into the

dull sky. Not so long ago, when she had been young and very romantic, she'd given herself stiff necks peering down at the receding island of Manhattan. She'd felt about the place so sentimentally, she could've written the song. No more. She didn't even turn her head. And how would it be when she was *really* old and jaded?

The stewardess was bending over her shoulder.

"I can get you a bloody mary if you like, Miss Channing, or something else."

"At eight-thirty A.M.?" Susan opened her eyes and laughed. "Thanks but no thanks."

What did they think she was, a lush who'd take a drink so early the in A.M.? Perish the thought. What would her public say? *Come off it, Susan! You're just one of the troops!*

Like hell she was! All the attention, it quite wrung her out. Was it worth it? Yes, it was. Life was tough, sure, but fascinating; exhausting, that too, in a physical as well as spiritual way. But she did love it and, asked if she would have traded it for anything, the answer was no.

Thinking of Nate—she always thought of Nate at moments of arrival and departure—what would *his* latest verdict have been? Guilty! Angel had fallen again. The freshest memory was unsavory... delectable. It was only bad if you thought of it badly. It only mattered at all if it mattered terribly to you. Nursey hadn't been able to help herself and, kissing the babyish lips, she had thought that surely he would come to a violent end. In all honesty, he was a truly evil boy.

After a bit of breakfast, Susan managed more serious sleep, or the closest she got to sleep these days. Tangled thoughts became scratchy dreams: Nate again, young and vital. With magical ease, memory wiped away his thick, wire-framed glasses, straightened his face, transformed him into something godlike. But Nate had been anything but wonderful looking. His great attraction had been personality, inner joy, derring-do; Susan had been too young and impressionable to go against a Nate Carleton. Oh, yes, they had been in heat, hot to breed; desire swollen by adrenaline, the living craving to reproduce themselves before it was too late. Her wildness seemed now to have been right for those times, days of fire and storm. The trouble was that she'd never gotten over it, put it aside, grown out of it. She had never recovered. Nothing since then had been real, as she'd told Harry. She was as dead as Nate was. Brain dead, feeling dead, nerve dead.

* * *

Mr. Dudley was waiting for her in San Francisco. The plane was a half hour late, but Dudley only shrugged.

"No problem, Miss Channing. I trust everything was all right in New York."

"That problem was not a problem."

In a very few moments, Susan was again on a Jasper International flying machine, a tiny one by comparison, for the jump over the coastal range to Big Sea.

Dudley went forward to inform the pilot they were ready to roll, flap wings, lift off; almost at once the small plane was in the air, buzzing busily, bearing north, across a corner of Napa, and down below couldn't she see the long, regular rows of grapevines, only a few months from harvest? Then they were briefly over Sonoma before heading west into the Hispaniola County wedge of Pacific coastline.

Mr. Dudley came back to offer her a drink which Susan again declined. Mr. Gates, it seemed, was already deep in meetings. Some sort of crisis? A certain problem, Mr. Dudley believed. But they'd already known that, hadn't they?

Susan had a pending problem of her own—how to handle Arthur Fineman. He'd be a climbing the walls by now, having seen *The New York Times* item and unable to reach her. Holy cow, she'd been out of touch, communication blackout, for going on twenty-four hours! *Hindsight* was being outrun by events, Fineman would scream.

She had been hoping for a respite, a couple of days to organize a plan. Now? Move more quickly? Postpone the whole thing? Get a camera crew up to Big Sea right away? Or let it ride until they got to Los Angeles? All this *presuming* that Jasper Gates, in midcrisis, was going to have the time or patience to submit to an interview.

It was incredible that Dick Lyons was still capable of causing so much commotion. Of course, it was not such a difficult thing to do. This would not be the first time in history that the Indians had been provoked, though usually it was by the dimwitted ways of the Washington bureaucrats, the Bureau of Indian Affairs at the Department of the Interior. She remembered how the tribes had seized the island of Alcatraz in San Francisco Bay to call the nation's attention to their grievances. Who was it had said Beau and Bel Custerd's father had been in on that caper? And there were the legal battles in Arizona and New Mexico over preferential oil and mineral leases let by the Bureau on Navajo land.

It was *very* complicated. Susan worried that she should have been further along. Fineman would say she'd been goofing off, spending too much time making whoopee and not enough on the job. She, who was usually so efficient. Whatever else was happening, no matter what, she was there! But in the past few days, since the first trip to Big Sea, followed by Mignon's death and the rumors about Sir Guy Bristals, she'd lost it. If, after all her rash and brash promises about nailing the Jasper Gates pelt to the wall, Susan screwed it up, there would be hell to pay. Arthur Fineman, permanently on the verge of breakdown, would go all the way; and, as likely as not, Simon Hayford, already on the skids, would join with AHB to make Susan Channing a ritual sacrifice before he himself was cut down by Sir Guy Bristals.

The trouble was that she had managed to make herself totally vulnerable. She was breaking with AHB, but could she really count on Jasper Gates? Trapped once more in one of his planes—how quickly she forgot he'd kidnapped her—Susan felt more than ever that she was actually flying into the untracked and unknown.

"We're coming in shortly, Miss Channing."

They had overflown the continent and were banking steeply over the ocean to return, the ocean an arm's length down below, white water crashing against the jagged coastline. Beer foam, Nate would've called it. More properly, pieces of white lace.

The pilot banked again to come up the coastal ridge. The plane bucked into the crosswind, and Susan was acutely aware of the accident, or miracle, of survival. The small craft fishtailed, dropped rapidly toward the forest, got between the trees, and found the ground. Wheels thumped. The plane bounced, then rolled, rolled to a stop.

"There'll be a car waiting, Miss Channing."

So far, there had been a sort of symmetry about this story and so Susan was not surprised to see young Ted Jay at the edge of the runway, leaning on a black Cadillac Seville. *Big Sea Center* it said in gold lettering on the door.

"Well, Ted, I'll bet you didn't expect to see me again so soon."

He was as shy as ever; he kicked at a tire and reddened.

"Hello, Miss Channing."

"How's your dad?"

Susan wanted to ask about Jenny too, but didn't.

"Fine . . . well, I'm not sure. But he was happy to hear you were coming back."

Yes, she thought, the last time she'd seen those two, she'd had to walk home to the inn.

Once in the car, Ted didn't start up right away. Was he going to say something important? He stroked the steering wheel, then spoke. "I got a promotion."

"I hope it doesn't turn your head."

"Bear would blow my brains out," he said gruffly. "But I wish I were going to school in New York City. . . ."

To be near her?

"If you did, I could see you once in a while, when you weren't busy."

"Bear says I should line up as many free meals as I can."

"I'd take you to my favorite restaurant."

Ted didn't react to her promise, instead went silent and in no apparent hurry drove away from the airstrip and into the tunnel of forest, dense, damp, and cool, which created the temperate climate of the Petertown area: the town itself, Indian Island, and Ross Lagoon, the body of swampy, tidal land across which Jasper Gates had built his memorial bridge.

"We weren't on this road when we went on Jenny Driver's."

"No."

"So, Ted, what's new in this neck of the woods?"

"Mr. Jasper is back." His big hands hung together over the burled wood steering wheel. "But you know that already."

It was a good thing the boy was leaving town for places more sophisticated. He was beginning to act like a native: close-mouthed, suspicious, unfriendly. For some reason he seemed disappointed in her. Why? Should she explain about her relationship, if any, with Jasper Gates? Or Arthur Fineman's incipient madness, AHB's life-and-death power over Simon Hayford, their concern about Sir Guy Bristals? Ted thought *he* had problems?

"Rumors!"

He blurted the word so unexpectedly she was startled.

"Yes? What kind of—"

"About . . ." He swallowed his Adam's apple several times. "Bear and Jenny . . . nasty things. That they . . ." He couldn't say it. "Somebody saw them! Horrible people here!"

"Ted, you shouldn't pay any attention to what people say." He shook his head bitterly. Of course, he couldn't know it was true. Those two were completely uncautious. Susan had seen it for herself. Affectionately, she touched his hands on the steering wheel, a jolly, comradely gesture. "People gossip, very narrow people who have nothing better to do, I promise you."

"Yeah." But he was not convinced. "I asked Bear."

"And he said forget it, right?"

"Bear told me to keep my mouth shut and ignore it. I'm glad I'm going away from here!"

"That's right, Ted. The big, wide world awaits you."

"He *knows* who's saying it."

"Oh?"

"Yes." Ted stared ahead, wanting to tell her, but embarrassed to do so. "It's Richard Lyons! And Moon Rivers." He glanced at her, face twisted. "And I respected Mr. Lyons. Moon Rivers, he's a bum but Mr. Lyons——"

"Now, come on, Ted. Dick Lyons, he's Jenny's husband, he wouldn't say a thing like that."

"That's what makes it worse," Ted muttered. "And he and Moon hate each other. But they're both saying that Bear and Jenny Driver . . . that somebody saw them in the back of the car up by the road . . . in the trees . . ."

"*Enough,* Ted! That's just not true! You are not to believe it. Just . . . believe your father."

"Mr. Lyons is in the middle of everything!" Ted clamped his mouth and glanced over his shoulder. No, nobody was listening. "He's got everybody in town stirred up. He's saying how can Jasper Gates be allowed to sell Indian land to the Japanese, when he doesn't even own it?"

"Ted, aren't we talking about two entirely different things?"

"Yes, two different things, but the same thing too." He cleared his throat, miserably, and Susan thought he wouldn't go on but he did. "My mother killed herself in Boston twelve years ago."

Susan's throat seized up. She couldn't speak, instead turned in the seat and touched his arm.

"He thinks I don't know about it. But I do," he murmured.

"It's . . . that was a long time ago, Ted."

"But why?" he cried softly.

"Nobody could tell you that, Ted."

He looked at her.

"Even Bear? He's a psychiatrist."

"Maybe he could," she said. "But in order for him to talk about it . . ."

"Well, why doesn't he just tell me then, Susan?"

"Ted . . . I don't know." What could she say? "It's something, I don't know. It's very sad."

"Sad to jump out of a window."

"Yes."

He would be worried about himself, wondering, wandering in a maze, asking himself if he was infected with the same dread urge. If she had known how to say it, Susan would have assured him, promised, sworn on a stack of Bibles that Ted Jay was as normal as normal could be, far more "normal" than Scott Blake, if it came to that.

After a moment, giving up, hoping to distract him somehow, Susan said, "Mr. Gates firmly believes he owns the island, Ted, and if anybody cheated the Baskets, it was done a long, long time ago."

"So, you're on his side?"

"Not particularly. I'm working on a story, that's all."

"Well, I'm on his side," Ted said. "I don't like Richard Lyons."

"Well, I don't blame you."

Whatever was building in the way of crisis, it seemed a quiet enough day in Petertown. Four cars were drawn up at the Rivers-by-the-Sea service station and maybe double that many in the supermarket parking lot. A little farther on, a cluster of men held down one end of the rickety porch of the Petertown Hotel; judging by the set of their tractor caps they were having serious talk.

"Moon Rivers." Ted grunted. "I'd like to kill him."

"Ted, forget it. He's not worth the trouble."

Rivers occupied quarterback position in the huddle, the same stained cap pulled low on his forehead, ever-present cigarette dangling off his lower lip.

"What do you think they're talking about?"

Ted had slowed down a little and he was staring hatefully across the street.

"The Indian Island War, that's what Bear calls it." He relaxed just a bit, adding, "Like the French and Indian War. Remember?"

"I wasn't around."

"Gosh, I know that! I was just—"

"I know, I know, sweetie." Susan wanted to hug him.

"Listen, Ted, what I want to say to you is everything seems confused. But it'll work out. It always does. You'll see."

"Yes, okay. But how do you know?"

"How do I know?" Good question. "Well, it did for me once." She drew a breath. He was waiting, so she had to continue. "I was in love with somebody in the Vietnam War and he got killed and I thought I'd die. But I didn't. I felt guilty for a long time, you know, that it was my fault, somehow." That was the one that hit; he blinked, he'd taken the shot. "Now, I know it wasn't my fault. It happened, that's all. Do you see? Do you understand?"

But had he heard? She was not so sure after all.

"Bear says Moon Rivers is an ugly little son of a bitch. He understands how Rivers can be crazy about Emma Bristals but he can't understand Richard Lyons because he has Jenny Driver who's really beautiful. Bear says Mrs. Bristals looks like the ass-end of one of her horses."

"Did he really say that?"

Susan laughed, much louder than she should have. But some things were easier to deal with than others.

She might never know whether she'd helped him or not. But apparently more cheerful, Ted picked up speed and got them to the Big Sea turnoff. In a tick, they were into the marshland and then whipping across the bridge. Ahead of them, a great ugly, red-goitered turkey hawk circled over the reeds.

A covey of gulls burst from under the bridge, disturbed by the noise of the Seville's tires.

"Oh, Bear says let's get together again when you've got a spare moment."

"I'm kind of at Jasper Gates's mercy."

"Whenever you get loose . . ."

Ted stopped in front of the inn and Susan did kiss him then, affectionately, on the cheek.

"Thanks, sweetie." He gulped. "Ted, I want you to take good care of yourself. Will you?"

He nodded, speechless, and Susan hopped out of the car, not waiting for more, or looking back.

As luck would have it, Ralph Teller was standing just inside the lobby door. Had he been waiting? A white-toothed caught-in-the-act grin broke across his face.

"Ralph!" Susan thrust out her hand, then, impulsively,

kissed his cheek too. For some reason, she felt very happy to be back here. "Surprise! How's Harry?"

"Fine, fine." He was guiding her to the front desk. "He's coming back over. Things are—"

"Things?"

"Don't ask!" He laughed nervously. "I put you in a suite next door to Jasper Gates. I hope that's okay." His expression was innocent. "If he gives you any trouble, scream—ha-ha."

"I will." She was not going to be embarrassed, not ever again, she swore it. "Ralph, is Guy Bristals here? From London?"

"And a Japanese friend of Jasper's, Sue. Doctor Guchi, that's Ishira Guchi, of the All-Nippon Prosperoso Company, trading company. Sue, do you have *any* idea what the hell is going on?"

"Only the rumors, Ralph, I don't know any more than you."

Susan slipped away; after all, she didn't owe Ralph any information. He hadn't been especially forthcoming with her. She had to call New York; they would be wondering where she was.

Which they definitely were. Fineman had just returned from lunch at the University Club. He came on the phone snarling.

"Where the hell are you, Channing?"

"In California, sweetie, where'd you think?"

"Why didn't you tell Jack and me about Lyons getting shot at, goddamn it?"

"They missed."

"We have to read about it in *The New York Times*? We coulda beat 'em by a week, Suse!"

"What the hell good would that do us, Artie?"

"Channing," he said, voice dripping sarcasm like acid, "let me remind you, *Hindsight* is part of the news department. Maybe not especially useful for us, but we could've gifted it to the *Evening News*. They might have been grateful for twenty or thirty seconds."

"Well . . . "She didn't have a good answer. "I didn't think it was going to get out, Artie." Meaning: she didn't think Harry Teller was going to use it. "I was hoping we could keep it for ourselves."

"So *happy* you didn't bother me with it, Channing!"

Moving right along, ignoring him for the sake of her equilibrium, Susan said, "Artie, I think we'd better be ready to move. I want you to alert a camera crew in San Francisco, hopefully not the same guys I had last time."

"Oh, is *that* what you want, Channing? Anything else? Goddamn it! Do *I* have to worry about your relations with a fucking camera crew?"

"Arthur," Susan said. "I want it arranged ahead of time. If *I* say I don't want to work with Julie whatever-his-name-is, you know damn well they'll give him to me, just out of spite."

She could see Fineman sweating, hating it, hating her. Was she asking him to stop the world? It was a moment of his time. His secretary could make the call. A measure of Fineman's decline was his neurotic response to the most routine requests. Nevertheless, she thrust at him again.

"Arthur! I need you to do this."

"Okay, okay! We'll take care of it," he shouted. "Would you mind giving me a reason, Channing? Is something happening, maybe?"

"Something with the Indians . . . it'll be part of the Gates story."

"Jesus, on a day like this! Simon is acting like Hitler, or Genghis Khan. I think he knows he's getting it."

Well, everybody else seemed to know—why not Hayford too?

"By the way," he added, irrelevantly, "remember that fashion flap? Well, now they want you for a cosponsor to some cockamamie fashion-award dinner benefit at the Plaza. I told 'em, Channing, that you're a journalist and you don't have time for that kind of horseshit, which you don't, do you?"

"No, I don't. Damn it, Artie, all this started just because I mentioned Scaasi's name once! I happen to like him. He's kind of chubby but—"

"You like him. I know."

Calmly, the ever-cooler Susan Channing said, "Artie, a bit of news: Small world department. Guy Bristals is here. It seems, believe it or not, he's a business pal of Jasper Gates."

"Fuck!"

"Arthur, just remember, my one purpose in life is to establish you as the leading edge of the *Hindsight* machine."

"Cut the shit! Listen, Channing, I want a full report. I want you to stick to that son of a bitch like glue. I want you to grill him, play up to him, kiss his ass . . . whatever it takes!"

"Sure. Artie, anything you say, anything for you, anything. . . ."

She hung up before he could say any more. No sooner had she replaced the phone than it rang, too soon for Fineman to have called her back. Susan took it on the bathroom extension.

"Sweetie! Me."

"Oh, Jasper, hello. I'm here, yes. Just having a quick shower."

"Sue! Welcome! C'mon next door. People for you to meet!"

"I'll be over in a few minutes."

"Flight okay?" She told him it had been fine and, hurriedly, he added. "Be waiting for you, *sweetness*!"

Sweetness? That was a new one. Just to show him, Susan took her time in the bath, then proceeded to the bedroom to unpack the suitcase which had preceded her to the Coast. She changed into the Big Sea uniform, a fleece jogging suit and pair of red Reeboks, then put in another five minutes brushing her hair, applying lipstick and a dash of perfume.

After all, she was about to meet Sir Guy Bristals, a man who evidently was going to be very important in her future, not to mention the Japanese gentleman whose name had an Italian ring about it. Of course, she was a little nervous about facing a roomful of strangers. Susan comforted herself as she walked up the hall to the next set of doors—who wouldn't be? God knew who else Jasper had assembled.

But there were only three of them there, Jasper, a blubbery man she assumed was Bristals, and the Japanese, all gathered at the round table next to the panoramic window.

Taking and holding Susan's hand like a trophy, Jasper led her forward.

"Sweetie, two of my *most valued* friends: Guy Bristals! For sure you already know him from the newspapers. *Sir* Guy, this is the well-known, *nay*, world-famous Susan Channing, the best thing American TV has to offer."

Who would not recognize Guy Bristals? Though of course her opinion was colored; Susan thought pictures didn't do him justice. Bristals was much uglier in person. But Susan smiled nicely, for Fineman's sake, causing Sir Guy to remove from his protruding mouth a sopping-wet and well-chewed cigar. He twisted it in sausage-shaped fingers, waiting for Jasper to finish.

"And my good old friend from Japan, Ishira Guchi!"

Bristals struggled to his feet but Guchi bounded up. Now, he, in comparison, was a fine figure of a man.

"Shira, Guy, this is my *fiancée*, Susan Channing. Meet Susan! You've both seen her on the box!"

Susan felt much as she would have if Jasper had torn off her clothes and spun her on her toes for the delectation of his chums. Fiancée? Of course, what else was he going to say? And what could Susan do but wince and let it pass?

"Miss Channing," Bristals said loudly, "a great pleasure." He touched his hand to hers daintily, then dropped it.

Bristals was such a wobbly old heap of flesh. She preferred to look at Ishira Guchi. No doubt Bristals's bulk made Guchi seem taller than he was and more slender, although slightly round-shouldered; he was thin-faced and bespectacled, like so many Japanese, and of no discernible age. His hair certainly didn't give him away: it was thick and very black, combed straight back. He looked more like a scholar or monk than the CEO of a huge trading company.

You couldn't imagine a man of Sir Guy Bristals's reputation being any different than he was. His hair style was baldness, though a few fuzzy strands of the stuff were slicked across his skull in hirsute conceit. Olive-shaded skin glowed like an oily lantern. Yes, Sir Guy had had his share of cake and ale. The Bristals eyes were a bit of a surprise, however: remarkably alive, deadly too, the pupils like black pencil points. His voice was atonal, jarred as he spoke by traces of cockney. He coughed, phlegm in the wings, testimony to the power of his Havana cigar.

"A great, very great pleasure," he repeated.

"I'm *glad* to see you," Susan responded.

Never mind what Bristals looked like. What mattered was that he was very possibly on the way to being the new power at North American Network.

Bowing deeply, Ishira Guchi whispered, "So honored."

Any friend of Jasper's was a friend of hers. Guchi's grip was firm and his smile toothy. Toothy, yes, but his teeth didn't jut; they were big and white and he had a whole mouthful of them. This was the man buying Big Sea? Why on earth should the Indians object? Ishira Guchi looked more like an Indian than any American of Jasper Gates's breed. Remembering Jenny's handyman, Susan thought Guchi could have been taken for the Custerd boy's older brother, or maybe father. No surprise there, if you considered the migration patterns from northern Asia several thousand years ago.

Taking Susan's hand again, Jasper said lovingly, " 'Bout

ready for a late lunch, Sue?" She nodded. "We been talkin'
the whole morning about the situation here," Jasper informed
her glumly. "Goddamn Lyons! Goddamn Indians!"

Susan asked, "What's happened now, Jasper?"

Jasper glanced at his friend Shira. Obviously, they'd been
going around and around. But Guchi's face remained impassive; he gave no hint that he was concerned about anything.

"As I've been explaining, Lyons is pumping up the Baskets
to go on the warpath. We had the title to this place *searched*
and re-searched to a fare-thee-well. But naturally, that doesn't
stop somebody like Lyons." Jasper paused, then altered
direction. "Sue's reported on stuff like this before. That's
why I'm keeping her clued in, Shira."

Guchi's dark, almond-shaped eyes probed hers.

"Frankly, sweetie," Jasper said smoothly, "Shira's not
having any part of a deal if there's a legal problem. Lyons
knows that. He's counting on it."

She wondered what he expected her to say. To confirm,
deny, elaborate, or what? To play the role of foil? She had no
idea.

Guchi said apologetically, "My board would toss me out
on my keester—"

"Well, they'd be remiss if they did!"

"Indeed . . . indeed," Guy Bristals chimed in.

Were Guchi and Bristals old friends too? Or linked through
the cosmopolitan person of Jasper Gates? What in the world
could they have in common? Why was Bristals in on the
discussion anyway? Indeed, what could Jasper have in common with the British media tycoon after he'd sold Bristals the
last of his media properties, the TV station in Michigan?

Susan decided Ishira Guchi must be in his late forties. He
had to be at least that old to have known Jasper in Japan those
years before and to have risen to the top of his company. But
he was not Jasper's exact contemporary. Aware of Susan's
interest—he must have been aware—Guchi had quietly sat
down again and closed his hands under his smooth-shaven
chin. He was a man who would know so well, as the Japanese
seemed to, how to wait, how *not* to speak or act rashly, how
to listen. They were never brash, these Japanese, were they?
It would take a bit of looking to find a Japanese Jasper Gates.

"I was telling the boys some horror stories about what the
Indians would do here if, God forbid, they won in court. First

thing, they'd open a bingo hall in our ballroom, or the Convention Center!''

Susan shook her head, demurring gracefully, trying to make Guchi see there could be another side of this. The Indians weren't all bad, if that was the message he was receiving from Jasper Gates.

"Jasper, you can't take it out on the Indians. They've had a rotten deal all around. You know that, being from Oklahoma—''

"I'm not from Oklahoma, Sue! And I don't know anything about Indians.''

"Poor sods," Guy Bristals blustered. "Emma tells me she has a few of them working for her at the ranch and you dare not give them anything to drink.'' He swung his eyes tellingly, as if they might not have heard of the very raunchy Lady Bristals. "Emma was my last wife.''

"I've met Lady Emma," Susan said helpfully.

He didn't hear.

"It seems to me, Jasper," Bristals said, "that one should find out what it is Mr. Lyons wants above all else in life and buy it for him.''

Glancing at Susan, Jasper grunted. "Already thought of that. It might backfire, that's the trouble.''

"Every man has his price,'' Bristals wheezed knowingly.

But Jasper, at this point, was plainly not interested in what the Englishman had to say about human relations. He was grinning at Susan, showing his own perfect teeth; she wondered if he'd had them capped. This thought caused her to remember the new suspicions August Blick had tried to plant in her mind, particularly the business about the Dinky Gang. Did she dare ask? Well, not right now.

"Sweetie, you and I have got a date in downtown Petertown this afternoon.''

"We do? For what?''

"With a notary, sweetie. We're gonna see a man about a house. . . .''

Susan started. She'd clean forgotten, though obviously Jasper hadn't. He had been serious after all! Oh, God, yes! She had to decide then—was it ethical to accept such a gift? Yes, well, no, probably not. She decided she'd have it out with him later about Greenswards.

Jasper was done with the subject of the Indians and Big Sea, but Shira Guchi suddenly was not.

Weightily, he addressed them, inspecting each word for flaws before letting it go.

"What bugs me the most, *Jas,* is the thing about the *legend.* Legends scare the bejesus out of the Shinto guys I've got on my board."

"He's talkin' the Indian graveyard we dug up," Jasper told Susan uncomfortably.

"I am not surprised."

"Oh . . . *crumbs,*" Jasper exclaimed, sensitive to Susan's seasoned look. "Lyons is making a federal case out of it. According to the legend—legend, my ass—we're all of us on the receiving end of a curse if we touch it. Can you feature that! Utter disaster will be visited on all our works."

"Balderdash," Bristals said.

"And, for God's sakes," Jasper complained, "we stopped work! We got it boarded up and we're paying for a really painstaking excavation. There's this local guy, a psychotherapist or something who's overseeing it."

Quietly, Susan corrected him. "No, he's a psychiatrist and social anthropologist and his name is Bertram Jay. He was educated at Harvard."

"See!" Jasper exclaimed. "Is she some reporter, Guy?"

But Guchi remained doubtful.

"What I'm telling you, Jas, is that ancestors are a big number in Japan. If we got involved here and it came out that the Basket's ancestors were rolled in their graves, there's *no way* Prosperoso could live it down."

Jasper stared at him for what seemed like five minutes.

"Jesus, Shira, that's what I'm trying to get across: we're taking utmost care not to shift a bone. This . . . Jay, he's our man. Our expert . . ."

The man cuckolding Dick Lyons . . .

" . . . Surely now, Lyons is ethically bound to advise the Baskets we're on the up and up. And the Baskets have got to be pleased we're handling their antecedents with kid gloves."

Guchi hammered it home.

"Jas, I agree . . . but it doesn't matter what I think personally. You been to my house, ate my food, do I lie to you? The heart of the matter is what the Japanese tourist industry would say about us messing with eternity."

Jasper couldn't disagree.

16

Swept along—that had to be it—at four P.M., in the presence of God and Notary Public Gabe Arrend in the town of Petertown, ethical or not, like it or not, Susan Channing seemed to have become legal owner of the Irish property called Greenswards.

Seemed was the operative word.

Susan had not believed that Jasper would go through with it and, being a realistic woman, she figured there must still be a catch, some sort of face-saving device that would allow him to slip out of the deal.

After all, she still had not delivered.

Anyway, it bothered her. Unable to stall or downright refuse him, she had accepted the gift, thus devaluing her independence. Was she so greedy? Or had she just gone along to avoid a fight? What if people found out, what would she tell them?

And Jasper was beside himself, so jubilant it made Susan wonder *why*. Why was he so happy? What had she promised, what commitment had she made without understanding it? Why, oh why, had he been so eager to have it done?

241

After a hurried thank you and good-bye to Mr. Arrend, and being complimented, to his annoyance and suspicion, on his plans to make of Indian Island a showplace, Jasper swept Susan down the slippery slope in front of the Petertown Professional Building. Possessively, he patted her hip and helped her slide into the front seat of another of the Cadillacs with Big Sea markings. Humming with self-satisfaction, Jasper eased himself in the other side, behind the wheel, grumbling that damp coastal weather froze up his left knee, which had been damaged during a barroom brawl at a white hunters' club in Nairobi, then banged about again while he'd been innocently involved in the Algerian war of independence. But never mind! Jasper sure as hell didn't want anybody driving *him* around. A man was pretty far gone if he couldn't handle a motor vehicle on his own, bad knee or not.

Jasper swiveled around in the seat and took her hand, carrying it to his mouth, kissing and breathing on it. He loved to fondle her hands.

"Tell me what you think of Shira Guchi, sweetie."

He was gazing at her so intently, waiting so indulgently for her opinion, that Susan was embarrassed. At any moment, she thought, the revelation would come: what Jasper Gates expected in return for Greenswards. Poor Jasper. He really was in a loss-leading mood. Susan felt for him.

"Mr. Guchi is an impressive man, I suppose."

"Suppose?" Jasper studied her keenly, a tight little smile on his face. "No more than that?"

What did he want her to say? That Guchi was a very good-looking man, the type of virile Oriental who drove Western women crazy, his presence alone enough to make them go slack in the thighs?

"He seems like a bright man."

"Bright?" he echoed her again. "Shira may be the smartest man you'll ever meet, sweetie—after me, of course. You realize how smart a man has to be to get to the top of one of those trading company pyramids?"

"Yes, I have a fair idea."

Jasper's face twisted unattractively.

"Which is why it's so unfair, so indefensible, for Shira to be thwarted by a Dick Lyons! Jeeze, I bring him over here in good faith and . . ."

Susan nodded, half agreeing, half not.

"What did strike me as strange," she said, "is that such a

man is traveling without a huge retinue. Don't they usually have a half-dozen advisors and secretaries and what have you—''

Jasper exclaimed wetly, "You are so right, sweetie. Shira is *so big*, they have to let him go it alone. He left his personal assistant behind in San Francisco, with *his* personal assistant . . . and the usual interpreters and secretaries. The *point* is, sweetie, we've got to do something about Lyons!''

That said, he finally started the car, reminding Susan to fasten the seat belt around her "dear" tummy. As they drove away, it occurred to Susan she had forgotten something important.

"Thank you, Jasper."

"For what?"

"For Greenswards, of course!''

"I said I was going to do it. And I did. I keep my word. Unlike some other people I can think of.''

He was referring, of course, to August Hugo Blick. Susan could not, however, offhand, think of anything AHB had promised to do that he had not done. He had simply never promised anything. And still Jasper gave no sign of ulterior motive. Despite dearly learned caution, Susan was beginning to feel quite bowled over by the gesture. Gone was any vague stirring of interest in Shira Guchi. Susan didn't want or need any more surprises, romantic or otherwise. Perhaps, against all odds, she *had* fallen for Jasper Gates, had, finally, found her kind of man. Had she been meant all along to walk at Jasper's side, or fly with him wherever he wanted to go?

"It means a lot to me, Jasper."

It was a token of something, a metaphor for something else: regard, esteem, respect. A person could never get too much of those things.

He glanced at her steamily.

"Sweetie, I wish to hell we could get the hell out of this place. I wish I could hand it over to Shira, *right now!*''

"Me too, Jasper."

His grip on the steering wheel was white-knuckled. Susan drifted toward him.

"Hey! Easy! Not while I'm driving, sweetie! Like I say, I wish we could scram-bolo." He laughed exuberantly. "Problems! I heard from Bulgaria this morning. Rusty rivets, leaky pipes . . . blistered plate!''

"I want to go with you!''

"You will!"

"I can't."

"Can't?"

"I heard from New York. My boss is sending me to Toronto as soon as I finish here. We're doing a big Canadian takeout and I've got to interview the prime minister."

"I know him!"

"Do you?"

"Bet your ass." He paused. "Look, Sue, you're gonna have to knock it off."

"Knock what off?"

"The job. I go in one direction and you in the other. Armand's wife *always* traveled with him."

"Armand Hammer, yes, but she didn't have a career, Jasper."

"And neither will you, after you quit NAN. I'll speak to them," he said with a grunt.

"Speak? How?"

"Get you fired." He chuckled about his life-giving, life-taking power. "Nah, I wouldn't do that. You'll quit of your own free will."

"But I don't want to, Jasper."

"I cannot talk to you properly from behind the wheel of this Cadillac."

Susan was stunned. He was perfectly serious. Then she was stunned again when she considered, for the first time in years, that she *could* quit, get out of it, dump her cherished post at *Hindsight*. Maybe Jasper was right. Did she really need it? What was so great about chasing your tail around the world? Susan had the wherewithal, her own and his, to say farewell. Traveling with Jasper, there'd be no end to luxury, high profile, even a small measure of fame. Was that what she wanted? To be Mrs. Jasper Gates, wife of the financial great man? Susan Gates, Patron of the Arts, Mrs. Big Bucks, Mrs. Charity Benefits? Would it be so bad?

Idiotic. Susan knew without thinking twice it wouldn't work. She didn't want it, forget it.

Coasting through the center of Petertown, Jasper whipped the Cadillac to the left and parked next to the post office.

"C'mon, sweetie." He jumped out of the car and came around to haul her out too, never thinking to ask whether this was her idea of fun. "Let's go in that pissant hotel barroom and see who's got the balls to say what's on their mind. I hear all kinds of undercurrent—"

"Is it safe?"

He laughed scornfully, pulling her along.

"Of course! What the hell are they gonna do, beat me up or something? I'd have their asses on a platter!"

The Long Bar at the Petertown Hotel, Susan finally learned at first hand, was spectacular, but only in that it seemed truly authentic. One could imagine what a wrench it had been just installing electricity a few generations before and indoor plumbing more recently.

A creaky door introduced them into the dark hole—less dark after your eyes adjusted, but still dank and damp. The ten-yard-long bar was heavy, of aged oak, and reminded Susan of the Long Bar at Victoria Station in London.

This altar to booze seemed to float a foot off the floor along one whole side of the rectangular room, sloping slightly, her eye told her, toward the west, the ocean. Dusty shelves held a variety of bottles; old porcelain handles advertised two or three brands of draft beer. The other side of the room was taken by a blackened fireplace with a carved stone mantle-piece Susan would gladly have carried away with her. Smoke-stained pictures crowded the walls, of men holding huge, gape-mouthed fish, of old locomotives and bridges that were no more. Left over, nobody had noticed, were a couple of recruiting posters from the First World War.

A baseball game was being played out on a color TV set, a small gesture to modern times, set high in the wall over one end of the bar.

As for patrons, a half-dozen stools were occupied by figures unmoving enough to be wax, their attention fully given over to the game.

Jasper chose two places next to shuttered windows at the end of the room away from the set and helped Susan up.

"What's it going to be, sweetie?"

As if completely unconcerned, he glanced down the rogue's gallery of faces—two camouflaged by full beards, the rest in varying degrees of hairiness.

And then Susan spotted Moon Rivers. Up close, he was nastier than at a distance. Thin, unhealthy looking, his un-pleasant features shaded by the peak of his cap, Moon was sitting all the way down the bar, separated by those few stools from the others. He was the only one not watching the game;

instead, he stared at them, fixedly at Jasper Gates, and not merely out of curiosity. There was, rather, an intense, single-minded belligerence about Rivers, as if Jasper had trespassed his property or stumbled across Moon's most awful shame.

But Jasper was right. Who were these clowns? She and Jasper had as much right to be here as anybody else.

"I'm going to have a vodka over the rocks with a twist of lemon."

"Good for you!" Jasper knocked wood to attract the attention of the bartender who stood gawking up at the TV, head thrown back in an unnatural angle. Jasper chuckled, not fondly. "I grew up in places like this, sweetie. I know these guys as I knew my own mother. *Hey!* How 'bout a little service down here!"

That would do it. The bartender turned, looked surprised, and ambled their way.

"Sorry, folks. Didn't see you come in." Which was a lie. "What can I get you?"

Jasper said, "The lady's having a vodka on the rocks . . . you got the Russian stuff? Some of that, friend. And I'll take a Jack Daniels with a glass of soda on the side. No ice. Okay?"

Poker-faced, at his own speed, the bartender got down two short glasses, piled ice in one, and set them on the bar. Stolichnaya bottle in hand, he poured a freestyle shot, then reached for the bourbon and did the same.

"Slice of lemon in the vodka, please." Jasper slapped a five-dollar bill down on the bar. "So what's cookin' in Petertown?"

Taking the money, the bartender finally looked at them. Susan noticed his resemblance to Moon Rivers, the same burned-looking, tight-skinned face, bony forehead, and sharp chin. Maybe they were related?

"Not a hell of a lot. You driving through?"

The son of a bitch, he knew who Jasper was.

"For crissakes, man, I own Big Sea! I'm Jasper Gates!" Taking the bull by the horns in every sense, Jasper shoved his hand out. "What's your name, pal?"

"Wiley . . . Wiley Casey."

He took Jasper's hand, not knowing what else to do. Jasper was at his overbearing best, or worst. He shook Wiley's hand enthusiastically.

"Glad to meet you, Wiley! I like your bar here."

Wiley nodded, but he wasn't comfortable with the flattery. Something was wrong; he didn't know what.

A husky, cigarette-ruined voice broke in. No surprise. Rivers had been waiting for an opening.

"*We* like our bar, mister!"

Jasper's eyes deployed, a tiny grin turning his mouth.

"That's good, pal. It'd be a poor place to drink in if you didn't like it."

"I ain't *your* pal." Jasper didn't answer, waited, coiled, until Rivers was forced to go on, his voice shaking, "And we don't give a good shit what you done at Big Sea!"

"Lady present!" Jasper called sharply. "Who're you, anyway?"

"Rivers!"

"I've heard of you."

Maybe this was what he'd been wanting to do, but anyway Moon sneered at Susan, "You're a friend of that bastard Dick Lyons!"

"So?"

Nonchalantly, Jasper said, "Maybe we could agree on that, Rivers."

"I don't need to agree with you, Gates. He's a bastard and you ain't no better."

Jasper shrugged and lifted his drink.

"I don't like you either, pal." Jasper drank off a goodly bit of bourbon, then, cold as ice, said quietly to Susan, "See what I mean?"

The words, which Moon had not heard but were obviously derogatory, sent him crashing off his stool. He strode toward them. The other patrons, Moon's friends or not, never took their eyes off the TV set. Moon Rivers must have a very bad reputation around town, whatever Emma Bristals thought of him.

Jasper remained calm, disturbingly calm, but Susan felt his small body tense. She wondered what she could hit Moon with, if it came to that.

Wiley tried to intervene, hardly forcefully.

"Okay, Moon, knock it off!"

"Shut up, asshole!" Moon came to a dead stop in front of Jasper and stood there, strung out, head down, glaring menacingly from beneath the peak of his cap.

Then, he howled, "Nobody gives a good shit about all

your money, Gates, so don't think you're some kind of hot
shit around here!''

"Piss off, pal!''

Moon was highly affronted that Jasper didn't flinch and
Susan supposed it was a miracle he didn't start punching.
Susan took a quick look at Jasper and at once understood why
not—something blazed red in Jasper's eyes, beat and throbbed
with the threat of vast destruction. Even a man as dense as
Moon Rivers would understand: It would not do to screw
around with Jasper Gates.

Immediately, Moon was out of bravado. His loud challenge
turned to clawless threat.

"And we don't want you selling Big Sea to a bunch of
fuckin' Japs!''

Jasper's voice cut like a precision blade.

"Who says I'm selling it to the Japs, you goddamn moron?
Now, go away. I'm talking to Wiley, not you. You better learn
some goddamn manners.''

"Like hell!" Again he turned on Susan. "And we don't
wanta be on your TV program either!''

Susan tried the Stolichnaya and found, to her disgust, that
Moon had made it taste bad. What would come next was
going to shock Jasper but she didn't have a choice. Susan
twisted around on the barstool, fixing her eyes scathingly on
Rivers. She spoke so quietly nobody except Rivers and Jasper
could hear.

"You ugly motherfucker, you won't ever be on TV, don't
worry. Now, get away from me before I kick in your goddamn
face!'' Moon backed up a little, but there was more to come.
"Emma Bristals must be desperate if she bangs an ugly
asshole like you.''

Moon's mouth opened but nothing came out.

Wiley broke in again, "Moon, leave 'em alone. Go sit
down!''

Dazed, Rivers shook his head, staring at Susan as if she
had indeed kicked him where it hurts. Then, he wandered
away. Glances were exchanged all along the bar.

But it was Jasper Gates who was most impressed.

"Sweetie—''

"Sorry, Jasper,'' she said lightly, "are you shocked?''

"No . . . well, you seem to know all the words.''

"Jasper, remember, I spent a lot of time with our armed
forces.''

Jasper downed his Jack Daniels.

"You leave me sort of breathless, sweetie."

Moon Rivers too. He had retreated to his end of the bar and was slumped in front of a fresh bottle of Coors Wiley had brought him, as a reward for good fellowship. Eventually, Moon lit a long, filtered cigarette and puffed on it bitterly.

Susan patted Jasper's arm. "Want to call it off, Jasper? See, I know these guys like the back of my hand. I was in the service with them."

Jasper smiled pallidly.

"You're mocking me, sweetie."

"I wouldn't mock you, ever. Are you disappointed in me?"

"Sweetie," he said, voice strained, "I want you to be a lady. That's all I want."

Jasper drove the car straight back to Big Sea, not tarrying for any more of the local sights. He even went over the bridge without reminding Susan how much it had cost and how, by rights, the Japanese should name it the Jasper Gates Flyover.

Jasper glanced at her once or twice, whistling tonelessly, then chuckling at nothing in particular.

Finally, as they pulled up outside the inn, he said, "Sweetie, you are really *something*! I never in a million years expected that nuclear explosion, believe me!"

"I explained, Jasper, people learn things, even women."

He turned sideways.

"Sweetie . . . Guy is right. Lyons *can* be bought. Offer him a half million."

"Me?"

"You, yes. You'll know how to do it. Hypothetically. In a way we can deny there was ever a real offer. Know what I mean?"

"I know what you mean, yes."

"Then do it."

Harry Teller had arrived. More than that, Harry Teller had stationed himself in the lobby so he couldn't miss her. And it didn't embarrass him in the least to trot right up and confront her and Jasper.

"Harry, what a surprise," Susan said, relieved to see him but probably showing only the tension. "Jasper, meet Harry Teller . . . Harry, Jasper Gates."

"Oh, yeah." Jasper shook Harry's hand, then looked up at him crossly. "Harry's your old journalist pal who's been writing about all my problems with the Indians, am I right?"

"Correct," Harry owned up, gladly. "Owner-operator of the *Rio Tinto Corsair,* Mr. Gates."

"Call me Jasper, even though you crucified me. No point being formal out here in the sticks. Hatchetman to hatchetee . . ."

Susan heard the almost audible resolution of Jasper Gates doing his best to be nice. There was not much hope. These two were of different species. Jasper would be unsympathetic to a man who made a living dredging up his secrets. He had no idea how to handle Harry.

And Harry, of course, he'd no real understanding of a Jasper Gates, or liking for him. Gates was the enemy, the man with the money *and* the secrets.

Where did Susan Channing fall?

She knew it then: not on Jasper's side.

"Well, Jasper," Harry said smoothly, "I'm not trying to do any kind of hatchet-job on you. Just reporting. The county is awash with rumors and it appears to me you're the only man who can straighten us out."

"Me?" Jasper laughed abrasively. "What the hell do I know?" Instinctively, he began to retreat, glancing at Susan for help he saw at once would not be forthcoming, and resenting it. "Say, I've got to get upstairs. I'm waiting for a couple dozen phone calls—L.A., Paris, you know.

"Bulgaria."

"Bulgaria? Yeah . . ." He nodded irritably. "Look, Harry, why don't you and Sue go have a drink and talk about old times and then, later, maybe we can get together. *Later.*"

Before either of them could think of a good reason why he should not go, Jasper whirled around and hurried for the stairs. They stood watching as he headed for the upstairs corridor. Susan didn't particularly want to be left alone with Harry. He was going to ask too many questions and Susan didn't have good answers. But she was stuck. She managed a smile.

"See how it is? He's impossible."

"Come on. Let's go in the bar and watch the sunset."

Susan didn't move. "I don't know if I want to, Harry."

"Why not? You heard Jasper's orders."

"Jasper Gates doesn't tell me what to do."

"Sounds to me like he does."

"Well, he doesn't!"

"C'mon, Miss Susie," he murmured, "what's the matter?"

All he had to do was touch her arm. Susan let herself be guided past the big stone fireplace and down into the bar area. Ralph's idea had been to create this instant tradition: that people *always* stopped by the Westward Ho! for a little drink at sunset.

"Not a bad idea, maybe," Harry had said, "homage to the Pacific and another day in the history of the universe gone forever." He sank into a chair. "Sit down, Miss Susie, take a load off your feet." Shrugging like he didn't give a damn, he queried, "So? What's up anyway?"

A smiling waitress hovered.

"Jasper and I were just down at the hotel . . ." She paused. Now he was going to ask her what she was doing out with Jasper Gates in the middle of the day and she'd say working on her interview. "I guess I'll try another vodka on the rocks."

Glancing up at the waitress, Harry said, "A Corona for me, Rita. Hold the lime. The hotel bar, eh? That's living dangerously. You wouldn't go when *I* asked you."

"As a matter of fact, we did have a slight confrontation with Moon Rivers."

"What's his problem—other than the obvious one?"

"I don't know," Susan said, "but we'd better take him off all the guest lists. He went after me because I'm supposed to be a big pal of Dick Lyons."

"And he hates Lyons."

"Gates scared him off. What a look! Malignant."

"It's Emma," Harry said. "It all revolves around Emma, our own Helen of Troy."

"Her husband is here. Ex. Guy Bristals."

"Ralph told me, yeah, and a Japanese guy."

"Ishira Guchi. Supposedly, Guchi is the Japanese party who's going to buy Big Sea. Why am I telling you this?"

"Why not? You're my buddy. Besides, you haven't told me anything I don't already know."

He smiled infuriatingly and nodded as she said, "You used the Lyons story after all, didn't you? You got it to *The New York Times*."

"That's right."

"How come, Harry?"

"I decided why not raise a little hell." He slid down in the booth and regarded her pleasantly. "Figured it'd pique your interest, Miss Susie... sorry, *Susan*. Might get you back out here. You left so goddamn suddenly."

"Or catch Jenny's interest."

"Jenny? How do you mean?"

"Jenny did a little talking," Susan said coolly. "She seems rather interested in you—to say the least. Bear Jay was touting a romance. She said you'd rendezvoused in San Francisco. Is that so?"

"Rendezvoused, holy moly!" He shook his head, shrugging and grinning at her again. "We bumped into each other on the street, for crissakes!"

"You're not... you gave me to understand you steered very clear of her."

"So I did. I do," he said. "Hey, take it easy, Miss Susie. All I said was she's an interesting woman. She is. An actress. Actresses are interesting, I would've said, wouldn't *you*?"

"Some."

"Is *that* why you took off out of here like a bat outta hell, Miss Susie?" Harry laughed softly. "Ha! I'm flattered. Pleased."

"You had an affair with her. She practically admitted it."

"I did not. She's stretching it—I didn't even try, not very hard anyway. I don't trust actresses."

"You bastard."

"What if I said I was lonely?" he needled. "What do you expect? You weren't around. I didn't know if you were still alive even. No, no, Miss... Susan. It's impossible, as I'm telling you. She's too fickle for me, too willful and moody. She's got the perfect match right now: Dick Lyons."

"You're so wise."

"I'm noted for it."

"The hell you are!" she said. "How do you explain Bear Jay then? They're thick as thieves."

"She's making Lyons pay for the dalliance with Lady Emma, that's clear as the nose on your... my face."

"Not serious?"

"Not for her. And he's half a nutcase. Doctor, heal thyself. I cannot figure him out at all."

"You're very clever, aren't you?" she said. "Our own little analyst."

A snide expression slid across his face.

"You think because I run a weekly country newspaper I'm a yokel."

Fortunately, the drinks came. Susan tasted her vodka while Harry poured beer into a tall pilsner glass.

"*And* you're pissed off at me because I didn't call, I suppose."

"I left a message on your machine in New York and you never called me back."

"You did not! There was no message."

Shaking his head vaguely, Harry said, "Doesn't matter." He held up his beer glass. "We have work to do. My pipeline says the Indians are planning something."

"*Lyons* and the Indians—"

"Yes, *Susan*, Lyons and the Indians. The dynamic of the situation, Susan—"

"Stop calling me Susan! And stop being such a smartass!"

"*Miss Channing*, what the goddamn hell am I suppose to call you?"

"Call me . . . Oh, I don't care. I'm angry with you, Harry!"

"Ha! So there's hope yet!"

"Harry . . ." What was she going to do with him? Nothing. Yes, she was going to go along. "You're right, we have work to do. Ishira Guchi, I am permitted to tell you, is the head of a Japanese trading company."

"I know."

"All-Nippon Prosperoso."

"I know."

"You're well informed for a yokel."

Harry continued to stare at her, straight-faced, controlling himself. He wanted to laugh, she knew it.

Instead, unabashedly, he asked, "So what's the deal with you and Gates, Miss Channing?"

"You're good-looking for an older man, Harry." That's what she was thinking, it slipped out. "Deal? No deal."

Yes, but there was, and should she tell him?

The Teller eyes were bright and much too alive, too clever, intuitive, knowing. For one thing, Susan felt he was seeing through her. And she didn't like it much.

"You seem mighty close."

"We're doing a piece, you know that. You know that his power and influence extend far beyond this place. Have you heard—just for instance—he's building the biggest cruise ship in the world?"

"I guess I heard it somewhere. So what?"

Wasn't that exactly how Jack and Artie had reacted?

"You don't think that's interesting, Harry?"

"Doesn't much interest me. We don't have a shipping section in the paper, even though we are the *Corsair*." She was tempted to slap his face. "Come clean, Susie!"

Susan lifted her glass, banging ice cubes against her front teeth, very conscious of her body and how it tensed and fell open to expose her and then, just as quickly, froze over.

Bitterly, she said, "Nate didn't leave me to you in his will, did he?"

"Now c'mon!" Harry muttered, coming forward in his seat. "That's not fair! If he did, then I've been a failure. For crissakes, Susie, we ran into each other again out of pure accident—doesn't that say anything to you? We went for a walk . . . remember? Doesn't that—"

"What should it say?"

"*Okay,* Miss Channing."

Grimly, Harry poured the rest of the beer into his glass and finished it with an impatient swig. He set the glass down and looked around.

"Can't we be friends, Harry?"

He mocked her, "Can't we just be friends, Harry?"

Daringly, she touched his hand with her fingertips.

"Well?" At least, he wasn't bouncing up and out of her life. "If I can't be your friend, how could I be anything more than that?"

"Lover."

"The way you say it, Harry. Hatefully. Aren't lovers permitted to be friends?"

"The most successful lovers hate each other except when they're in the sack."

"That's not true and you know it."

"It doesn't have to be true. It sounds right."

"You're dodging, Harry. I refuse to take you seriously. Everything is ultimatum with you, Harry. Either . . . or? Yes or no? Are you with me or against me?"

"*Well?*"

"Harry, I've got something to tell you."

"Finally," he growled.

"Harry, please. I need to tell you something important."

He waved for another beer, then settled back.

"Okay. Go ahead."

Susan looked around carefully, then said, "Gates wants me to offer Dick Lyons half a million dollars to lay off Big Sea."

"You can't do that."

He answered instantly. There was no doubt in his mind.

"I know, but he wants me to try it on him."

"Sure." Harry laughed nastily. "What would you say, Dick, old boy, if somebody, some faceless individual offered you a bundle to stop making trouble? How would you respond to such a situation, Dick, old boy? And Lyons is supposed to fall on his ass and roar, Man, if somebody would finally, after all these years, just offer me something I'd be outa here so fast—"

"Exactly."

"Well, you cannot touch it, Susie! That little fucker! Plausible deniability, they call it at The White House. Remember?"

"Could I forget?"

"If he wants to buy Lyons he should get his own boy to do it, Susie." Harry smiled. "But I must say I'd be very intrigued to know if The Great One would accept."

"Harry," she said, feeling she should say it, "Jasper *has* become something of a friend."

"So? Is that why he thinks you should do this for him?"

"No, no, nothing like that."

"Now, Miss Susie, now, now..."

She lied through her teeth, stared him down. He had to believe her, for there was no alternative to believing her. The alternative was preposterous. Susan was telling the truth as she saw it.

"I admire men like Jasper, Harry, and so do you! He's self-made and that rare thing—an honest businessman—"

"Honest!" he exclaimed. "He's selling Big Sea down the river."

"Harry, a sale to the Japanese could be good for Petertown."

He gazed at her so patiently that Susan went into a spin.

"Knock it off, Susie."

"What?"

"Look, I'm your friend too—very much so. I'm extremely interested in your welfare and well-being."

"Thank you so much—"

"Susie, you ask for friendship and I give you friendship. Can I take you to dinner or are you promised?"

"Are you staying over?"

"Yes, for the simple reason something might happen tomorrow morning . . . and other reasons."

"Where are you staying?"

"There's a leading question. So far, at least, my plan is to stay up at Ralph's."

"So far, you're saying."

"Yes."

"Leave it that way for a few minutes." Susan leaned toward him. "Camera crew, Harry? I'd feel like a horse's ass getting them up here for nothing."

"I would not mislead you," he said. "I *am* your friend."

"It's true," she said softly, "I think you really are. And I'm your friend too, Harry."

"Glory be," he said in that way he had that made her want to slap him or caress him, very gently and tenderly.

17

"Sod the sodding savages!"

Sir Guy Bristals sprayed saliva as he delivered himself of the judgment. Something must have happened upstairs to displease him mightily.

"Ah, my sort of people," he cried. "May I join you? Of course! Jasper G. said you two would be down here and I am *delighted* to see you both."

Susan had to introduce Harry and naturally they couldn't object when Bristals, not waiting for an invitation, spread his formless bulk next to Susan on the banquette facing the window and evening sea. Jasper, it appeared, had just agreed to a "powwow" with Dick Lyons—was this possible? All too possible—Bristals sneered. Jasper was going "to treat" with the savages, no, actually with this man Lyons who, by all accounts, was worse than a savage. Emma had once mentioned Richard Lyons, Bristals recalled, and not in a very complimentary way.

What Jasper should do, Bristals said, was simply sell Big Sea and fight about it afterwards. The cost of litigation would break the Indians' bank . . . and *damn* the adverse publicity. Bad publicity had a way of being devastating at the moment, and a week later gone and forgotten, like a bad smell. He should know, Sir Guy opined. It had happened often enough to the Bristals London Group, indeed most recently when he had taken over the company that put out the magazine *Fast Set* in New York City.

"I just met one of your people," Susan said. "An Ivy Eva Smith."

"Smith, yes," Bristals said with a smirk. He winked at Harry like a music-hall comedian. "Pleased to meet you Mr. Teller. I know of your newspaper—the *Corsair*."

Harry, proofed against this form of flattery, said rudely, "Oh, come on!" Susan wished he wouldn't do that, not at this particular juncture anyway, when so much was up for grabs. "You heard about the *Corsair* five minutes ago from Jasper Gates."

"Not so!" Bristals exclaimed. "I'll have you know, sir, that when I am about to visit a virgin territory . . ." He clucked. "I mean in the sense of it being my first visit here and in this sense virginal, as it were . . . before I set out, I have my people look up all the salient information on local media . . . radio stations, TV, newspapers, magazines, printing plants, newsprint resources, and the like. And, therefore, you see, Mr. Teller, and I have decided to call *you* Harry, I was briefed *by my people* about the *Corsair*, the flagship paper of Hispaniola County."

His eyes danced and for a second, just a second or perhaps two, Susan found herself rather liking the chubby knight.

"Circulation, one hundred and seventy-five thousand!"

Harry nodded, slowly, reluctantly.

"One hundred seventy. It's just a small county, Mr.—"

"Sir," Bristals barked, "but I want you to call me Guy. Both of you! We're friends, united in media. I will wager you that I can tell you the name *and* circulation of every newspaper on this planet, give or take a few thousand. What say you to a bit of bubbly, dear media associates?"

Susan nodded. She was easy if someone mentioned champagne—why hide it? Plus the fact, if Bristals was buying, she'd take what she could get.

"I'm sticking to the Corona," Harry said.

"Suit yourself, dear boy," Bristals wheezed. "Two people enjoy a bottle better than three."

Well, now? Harry was watching her surreptitiously, waiting for Susan to make a point, if there was a point to this.

"I'm surprised to hear Jasper has agreed to meet Lyons," she said.

Bristals agreed. "Not my idea of good sport. And nothing to do with me, I might add. I could *care less* about what happens to this place. Besides which," he added, "never negotiate, never compromise, never falter. My family motto: *Non Parlare* or words to that effect. My unions will testify to that. I've broken them all!"

Bristals laughed moistly and slapped Susan on the knee, as if to get across the message he was only joking, or at least exaggerating.

"So? What does bring you to Big Sea, Big Guy?" Harry asked.

"Dear boy! Jasper G. insisted I have a look at his new venture. And here I am!"

"Come, come, Sir Guy."

Predictably, Bristals giggled. "Oh, you two newsies will get it out of me, won't you? If you insist—*entre nous*, yes? I'm really here to meet Doctor Guchi."

"So you're not taking a piece of Big Sea?" Harry followed up.

Maybe, eventually, she and Harry would make a good team. He was good at this; so was Susan. Hadn't she been doing *Hindsight* long enough? A smile, the proper question, and they dissolved, the hardest of them, and Sir Guy Bristals, being so full of himself, would be one of the easiest.

"No, dear boy, heavens forbid!"

As Sir Guy downed his first glass of champagne, Susan felt free to ask, "Tell us about you and Doctor Guchi."

"Ah, *that* would be telling!" he said playfully.

Which was what she wanted.

Bristals emptied a second glass of champagne into his large pink mouth, then leaned back, his heavy eyelids half-closing, cheeks quivering.

"Briefly this, no sense keeping it secret: Bristals London Group intends to spread its wings in the Orient . . . in Japan, to be more precise," Bristals snapped. "People say it cannot be done but Guy Bristals has heard those words before . . . and ignored them!"

Despite herself, impressed, Susan said, "Is there any hope? Would the Japanese government allow it?"

Harry was at least as doubtful. "Hell, Guy! We have a tough time just selling them citrus products. You've practically got to go to war to get tariffs lowered."

"Amen . . . Amen!" Bristals agreed. "However, we can but try. And I am hopeful that Doctor Guchi will be able to help. Do you *begin* to understand?

Did Guchi have that kind of influence? He'd have to be a powerhouse to help Bristals on this one.

"Of course, it must need be a joint venture," Bristals said intensely, glancing at Susan as if to tell her to pay attention. Was there some subliminal advice she was not receiving? Then she got it, loud and clear. "Frankly, dear girl, I'm counting on you to help me in this."

"*Me?* How?"

Smiling wisely, tolerantly, Bristals suggested, "The Japanese know your program."

"Certain pieces have run there, yes. But—"

"*Darling* Miss Channing! You are *very well known* in Japan! Don't minimize! As well known, I'm told, as some American rock groups."

Susan smiled back at him thinly.

"Thank you for making the comparison."

"Not an insult, believe me!" Bristals slapped his hand down on hers. Harry chuckled throatily and Susan wanted to tell him to just shut up, if he hadn't anything to add. "You *can* help me with Doctor Guchi, Susan."

Harry interrupted rudely. "Is this guy a doctor, or is that just a manner of speaking?"

"He *is* a doctor of business systems, or something."

"*Quite!*" Bristals glared, then said frankly, "Dear Susan Channing, one of my motives in involving Bristals London Group in North American Network is to have access to your special abilities."

Special abilities? It was a Bristals flaw that most everything he said had a double meaning.

As Harry rolled his eyes, Susan repeated, "You're taking over NAN to get *me*? Please!"

"Believe it!" Again, Bristals showered saliva. "And also believe I am determined to get a foot in the Japanese open-door. I believe very deeply in the Pacific Basin, and in the overriding position of Japan. Good God, the Japanese are far more powerful than if they'd won the war. And working with the Chinese in the next century, my dears? Well, I hesitate to speculate. . . ." Sir Guy paused to breathe raspily and help himself to more champagne. Then he owned up proudly, "I, too, am an empire-builder. Bristals Group is all-powerful in London. Bristals Group is well represented in continental Europe. We are moving ahead briskly in this country. Next, the Orient. With a power base in Tokyo, there is no city in the Far East that Bristals London Group cannot storm. *This is my belief!*"

Susan's reaction, she supposed, was respectful but, as for Harry, Bristals glanced at him coldly, not liking Harry's attitude one bit. Harry responded in kind—by lifting the Corona bottle to his lips, pointedly not using the glass, determined to outredneck anybody in the place.

"You *could* also be part of this, young man!"

"Who, me?" Harry pointed at himself. "How would I fit into such a grand scheme, Guy?"

"You've worked in the Far East!"

"I have a newspaper to run."

"Harry, you could at least listen to the man."

"I am listening."

"No champagne, Harry, are you sure? Another beer?"

"No, thanks."

Harry muttered something about not wanting to pamper his taste buds. Harry could be such an almighty pain in the ass!

Bristals shrugged dismissively, put his glass down, and reached into an inside pocket of the rumpled white linen jacket—he'd already shucked his London duds—and withdrew a fresh cigar, still comfy in its airtight metal tube.

"As to your newspaper, Harry," he said in lordly manner, "that's easily taken care of. For some considerable time, I've considered acquiring a chain of American provincial papers . . . such as yours. Countless numbers of them struggle year-in, year-out to make ends meet. I would suppose that great savings could be achieved—re: purchase of newsprint, per example—by operating in concert, rather than independently, as you do." Harry had gone rigid. "Harry, tell me the return on *your* investment? One percent . . . two percent? I'll wager it's no more than three percent."

He'd hit where it hurt, right in the bull's eye; you knew that from the defensive tone of Harry's reply.

"Nobody ever said you were going to make a fortune running a county weekly, Guy. If I wanted to make a fortune, I'd sell used cars."

"Yes, yes, dear boy, of course! God knows, we are in this business because *we love it!*"

"And to make enough to buy diesel fuel for our yacht."

A cheap shot, but Sir Guy said calmly, "That too."

"Sorry," Harry said, a bit contritely, "I . . . well, I've got nothing but admiration for what you've built. I know how tough it is. It's just, we're in a different league."

"Of course we are!" Bristals grimaced. "It's of no real importance what you think of my properties, Harry, but I am happy to hear you say what you just did. There is another person," he said balefully, "who happens to work at NAN, who has a far different opinion."

"At NAN?"

"Oh? You don't recall a piece your colleague Jack Godfrey wrote for one of the journalist organs?"

"No, I don't recall," Susan lied.

"Well, I will tell you! Godfrey heaped abuse on my London evening paper, saying all my success is due to T and A."

"I didn't know he'd even written such an article," she lied again.

"Dear girl, accept my word that he wrote it. Also accept my word that I do not think kindly of Mr. Jack Godfrey."

Susan said faintly, "Jack tends to express himself in hyperbole."

"I'm sure he does."

Bristals placed the still-unopened cigar tube on the table next to his napkin. Belching politely behind his hand, he continued. "I've seen any number of *Hindsight* shows, Susan, and in my *humble* opinion, Jack Godfrey adds *very little* to the format." He looked straight at her, his eyes narrow with decision. "I certainly expect a sensible management team and an astute producer, such as your Arthur Fineman, would recognize that *Hindsight* can do better, and with better cost control, with one, *not* two anchors."

Nervously, Susan tried to argue. "But Sir Guy, the way we've operated, it's become our M.O., method of operation—"

"I know what it means," he interrupted imperiously, "and no, the show most definitely can go on without Jack Godfrey! An unnecessary and *expensive* luxury!" Bristals nodded for emphasis, then went on, astonishingly, "For instance, I would far prefer a Harry Teller sitting in that spot, if we had such a spot, than the present incumbent—and Harry has no TV experience whatsoever!''

''I don't do TV,'' Harry murmured.

Susan was speechless. In truth, there was nothing to say. Bristals had decided. Jack was out, and nothing would convince him otherwise. But Harry? Was Bristals serious? It wouldn't be beneficial to one's health to ask. As they had feared, disaster loomed. If there *had* been any hope, Susan could've argued that *Hindsight* was Jack and Arthur's show, that she'd come on board only later, initially as an experiment, one that, fortunately, had worked.

But Harry? Harry wasn't talking. He just sat there, smiling tightly.

To her relief, despite the peculiar smile, he was not making light of this. He worked the Corona bottle with his fingers. If she asked, of course, Lucky Harry would murder Sir Guy for her. Lucky Harry: he'd removed himself from the fray. It was a ruthless way of life. Dog eat dog didn't begin to cover it; when so much money was involved, palace revolutions such as this pending one at NAN tended to be very bloody. Think of it, Harry, at *The Rio Tinto Corsair,* a man such as yourself is immune, his own boss; Harry hired, he fired. He'd be crazy to go to work for Sir Guy Bristals. He wouldn't even consider it.

''Well,'' Susan murmured, stating the obvious, ''judging by the way you're talking, Sir Guy, the rumors must be true: you're taking over NAN.''

Bristals preened.

''*Aye,* ready or not, NAN is in for a facelift. Of course, I'd be present in a minority position, due to your strange laws vis-à-vis media control.''

''The rumors have been rampant, I can tell you that.''

''And I suppose everybody is *pissing* their pants,'' he said happily, ''as no doubt they would be if they've been listening to Simon Hayford on the subject. My informants tell me Simon H. has been spreading atrocity stories about kindly Guy Bristals. Ahem!''

With that, smirking, Bristals prepared to enjoy his cigar. Unscrewing the cap from the metal tube, he extracted the Havana-rolled weed, releasing the pungent aroma of choice, Communist-oriented tobacco, directly from Cuba, embargo or not. Sir Guy slipped and slid the cigar through his lips, like a carwash, wetting, soul kissing the Marxist-Leninist product, prelude to the prescribed lighting ceremony.

After the cigar was afire, Bristals dribbled more information and this next bit might have had Susan Channing's address written on it.

"It seems," he confided, "that at long last I shall be able to acquire August Hugo Blick's holdings in NAN. Blick has, in the past, been unwilling to give up his seat on the board but, finally, my people and his appear to have struck a deal. As a consequence, if—I emphasize *if*—all goes well, Bristals London Group will hold the largest minority interest in your company, Susan. I stress *minority* which, I trust, will keep me clear of your FCC rules. Elsewise," he said elfishly, "Sir Guy may be forced to become an American citizen...."

"Like Rupert Murdoch," Harry said.

"Exactly. But we shall see. In any event, *if* we are fortunate, BLG will carry the day." Bristals sucked smoke. "And, Harry, I have no reason to think citizenship would be refused. I have friends, well placed indeed within the present administration. My American media properties, as a matter of fact, have come down very supportively of this administration and very anti the Democrats. Adept political contributions of a different sort have also not gone unnoticed—"

"Guy!" Harry eyed him sternly. "Be advised: *Nothing* is off-the-record."

Smiling, Bristals went right on. "I could bring a good deal to this country in the way of culture."

There was no false modesty about Guy Bristals. He mugged profusely, knowing he was tantalizing them. At the very least, Susan thought, they should denounce him for smoking Cuban cigars.

"*Heaven.*" Bristals sighed, blowing smoke, squeezing the cigar fondly in his fingers, and then, out of the blue, having paced himself in the best theatrical manner, dropped the big one. "Mr. Blick, I understand, is a very dear friend of yours."

Harry was watching... Harry was alert and listening.

"He's my former father-in-law."

Mischievously, or so it might have been interpreted, Bristals said, "He resisted us for months. Then, suddenly, in the past week..." He snapped his fingers. "*Poof!* It was done. Simon H., as you probably know, has been begging Blick to stick it out. Because, without August Blick, Hayford is nothing! And deserves to be nothing.''

So, Susan thought, their worst fears were substantiated. Hayford was a dead duck. Susan wondered if it was also true that he'd built for himself a beautiful "golden parachute"? Hopefully. Simon should be good for at least two or three million in good-bye money. Jack always said he wouldn't be pushed out for anything less than one million and Susan figured, at that rate, her going-price should be in the vicinity of three-quarters of a million. But, wasn't that supposed to be beside the point? Weren't they in this for more than money? Though a Guy Bristals might not believe it.

The man, it seemed, was still not done with her. Finally, Susan had to wonder just how friendly his intentions were.

Hidden within a made-in-Cuba smokescreen, Sir Guy continued insinuatingly, "My hope is *your fiancé* might join me in the NAN endeavor, but he cannot decide yea or nay, so preoccupied is he with the *bloody, sodding* savages! Another four-point-five percentile of voting support would not hurt my cause."

"My fiancé?"

Harry Teller stopped being an innocent bystander. He thumped the beer bottle on the table, face flaring with irritation, then anger.

"Jasper G., of course," Bristals said, "or am I mistaken? Would that I were! What do *you* say, Harry? Better if this beautiful *gel* stayed on the free market, *what*?"

"I say I'm going for a walk," Harry said with a growl.

He was already out of the booth. And all Susan could think was: No, it just wasn't in the cards. Susan wouldn't let him out of her eyes, though. He wavered, flushed, stared back at her in dismay. He couldn't believe it. What had she done this time?

"I gotta go, Susie, I gotta go for a walk."

"Okay, so go."

Harry looked away. He nodded at Bristals, then once more, sideways, at Susan.

"I'll see you later."

"Yes." The good-bye was interminable. Why didn't he just turn around and get going? "See you later . . . pal."

Then Harry did go and Susan wanted to shout after him, *Hey, you forgot to pay for the drinks!* But she didn't and he kept going, finally disappearing around a corner in the lobby.

Pleased with himself, Bristals stuttered, "Did I . . . uh . . . say something untoward, dear girl? Your friend Harry is gone off in high dudgeon."

"He gets that way."

Bristals didn't worry about it. As if relieved of a great burden, he turned his attention to the last of the champagne.

By then, Susan was sympathizing with Emma, Bristals's former wife. As slovenly as Emma had appeared to be, marriage to such a slob as this would've been a terrific ordeal. Was it possible to imagine, for instance, actually going to bed with the lardass?

Indolently, Bristals lolled back, tapped ash off the chewed-over cigar, and looked at Susan with a patronizing kind of amusement.

"You mentioned dear Ivy Eva," he mentioned. "I rogered Ivy for quite some considerable time."

"I thought perhaps you had," Susan said dryly.

"Does it show? If I do say so, darling, when I roger a *gel*, they stay rogered." Susan's disapproval didn't register. Bristals went on heartily. "Jasper looks a randy little bugger. But I would've thought a woman like you, Susan Channing, in the prime of life, well, that you'd prefer something a bit livelier. . . ."

Her reaction was more vehement this time. Susan shrugged her shoulders violently, distastefully.

But on he pressed.

"I think you are wonderful! I quite worship your style, speculating to myself whether you'd have been finer as a print, rather than TV, journalist. Unable to decide, I watch your shows whenever I can. Your camera presence is quite remarkable, your photogenity wondrous—though Godfrey is a turnoff, as I've said." Bristals reached boldly for Susan's hand. "I want us to be *very* close. I have *big* plans."

"Do you?"

Susan responded coolly, cautiously, thinking that, after all, there was no way she could help Jack if she poisoned the well.

"Yes! I *want* you to be part of Bristals London Group's Pacific Phase. I'd like you to get *very close* to Doctor Guchi." Close? Bristals nodded, with the grin of an overfed cobra. "We want the good doctor to think well of us. I'm told you know what to do."

Finally, there it was.

"I don't understand what you mean," Susan said frigidly.

Bristals blinked disingenuously.

"I think it was J. Gates who *indicated* you were the most brilliant woman he had ever met."

"Somehow, I don't think that's what you're trying to say."

"Very well," Bristals said, dropping the surface gentility, resorting to the language with which they were both more familiar. "The word is that you are totally ruthless, no-holds-barred when it comes to getting into a story. Think of this as a story!"

Somehow, Bristals had become convinced that Susan Channing was as skilled a courtesan, in this case geisha, as she was interviewing for *Hindsight*. Were these the special abilities to which he had referred only minutes before? And if so, where had he gotten such an idea about her? What *had* AHB told Jasper Gates and Jasper passed along to Bristals? What, indeed? It was not as though Susan performed tricks. AHB might be famous for cunnilingus, or Emma, Lady Bristals, as a fellatiste, but Susan Channing? Boring old Susan Channing favored the boring old missionary position. Of course, she threw herself into it with truly missionary zeal, if that counted.

Susan began to do the proper thing. She collected her pocketbook and slid toward the end of the leather booth.

"I think it's time I go see how Jasper is doing."

Or find Harry and try to explain to him the inexplicable.

"My dear," Bristals protested, "take what I say as a compliment! I admire your pragmatic mind. We're of a kind, we two!"

"Compliments like that I don't need, Sir Guy."

Good! She had done well, put things on a strictly personal basis. It had nothing to do with Jack or Artie or the show, the way Susan Channing reacted to his personality.

Bristals's hand shot forward, grabbed at her thigh. His fingers dug in.

"Hear me out!" His voice was urgent, commanding. "My dear Susan, I consider you the quintessential anchorperson, I repeat, *quintessential*. We have a great future *together* at NAN."

"Really? On what basis, Sir Guy? My *special abilities*, whatever it is you mean by that?" Bristals tried to smile but his oily face showed mere puzzlement. People didn't talk to him this way. Susan plugged away, testily. "I think you should be in touch with my agent."

"I shall be, darling," Bristals said. "I will want to discuss

with your agent the status of your current contract with NAN.
I will warn him in no uncertain terms that I will not tolerate
any attempt to break that contract. You may scream and yell,
Miss Channing! But it *is* true. I am taking NAN in order to
have access to *your talents*!''

''Now it's talents, is it?''

''Be insulted, if you wish!'' Bristals had removed his hand.
He stared at her like a blowfish. ''What I am acquiring is
you! You, your person.''

''Excuse me. I'm going upstairs.''

Susan managed to get out of Westward Ho! without trip-
ping and falling. Sir Guy Bristals had made one hell of a
mess of things. But Susan guessed she had too.

There was no sign of Harry in the lobby.

Well, bother Harry Teller! She crossed rapidly, not slowing
down until she had climbed the shallow steps and reached the
second floor. Bristals had bought her, had he? If he had
bought Susan Channing, it could mean only one thing: that
August Hugo Blick had *sold* Susan Channing to Jasper Gates,
who had sold her to Sir Guy Bristals of London, England.

Perfect! And they said slavery was dead!

Bristals would have to fire her too. But Susan accepted
that. The risk was everpresent; it came with the territory. One
minute you were up and the next you were on your ass.
Maybe she should have kept her mouth shut. What, then,
would Bristals have offered for her cooperation in the matter
of Ishira Guchi, especially if she became solely responsible
for getting the Bristals group into Japan? Surely, that would've
been worth, as they said, plenty.

Angrily, Susan punched the bell at Jasper's door. His voice
finally came, a bellow, when Susan hit the bell a second time.

''It's open!''

Once inside, Susan stopped and stared at him—Jasper was
at the table by the window—trying to decide whether it was
really possible he was simply using her. Did he bother to look
up, possibly to ask her what was wrong? No.

His greeting was a frustrated grumble and before Susan had
time to ask what was his problem, he exclaimed, ''*Don't ask!*
Son of a bitch Lyons was here, he and his faithful Indian
sidekick, Beaumont Custerd. *Don't ask!*''

Coldly, Susan didn't ask, she said, ''You offered him the
money.''

Jasper's eyes bugged.

"I had a wild idea at first that you'd already tried it," he said, "then I realized there wasn't time. He called five minutes after I got upstairs and I'm thinking, man, that is fast work on Sue's part—"

"I haven't talked to him."

"Now I find out." Jasper shook his head groggily. He was in shirtsleeves, not surprisingly rolling a glass in his hand. Ice cubes clinked. "Lyons is a steamroller. I should have brought my bodyguard."

"Where's Mr. Dudley?"

He scowled.

"Gone to San Francisco to collect my lawyer, whom we're going to be needing desperately. Dudley's not a bodyguard anyway. Lyons could drive a man stark, staring mad, sweetie. Like being in a barrel for two, going over Niagara Falls."

"So . . . what happened?"

"Nothin' . . . that's just it. Nothin'—outside of damn near a whole bottle of gin down his gullet. We didn't get anyplace. Here I am, ready to make all kinds of concessions, anything to get them off my back, like an elephant trying to shake a flea off his ass. But no way! The Basket tribe has got to share in everything at Big Sea and, if we sell, mind you, the buyer has got to guarantee a certain number of jobs for the Baskets, and medical care, scholarships. *Shit!*" Jasper bellowed. "Impossible! Nobody could go for an open-ended deal like that."

It was immediately obvious to Susan and should have been to Jasper too—Lyons didn't want a settlement. The demands were too outlandish. He wanted to keep it going.

"Ego, Jasper."

"Tell me about it! Newspaper coverage. And . . ." He frowned at her. "TV too, I have no doubt."

"And? If you don't go for it?"

"Lyons, very calmly, you know, tells me they're already at the county court for an injunction against any further development, or negotiation, for example with Shira, unless the Baskets are part of it. Highway robbery, sweetie, don't you get it? Months, years." Jasper laughed mockingly. "In the meantime we've got all this money tied up . . . not only money, but the sheer goddamn aggravation of it, when I got better things to do with my time. *Chickenshit!*" he bawled.

In that case, she thought, why sell? You might reasonably expect that building Indian Island into a world-class resort

would interest Jasper Gates. After all, he was in that kind of
business. He should buy out AHB; August would be interested only in retrieving his investment anyway, his philosophy being money in, money plus profit out. August wasn't interested in building anything.

Some day, Susan thought, vindictively, the scandal of August Hugo Blick would be exposed to the world. Mister Anonymous Moneybags would be revealed. And, if Jasper Gates was hurt in the fallout, so be it.

"Son of a bitch, sweetie," he wailed, sweating from the bourbon, "and right in the middle of this I get a phone call from Varna, Bulgaria, from my engineering *maven*, Chuck Detroit, and you know what?" Before she could say no or even shake her head, Jasper shouted, "Chuck says if we launch the SS *Freckles* the way she's shaping up now, she'll roll over and sink! Sink at launch, sweetie, and nothin', sweetie, *but nothin'*, can be more humiliating for a ship owner. Like having your horse stop for a leak in the middle of a race."

Susan laughed. She couldn't help it.

"What's' it?" Jasper cried, not seeing the humor, then grinning uncertainly, as if she'd caught him in a good one. "This is serious, sweetie, sometimes I wonder if it's worth living, continually being harassed. I may just . . . one of these days I'm just gonna cash in my chips and to hell with all the flak! *I'll retire!* Y'ever think of retiring, Sue?"

"Lately, a lot," she muttered.

Like in the last fifteen minutes. Sir Guy Bristals was enough to make one consider it.

"Sweetie, I'm hamstrung," Jasper admitted. "Can't you do what I asked you, or is too late? What about having a word with Lyons's wife?"

"They're not speaking, Jasper, and I'm not going to do it anyway," she told him.

"Lyons needs help. Here I think we're gonna get to the point, you know—money, *wampum*, shiny beads, or whatever. And Lyons doesn't want to hear about it! I begged your help, sweetie," he reminded her.

"Jenny's given up on him. She's . . . it seems she's in love with another man."

"And I don't blame her. And just as well. Jenny Driver better get back to acting, where she belongs, and *fuck* that psychotic Lyons.'' Jasper tilted his head. ''I was engaged to an actress once, didn't know that, did you?''

''No.''

''Yes, soon after World War the Two. Her name was Davis. You're thinking Bette. No, Jeff, they called her Jeff for Jeffiner. She was fast, sweetie, very fast. Guy asks her if she wants a quickie, before he can get the cork out of the bottle, she's got her panties off. . . .''

Jasper guffawed.

''You told me that one once or twice before, Jasper.''

''No matter.''

''Look, Jasper,'' Susan said impatiently, ''I'm a little out of sorts . . .''

''I *know* you are, sweetie,'' he said, ''Mother Nature's way of saying, Hi, remember me?''

''I do not mean that. I'm talking about your piggish friend Bristals.''

''What? *What* happened?''

''I'm saying, I don't feel like talking. I say this, Jasper. You're spinning your wheels. You know you won't get any place with Dick Lyons. And I am *not* going to offer him a bribe!''

''Thanks. Some friend. I appreciate it very much.''

''Isn't there some other way? What about Guchi?''

''What about him? What's he supposed to do? Jesus, sweetie, people blame the Japs for everything, but it ain't their fault if Americans are stupid!''

''What I'm getting at is that Guchi would look like a hero if he could do a deal with the poor, downtrodden American Indian . . .'' Jasper's eyes warmed, and even more when she half promised, ''And wouldn't *that* be a hell of a story, Jasper?''

He liked it, but Susan saw he was reluctant to admit she might have something there.

''Make him look good?'' he said doubtfully, ''him and the Indians, all happy as clams? They wouldn't have looked so good, PR-wise, since Pearl Harbor? You think so? Well, talk to him, Sue!'' Jasper glanced anxiously at his telephone. ''See how it is, sweetie? I spend half my life waiting for Bulgaria, never mind about that . . . *Lyons*? You gonna make yourself a drink?''

''I had champagne with Guy Bristals.''

''Say, what happened there anyway, sweetie?''

"He just behaved like a goddamn pig! Made all sorts of suggestions which I really found disgusting. Particularly from him. He's as ugly as a . . . I don't even know what."

"I know that," Jasper chuckled. "He's as ugly as I don't know what either." He laughed loudly, then stopped. "You really could do me a favor with Shira. If you were nice to him . . ."

"I was nice to him. I am nice to him."

"Yeah, I know you were," he responded unsteadily, "but . . ."

"And I will continue to be nice to him, Jasper."

"And Shira's just wild about you, sweetie. He collects all your shows he can get his hands on. Maybe, between the two of you . . ." Jasper, amazingly enough, was slightly embarrassed. "As for me, I'm about ready to walk away from this mess. I'll just let it take a dive, absorb the loss and to hell with it. That'll teach them they buttered their bread on the wrong side. And it'd be a lot easier than getting hauled over the coals by Lyons and his faithful Indian assistant."

"Do what you want," Susan said distantly.

"Aw! Sweetie! C'mere." Jasper held out a hand to her. "Too much with the business. I forgot. I'm sorr-ee."

Susan remained well away. She was not about to fall for that all over again.

"Crazy about you, sweetie."

She stood her ground.

Jasper leaned forward to put down his glass, preparatory, Susan feared, to making a rush for her.

"Hots for you, sweetie," he whispered, "*mucho hots*! Soon's I get this Bulgarian stuff out of the way, I'm going to talk turkey to you—"

"I've never been to Turkey, Jasper."

"Hey, hey, you know what I mean!"

"Do I?"

All the way across his room, Susan fancied she could smell the Jack Daniels, the marshmellowy cooked-out, wafting scent-flavor of the Kentucky brew.

Jasper had gotten to his feet. Susan backed to the door.

"I'm seeing you later, aren't I, Jasper?"

He was at her before she could escape. His nose struck her bosom level and he burrowed in. Fortunately, she was well protected by the fluffy jogging suit. But he tried to get his hands underneath. Susan for a second, irritably, considered pulling him to her, smothering him in her abundance. What a way to go, he'd laugh. Then lose his breath.

"Jasper," she murmured, "please. I think . . . I might be sick . . ."

He jumped back.

"I understand . . . understand, sweetie. Is that the effect I have on you?"

He was joking. She was too. She smiled fraily.

"You know better . . ."

The telephone rang. It could not have picked a better time to do so.

Jasper spun around.

"Bulgaria!" he cried.

18

Lyons was drunk. Smashed was the squire of Rancho Mondo. He leaned in toward Susan, a hand on each side of the door frame, gazing at her blearily.

"What are you doing here, Dick? You're plastered."

"So I am and so what, Sue? Ask me in."

She looked him over. He was drunk enough, perhaps, to be harmless. Or was he drunk at all? Even cold-sober, Dick Lyons had often seemed to be under the influence of something or other. That, supposedly, had been one of his attractions: his mad, driven, possessed vitality, his—let's admit it—charisma. Unfortunately, the years and bad habits had robbed Lyons of his ruddy-faced good looks; the thick foliage of reddish tinged John Brown beard couldn't hide the fact he was no longer vibrant and handsome.

But better to have him inside than outside screaming if she closed the door in his face.

Lyons waddled past her.

"Reason I'm here, Sue, is to advise you to get ready for the fireworks. Big doings in the morning."

"The meeting with Jasper didn't go well, did it?"

"No, it did not!" Lyons looked around. "What have you got to drink?"

"Nothing. Not a drop." Susan stood across from him, more distant than the four yards that separated them, her arms folded across her chest. "What's going to happen?"

"Ah . . ." His laugh was disorderly, like most of his conduct. "That'd be telling, hon. Just giving you fair warning. Be ready to roll 'em, bright and early."

"I don't have a crew with me, Dick."

"Better arrange one then."

"Did you warn Jasper too?"

"What! Do I look crazy?"

Lyons was enjoying himself, wasn't he? How long since he'd played white knight, champion of the little man? Yes, yes, he'd be saying next, it was like old times. A cause! My kingdom for a cause!

"And you'll tell him anyway," he added scornfully. "Aren't you his girlfriend now, his mistress? Isn't that what he told me?"

"No, he did not! What he's been telling everybody who'll listen is that I'm his *fiancée!*"

Pulling at his beard, delighted to shake her up, he crowed, "Hey, little Suzette, the same thing, isn't it? Fiancée equals mistress in this day and age. Suzette, it's Dick here, remember? *Big Dick?*"

"Don't talk like a fool."

How dare he remember something that had been in no way memorable, if he was referring obliquely to an episode of so long ago Susan was positive everybody, especially a man with alcohol-related brain damage, must have forgotten? Susan herself had put it out of mind, beyond recalling that she probably could've had Dick Lyons arrested for rape if she'd wanted to expose herself to the attendant embarrassment. It had happened, God knows how, somehow. Susan had been careless with Dick, in the back of a car, in the dark, in the woods, in Westchester County where Jenny and he had been living then. Lyons had been taking Susan to catch a suburban train back to New York, or something like that, she couldn't remember exactly, except she had been a lot younger and Lyons had not yet completely lost it.

"I was in the bar," he said spitefully. "I saw *you*, with the Englishman."

"Bristals."

"I'm friendly with his wife, you know." Lyons fidgeted; he wanted that drink. "Or ex-wife, whatever she is."

"Jesus, Dick, I do know that! She came calling when I was at your house. Don't you remember?"

Sure, he'd recall something from ten or twelve years ago and forget last week. So typical; so tiresome. His brain was rotting.

He shrugged indifferently. But, for a second, worry slicked his eyes. He wasn't sure at this point what he did remember and didn't.

"What were you doing talking to that slob anyway?"

"He's buying the network, Dick, or so it seems. What should I tell him, to get lost?"

"They ought to run him out of the country!"

"Why don't you go on home, Dick? You've got to drive that awful road, don't forget."

"So" he demanded balefully. "And from you, little Suzette, I get no drink?"

"I haven't got any drinks here."

"Well . . ." Undecided how to proceed, he muttered, "You heard what I said about tomorrow?"

"I don't know whether to take you seriously."

"It's going to be very, very visual, I guarantee it!"

"You *are* known to be a publicity hound."

"Yeah." He nodded, eyes dancing out of focus. "Sure I am. But I wouldn't kid you, would I? I'd know better than that."

"I wouldn't come near you again if you gave me a bum steer."

"And have I ever pissed on you before? Haven't I always delivered?"

"Yes, I guess."

"Suzette, you know what I'm like," Lyons mumbled, suddenly sounding gooey. "Remember our times together?"

"Times together? You mean *time,* don't you? One time, Dick, and you forced me."

"Forced you?" He flung his head back in mock outrage, pointing the unkempt beard at her. "That's a good one. *You* handed Dick the apple, Suzette! You couldn't wait for me to take the first bite."

"You are crazy! You pushed me into the backseat, Dick."

"I *helped* you into the backseat, Suzette." He smiled

knowingly. "Never mind, it doesn't matter now that you took advantage of Old Dick."

"Why *don't* you go home? I invite you to leave!"

"No, no. Sue, *you know* I'm a straight-shooter, especially with you. You *know* I don't give a damn about anything, or anybody, unless they're on the up and up. I'm untamed, Suzette," he announced, "and untamable."

"Untamable for sure."

Next, he fixed on her that disturbing, disarmingly blind stare, as if he were looking through her, or didn't see her at all.

"Your friend Gates was getting ready to offer me a bribe, you know," he said sadly, his mouth twisted. "He didn't quite. Good thing. I'd blow him out of the water. He'd do that only because he thinks I'm past it."

"Why should he?"

He laughed cynically.

"Maybe because I am."

"If you mean you're no longer a public figure, Dick," she suggested, "you can start suing for slander."

He stared at her, nodding almost menacingly, the eyes flaring and dimming and flaring again.

"That's a point. Suzette, please . . . I thought we were on the same wavelength." Again, his attention wandered. "You know, I always thought, if you hadn't been such a pal of Jenny's . . ." He grinned. Then, as Susan was about to insist that he leave, to tell him frankly that she was worn out and, moreover, believe it or not, bored by all this, he asked, "Where is Jenny, by the way?"

"What do you mean, where's Jenny?"

His disorganized look disappeared with a single blink of his mad eyes.

"I mean . . . she's gone. And I understand she's checked into the Petertown Hotel."

"Or has she gone East like she was planning to?"

"Not if she's at the Petertown Hotel."

"Well . . . I don't know anything about it, Dick. I didn't know she left or that she's moved into the hotel. Are you surprised?"

If Jenny Driver had decamped, it suggested to Susan that she'd committed herself fully to Bear Jay.

"No, I'm not surprised, the way things are going. You'd take Jenny's side, wouldn't you?"

Susan nodded. "Yes, I probably would."

"And if Jenny did take off, you'd say about time she did, right? That's what you're saying?"

"Well . . ."

"Even though she started this thing with Bear Jay long before I—"

"Emma?"

"Long before that, Suzette." He sighed. "Emma was just my desperation move."

"Oh, c'mon."

"Jenny *always* banged around, Sue, you didn't know that, did you? Of course not. It was always: sweet innocent Jenny! That's the way those people are. They're a gypsy breed, actors are. And it was always old Dick, the lecher and roué! But, lo and behold—*Now* we find out!"

"Oh yeah?"

"I guess there's not hope for *us*, Suzette. . . ."

"Nope."

"Just as well." He sighed again. "I've got my work cut out for me."

"Good. It's better to keep busy."

"Well? It *is* good, Susan!" he said stridently. "Somebody's got to do it. Besides, I am just nuts about the two Custerds. You've seen Beau—well, his twin sister, Bel, is absolutely beautiful. Jesus Christ, forget Emma, built like a dump truck! I'm half in love with Bel. More than half. But that's hopeless too. . . ." His voice trailed away. "She's so young."

"I'm confused, Dick," Susan said tiredly.

He made a face, yanked his beard, and laughed hoarsely.

"*You're* confused? Look, one is not *fond* of Emma Bristals. One walks into the tornado once in a while, when one has nothing better to do. The tornado, hurricane-force monsoon, whirlwind . . . The Big Blow."

"I see." Did she see? Only if she chose to. "And what about Moon Rivers?"

"That moron? I hope he survives it. 'Course, he's got more stamina." As he babbled, Susan wondered if she was going to hear from Jenny, wherever she was. Then, with a kind of enraged, frustrated roar, Lyons leapt up, thundering so loudly she thought Jasper would hear if, indeed, he had finished talking to Bulgaria. "It's that son of a bitching psychiatrist. I'd like to know what he does for her?"

The question, of course, would be what had Dick Lyons

stopped doing for her? For one thing, he'd stopped being a household word, either hated or admired. Peculiar, Susan had never taken Jenny for the sort of woman who needed to be mated with Star Quality.

"That son of a bitch inveigled himself into our life, don't ask me how. He was practicing shrink on me, ha! But all the time, he was working on Jenny. They know all the tricks of the trade, those bastards! And now, lately, I'm telling you, they've been seen . . . in the back of his car, bangin' away."

"Seen by whom?"

"Up at the edge of the property, by any number of goddamn people, like they don't even care, and what does that do for old Dick's image, one may ask?"

"And you've been passing it along, haven't you?"

"Me? What do you mean? I'm going to tell anybody my wife is doing the two-backed beast out in the full glare of daylight?"

"Bear's son is very disillusioned—he told me you *and* Moon have been telling everybody about his *dad* and Jenny?"

"Oh, shit!"

"Exactly."

Lyons blew air and sat down again, deflated.

"Lemme ask you, Suzette, are you sure that kid's his son?"

"You're bananas, Big Dick."

"Maybe. But I'm convinced Bear Jay is nuttier than any of his patients, including Miss Jenny Driver."

That would not surprise her. For once, Lyons might have tripped and fallen over the truth.

"He's fucked up," Lyons elaborated. "Old Bear can't figure out whether he's in love with Jenny . . . or me."

What Dick Lyons suggested or hinted or intimated was, of course, in no way impossible. But it would certainly be a shocking departure if either speculation were true. However, as Susan reeled, Dick completely forgot about it.

Crossing and recrossing his legs, stroking his beard, hoping against hope she'd finally offer him a drink, he made no move to go. Susan, having no intention of satisfying him in any way, strolled to the window, waiting. The sunset was finally fading and the long shadow of night was covering the meadow and rocks and reaching out to sea. Should she turn on a light, or just . . . wait? Time was reaching past the dinner hour; Susan didn't care anymore.

"Listen to me, Suzette!" Dick eventually said. "I really *love* these fucking Indians!"

"Miss Custerd."

"Yes and *en masse*. Don't be jealous, darling!"

"*Jealous?* Are you mad?"

Laughing brightly, hopefully, vividly, he exclaimed, "*This* is where it all began, Sue. It's so exciting. Nobody gives the Noble Savage any credit, these people we take so much for granted. They're completely different from us! They're smarter, you know, just all-around brighter, they have more sense than we do. They're intuitive, a sixth or seventh sense we've lost, or killed off in a swamp of junk food and soda pop and TV—*sorry!* They feel stuff and we've been blinded and deafened. Lost all sense of direction in this country, Sue! Just look at the politics! Our affairs are being managed by morons and thieves!"

"Haven't heard you like this in a while."

"You bet. I'm back in action, hon! Us, and our fucking moral superiority! Genocide?" He was angry. "We've done it. Forced migration, read: resettlement. We've been there! Do you know what I'm saying, Sue?"

"Of course I do."

"Have you seen the graveyard here on the island?" No, she hadn't and didn't much want to. "Come on with me now and I'll show you!"

"Now? Dick, I'm tired. I don't feel like—"

"It's not far. This is the best time of day, Sue. Come on!"

He was out of the chair and at her before she could turn around. Chuckling gleefully, Lyons seized her around the waist from the back and hugged her to his burly self, pushing himself against her roughly. His strength had not waned. Nor the stench of his alcohol-breath which might have knocked her out sooner than the crush of his arms.

"Dick, stop it! All right."

Susan got away, evaded his hands once more, darting to the door.

"Right," he said, disgruntled, "especially if you're not going to bed with me, which I gather you're not."

"Let's go, if we're going," she said impatiently.

"You and me, Sue," he said as he leered, "you'd be good for me and I'd be good for you." But he saw there was no hope. "Okay, let's go."

In the hallway, Susan put a finger to her lips for quiet, then went to listen at Jasper's door. Naturally, he was on the telephone again, talking to God knows who, loudly, bossily, impatiently. Not letting Lyons get too close, Susan led him down to the lobby. There was still no sign of Harry. By now, he'd be up at his brother's and they'd all be sitting there talking about Susan Channing, poor thing.

"Want to walk or take a golf cart?" Lyons asked.

"Walk."

They stepped into the warm June night. Susan breathed deeply; the air was proverbial, the perfume or ambrosia, or whatever it was supposed to be.

"Take my arm."

"That's okay, Dick. I'm fine."

At least, there were still a few people splashing around in the Olympic-size pool inside the spa building; she could always run in there if Lyons tried to pull her into the trees.

"Not far now, hon."

The Lyons head had cleared. He'd lost interest in doing his worst. They walked along in silence, as if between acts—day was gone, night was on the way. What next? In a few minutes, they reached an open space in the forest, surrounded on three sides by tall, spindly, wind-blown pine trees and opening precisely to the west, in the direction of the bleeding horizon.

"This is *the spot,* Suzette."

Mumbling with uncustomary reverence, Lyons pointed at heaps of red-colored earth that lay along the edges of the excavation. Carefully, he led her to the waist-high siding that had been erected to protect a network of trenches and pits dug six to eight feet deep, some places covered by sheets of plywood or canvas tenting. In the tricky twilight Susan discerned the shapes of tools and more arcane archaeological aids such as brushes, brooms, and large dirt-sorting sieves.

Here was a garbage dump of past life. The idea was chilling but so too the thought that, even in this unlikely corner, ever-inquisitive man was monkeying around with the earth, with the past, for evidences, for some odd reason reassuring in the present, of long-gone civilization—as if it mattered one damn bit that just here other people had buried their dead on the very edge of the continent with a view of the end of the world.

"See, Sue, they were digging out holes for a foundation or something and *very* accidentally the tractor clawed up an old clay pot, almost intact, a miracle it wasn't broken to smithereens.''

"It's eerie, Dick,'' was the best she could say, shivering, suddenly cold.

"Like I said!'' Inquisitively, he studied her; she *was* impressed, wasn't she? ''A hundred, hundred-fifty years old. Luckily, Ralph Teller had enough sense to stop work.''

Nobody had ever said the Teller boys were dense. Other things, yes, but not dim-witted.

"Bone fragments, bits and pieces of pottery, a couple or three Russian coins, pieces of cloth,'' Lyons added somberly. ''A bottle or two, one that smelled of bourbon.''

"So, Dick,'' she mentioned, ''in fact, you *don't* really know who's buried here, Basket Indians or Russians? Doesn't that weaken your case?''

Lyons turned on her furiously.

"I know, don't tell me! Your cynical little mind is already figuring out that somebody planted that stuff! Why? Of course! To get their hooks into the Big Sea Development Company! Isn't that what your boyfriend says?''

"No such thing, Dick.''

Lyons shook his head violently, vastly disenchanted.

"You guys are really something! You don't believe in anything. *Nothing!*''

"Oh, yeah? Since when are you such a Boy Scout, Mr. Lyons?''

Lyons didn't answer.

The response, if it was that, came from behind them.

"*Mr. Lyons?* And good evening to you, Miss Channing.''

Smothering a bad word, embarrassed to be caught here alone with Lyons, Susan turned. Ishira Guchi appeared, his agile figure sliding out of the shadow of the redwoods.

"Doctor Guchi!''

"Sorry. I didn't mean to surprise you. I was having a swim and decided to take a walk over here. Hearing the name Lyons, I was emboldened to interrupt.''

Guchi came closer. He was dressed like a wraith, in an ankle-length, black-and-white-figured robe. Thonged sandals were on his feet. He smiled, mystically, like a friendly monk.

"Lots of artifacts kicking around this place,'' he said softly.

There would be no argument about that, not from Dick

Lyons anyway. Breathing hard, as if alarmed to meet the man face-to-face. Lyons stared at Guchi.

Then he put out his hand, straight at Guchi's middle.

"I'm Dick Lyons."

Guchi grimaced, perhaps at Dick's macho pressure.

"Ishira Guchi."

"Mister or Doctor?"

"Doctor...mister, call me whatever you like. Just don't call me late for dinner..." Out of him, like gas, rushed a hissing laugh. "One of Jasper's jokes. *I love it!*"

"Yes, I'm familiar with it too," Susan said.

Dick continued to stare as if the future itself hung on his assessment of the man. This didn't bother Guchi. He was very comfortable with himself, and that was important. He and Susan traded smiles. No, he was not intimidating. As she'd noted, he was big for a Japanese, but nothing like as tall or broad and heavy as Dick Lyons—or as sweaty and smelly. Shucked of his black mohair business suit, Guchi seemed a good deal younger and much more handsome. His course black hair was still moist from the pool, his face soft, pliant, as if God had kneaded it like dough during the act of creation.

His penetrating eyes, sparkling behind the wire glasses, made Susan shiver and for a moment she forgot Lyons. She was alone with Ishira Guchi. He had ceased all movement; the body language was shattering. He was at rest, watchful, stealthy, like a cat stalking prey. Not a quiver, not a heartbeat, came from beneath the robe.

Finally, he relented, and turned to Dick Lyons.

"Your meeting with Jasper was a big flop."

"Look..." Dick burst out impatiently.

"*Shira*, please." Guchi regarded Lyons confidently, but so pleasantly; in another minute, he'd have him in his pocket. "Dick, I'll level with you. Prosperoso is interested in Big Sea. We've got the money and the know-how—"

"You're after the land," Dick lashed out. "That's what you want: the land, the acreage—"

"Whatever..." Guchi's face was earnest. "We're ready to deal. I'm sure we can fashion a compromise peace to the benefit of everybody."

"You think so?"

"I'm *sure* so, Dick!" Inscrutably, Guchi murmured, "The problem is so big we cannot encompass it with our poor arms.

But the solution is as small as the palm of the outstretched hand."

"Well . . ." Lyons thought that over, then stammered, like a lummox, "I can say we believe in negotiation, always have . . ."

"So, then?"

Lyons stepped back, lowering his head as if to guard his eyes from the Guchi onslaught. He jammed his hands in the pockets of his baggy tan working pants.

"Shira . . . you have to understand, *certain things* have to run their course."

He ducked into a bargaining position, doggedly swung his shoulders. Susan understood, even if Guchi didn't, that there couldn't be any kind of a deal until Richard Lyons, the great advocate, had harvested full media exposure.

"This is a very special and probably unique situation, Shira."

"I *buy* that," Guchi replied. "What say we walk back? It's getting kind of cold." He gestured broadly. "Beautiful spot. Talk about ambiance! Great place to be buried, if you've got to be buried."

So saying, he had the nerve to put his hand on Susan's arm. He barely touched her, but she almost jumped out of her skin.

Shakily, Lyons stated, "We want nothing more than justice, a fair shake for the Baskets and their ancestors—*and* their descendants!"

Guchi made acquiescent sounds, having taken a firm grip on Susan's elbow.

"This is going to remind our people of certain localities in Hokkaido, I guess, yes, especially in the morning, you know, with the trees outlined in the fog, like spirits. Japanese artists try to catch the mood, you know? You've seen those etchings, Susan? If not, I can . . ."

Jesus! What was this one up to? Etchings too?

"I've been to Japan several times."

"Back in the country, Susan, in some localities, it's still like it was in medieval times."

Sure, sure, she told herself nervously, too aware of his hand.

"How did you come to meet Jasper Gates?"

"Ah!" Guchi laughed disparagingly. "That was years ago . . . And you were working as a reporter in Japan?"

"I interviewed several of your politicians. And some businessmen."

"But not me."

"No."

Lyons interrupted. "*Shira,* let's plan on getting together tomorrow. In the late afternoon? Does that sound workable?"

"You bet, *Dick!*"

"I'm kind of busy in the morning."

Indeed, as soon as they walked within sight of the lighted spa, Lyons began to prepare his getaway. There were things he had to do, people to see, matters to arrange. And it was getting late.

And then Susan had done it, got herself talked into going with Shira Guchi to his suite, down the hall from her own. Like a virgin to the slaughter, she couldn't help thinking, if that was what Shira had in mind, bless his heart. Strange: you met a man like Guchi and the first thing you asked yourself was could I handle an affair with a man like that?

"Please sit down."

Guchi was going to make her his own very special tea, the very thing for beddy-byes; or that was what he'd promised, to get her upstairs. Hustling to the wet bar, he began fiddling with an electrical water-heating gadget which was not part of the lavish furnishings.

Then he bowed very politely and asked to be excused for a moment and, of course, Susan gave her permission, assuming he was going for a leak. But she was feeling somewhat bewildered. It was hard to imagine a Japanese anymore westernized than Ishira Guchi. But on the other hand?

The good doctor's window, like her own, faced the Pacific. It occurred to Susan that people spent entirely too much time staring out of it. There must be something else to do.

What did she see? A shadow, a perception of movement against the backdrop of the sea. A man? Tall, the figure glided insubstantially across the horizon. Harry! Susan jerked forward. *Be careful!* Then, as suddenly, the substance, man, Harry, ghost was gone.

Who was she kidding anyway? Careful? Why would Harry heed any warning from her? And now she was confusing everything all the more.

If you didn't know better, you'd think Susan Channing a disreputable character. But mightn't it have looked a little odd to have tea in the bar, with Guchi dressed as he was? Propriety? When in California, well, she hadn't wanted to insult him. Wasn't it taken for granted that Ishira Guchi was a responsible, respectable businessman and a very important one too, at least so said Jasper Gates and the awful Guy Bristals, both of whom, Susan remembered, had asked her to be nice to Shira Guchi. So be it.

By the time she'd finished deliberating the pros and cons of the situation, he was back.

"Hello. Here I am, the bad penny!"

The good doctor had changed into a slick pair of red pants with drawstring closure, Japanese-Cardin by the look of them, and a tight red-and-white-striped sports shirt with the animal insignia of some brand or other on the pocket. These people were mad for labels: Chanel, Vuitton, Weitz, you name it. But his feet were bare—what, no Gucci slippers for Dr. Guchi? He squiggled his toes in the carpet.

"Or would you rather have a *belt*, Susan? It came to me you might like that better."

Hearing language she understood, Susan said boldly, "A belt, Shira, if you don't mind. Vodka rocks, light on the rocks."

That old adage did not, in his case, apply. You could take the boy out of Japan and a lot of Japan out of the boy too. Not only was Shira Guchi Jasper's pal; he acted a lot like Jasper Gates.

Guchi turned with relief to the vodka bottle. He unscrewed the top and sniffed and sighed. The very healthy sound of ice cubes rattling in glass made her drool. No, goddamn it, she was not an alcoholic. What was Guchi trying to prove? That he was unbelievably clever, that three or four thousand years of civilization gave him an advantage over such a savage as Susan Channing?

"Very nice, thank you."

The good doctor, with a Gatesian bourbon in hand, sat down very gracefully on the sofa, not hustling her, so far at least, and with a sneaky move, collected his beautiful feet under him, assuming a variation of the lotus position. He was as limber as a cat; that *was* impressive, like everything else about him.

Suddenly, however, Susan realized she had nothing to say. Her previous Japanese experience had not been very satisfacry; why had she conceived the idea that Guchi would be any better? He had so far not shown himself to be a ball-of-fire conversationalist and if he resembled her old friend Jojo or Yoyo Kimona in other ways, the evening promised to be a dud. Add to that, she hadn't eaten anything. A couple of more drinks and she'd be crawling home.

"Do you think we should call Jasper about some dinner?"

Guchi nodded indolently, but made no move to untangle his legs.

"That naughty boy, Jasper Gates?"

"Why so?"

"Hiss ... hiss." He chuckled. "When I came to this country to study ..."

"In Boston ..."

"... Jasper told me Western women were different from our own."

"How so?"

Guchi made that familiar motion, drawing his finger sideways, then clutched himself around the middle, laughing destructively. Susan blushed. Damn! She had fallen for it, the oldest one in the world, though ordinarily used by Western men to denigrate Oriental women. Naturally: it was distinctively a Jasper Gates type of joke, and not funny.

Staring at her drink, she murmured, "Presumably you found out differently."

"A joke, Susan. In Boston. I had an Irish mistress and she couldn't take a joke either. Her old man was a well-known politician ..."

"Not an Irish warlord?"

Guchi looked blank. Maybe the one story he hadn't heard was about Jasper's daughter-of-the-warlord.

"Whatever, she became a nun and broke my heart. I fled to Chicago and then went to work on the Mississippi as a card sharp, the only Japanese card sharp in that part of the world, believe it or not—"

"Oh, I do believe you."

"Then I went back to Tokyo, and work became my mistress."

"And you married?"

"Yes. I have a wife, or two."

"Or two? You've been married several times?"

"I have one in China and one in Japan."

"Is that permitted?"

"No—and yes." Guchi shrugged in such a way Susan was

pleased she would not be Wife Number Three. "My wife in
China is treasurer of the Bank of Yang'tse, Canton, Shanghai—"

"You keep a woman in China is what you mean."

"Cecilia . . ."

"Cecilia, a beautiful name, un-Chinese though, isn't it?"

"She's a saint, believe you me. And a baptized Catholic."

Susan smiled. "You seem to like Catholic girls, Shira."

"You're not a Catholic?"

"No, I was brought up in the Episcopalian faith."

"Close to the Catholic," he pointed out. "In fact, Catholic, if it weren't for King Henry."

"Yes, if you're high Episcopalian."

"As you are?"

"Yes, *fairly* high. And low. I don't go to church much
anymore. And you?"

"I do Shinto, that's the religion of big business. Strict.
Discipline. Very warlike, the way we operate. Stand and
deliver! Damn the torpedoes. Total war! But I also like atheist
girls, Susan." Guchi strung it out. "I met several of them in
Moscow. They are quite good. But it is true, Catholic girls are
my favorite. Cecilia is the daughter of a good friend of
Jasper's from the old days."

"Don't tell me! Jasper's own daughter. The granddaughter
of the warlord!"

"No, no, why do you say that? Her grandfather was a
wrapper in the Boxer Rebellion!"

Guchi smiled broadly, magnificently, joyously, like Jasper
did sometimes, showing those big, white, regular teeth, and
Susan smiled back, as vivaciously as she dared.

"Catholic girls fascinate. They have an acute sense of sin.
Pleasures which are forbidden are the most satisfying. Time
and motion shows . . ."

Now, Susan had to interrupt, disbelievingly. Enough was
enough.

"Don't tell me *sin* is a time-and-motion study, Shira,
you're making me laugh."

"But it's true, Susan!" Quivering with sincerity, he put the
bourbon to his mouth and gulped. "Is not orgasm a function
of time elapsed and motion? My university studies showed
that orgasm is attained much more quickly, easily and effectively
by girls given to exquisite awareness of guilt."

"Psshaw!" Susan mocked. "You're telling me this was
your thesis at MIT?"

"Sweetheart," he whispered, "it made my name."

Sweetheart? Was that a Japanese word? Guchi's sense of humor, it had to be said, was more primitive than Jasper's. Susan was not required to encourage it. Nothing more was expected than she was putting out right now. Be nice, humor the Japanese gentleman, all well and good. Fine. And?

And change the subject.

"You know, Shira," she said, careful not to promise anything, "if you did make a deal with the Baskets, we could talk about a *Hindsight* segment that'd knock your socks off. Like: Japanese company harmonizes with American Indians. Everybody lives happily ever after! *And beyond!* Y'know, speaking of ancestors—"

"*Swell!*"

"You'd agree to do it?"

"Would I agree? You bet, sugar!"

"You'd talk about your whole company, philosophy, aims, ambitions, the story of Prosperoso?"

"Baby, the time has come for Prosperoso to tell its story! All-Nippon Prosperoso is the nightmare of all good American capitalists and it's time we tooted our horn!"

"It'd be a first, Shira," Susan warned him. "There's *never* been an in-depth on a Japanese trading company."

"Tell me!"

Goodwill surged, a swell of excitement caused Susan to shiver, uncontrollably. Was she one hell of a journalist, or not? Such a scoop! She should give the handsome Japanese devil a big wet kiss.

"And what's the deal with Guy Bristals, Shira?" she pressed on, figuring she might as well hit him up for everything.

"*Oh?*" He reacted cutely, like those of his feather did. "You've heard?"

"From the birdies, sure."

"Ah, ah! Guy proposes a heavy-duty partnership in Tokyo. *And...*"

"*And?*"

"...and you will be in Tokyo as chief media advisor. *I love it!*"

Susan was flabbergasted and didn't let on that she wasn't.

"I? Who says so?"

"The great one. The fat man."

"Well! Sounds terrific, but that's the first I've heard of it."

"I will welcome you with open-arms policy, cutie pie!"

His euphoria was well nigh out of hand. Decisively, Guchi undid his legs and jumped up, like a grasshopper, pranced to the window and back, circling her, reaching for Susan's glass, saying he'd make her another drink. Same again! More than ever like Jasper. And, like Jasper Gates, totally unpredictable.

"I discern that Richard Lyons is a very troubled man." Maybe yes, maybe no, the good doctor would find out about Dick for himself. "Not long ago, Richard Lyons was a hero among our students," he pondered. "I have your show in which you interviewed Lyons and his wife . . ."

"Jenny Driver."

"Yes, Miss Driver was also much in the public eye. Her movie . . ."

"Dark and Shining Nights . . ."

"Yes. But Richard Lyons was much more famous, beloved by our youths, due to the nuclear protests."

"You should tell him that, Shira. He could do with a bit of a morale boost."

"And what has happened to this good man? Why has his country forsaken him?"

"I wish I could tell you. Times change. He's older."

She didn't mention the booze, or Dick Lyons's concept of permanent revolution. Guchi wouldn't want to hear about that.

"We *must* help Richard Lyons," Guchi whispered. "We will put him back on his pedestal."

Yes, maybe, but how. And why? Susan doubted even Lyons would consider himself so important in the world scheme. Guchi's motive? Who could say but, nevertheless, wasn't it bittersweet to hear a world-class financial player express such concern for a rabble-rouser of international ranking? By all that was holy, Guchi should be cheering the demise of Dick Lyons.

Yes, the good doctor *was* inscrutable. Or perhaps an imposter. Whatever, he plopped down again and rocked on his lotus seat, eyeing Susan searchingly, making her dizzy, if anything; and Susan, as always, became instantly suspicious that somebody, never mind who, had given him to understand that she was his for the asking.

"We two will be such friends!" he quavered. "Have you known a Japanese man, *cherie*?"

Her reply was quick, unconsidered, misleading.

"Oh, sure, several."

"Several?"

She had wasted him and, too late, understood why.

"Friends, of course, you know..."

"Susan Channing," he cried, voice wobbly, "we Japanese men suffer too!"

"You're suffering? I'm sorry. What's the problem?"

"We also fall in love! We faint at nonreciprocation!"

Susan smiled foolishly. The idea was to keep him happy, pliable, cooperative. Be nice to me; then I be nice to you, the Balinese song went, the one she'd quoted to *People* magazine.

"There is no difference between Oriental and Occidental love," Guchi exclaimed.

"Probably not."

His face had turned an unlikely, if not unnatural, shade of white. Did one ask Shira Guchi about the purely mechanical functioning of his heart, that is leaving aside the poetic aspects of the thing?

"This Japanese fella is one of your great admirers!"

"Shira, please."

Gutturally, he gasped, "For you to do a *Hindsight* on me, you know that'd be a hell of an honor."

"Well, we just might, you never know!"

Emotion ripped out of him; he became incautious.

"Fly with me! To Tokyo!"

"Shira, Shira..." Susan tried to murmur his name in a soothing way. "That's got to be arranged by my producer."

"I mean now!"

"I can't just hop on a plane at the drop of a hat."

"Ah, ah!" He groaned and, again, the words rushed. "I invite you to my home in Japan, honeybunch! I own four thousand square feet of prime property in Tokyo."

And why didn't he go ahead and tell her it was worth a million per square foot, or whatever?

"... my condo in Hong Kong, my estate in Inner Mongolia, where I keep my ponies..."

"Shira, Shira." Susan protested quite vocally. "What are you suggesting?"

"That we take off, beautiful!"

Perhaps it *was* his heart. Without stretching the exertion much more, he would strangle, or collapse. His eyes sagged shut, his body went limp. Susan hadn't seen a man behave like this in years.

"Now, Shira, please!"

"Please *yourself,* doll face!"

Funny, Susan had figured Guchi for a reserved, dignified gentleman and now he'd come apart. Interesting, just beneath the surface, he was so very emotional. Susan was reminded of the Indian men she'd met, Indian men from Calcutta and Delhi and Bombay. One had a notion that the Indians were a soft-spoken nation of philosophers; lo and behold, when aroused they turned more hysterical than a mob of Italians.

Susan got up hurriedly, not pausing to finish her second drink.

"Shira, I'm going to take a raincheck."

As Susan made for the door, a wail burst loose behind her, an unlikely sound to come out of a Japanese financial samurai. It stopped her in her tracks. She turned. He was on the floor. Not thinking straight. Susan came back and knelt beside him, putting one hand on his forehead. He moaned distress.

"I die . . ."

Show me where it hurts. Should she ask? No. His problem was obvious. Those elegant Cardin-of-Japan pants were much too tight all around: hips, crotch, thighs, calves, wherever. His body seemed to have swollen; he was about to burst the fabric.

Guchi frightened her. She had to hold his hands to keep them off her and, at once, Susan developed a mental picture of herself being pursued up and down the Big Sea Inn corridors by a Japanese gentleman, robe flying about him, fixtures and fittings in disarray, then catching her and . . . don't think about it. Susan remembered the etchings Guchi had mentioned. Nothing about them had ever suggested pleasureful passion; what they got up to, limbs all twisted, men like beasts and women all-suffering. Doesn't look like much fun, sweetie.

But she was saved, if it had come to that, by an outburst of noise in the corridor. With a grunt, Guchi sat up, suddenly quite well. Somebody shouted, somebody screamed. Perhaps somebody had heard Guchi's groans and called for medical help or the police.

"Hark!" Guchi said softly.

Another shout exploded, the cadence of it familiar.

"Anarchy! Goddamn it, Gloria, anarchy! *Is there no hope?*"

19

Susan had awakened just before Jasper came banging on her door, into the bright morning of California but thinking of New York. Eight o'clock in California, it'd be eleven in New York and all life was calibrated to New York. Wherever you were in the world, you woke up asking yourself what time it was in New York.

"Who is it? Who's there?"

His voice came back, a loud whisper.

"Hots for you, sweetie."

Susan opened the door and Jasper darted inside, all smiles and apology about the evening before. He was bright as a button. And why, when the day promised to be so difficult?

He backed her to the wall, kissing her cheek eagerly, then trying her lips with the rough tip of his tongue.

"Oh . . . Jasper!"

Somehow, it wasn't right. Certainly, it was not the right time. Susan had to get downstairs; her crew was due any minute. And Jasper was ready for business. He was freshly, closely shaven, his breath smelled minty, and his thin hair was brushed down smoothly. He was wearing one of his natty Savile Row pinstripes with vest, a stiff white collar, sober blue tie, and shoes so highly polished they reflected her red-painted toenails. Mr. Dudley had been busy.

"Please, sweetie . . ."

Jasper leaned against her, breathing forcefully, lips slack with lust.

"Jasper, I've got to get dressed."

She was still in her robe, defenseless. She should never have let him in. Too late now for, eyes shining, he ran his hand up and down her arms, caressing the silk, staring greedily at her neck, her throat, the place where robe met breast.

Susan pulled the garment closer around her.

"Sweetie, I need comfort and encouragement as I'm going into battle."

"Battle?"

"You better believe it!" he cried, eyes running riot. "Lyons and his boys have put a barricade up on my bridge. This morning! Did you know?"

"I just got up."

And she was worn out. It had been late by the time she'd escaped the good doctor and finally got through to a person of responsibility in San Francisco. Yes, it seemed somebody had heard from Mr. Fineman. Yes, it seemed *somebody* had been assigned to her.

"*On my goddamn bridge,* of all the fucking nerve!"

"Jasper, that's not serious. It's just a gesture."

"A gesture! Those bastards have closed the bridge, Sue! Don't you understand? They're charging *tolls* for people to come across!"

This was the dramatic happening Dick Lyons had promised? Susan's heart thumped. She had ordered up a camera crew for this? Artie Fineman would skin her alive.

"Wouldn't it be considered a public road, Jasper?"

"Oh, yeah, and I can *claim* the bridge belongs to me and what right have they got? I built it. And they've closed it! The Indians are making people pay to get to the goddamn island, sweetie!"

So they'd call the police and by the time her crew got here, the Indians would be gone and then what? Well, at least take some stock shots of the Big Sea layout. They'd be needing those for the Jasper Gates profile, whatever happened today.

And really, what had she expected was going to happen? Cowboys and Indians, a shootout, scalpings, and burning wagons? This *was* the twentieth century, after all.

"That prick Lyons is trying to position Jasper International for a killing, sweetie!"

Jasper held Susan's hands tightly in his own. Slowly but surely, he was working her across the room, toward the couch.

"Hotter than a firecracker, sweetie," he gurgled. "Pull my fuse, haha!"

"Cute."

"Sweetie, si'down, just for a minute."

"Jasper, I must get dressed."

"*Uno rapido*, sweetie?"

He held her tightly, trying to push her down. Susan resisted with the back of her legs against the arm of the couch. Ingratiatingly, he stuck his tongue tip into the curl of her ear, huffing and puffing excitedly.

"Jasper, what is it with you?"

Susan heaved and finally forced him back.

"Dunno, sweetie, dunno, I'm just powerfully motivated, that's all."

His eyes glistened all the more.

"This *game*," Susan said, "it's got you going. I thought *power* was the aphrodisiac."

"No, no," he cried, "in my case, the *battle*, sweetie! The smell of war! What about it, Sue, what about it? I've got twenty minutes before I'm meeting Gloria."

Gloria, the person Jasper had been shouting at so raucously the night before.

"Twenty minutes? Wonderful. Can you spare the time?"

Chuckling wildly, he said, "Our lawyer, Gloria Goody. She's a star, sweetie, one smart little lady-lawyer, let me tell you! Besides being as cute as anything . . ."

"Goody, goody."

"Her idea is to *talk* 'em off there. Sweetly and reasonably. Not to give Lyons any publicity. Gloria thinks the schmuck is trying to establish some kind of a stupid precedent—like our access to the island was always thanks to some kind of an easement. Understand?"

"I guess."

"It won't work! They can't prove they *ever* closed the road before."

"Can you prove they didn't?"

"Whose side you on, sweetie?"

And now, she realized, even more discouraged, Jasper was telling her that Lyons's dramatic event was going to dissolve in a legalistic stew. For God's sake, why hadn't Dick Lyons organized a day of native dances and speeches in dialect, picket lines, and a standoff with the National Guard? Those were picture opportunities, not bridge tolls.

Jasper pushed forward again.

"Sweetie, come on! A quickie! *Uno rapido!* Take ten minutes out of your busy schedule. No more!"

"No."

What the hell was he talking about—an Italian express train? Susan turned rigid, unresponsive. He must have felt her whole body freeze; neither lust nor desire was in her.

"*Hots* for you, sweetie!"

"I wish you would *stop* saying that."

"*Truth,* sweetie!"

Jasper's cheeks flushed. He tried to laugh, to undercut her resistance.

"Absolutely not."

"Absolutely not?" Jasper repeated it. "What do you mean, absolutely not?"

"I mean: *Absolutely not!*"

"Sue! Sue . . ."

His lips tightened; lines washboarded his forehead.

"And I'm going in to get dressed. Stay here, or go. Suit yourself."

Not waiting to see which he would choose, Susan turned and walked through the bedroom, into the luxury bath. She shut the door and locked it. Would he finally get the message that there was a time and place for everything and right now was neither?

Susan turned on the shower, removed her robe, and stepped in. The noise drowned out the exterior world. She soaped and rinsed, thrusting her face into the spray, clearing cobwebs, straightening out her world. Five good long minutes and by now Jasper Gates should be on his way.

But he was still there.

"At two bucks each way per car," he yelled, as soon as she

turned off the water, "it'll take ten thousand years for the thing to pay for itself!"

He couldn't hear the mumble, "Poor Jasper Gates Memorial Bridge . . ." and there was nothing sincere about her compassion. Jasper Gates would certainly survive Dick Lyons and the Basket Indians.

Susan wrapped herself in a bath towel and now Jasper was making horrible, kissy noises at the door.

"Sweetie! This boy is going into *battle*."

Spitefully, she muttered, "Then you better go sharpen your lance, Jasper."

"What? I can't hear you, sweetie. Hey, c'mon! Sweetie, what'd you get up to with Shira last night?"

Ishira, mon amour.

Well, she had turned down the good doctor, that was what! She'd just said no—it wasn't so hard, wonder of wonders, even though, for all she knew, Guchi might have been lover *extraordinaire*. But it had never even been close; and, once again, for all she could say, she and Shira might've hit it off so splendidly that within hours she'd have messaged Fineman to take his job and shove it and been off to the foothills of Mount Fuji. It could have happened.

"We talked."

"Talked?"

"Talked."

"You can't trust him!"

"Now you tell me," Susan said loudly.

"Why didn't you call or come over?"

"It was late, Jasper . . . very late. I didn't want to bother you. You were on the phone, Jasper, you're *always* on the phone."

Let him sweat, if he didn't believe her.

"Not now, I'm not!"

"So?"

"Sweetie, sweetie . . ." He was up close to the crack in door closure, panting. "I wish to hell we were in my airplane flying someplace. I'd rather be in Bulgaria right now . . . or Yemen, raking camel shit."

"I'm with you, Jasper!"

Was she? She lied.

Susan put lipstick to her mouth, staring at herself in the mirror. At last, she had to stop playing around with him. It had come to her in the shower and again now, in a gory slash of realism, finally, that she could *not* accept his gift of Greenswards. It would not be honest, or ethical, or wise in any way. Susan looked at herself, with no great sympathy.

The problem, her problem, was, never mind about ethics or honesty, that she wouldn't know how to explain Greenswards to Harry.

Ah, so, Miss Susie, caught! At last!

But how to go about explaining to Jasper without destroying all hope of doing the *Hindsight* show? Was he man enough to accept the plain truth? Whatever happened, Greenswards was not worth the price she was expected to pay for it, from now onwards, into something like perpetuity.

And, boy oh boy, perpetuity was a long, long time.

Susan put her robe back on and opened the door.

"Sweetie!"

He was there, waiting, grinning like a schoolboy. He had taken off all his clothes, except for a pair of electric-blue bikini shorts.

"Well!" Of course she had to notice, she wasn't blind. "Are those Savile Row too?"

"All coordinated, sweetie! From head to toe and in between. Light my fire!"

Susan saw without making it obvious that it was already lit.

"Jasper," she said laconically, "seems to me you've got an appointment with the Basket Indians."

"Appointment with destiny, sweetie, is what it is."

"There's not time."

"There is time, always time for *love*." Jasper snapped the elastic of his shorts. "See, I don't care, sweetie. I just don't care anymore! C'mon! Off with the robe! You realize, sweetie, in all this time I haven't seen the goods."

"Jasper . . . please!"

"Seen some of the goods some of the time but not all the goods at one time."

"Are you . . . okay?"

Susan stared at him curiously. He was ahead of her now. She had never expected this. She tried to keep out of the way but Jasper approached her as if they were going to wrestle, warily, looking for an opening. Susan had not seen *him* this way either. His was not a bad little body—neat, well formed, muscular without being muscle-bound, with a modest set of pecs and shapely legs.

Catching her observation, Jasper ran a hand across his

chest, pulling at a little tuft of hair. He pulled his shoulders back and seemed about to pose.

Then, without warning, he leapt forward, grabbed her robe and stripped it away, off her shoulders, baring her from top to bottom.

He reeled, as if blinded by the spectacular sight.

"Holy God! If I'd ever known!"

"Stop it!"

Susan tried to regain control of the robe but couldn't and it didn't much matter anyway for, frantically, he spun her around and down on the bed, lifted her ankles and spread her legs and lowered himself into the breech.

His face was up close to Susan's; he was snorting hot minty flavor.

"I don't want this."

How could she ever have trusted him? This might've happened on the airplane, with less chance of escape. Why now? There must be some explanation for his present madness.

At least, she believed, he wasn't the type to kill her or really hurt her if she resisted. And Susan knew how to do that. She drew up her knees, intending to kick him away, but Jasper twisted and hung on, his mouth fixed to her throat and that *was* going to leave a bruise. Like a rock between them, she felt the bulge of his blooded genitalia. That was where she'd kick him.

"Off!"

"On!" he gasped. "I told you I don't like to be teased."

"I never teased you!"

"You never stopped teasing me, sweetie!"

"I'll hurt you."

"I'm already hurt. I'm suffering. And I'm going into battle. What about, one time . . . lemme . . . it's no big deal!"

"Jasper!"

Susan didn't quite scream; the sound was a few decibels short of that.

"I'm not taking Greenswards . . ."

He seemed not to hear. Perhaps he really had gone crazy. He continued to fight her, holding her arms, her wrists, trying to catch her legs, but he was not big enough or strong enough. No, he wouldn't succeed, not even if he put a gun to her head, or a knife to her throat.

Jasper was losing his purchase. His body was all sweaty against hers, and Susan was perspiring with outrage. He was slipping, sliding, slithering down her, his head momentarily at her breast, thin-lipped little mouth slurping, lips nipping, and still he slipped until he was on his knees, crouched between her legs. He thrust forward, daringly, with a snarl of passion, his face twisting at her center, striving, the mouth, the tongue.

"Just as good as Augie, just as good..."

He gasped hoarsely, croaked.

"Jasper, I'm giving you back Greenswards."

Tearfully, he peered up at her. He must have seen she was frightened, and embarrassed, that there were tears in her eyes too.

"Don't be silly! I...no deal!"

"I'm ripping up the deed, I promise you."

"You can't."

"Why can't I? Who says?"

He didn't answer, instead shoved forward again, mercilessly, or so he might have thought, not understanding he was so defenseless, and at her mercy.

Susan adjusted her legs, cocked them back, summoned energy, and slapped her thighs together. Thwack!

Jasper lurched back, to the side, fell over, and clapped his hands to his head.

"Jesus! My ears!"

"I warned you."

"Sweetie! You've busted my eardrums!"

"No, no, you'll just ring a few minutes. I'm sorry, Jasper, but..."

Quietly, in full possession of her senses, and dignity, Susan got up, picked her robe off the floor and put it back on, quite simply, not rushing to cover herself, not taking her time either.

Jasper got himself together, miserably, for he realized he had been humiliated. But what was humiliation with only a single witness? Still a bit dazed, he shook his head from side to side.

"Sweetie, a knockout blow. How could you do that to me just when I'm going into battle?"

"You're going to be late for the battle if you don't get going."

"It's my show, Sue," he whined. "I can get there when I want."

"Jasper, did you hear what I said before?"

"Uh-uh," he said perversely.

"I said I can't accept Greenswards. I appreciate the thought, you know, but . . ."

"Are you crazy or something?"

"No. I've been thinking about it and it wouldn't be right."

"I promised you!" he stormed. "Whatever happens, it's yours. No-holds-barred. Whatever happens. You *know* that."

"No, it doesn't work that way. You assume, just because . . . and I don't blame you—"

"No such thing! I never assumed any such thing!"

"Then why?"

"Because I had the *hots* for you, sweetie," he said, sorrowfully. "Not anymore though. Now I got the *colds* . . . and the deafs. Jesus, where'd you learn that trick?"

Steadily, not answering the question, though she could have, easily enough, Susan said, "I can understand you might want to call off our interview, the *Hindsight* show, I'm sorry . . ."

"Hey!" He regarded her adoringly. "Are you kidding! I gave my word! We proceed normally, full speed ahead, sweetie. I know that eventually, given time, I can win you over."

She nodded uncertainly, reluctant to encourage him.

"I appreciate that," she said slowly. "But now, look, really, Jasper . . ."

"Sweetie, sweetie . . ."

"I've got to get ready. I've got a camera crew downstairs—"

"*What!*" He was horror-stricken. "Do you mean you're gonna film this fucking thing, Sue?"

"It'll be worked into the big picture, Jasper, sure."

"Jesus! I do *not* believe it! I thought you were my friend! We agreed, no ink or film for Lyons! First your friend Teller . . . now you? The son of a bitch is going to be famous all over again—at my expense!"

"Jasper," Susan said calmly, "we can't pretend it's not happening. Lyons has already made the newspapers; we're just following along, if not us, then another of the networks, or *all* of them. In fact you could argue—"

"Don't! Don't argue! I don't want to hear it!"

Jasper backed away from her, as if she'd suddenly become too hot to handle.

"Now, don't forget, for purposes of *Hindsight,* this is going to illustrate how you dealt decisively with the Indians, what kind of a corporate statesman you are, how you and Shira Guchi made peace with the Baskets, to *everybody's best advantage*."

Jasper stared murderously.

"What are you saying?"

"That Shira is going to do a deal with them."

His look hinted that maybe he was trying to figure the most convenient time to have her assassinated.

"Who says?"

"I do. He and Lyons are going to have a meeting, don't you know? Didn't Shira tell you?"

"Tell me? I told you he was shifty."

"He agrees it'll make a wonderful *Hindsight* program, *All-Nippon Prosperoso-USA*!"

Jasper tottered to the other side of the room where he had carefully piled his suit and shirt on a chair.

"You're doing a show with *him*?"

"Yes. He agreed; in fact, he's eager."

"*Shit!* Cave in to Lyons? Me? No way! And now you're doing a program with the Japs? What the hell kind of treachery is this, sweetie?"

"We'll do shows with *both* of you, don't you see?"

"Horseshit!" Brow furrowed, Jasper spit, "Goddamn disloyalty. How does Shira dare make a deal? *You* arranged it!"

"I offered to help. You asked me to help."

"Then . . ." He was confused, but who wasn't? "Why all this theatre today?"

"That's Lyons, for himself. He had to go through with it, to impress the Indians, I suspect. And me. He got me to call up a crew."

Jasper thrust his arms into his shirt and began buttoning it, his mind so far away he wasn't at all shy or embarrassed about his body.

"Holy shit! Judas! Female Judas. Judas-person!" All hope of a quickie now gone, he climbed back into his pants and, for some reason, turned his back to tuck in shirttails and zip up. "So this is what you're gonna do to me!" Any second now and he would renege on his promise. "You kick me off your body and now you got a TV crew up here without even warning me. And you probably knew what Lyons was up to, all along."

"No. I didn't have any idea. Please believe me!"

He pouted, wanting to be cajoled, and, indeed, a sweet sort of smile flickered across his unlined face.

"Never mind, I believe you. I need to believe you, sweetie. And you're not to worry about Greenswards." Jasper tried to grin, to bear it, to bluster through. "I'm sorry about that, sweetie, and hope you'll forgive me. I didn't mean to come in here and rape you."

"Well, you didn't."

"No thanks to me! It's just, before battle," he explained, so objectively, "the old juices run high. Like at the grand opera. I was engaged to a soprano once and when she came off the stage, you know, after singing *Carmen,* well, she was fit to be tied. She used to slam shut her dressing-room door and God, well . . . every man for himself! See what I mean, sweetie?"

"Oh, sure I do."

Eventually, Susan supposed, Jasper would leave. He was remaking the knot in his tie.

"I think the world of you, Sue, you know that."

"Yes," she said, "and that reminds me what I said in my interview with *Newsweek*—maybe you saw it."

"Sure." Jasper beamed, not hearing a word. "I wish *to God* you and me were on the Jasper-rocket on our way someplace, Sue! Would you go with me now, fearing me as you must?"

"You always want to be where you're not, Jasper."

"*The truth!* I flee reality!"

"Jasper . . ." She had to get him out of there. "It's almost nine."

Sam smashed his fist into the palm of his hand and reached for his suit jacket.

"I muster my forces, sweetie, and we march on the bridge. *To make peace!*" he announced with a brilliant smile.

"Dick Lyons will be very surprised."

"And probably disappointed," he said wisely. "Sweetie, forgive me my trespasses. Kiss me, fair lady, and I am gone!"

So there was some hope after all.

Feeling generous, she let him put his parched lips to her cheek, didn't recoil when he hugged her, briefly, awkwardly, and smiled tolerantly when, shamelessly, he caressed her breast with the back of his hand. Of course, a man like Jasper

Gates was never going to learn, was he? Amazing, a few moments before...and now...and she, such a simp!

Jasper Gates clutched at her again and whispered, "Sweetie, got the hots for you! No kidding."

Her phone rang.

"That'll be New York. Jasper...*don't* start without me."

He waved flippantly and ducked out the door.

Susan picked up the phone.

"Hello, Arthur."

"Hello yourself, Channing. How'd you know it was me?"

"I'm psychic."

20

Private Property of the Basket Nation

Right of Passage $2.00

The beautifully provocative hand-painted sign hung off the red-and-white-striped barber-pole barricade across the middle of the Jasper Gates Memorial Bridge, and as the Jasper group neared, Dick Lyons pointed at it proudly and boomed his challenge.

"Take a look at that, Gates!"

Legal-eagle Gloria Goody, dressed in a tailored tweed suit, hair pulled back in a businesslike bun, halted the entourage in the middle of the road. She shook her head at Jasper. He was supposed to keep his big mouth shut. Ms. Goody was her name, the law was her game, and she was in charge. Or so she might have wished, obviously not taking her boss into consideration.

Jasper's face knotted and turned fiery red. Ignoring his promise to Susan that he was going to be good and ignoring

Ms. Goody too, at the top of his lungs, he took Dick Lyons's bait.

"I paid for that goddamn bridge, Lyons. It belongs to me! It's *my* property!"

"Says you, Gates!"

Lyons jeered at him mightily, in a manner that was bound to infuriate Jasper all the more. What had become of the peace-making mission?

"*Far enough,*" Gloria Goody commanded. "And: Quiet, please!"

Her voice was remarkably loud, truly a courtroom baritone that had no trouble carrying across the stillness of the marsh.

"*Who she?*" Werner demanded.

Yes, much to Susan's disgust, she'd been given Jules again. Acne-faced, long-haired Julie Werner and his crew had arrived just before the long march began from inn to bridge. Did he know she had specifically asked for *not* him? Neat.

"Gates's corporate lawyer from L.A., Jules."

And the rest of them. Harry Teller was standing with his brother, a bit to the rear of Jasper, Gloria Goody, three of the uniformed Big Sea security force, Mr. Dudley. Bear Jay was with them too, because he was in charge of the dig. Jay had come bumbling up to her in the lobby as soon as she'd come downstairs; happy she was back! Jenny wanted desperately to see her, to talk, to explain, etcetera. But Susan had sort of brushed him off. Harry, he'd nodded at her from across the room, about as cordially as AHB would have at this point. And now he just happened to glance her way, mouth twisted, eyebrow cocked. Which made her furious. She hadn't actually done anything to him to deserve this. He hadn't given her a chance to explain.

Laughing scornfully, minicam tucked under one arm, Werner lit a cigarette. He had parked the NAN van off on the gravel shoulder of the road, perhaps fifty yards from Lyons's position smack in the center of the bridge. Of course, Werner wouldn't be impressed, not at all, a man who'd seen it all twice or three times, behaving as if they had all the time in the world.

"Crazy bastards," he mocked, so cynically that it broke her heart.

"Would you just go take some pictures?"

In no hurry, Julie drew on the cigarette, inhaled hatefully, and scratched a three-day-old beard.

"The plot is that this island is the ancient property of the Basket Indians? And Gates stole it away from them. So what? What the hell are they trying to prove?"

"In essence, that they still have a good claim on the island."

"Crazy bastards. Good luck to them."

Sure, tell it to city hall. Susan had tried, as best she could, to arouse a little interest in the assignment, but that was very much uphill. Julie wasn't about to forgive her for not wanting him in the first place, and then dragging him and his two assistants out in the middle of the night just made it worse.

"Look," Susan said impatiently, "you were a pain in the ass in Sacramento and I don't want a rerun of that. Just do your job."

"Don't worry about me, *Miss* Channing."

Then Sir Guy Bristals chugged up, winded after the walk from the inn. He wanted to know what was going on and said he was very eager to see how Susan worked. She was about to introduce him to Jules Werner, whom Sir Guy surely would not want to know, and maybe he saw it coming, for just as quickly he decided he'd pop over to Jasper and see what was happening.

"*Hallo!*" Dick Lyons was waving at them with both arms. "*Hallo!*"

"Richard Lyons."

"He sure is," Werner muttered. "And has *he* gone to seed!"

"He still knows how to get out the press. You're here."

Werner just looked at her. The reason he was here, he didn't have to say it, was because of Susan Channing who'd called the city late, promising a great story. Great story? Six guys standing out in the middle of a bridge? They might have expected more, given that Lyons had a lifetime of populist hell-raising behind him. In his heyday, Lyons had invented behind-the-scenes dirty tricks in a variety of presidential campaigns; after that had come the causes—versus big oil, power, the nuclear industry; greenhouse, acid rain, clearcutting; disarmament, abortion, civil rights. Think of a good one and Dick Lyons had been there. And of course, way

back, the Vietnam *thing* which over the years had brought
him more grief than celebration.

Now this?

At least, he had picked a nice day for it. Bright sunshine
poured down on Indian Island and upon the Horatio-at-the-
Bridge scene he had created especially for the *Evening News*.

"Hallo!"

Lyons waved at them again, motioning for Susan and the
crew to come closer. Crank, ye cameras! He planted himself
behind the makeshift tollgate, surrounded by his stouthearted
men, all Native Americans, by the look of them. Legs spread,
fists on hips, Lyons looked huge, like a colossus, his bulky
chest and protruding gut tented in a flannel shirt, pants tucked
in high boots. Paul Bunyan, sans ax? The Lyons mane, his
beard, was ferocious, its reddish tone highlighted by the sun.
A Biblical prophet? Jut-jawed warrior-militant? Crusader?

All these things.

"Shit!" Werner sneered.

"Next to Lyons, the Indian chief, or whatever: Beaumont
Custerd."

"Cute."

Werner claimed to know Harry from the old days, but
Harry wasn't rushing over to say hello, was he? Thank God,
Nate Carleton somehow slipped through the crack. That was
all she'd need, for Julie to start bleating about good old Nate.

Harry had a still photographer with him from his crummy
county rag and was still doing his best to pretend Susan was
not within a million miles. No good saying she'd tried to call
him. She hadn't.

Julie had a point about Beau Custerd. Alongside Lyons, he
looked like a cream puff, slim as a girl, and, it had to be said,
at least as beautiful. In the clear light, perhaps the way the
shadows were arranged, there was a slick Mongolian look
about him, a housebroken Genghis Khan. No reason to doubt
that a woman like Emma Bristals aspired to eat him alive.
Beau, like Dick, was staring in their direction, but there was
no fierceness in his expression, real or simulated. Dreaminess
emanated from him, even at a distance.

Beau had been dressed like a bridegroom for the occasion,
in a fringed leather suit—à la Buffalo Bill, a very soft doeskin
number, or at least that's how Susan was going to describe
it—and a headband around his jet-black hair, with a single,
long red feather sticking up in the back.

Beau was going to look terrific on TV.

Unfortunately, the half-dozen of his cousins would not be quite so telegenic. There was an interesting black hat and one dirty leather vest in the mob but otherwise, Susan saw, as she and Julie approached, costumes were by Redneck: blue jeans, T-shirts, one pair of greasy Bermuda shorts, a weird Hawaiian sports shirt . . . and, in the way of armaments, one pathetic unstrung bow and quiver of arrows.

Scathingly, Julie Werner said, "So I concentrate on Lyons and the chief. The rest of them look like bums."

"So sorry."

"Hey, we're with you."

Julie offered Susan the mike.

"You write anything for this or you going to wing it?"

"Wing it, of course. I'll over it later. I want pictures and sound."

"People, bridge . . . trees . . . The fat guy sitting in the golf cart. *Who he?* He said hello to you."

"Ah, yes, don't miss *him*, Julie." Susan could find out how far the news had spread. "That's Sir Guy Bristals, the London press baron."

Julie looked panicked.

"You could've told me."

"Is the mike on?"

"Yeah! Shit!"

Ignoring Harry with all her might, Susan drew up to Jasper Gates. Gloria had stopped the contingent ten or fifteen feet from the barrier and there they stood, in uneasy confrontation. Jasper remained highly excited, hopping up and down as if he had to go to the bathroom, holding himself back impatiently as Gloria Goody rifled around in her attaché case, and all the while glaring past Gloria's shoulder at Lyons and his Indians.

"Oh, good morning, Miss Channing," Jasper said, winking broadly, "so pleased you could make it."

"*Mister* Gates . . ." Susan was drop-dead cool, making sure she didn't so much as glance in Harry's direction. She held out the mike. "You might tell us what's going on here this morning, Mr. Gates. The Indian Island Bridge seems to have been occupied by a contingent of Basket Indians led by Richard Lyons, the very well-known—"

"Well-known troublemaker and *pain in the ass*!"

Julie snorted with glee, but Susan wasn't amused, even

though it didn't matter. The picture was everything. They'd cut and paste Jasper's words at will, make him sound a jackass or great intellect, just as they pleased.

"A moment, please . . ." Pint-sized Gloria Goody, up close a buxom little redhead with well-powdered features. "Mr. Gates has nothing to say. The group you see on the bridge, *whoever* they may be otherwise, are trespassers."

Taking his cue from Ms. Goody, Werner, professionally enough, tracked his camera from Gates, past Gloria Goody, toward Lyons, Beau Custerd, and their men, lined up in such perfect order on the other side of the red-and-white barber pole.

Dick Lyons challenged Jasper Gates again.

"Hey, Gatesie! We collected seventeen dollars so far this morning!"

Jasper jerked around and hollered back. There was nothing Ms. Goody could do to stop him.

"You're crazy, Lyons! You think you and a couple of kids can shake us down?" He stopped, suspiciously. "What's the extra dollar for? Your goddamn white horse?"

"Mr. Gates . . . please! We'll be issuing a statement." Ms. Goody snapped. "Please . . . Mr. Gates! The legal status is obvious: The trespassers have erected an illegal barricade across the bridge—"

"They're charging people to get through."

"That appears to be the case."

Jules had the camera on Gloria, good and tight.

"What do you say to the Baskets' accusation that Jasper International and the Indian Island Development Company fraudulently acquired Indian Island?"

She wasn't getting an answer to that. Jasper made a nasty sound and looked insulted and Gloria Goody spun away, at the same time removing from her attaché case a four-by-five-inch file card.

The time had come to recite the riot act.

"Mr. Lyons," she read, "the Big Sea Development Company requests you and your friends to remove the obstruction you have illegally raised on the Big Sea bridge. The Big Sea Development Company does not recognize the claim that is being made to Indian Island by the Basket Nation. The Big Sea Development Company legally and properly acquired title to Indian Island. The purchase was duly recorded by Hispaniola County, which raised no objection to the transaction, and at the time of purchase no other legal objection was raised and no liens brought forward against the transaction.''

Head cocked toward Ms. Goody, Lyons listened politely. He let Ms. Goody's voice ring on for a moment after she finished, then dragged out his own piece of paper and read:

''We are mounting this protest, Mr. Gates, and friends, to call attention to the fact that the Big Sea Development Company has refused to make any sort of accommodation with the Basket Nation, or to compromise with the just demands of the Basket Nation which believes it was unfairly, unjustly, and illegally done out of Indian Island more than one hundred years ago by the failure of the Bureau of Indian Affairs, Department of the Interior, properly and in good faith to protect its interests as provided for by treaty with the United States Government!'' Lyons waited a beat, then added, ''I've got copies of this statement for whomever wants 'em.''

Ms. Goody couldn't hold Jasper back now. Perhaps she didn't try. In any event, he ducked away from her and rushed to the barricade. Bear Jay was close behind him, as if to prevent a collision of the two mighty men.

Face-to-face with Lyons, even though a good head and shoulders shorter, Susan noted, Jasper bellowed, ''You bastard, Lyons, you're misrepresenting! You're misleading these poor people. You're in this for yourself, for the publicity. You do not give a good goddamn for these Indians!''

Julie Werner thrust his camera right in their faces. Give him full marks—he was getting good stuff. What it amounted to, God knows—two grown men, yelling and calling each other names?

Worth maybe fifteen seconds, on a slow evening.

''Dick,'' Bertram Jay interjected, ''you know we're taking the greatest care of the burial ground. The excavation—''

''Shut up, you!'' Lyons roared. ''Keep out of this!''

Gloria Goody helped little by observing, ''I see, Mr. Lyons, that one of your men is carrying a weapon!''

''Weapon?'' Lyons glared. ''What weapon, for crissakes?''

''That bow! And those arrows. I see them with my own eyes!''

''Jesus Christ, that bow doesn't work. It's a prop.''

''*You* say.''

''Yes, *I* say!''

Gates aimed his forefinger at Lyons's bulby nose.

''I'm giving you fair warning, Lyons, we'll bust your ass.

We'll take you to court . . . not the Indians. *You*! For inciting riot, and anything else we can nail you with."

Not thinking, Jasper stretched across the barricade and grabbed at Beaumont Custerd's arm.

"You! Beau, that's your name, isn't it? I want to talk to you! *I have a deal for you!*"

"Get your hands off him!" Lyons shouted.

Lyons jumped toward Gates and Beau slid away, out of Jasper's reach, like a wild thing. Jasper pawed at Lyons and Bear Jay struggled to get between them and, in the confusion, Lyons struck out wildly. Wildly? Lyons's fist caught Bear in the temple. It was a huge blow; Jay staggered backwards and tripped and fell.

"Oh, my God!" Gloria Goody screamed. "I saw that, Lyons. Assault!"

"Self-defense," Lyons yelped. "They were attacking me!"

"It'll be on the tape," Goody screamed again.

And she'd never get her hands on the tape.

Bear was getting to his feet. He might once have been a big football hero, but that hadn't prepared him for Dick Lyons. Even gone to seed, Lyons was a very powerful man. Jay gripped his head with both hands. For all to see, a bump was already rising on his forehead. Tears were running down his cheeks and he shook his head painfully. That hit had been a concusser. He limped out of the way.

"Sorry, buddy," Dick said loudly.

But he was smiling behind his beard, Susan knew it.

"How long do you propose to continue this charade, Mr. Lyons?" Gloria Goody demanded, glancing at her watch. "We propose to call the sheriff if the bridge isn't cleared by . . ."

Well, Lyons had made his point and what more was to be gained? Besides, he had to call it off in time for his meeting with Ishira Guchi who, Susan noted, had wisely come nowhere near the bridge.

Harry had pushed his photographer up beside Julie. Too late, though. Julie had the punch on film. And so what? The story was still not of national caliber. Ugly little incident at Big Sea? So what? Harry understood that just as well. His icy expression ruined his face. Stupid, he'd be thinking, in more ways than one, including Susan Channing in the summary.

Susan was also aware of Guy Bristals. He had wedged himself into the seat of a golf cart, scowling at her and

evidently none too pleased either with his *dear friend* Jasper
Gates who had mysteriously turned into a trained bear, not so
well-trained at that.

"Hey, kid . . . Beau, listen to me!"

Beau didn't speak. Had he ever spoken?

"Gates, you're too obvious," Lyons snarled. "Pay him no
heed, Beau! He's trying to divide us, it's only a tactic—
divide and conquer, like Geronimo used to say."

"Kid, I shit you not!"

"Anyway"—Lyons shrugged—"this is all academic, Gates.
You can rave all you want. It's out of your hands."

This Jasper Gates was a new one on Susan. His blood
pressure must be rocketing and worse—he knew what Lyons
meant: that they were going to deal with Guchi. And that was
going to make Jasper look like a loser. He couldn't bear it.

"Kid Beau, *trust me!*"

Trust me was written all over Jasper's earnest face.

Lyons shuffled back, shaking his head at Beau.

Susan should have had her wits about her. She should have
checked the time.

She noted or heard or perhaps sensed a high-pitched winged
sort of noise, followed swiftly, no, faster than swiftly,
instantaneously, by a thump, a solid, fleshy thump, a pinched-
off scream, a terminal grunt. Instinctively, figure *that* out, she
turned toward Harry, aware of a span of dead silence broken
only by the low hum-whir of Jules Werner's camera.

Something had happened that was not in the Dick Lyons
scenario.

An arrow, yes, with long shaft and feathered end, was
sticking in, and out of, Jasper's chest, the very blue-black
metallic butt of the arrowhead plunged with sickening definition into the white shirtfront at the top of his vest, being wet,
stained, slowly, faster, by an oozing, spreading, pumping
blood.

If not for the blood, Susan wouldn't have believed it. This
sort of thing didn't happen anymore. It hadn't even happened
very often when it was widely supposed to have happened—
that is, during the days when the Indians had mounted their
guerrilla wars and freedom-fighting campaigns against the
white man invaders.

Jasper was done. Nobody thought to catch him, to ease his
way. Lyons tried. He reached, but he was too late. Jasper

went down, not making another sound—and why should he, how could he, if he was dead?

"Hey!" Lyons roared. "What the hell! Crossbow!"

Jasper's body jerked, trembled, legs kicked reflexively, and before anybody could move, there came a final expulsion of air, and a rattle that said he was gone.

Madly, Lyons darted to the side of the bridge, his eyes searching the undergrowth, the swampy grass that grew so profusely in these tidelands.

An arrow! Such madness! Who would shoot such an arrow into the sky, to land in Jasper Gates's chest?

And all Susan could think was that she *had* seen it all before. And, again, she wanted to die. Harry crashed toward her, making such a hell of a racket. And all the while, the camera whirred politely, unobtrusively. Julie Werner never stopped. He was muttering to himself, sort of moaning with happiness, and repeating, over and over again, "Holy shit . . . ho-lee shit . . . holy *shit*!"

Gloria Goody had obviously never seen anything like this in the raw—she jammed one hand in her mouth and tried to eat her knuckles. She began to sob and wail, stumbled backwards to get away from Jasper, and finally sat down on the bridge and held herself together around the knees. In the confusion, Susan could hear Guy Bristals panting, gagging.

Fortunately, Susan was a pro. Like Julie. And Julie had it all on film, every second of it. *Holy shit!*

Sixty seconds, at the very least, on prime-time news. Hey, how many times do you get a shot of an arrow actually penetrating a man's chest? The shot has been faked in the movies a thousand times. But this was for real! Death in real time! They could slow it down, to the instant the tip of the arrow touched Jasper's shirt, or take it back to real time, whatever they wanted.

"Somebody . . ."

Ralph Teller dropped on his knees next to Harry and Mr. Dudley. Unshakable Dudley had taken off his coat and placed it under Jasper's head. He picked up Gates's hand and felt for a pulse. Bear Jay slumped down beside them, making as if to help, but Dudley pushed him away.

How could he be so cool? Harry said, "Beau, run like hell down to the inn and call the paramedics . . ."

"Yeah and the police," Ralph added.

"Yeah, and the police, Beau."

Sir Guy Bristals's rotund body rocked against Susan.

"Oh, Lord, Oh, Lord . . ."

Beaumont Custerd took off like a deer.

Very precisely, Dudley said, "Mr. Gates is dead."

"I think you're right," Bear Jay muttered.

And he was a doctor, of sorts.

Dick Lyons yelled, "You guys, fan out . . ."

"You'll never catch him now," Harry said.

"We can try."

Richard Lyons took it very personally. *Somebody* was dumping on his program.

"Be careful, Dick."

Was that herself speaking, Susan, so amazingly controlled? Yes, Julie, yes, follow Lyons and the Indian boys. They were climbing off the bridge, sloshing in the mud, looking underneath the bushes. But Harry was right—whoever had done this was long gone.

"Susie, you don't have to stay here. C'mon . . ."

She was looking at Harry. But what the hell was he talking about?

"Harry, I'm working!"

Bristals ogled, his milky eyes dazed, thinking God knows what.

"C'mon," Harry insisted.

"Julie, we've got to feed this to San Francisco. Julie . . ."

"And you're gonna have to give voice." Julie was gazing at her, stupefied. "Did you . . . how did you . . . did you have any idea of this?"

"How could I? Don't be stupid . . . Harry, goddamn it!" Susan yanked her arm away. "In case you didn't know, this is the *stuff* of TV, Harry. That's why I do what I do, Harry."

"Susie, I know that!"

She was crying a little, just to show him.

"You think I'm a monster."

"I do not."

Monster or not, she was having trouble with it. So was the great media mogul. Bristals stuck close, trying to get Susan's arm, more to help himself than comfort her, but with Harry's help she stayed out of his reach. Harry even stopped and turned on Bristals and grunted nastily and Sir Guy sidled away, pathetically. Of course, what would he know? He was the king in his counting house. This was something new for him too.

"I don't know," Susan heard herself saying. "Get the kids out of the room, Harry. It's *too* graphic, wouldn't you say?"

"Could be, Susie."

Wait just a minute, they were talking here about Jasper Gates who, less than an hour ago, had been telling Susan he had the hots for her, and whom she had pushed away.

They reached the NAN truck and, by now sputtering indignantly, Sir Guy got up next to her, avoiding Harry's shoulder block.

"Are you quite all right, my girl?"

"She's fine," Harry muttered.

Cheeks quivering with excitement, as if in self-congratulation for an amazing survival, Bristals patted himself down, caressed his dear body, arms, chest, felt his crotch, nodding as he found he was as A-OK as he was ever likely to be.

"Remember most faithfully, old girl," Bristals ordered, "we shall need stills from your footage." He glanced at his watch. "It's evening in London. For tomorrow evening's paper then! Most dramatic exclusive to the *London Final*: Jasper Gates, American financier, assassinated by California savages!"

"Easy, Guy," Harry cautioned. "We don't know yet."

Bristals didn't hear.

"Exclusive to the *London Final* from its own correspondent, Sir Guy Bristals."

He had recovered from the shock, it might be said.

"Oh, so sorry, my girl! I know how *close* you were!"

"Jasper was a friend," Susan murmured, daring them to disagree. "A very good friend." Then added, for Harry, "He was not my fiancé."

"Guy," Harry said softly, "no reason for you to hang around here. You'll want to start writing your story. I'll tell the sheriff where you'll be in case he wants to see you."

"Me? But why?"

Harry smiled evilly.

"For all we know, the guy was shooting at you. Think about it."

Bristals did and turned pale.

"Well . . . that's out of the question," he stammered. "Susan, we must talk, dear girl. I know you . . . you're feeling miserable about this bloody awful business. But *later*, when you're ready, we will talk. About Japan. Other vital matters!"

She shrugged, indifferently, neither agreeing nor disagreeing, leaving Bristals hanging.

Finally getting the point, he said petulantly, "Well, I'm not needed here any longer. If a statement of any kind is required, I'll be available at the inn. Now, if you'll excuse me, I think the good doctor is going to be very interested in my report."

"You can say Gates never knew what hit him," Harry said, "that for all he knew, it was a terminal nuclear strike and everybody in the world died at the same time he did."

"Thank you, Harry, such a *comfort*," Guy said testily.

Sullenly, he finally turned away and, alone, made down the road toward the inn, his rotund body swaying on feet that seemed far too tiny.

How much would they need from her, thirty seconds? No more; more would be excessive. The film would speak for itself.

"At approximately ten A.M. this morning, Pacific time, Jasper Gates, chief executive of Jasper International, Los Angeles-headquartered shipping, real estate, and energy conglomerate, fell victim to a steel-tipped hunting arrow... dense forest and desolate marshland of the Indian Island resort development called Big Sea, in northern California... scene a century or more ago of a bloody massacre of Basket tribesmen by a renegade U.S. Cavalry squadron... incredible and exclusive footage... Gates is cut down... heated negotiations with representatives of the Basket Indian tribe and their champion Richard Lyons, the well-known people's advocate and tireless human rights campaigner... the rightful ownership of the island, which for centuries was the home of the Basket Nation... recent weeks saw the dispute vastly complicated by the discovery during renovation work of an ancient Basket Indian burial ground on the site of the massacre... artifacts, human remains dating back many years... any disturbance of the land and burial ground would verge on sacrilege and, *as the Basket elders have warned,* bring down a *curse* on the heads of the perpetrators..."

Or something like that.

Harry watched her closely for signs of cracking as Susan scribbled her report. Beyond them, men had gathered in a protective shield around Jasper's body, Dick Lyons towering above, distraught but pensive. He had never meant for anything like this to happen.

"Jasper Gates, much in the public eye, known for a number of daring and colorful projects, including forestry in the Amazon rain forest . . . most recently, the talk of the international cruise business, contracting to build the world's largest cruise ship, a veritable floating city block of luxury hotels, casinos, night clubs . . . a project Gates himself called Las Vegas Rides the Waves. The ship, to be christened S.S. *Freckles*, part of Jasper International's SunSpots Cruise Lines, being built in Varna, Bulgaria . . ."

Or words to that effect.

Then she had to stop. The sound of sirens signaled arrival of ambulance and police. Harry left Susan in the truck, went back there for a moment, then quickly returned to her. He expected her to cave in, didn't he? He couldn't figure out what was holding her together, could he? And he thought he knew everything about her.

"I'm not very good luck, Harry."

"Now . . . forget that, Susie!"

But there were certain things she should say to him before they talked to the police. There were certain things he should know.

"Harry, I liked Jasper. He was a . . . character. I have to say I really liked him and I admired him, Harry."

"That's okay. Believe me. I liked him too, in a way."

"But I didn't love him, Harry."

"Okay," he said, "I never thought you did."

"Even so," she said morbidly, "I'm not a lucky token, Harry, Susan Channing is no good-luck piece."

"Susie, knock if off! I suppose next you're going to mention Nate."

"Not smart to get mixed up with Miss Susie, Harry."

Harry took her by the arm so tightly he squeezed off any further words. Maybe she did protest too much.

" . . . and so death came for Jasper Gates in a very public way, too public for a man who ran from personal publicity . . . tragedy of the purest sort, out of conflict between tradition, ancient ways, and modern times . . . [Facing the camera-eye earnestly] . . . a story as old as this country. Jasper Gates, a man from nowhere, returns to oblivion . . ."

Perhaps a little purple but if they didn't like it in New York, they could just go ahead and shove it . . . or rewrite it, or cut it, or suit themselves.

"*Curse*, Miss Susie?" Harry asked, referring to the spot she'd just finished.

"The ancient curse of the Baskets, Harry, that's right. Jasper told me."

"You made it up, Miss Susie."

"Harry, I swear it!"

Liar.

Harry hadn't let up since it'd happened. No matter what he said, kidding aside, kidding her along, he hung to her arm for dear life.

"I don't buy curses laid on people." He squeezed. "That was good, Miss Susie. And, man, sensational stuff your boy Julie got. Though I don't remember the ugly son of a bitch from Adam—"

"You think Sir Guy is going to let us live?"

His hold tightened.

"That egotistical bastard. He's world-class, Miss Susie. You're never going to make it with him."

"What do you think I should do, Harry?"

She leaned on his arm, why not, she had him here with her, remembering that last time when they'd made love in the moonlight. She'd said she would never forget. And she hadn't, even if he acted as though he had.

"That's your decision, honey."

"What would you do, Harry?"

"I dunno, Miss Susie. I wouldn't ever take the responsibility for interfering with a money machine like yours. I mean what are we talking . . . No! Cancel that. I didn't ask."

"Mercenary me, Harry, I wouldn't tell how much, don't worry."

Oh my Gawd! Greenswards!

How to explain? Practically the last thing she'd said to Jasper was that she was going to tear up the deed. And now? Tear it up? She couldn't tear it up; it would probably be against the law to tear it up. She was so sorry. Poor Jasper. But think, if Jasper's end had been ordained for this day in June, then the snuffing had been a kindly one. And he could take comfort, if he was in a position to take any comfort, that he was in no way to blame for what had happened. It wasn't as if he'd smoked too many cigarettes or drank too much gin!

"You know something, Harry?"

"What's that?"

"We're alive."

A Truth: Jasper Gates was dead and they were alive. Susan remembered from the old days, and maybe Harry did too, thinking whilst in the midst of death, surrounded by death, almost as a participant in death, how *she* was still alive and how extraordinary that was. The knowledge or awareness of survival, of continued existence, versus the nothingness, the unmeasured zilch of the other, i.e., death, had always served to add zest to the smallest, most ordinary acts of living. And to make you wonder with great, crushing wonder why you were alive and everybody else was dead.

"It's very good to be alive, Miss Susie. I'm glad you noticed."

21

There was precious little anybody could tell the sheriff's deputy. Nobody had seen anything, before or after the arrow met its target. They were barely able to agree about which way Jasper Gates had been facing—toward Lyons, then turning, reaching for Beau Custerd's arm, Beau twisting away, Lyons lunging and suddenly! Gates hit, his outcry cut off in crescendo, falling.

Lyons and his gang couldn't be blamed. Dick swore the intention was only to dramatize the Basket complaint. The tollgate was to have been dismantled before lunchtime, whatever happened.

No, no, the whole ugly business, simply stated, boiled down to the mystery archer who, as if advised perfectly of a timetable, had hidden himself in the bulrushes, loosed his deadly arrow, and then made his escape, precious seconds before a search was begun. And nobody could help with that.

When they had finished with the law, this assorted group, now much subdued, went in their various directions: Gloria Goody to begin an afternoon on the telephone with headquarters; Bear Jay, holding his head and a grudge bigger than ever, presumably back to Jenny; Mr. Dudley, trailing Gloria; and Dick Lyons with Beau Custerd up the hill to Rancho Mondo. In the next few hours, as soon as possible, Ms. Goody had told Lyons, they would arrange a meeting and settle the Indian Island dispute.

Harry lingered while Susan finished up with Julie Werner. Julie was to rush back to San Francisco. Susan would stick it out at Big Sea. Stay tuned . . .

Susan was not sure about anything else, but she did know it wouldn't do to be alone.

As soon as Werner was out the door, she turned to Harry.

"You're not going to run away, are you?"

"Don't worry, Miss Susie."

"I've got to call New York. Will you . . ."

"I'll go upstairs with you."

At the top of the steps, she remembered.

"What about *your* story?"

"I've got time. Remember, I'm a weekly."

"In that case—" she continued down the hall and unlocked her door, "you can come in."

"Yes, I plan to, Miss Susie."

And it was done. Harry was in the room, and now that he was and they were alone, she didn't know what to do next. She wanted most of all not to frighten him again.

"Harry, can you stay? Can we have dinner together, just the two of us?"

"Yep."

"When do you have to leave? I know you come out before the weekend . . . I *know* you have to do that."

"Later tonight, Susie."

"I want to take a shower, is that okay? And call Fineman."

"Well . . . sure."

"You can have a drink. There's all sorts of stuff there."

"Okay."

She hesitated and Harry looked at her so blandly she wondered if he were playing some kind of a trick.

"What would you like?"

"Susie, I'll make it. Go ahead."

"Will you be all right?"

"Absolutely. *Go ahead*."

And she went, looking at him over her shoulder, back where she'd been with Jasper Gates. Should she lock the bathroom door? Yes. No. She didn't. Swiftly, she undressed and did her best to wash the morning away. It stuck to her though, the very subtle odor, the dingy body-slick; she couldn't get rid of it. When she'd done all she could, Susan wrapped herself in one of the big SunSpots towels and came out into the bedroom. Peeking around the door, she saw Harry was sitting in front of the window with a long drink of something or other in his hand, staring out at the ocean. He didn't hear her come up behind him in her bare feet—but he wasn't startled either when she put her wet hair next to his face and kissed the side of his forehead.

"Hi," he said. "You know, you mentioned dinner and we haven't even had lunch yet."

"I know. It seems a lot later."

"A kind of a long, dread day."

Susan came around and sat down in the other chair there, her towel tucked neatly, chastely around her like a full-length cloak. Harry noted it, said nothing. Maybe he was used to sitting around with half-clad females.

"You look like you were just reborn, Miss Susie. Did you make the call, I didn't hear you?"

"I will, later. Harry, I suppose you'll put the Gates story on page one of *The Corsair*?"

Harry let go a scarcely amused laugh.

"You kidding? Susie, how many really sexy murders, death by arrow, for heaven's sake, do you think happen in these parts? Not very many, you can be sure. Besides, I've got to follow up last week."

"Dick delivered quite a bop to Bertram 'Bear' Jay," she recalled. "Accidental, of course."

"Sure . . . with great *élan*, as we used to say in the French Foreign Legion."

"Harry, I didn't know you were in the French Foreign Legion."

Funny, that was the sort of aside Jasper Gates would've passed off as biographical material.

"Yeah, Fort Dummy, near Marrakesh . . . You know, Miss Susie, I want to talk to Lyons about this. I kind of think that arrow was meant for him."

Susan leaned forward, nodding, elbows on her knees.

"It was so haphazard, yes, that makes sense, Harry."

"It does if you agree nobody was mad enough at Jasper Gates to kill him. I mean, most people in these parts don't know him at all, much less that he's mixed up in Big Sea. I doubt if any of the Baskets feel that strongly about it. On the other hand, Dick Lyons *is* known and *is* hated by any number of people, here and all around the world. Don't forget, somebody shot at him once before.''

"True.''

"If I were him, I'd really be watching my back.''

Downstairs, Lyons had tried clumsily to make amends to Bear Jay, potentially a new enemy, even to the extent of hugging him, then loudly announcing he was going to bless Jenny and Bear by leaving Rancho Mondo. They could just damn well go ahead and move in there together and old Dick Lyons would be on his way. Then, a minute later, he'd been whispering gleefully to Susan that all he was doing was going up the hill to Bel Custerd's trailer.

"You know, dick around, write some poetry, like I've always wanted . . . I'm too old for her, but if the child loves me, what the hell am I supposed to do?''

"My big scoop, Susie. We don't get many, you know.''

"I'm not going to steal it. Harry . . .'' She put it to him straight. "You don't much like it, do you?''

"What?''

"The paper. Working here in the sticks?''

"Who says so? Did I say that?''

"You're brilliant, Harry!''

"Of course I am.''

"But maybe you're a little too young for Rio Tinto, as well as too brilliant.''

He only smiled. He would never answer such a question.

"So,'' she repeated, "who wants Lyons dead?''

"Can you think of anybody?'' he parried. "I can. Jenny? I didn't know she'd left the big buffalo. Bear Jay? Especially now, after getting socked like that.''

"I don't seriously think they'd try to kill him, do you?''

Susan thought he would never ask, but, anyway, finally, he did: Why didn't she come along? She'd never been to Rio Tinto and it was sort of an interesting, provincial little place. Besides . . . besides what? Well, Harry just wished she would. She'd like his house, if she went for kind of quaint, turn-of-the-century California bungalow architecture, freshly painted white, with gray trim. Or? Actually, she might not be interest ed at all.

"I'm interested in *everything* about you, Harry."

For a second, she was tempted to drop on him the info about her house, that old Georgian job called Greenswards, which, but for Jasper's untimely end, would have been returned to its previous owner, and which she was now stuck with until she'd at least had superior legal advice.

But, what the hell, she couldn't leave Big Sea now. They were still somewhere in the middle of the story. Susan would be hearing from Fineman if she didn't call him first. And then, what about the Gates profile—was it shitcanned or would they rejig it as a retrospective, weave it into the big takeout on Ishira Guchi and All-Nippon Prosperoso? This remarkable footage Julie Werner had shot could be, should be, used and reused, used ad infinitum. *The American experience!* Perhaps, thanks to Jasper Gates, that is to say his dramatic death, the Indian Island War would turn out to be one for the books. It had everything: cityslicker developer Jasper Gates, the beautiful and/or handsome Basket Indian twins Beaumont and Belmont Custerd, people's hero Dick Lyons, and foreign financial forces in the person of Ishira Guchi. Put all this together and what did you get? A homespun *American experience*: Death by Arrow.

"Like that, Harry, see what I mean?"

"Look, Miss Susie . . ." Harry stared at her, rather anxiously, pleasingly concerned, Susan thought. "We're not going to split up again, *are we*?"

"No."

"We've got to talk, Susie."

"East Coast, West Coast," she mused, "and never the twain shall meet?"

"Oh . . . Susie . . . for chrissakes!"

Harry looked genuinely wasted when she said that. Susan eased herself forward, down on her knees, and crossed her arms on his knees.

"Harry, my next assignment, as far as I know, is to go to Toronto. I've got to do it." What was she saying, that she had a certain number of commitments to fulfill and then . . . what? "I don't know what we're going to do about the Gates story now." She smiled up at him. "Jack and I are doing a job about Donald Trump in Atlantic City and Fineman is working on stuff in Warsaw and Moscow."

"Your feet won't touch the ground for a year."

"I'm telling you how it is, Harry."

"Well . . ." He drew a long breath, staring at her worriedly. "Look, I . . ." He started again, "I wouldn't want you to quit doing what you do. I wouldn't expect that of you, Susie."

"Harry," she teased, "are you getting a little ahead of yourself?"

C'mon, Harry, first things first.

"Ahead of myself?"

"Why should I want to anyway? Quit?"

Harry scowled patiently. He was not doing well and he knew it.

"Well, the reason . . ." He stumbled. "The reason would be so we could be together . . . but, like I said, I'm not asking."

"Define *together*."

"The condition of contact. Coming together: collision. Bang! Joined. As one. The opposite of separate, divided, apart . . . alone."

"You're very romantic."

"Yes, I know."

"And I," she said, "I couldn't ask you to dump the *Corsair* and move back to New York, Harry, just for some casual reason."

"Casual, what would be casual about it?"

"Well . . ." Then, risking it, she said, "I wish you'd at least touch me nicely. Just once. Ain't I deserving?"

Gravely, he leaned down and put his lips to her forehead and, as she closed her eyes expectantly, her lips.

"Thank you."

"My pleasure."

Susan opened her eyes.

"Isn't it strange? After all this time? I think we can do a lot better. Last time, it was like it didn't happen at all, you know, and then all of a sudden you're talking about ghosts, Harry."

"I know," he said glumly.

"You were shocked. I went too fast."

"No."

She held the back of his hand to her mouth, kissed the knuckles, then the palm. He didn't move. Harry, of course, would not give in all at once. Susan clung to his hand, holding it to her chest.

"Harry, I absolutely do not want to scare you away again."

"Don't worry."

"You said together means collision."

"Right. A collision so powerful you see stars."

"Is that serious, Harry?"

"Sure. And if it isn't, who says we have to be serious, Susie?"

"Then kiss me again."

He did and asked, "What're you thinking now, Susie?"

"That I like your skin. Does that surprise you?"

"I should say not."

"What about . . . me?"

He never stopped smiling.

Susan blinked tearfully, feeling as she had that other night, very vulnerable, undefended, like a city open and ready for the sacking.

"I don't know, Harry, it's like it's been a long, long trip. And here we are. But *where* are we?"

"Right here, in your room, at Big Sea Inn, that's where."

"Harry, I wish you wouldn't leave tonight."

"And I wish you wouldn't go back to New York."

And then, in a flash, he folded: no more second-guessing. He put his hands on her bare shoulders, thumbs digging in, and pulled her up, toward him, kissing her again, aggressively. Beautifully. Susan was hardly prepared for the onslaught of his wide, strong mouth. She kissed him back, urgently, forgetting to breathe, then gasping for air. The radical movement loosened her towel and it slipped. Harry pulled it away, threw it on the floor, and pulled her up in his arms, then half carried her into the bedroom.

All she could think was to mumble stupidly that he'd give himself a hernia and so on. Susan was not a little girl. But he was strong and it wasn't far to the bed. She held on to him while he undressed, throwing clothes every which way, then dropped beside him, dissolving, like sugar, sticky and wet, turning to liquid, the Susan Channing ice cube melting, that's how Jack Godfrey described it, and what a stain she left behind. Even her eyes became gooey, swollen so badly she could hardly keep them open, though they needn't be open, did they? An allergy, yes, the well-known one occasioned by need. Opening her mouth to kiss, she heard a whimper, her own, and sought his tongue, hot, scrambling, the fleshly metaphor. Harry took her to himself, her breasts, aching, and her belly. Susan opened to his hand; her legs, her body heaved. She could not handle it.

"Harry! Yes, please!"

He didn't stop now, didn't pause, punishing her, perfection himself. Susan grappled desperately, fighting him off, not letting him escape either, capturing him for her own, taking him within her breathlessly, at length, fully encompassing, unlike any other being, in a tangle of long legs, so confused she couldn't tell limb from limb.

Though Harry might think otherwise, Susan was in full control. This was her thing, her way, her norm. Desire piled on desire, built, bloomed, burgeoned, a fragrant growth, lush and decadent, half decayed, half dead already, even as it blossomed. Dragged by passion, pulled, driven, Susan lost ability to speak; this was also her way. She would communicate in primitive grunts and screams. Was there anything wrong with that?

Susan wanted Harry, all of him, every last bit of him, absolutely, without qualification; this was imperative and had not been so imperative for a long, long time. Between her legs, he came forward, then down, by the numbers, slowly, so intently really, as if approaching from a mile away, the leading nub of him touching her first and then the main force a yard or two later, as she directed the coupling, a new world entering her, the universe of Harry Teller, sun, moon, stars, gravity itself. She held on tightly as he pulled and thrust, lifting her until she cried out, taking her much farther along the road than she'd ever been.

"Susie, Susie . . . it's fine."

Her voice was mashed and choked.

"Make it fine then, Harry."

Of course, she was really asking to be saved, from herself, from life, a lonely future. In bed with him, which was what she'd wanted, Susan couldn't stop herself from crying, but so silently, Harry couldn't have known. Why? What was she mourning now? That she'd be fresh out of Harry?

His body was long and hard, and, as lightly as he was built, he made her feel weak and frail, the vessel, the receptacle filled, desire spiked. She twisted and squirmed and adjusted until enmeshment could have been declared complete, if anybody was making such announcements.

Then, suddenly, he stopped. All forward movement ceased and you were listening for voices calling for help. Within the silence, Susan heard, felt, his heart pounding, his blood racing within her.

"Hello there, Miss Susie."

"Harry..." Her lips were thick, gluey. "Joined, *together*, at the hip. Is it all right?"

"Miss Susie..." How could he compliment her? "Pacing is everything. You wouldn't want me to finish before I begin."

Susan knotted her arms around him, kissed him, mouth wet and sloppy, tightened her legs, rolling under him, sucking him forward, cavorting, the very word.

"Harry, I think you can stop calling me Miss Susie now."

"All right, what do you require. Susan? Miss Channing?"

"Are you okay, Harry?"

She felt his lips crinkle.

"Yeah. Fine. I'm glad I saved myself for you, Susie."

"Dog!"

Well, he didn't have to be serious. That didn't matter now because she had him and she held him fast. At your servicing, Channing! His weak male body was secure in her legs, the long prong deeply imbedded. He knew it too. Carefully, cautiously, for he wouldn't want to disappoint her, assuming, as all men did, that he was in control, so deliberately that she could have screamed with laughter, and glee, Harry resumed, searchingly, reaching, overreaching, though she didn't say so, of course.

Susan couldn't think of Nate now. He was but a glancing memory, the way it should be, a recollection of heat and noise.

And she still made a considerable amount of noise. Enough so Harry cut off her cries with his mouth, holding her down with brute force and breathing hard.

God forbid she should damage him.

Thinking... thinking. Doing... doing. All that mattered, basically, was his weight, the maleness, the driving, incessant, regular presence inside her; the sweet, raw, inciting smell in her nose and taste in her throat; then, distantly, a narrowing, converging, cresting. Nerve ends, finally, touched like hot wires, flashed and showered sparks.

Susan heard that voice again, her voice, in triumph. Skillfully, she held the crest, riding the climax like a surfer, replying to him ever more fervently, arms and legs spread away from him, akimbo, as she reached for him with her very heart and soul and brought him forth.

Coming down to quiet again, Susan was conscious of the absurdity of it, a split second of infinity and how little it mattered. How little? It mattered not at all! And yet, it was everything. And how many man-hours thus expended since the beginning of time and until the end of time? Light years, billions, trillions, uncounted, uncountable.

Harry finally spoke: the god broke whispered words.

"I do love you, Susie."

It made her so sad. She held him fast in her arms and legs, hugging.

"Harry, what're you doing here?"

"Everybody's got to be someplace, Susie."

"I don't mean that."

"You mean, how did it happen? Timing, Susan, timing is everything."

"Harry, have the ghosts all been laid now?"

"Well laid, Miss Susie."

22

Susan broke away from her new best friend Gloria Goody long enough to speak for a few moments to Harry's brother who just happened to be loitering by the front desk.

"I'll be in shortly, *sweetheart*," Susan sang cheerily, to the lady attorney's back.

Making no sign she'd heard, Gloria continued down the steps toward the dining room. No, she was not altogether happy with Susan Channing's attitude.

"Any news, Ralph?"

Watching Ms. Goody's back, Ralph Teller sighed. "Have I aged ten years? I had that woman with me all morning." He hesitated. "I saw Harry. We had coffee before he left."

"*Dear* Harry Teller!" Susan regarded him impassively. "How was he?"

"He seemed just fine, Sue."

"Ah, good. Good."

Although no doubt just a little bit tired? They'd finally eaten something at eight, then again retired.

"Sue, this Goody bitch tells me J. I. wants out of Big Sea pronto. They'll accept practically any terms. Jesus, open one day and sold the next."

"Yes, that's what Ms. Gloria told me too."

"*If* Blick agrees." Ralph looked not just weary, but worried. "He's due in tomorrow morning."

"Gloria told me that too."

Unbelievable! She'd just finished assuring practically everybody that AHB *never* traveled. And now? Mignon's demise had unhinged him. But of course there was money involved at Big Sea and that was a powerful incentive.

"That woman is a ball-buster, Sue."

"Ralph," she said disapprovingly, "don't *macho* me."

He didn't get the point, just went on moaning. "I figure my days are numbered."

"Surely not. The Japanese are going to want continuity . . ."

"For how long? A month or two?" Ralph looked mournful. "I miss Jasper Gates, Sue. He was an irascible little guy, but you knew where you were."

"Yes," she agreed. "He was not a bad man. I'll remember him, that's for sure."

But not for the gift of Greenswards, which Ms. Goody claimed by rights belonged to the company and he'd had no business deeding over to her. Funny, Susan had been ready to throw it back in Jasper's face. Now? She didn't know, except she didn't intend to be pushed around by Ms. Gloria Goody.

"Harry says I better start thinking about getting into the newspaper business."

"Why not?"

"Sports column."

"That's not a bad idea."

Finally, Ralph mustered a grin.

"He doesn't know what he's saying. He's crazy about you. You know that?"

"Well . . . nice to hear it from an impartial observer."

"Not impartial."

Ralph's face turned red. What, was he going to leap up in the back of the church, not forever hence prepared to hold his peace? What could there be that Ralph knew about her? She had never once misbehaved in the Big Sea Inn, at least until last night.

"I want him to be happy," Ralph muttered.

"So do I."

"Good." Ralph glanced at her keenly. "Blick showing up is not going to make any difference, is it?"

"Blick? Why would it?" She looked him in the eye. "Because I was once upon a time married to his son? That's got no bearing on *anything*, believe me, Ralph."

"Good," he said again.

Susan could have been less concerned about what to wear to lunch. Of course, she had been put off by Gloria Goody's visit and just watching Gloria hopping around in her little career-girl knit suits tainted one's judgment—as Susan should've realized before Emma Bristals charged into the inn in her sweaty trail clothes, by the look of them the same she'd been wearing at Rancho Mondo that other day. Susan had just kissed Ralph on the cheek and he, in brotherly fashion, had kissed her back. Then, sighting Emma, he muttered good-bye and ducked behind the front desk and into his office.

"Sue Channing," Emma bawled, "remember me?"

"Of course I do."

And Susan looked just fine in her jeans, denim shirt, and a red bandanna around her neck to cover Harry's lipmarks.

"We're lunching, are we? Guy-balls said us and a Japanese chappie who is said to be immensely well set up! You've seen the stud in the flesh, Sue! Is it true?"

It didn't matter in the least who might be listening.

"His name is Ishira Guchi."

Emma seized—didn't take, didn't grab, seized—Susan's arm.

"Well then! What *about* our incident at the bridge!"

"Have you seen Dick?"

"No, not since yesterday noon, just after they came back. Then, Saladin dropped in and, as you may have heard, Saladin is not a great admirer of Dick's. The two don't tango, as we say, far from it."

"Has Jenny really moved out, Emma?"

The Lady Bristals nodded, rather guiltily for her.

"So I believe. But needn't have on my account. No, I think it's this thing with Bear Jay. He's confused her somehow. Dropping all caution to the wind, you've heard the stories. Practically doing *exhibitions* for all to see . . ."

She tendered the word its French pronunciation and, of course, in French it had a particular connotation.

"Some form of therapy?"

"Sue! She's *your* friend." Emma laughed sharply. "Psychiatrist, cure thyself. Shall we make for the bar, Sue? I see no hint of Guy-balls and I could use a stiff one, darling, believe me! I do mean *drink* of course!"

Given the circumstances, it was not half bad Lady Emma was to be in the party. She'd take the heat off the Gloria-situation and also serve to keep Guchi at bay. Why Sir Guy had invited Emma, of course, that was something else.

Emma pulled Susan with her into Westward Ho!, then abruptly stopped. Bristals and Gloria were sitting in the leather booth that had become Sir Guy's home-away-from-home.

"Oh, bloody hell," Emma sputtered, "there he is. His Bloatedness! How much I'd forgotten." She stood very still staring across the bar. "He's no Saladin Rivers, Sue, I don't mind telling you that." Luridly, she added, "Saladin's achievement in the Eros department is quite phenomenal, if I say so myself. A jumpy little stud, but if you like 'em that way, which I happen to, nothing matches for a mount."

She slapped Susan's shoulder and guffawed, as bawdily as a country squire. Bristals whipped around, beamed pudgily, and waved.

"Well, into the fray," Emma groaned sportily. "I'll tell you one thing: Saladin will never be the same, *après moi*. There's porking, Sue, and then there's *the other* which a native boy such as Saladin can't ever have experienced, at least as practiced by an expert such as myself!"

The other? Susan thought she understood what Emma meant, but for the sake of argument she looked blank.

"Sue, for God's sake!" Emma said, much too loudly. "Don't tell me you don't know that back in London, I'm called the Marie Antoinette of fellatio: *Let Them Eat Cake!*"

Susan writhed over a fire built for a witch. Even giving Emma credit for being disreputable, a drunk, a horsewoman, an Olde English vulgarian, barbarian, still in all, wasn't she a little too awful? Hotly, shamelessly, Emma stared at her, watching for just such a sign of distaste as was in Susan's mind.

"Emma, give me a break! I've been shocked by the experts."

Rumbling with laughter, Emma said, "C'mon, ducks, let's join Guy-balls and his friend . . . that the lady lawyer?"

Sir Guy tottered to his feet as they approached. From afar, one might have conceived the notion he was pleased to see

Emma again, but at closer quarters his lively grin seemed more spiteful than cordial.

"Hello, old dear."

"What ho, Guy-balls."

Bristals said, "I want you to meet Miss Gloria Goody from Los Angeles..."

"Ms...."

Bristals blinked.

"Yes, yes, beg pardon, *Ms*. Goody who's on the legal staff at Jasper International, Emma."

"Not *your* solicitor then?"

Gasping merrily for breath, Bristals said, "Oh, no! Oh, no!" He went up on his toes to kiss her heartily on the cheek. "You'll be needing a drink, old dear... and Susan too."

He turned and snapped fingers at the bar.

"How do," Emma greeted Gloria Goody, not bothering to take her outstretched hand.

She dropped carelessly into the leather banquette, butting Gloria unceremoniously toward the middle so there would be room to her right. Obviously, Emma meant for Dr. Guchi to sit there when he arrived. Not what Sir Guy had in mind, for he frowned biliously, then sat down again next to La Goody, thank God, which put Susan on the outside.

The customary bottle of champagne arrived at the same time.

"Dom Ruinart, thank you, Rita!" Bristals announced. "Your favorite, dear Susan."

"Make mine a pink gin," Emma said crustily, "a double."

"I'll drink your champagne, Sir Guy," Susan said.

"And an iced tea for Ms. Goody who's working," Bristals said. "All right, Rita?"

"Yessir!"

"Good girl!"

Bristals tried to slap her rump, but Rita dodged too quickly, already onto Sir Guy's London tricks.

"Nice gal," Bristals noted.

Wasn't he aware of Ms. Goody? If looks were lethal...

"How are you keeping, old girl?" Bristals asked Emma bluffly.

His tone was so patronizing you wondered how he got away with it. Before answering, Emma glanced at Susan, then Gloria Goody.

"Very well indeed, Guy-balls," she said breezily. "I have my horses and my hounds. Life is good!"

"Though perhaps not as set and stylized as life in Ireland?"

"Better," Emma responded instantly. "Life here, as you say, is not as structured, Guy-balls."

"Ah-ha!" he clucked unhumorously, "I have heard, old thing, *apropos*, that you're living dangerously, on the very brink..." Emma glanced at him haughtily. "What truth to the rumor, Em, that you're *thick* with a local lad *and* also much in the company of the *man of the people*?"

"Man of the people?"

"That monstrous troublemaker: Lyons, is it not?" he asked of Susan. "The man responsible for the death of our friend Jasper Gates..." He was pouring champagne in his glass, Susan's. "...whom I toast. Absent friend: Jasper Gates."

Emma sneered pityingly.

"Don't act the fool, Guy-balls. Bring an action, why don't you?"

Bristals hruumped and drank again.

"Bit late for that, old shrew."

Ignoring the last endearment, Emma gulped a good half of her gin, then simply turned sideways and slapped a hand on Gloria Goody's forearm, living dangerously once again, if she had but known it. Or did she? It seemed to Susan that when it came to such matters, Lady Emma was no slouch.

"What a place this is, Ms. Solicitor, let me tell you! Work aplenty, if you're interested. The natives are all half crazy. Maybe it's the air, or what's in the air."

"Not my bag, I'm afraid. I do corporate law, Lady Emma."

Gloria smiled hesitantly, not knowing what to make of her.

"Call me, Emma, darling. I'm no lady." Emma said with a cackle. "The fact is I enjoy Lyons's company. He's a wonderful drinking chum. Something Saladin Rivers is not—Saladin couldn't drink his way out of a paper bag! Lyons and I sit about telling tall horse tales and regaling each other with alcohol!"

So saying, Emma downed the rest of the gin and twisted around for Rita, pointing at her empty glass.

"And," she added, "speaking of living dangerously, Saladin's wife, a totally wilful bitch, tried to kill *him* once before and, for all I know, she may end my days with a bullet. The law of the Old West, Guy-balls. Just remember, if anything *happens* to happen to me, have 'em ask *Maudy Rivers* where she was at the time in question. . . ."

Emma laughed loudly, boisterously. As Dick had said, she was her own force of nature: windy and stormy: the big blow, indeed.

Gloria Goody began to look very nervous, and undecided, evidently, whether to stay put or edge away. Bristals regarded his former wife stoically, but there wouldn't be any trouble divining what he was thinking, or rather hoping.

It was at this appropriate moment that Ishira Guchi appeared at the top of the steps into Westward Ho!

"And," Emma added vivaciously, "ten to one that's our Japanese friend!"

"Since he's the only Japanese registered at the hotel—"

"All right, Guy-balls."

Understandably, Ishira Guchi looked very solemn, his heavy lids perhaps like funeral canopies, even more sadly long-faced than usual, although making such a comparison was useless. Each time Susan had seen him, Guchi seemed that much more overloaded with the world's problems than before.

Bristals jumped up spryly.

"Doctor Guchi!"

"Good evening . . ."

Guchi had reason to be distraught. Jasper had been his dear friend, for all Susan knew his *dearest* friend. Given his position in Japanese society, his international preeminence, Guchi must live a very circumscribed sort of life. His every move would be measured, debated, every remark researched before delivery and every decision counterweighted with consequence. Jasper Gates might have been Guchi's only escape to a less deadly world. Of course, the good doctor couldn't know that Gates had considered him shifty.

"Ladies, Doctor Ishira Guchi!" Bristals puffed. "Susan, of course, you know, Shira, and I think you've met *Ms*. Goody. *This* lady is Lady Emma Bristals, my estranged wife."

"Doctor!" Emma blustered. "Sit down, right here, beside me!" She smacked her hand on the leather. "Heard so much about you. Terrible business this morning."

"Yes, right," Guchi said, seating himself cautiously, "and in honor of my friend, Jasper Gates, I would like to drink a bourbon, with a glass of soda on the side."

"And so you shall!"

Not pausing, Sir Guy took a bulky envelope off the seat and laid it on the table.

"I've brought for you all to see a *dummy* of the *Tokyo Express*."

"Ah, ah."

Guchi hissed agreeably, but his face showed little interest.

Pushing drinks and napkins aside, Bristals spread upon the table a much-thumbed tabloid-sized newspaper. At first glance, as far as Susan could judge, it seemed nicely done, professional, at least, without question, the striking crimson rendering of the *Tokyo Express* flag across the top of the front page—or page twenty-four, depending where you started to read. Before they could have a proper look, Bristals flipped pages, bubbling over with sales pitch.

"Sports . . . financial . . . politics. Of course, this is a sample product, prepared by my people in London and the content is mere gibberish. You do understand that, Shira, it's the way we work. But isn't it true the Japanese male is a sports fanatic? Therefore, eight full pages of sports. Baseball, Shira, a favorite Japanese sport, isn't it, next to sumo wrestling? And golf! I'm given to understand that *all* Japanese businessmen play golf. Millions of 'em; even if they hate it, they're forced to play for business reasons. Enormous sums are spent on golf clubs, isn't it so?" Tapping his glass against Guchi's, Sir Guy said, "To Jasper Gates . . . football, darlings! I mean European-style football which in this country you call soccer—"

"No," Guchi interrupted, "a lot more baseball than football."

"Yes, yes." Bristals raced on. "And finance in the same exhaustive mode. It is possible we can front-page the financial news and start political stories on the back page. Thus, if our reader would prefer to read back to front, in Japanese style, fine . . . or front to back, as in Western countries, fine too, he can begin with a blockbuster financial story and finish with boring old politics . . . or vice versa."

"Ah, ah."

Guchi was too polite to react.

"Dear Doctor!" Sir Guy exclaimed, "please study this well. We're prepared to answer any questions you're likely to have. *Right, Susan?*"

"Yes . . ." Well, all right, just for now. "As best I can."

"I've explained to Doctor Guchi..." Bristals began.

"Ishira," Guchi interjected, for the first time that evening trying a meek, entreating smile on Susan. "Call me Ishira, please."

"Ishira!" Emma snatched at the name. "And you're to call me Emma, or whatever's comfortable."

"Emma... please."

Emma was not going to make it easy for him. Or for Ishira Guchi. He was already looking uncomfortable.

"Thanks, Sir Guy. I... what about pix?"

"Sure! Of course! Pictures! We have the biggest picture archive in the world."

That was an answer, but not, evidently, for Guchi's question.

"The girlie pictures..."

Of course, Guchi was referring to circulation-building T-and-A shots for which the Bristals papers were so famous, or notorious, if you listened to Jack Godfrey.

Bristals beamed reassuringly, but Emma got there first.

"Guy-balls, the *dear* man is talking about the knocker pictures on page three, the girls with the big lungs. *Garbanzos,* they call 'em here."

"Emma!" Bristals shook himself in and out of fury and beamed again, though less effectively. "Shira, Shira, nothing, believe me, out of bounds of the best of good taste!"

"Just, you know... that doesn't go over in Japan."

"Guy-balls, ultimate bad taste to show tits in Japan," Emma expanded. "Everybody knows it. Surprised you don't."

"But I do know, *old thing,*" Bristals grated. Irritably, betraying a definite nervousness by reaching for a torpedo-tube of cigar, he went on, "If I may say so, Shira, you have the advantage over us in design of automobiles, but when it becomes a question of newspapers, London is the capital of the world and will always be. Am I right, Susan?"

"I wouldn't disagree."

Sir Guy went on, "Therefore, Shira, I hope you'll agree our proposal is worthy of consideration?"

"*Yes...*" Guchi frowned anxiously, as if he wouldn't have known his way around the block, "*and no.* I'm up against it, Guy. TV, yeah, yes, I can see it, but I'm telling you when it comes to newspapers, there's a ton of competition in Japan."

"Susan..."

This was her cue, she understood, to back him up.

"I'm not a newspaper person," she said bluntly.

"Media is media."

Guchi suddenly chortled. "You can bet the farm, Guy, this boy is gonna steal Susan Channing from North American Network and put her on Japanese TV. She's gonna be a big star! *Susan Channing, Star Face*."

"*Ishira*, Susan Channing is already a big star," Bristals said, his voice strained, "and destined to be an even bigger one!"

Emma hooted, "Heh, heh! I've heard that one before and I'll bet you have too, Sue!"

"Emma! *Please!*"

The time had come for Susan to talk sense, cold logic.

"Since I don't know one word of Japanese, Ishira, there's not much hope of me being a TV star in Tokyo."

But Guchi's smile broadened, unrealistically.

"Have no fear, for Shira Guchi is here!"

Spoilsport Susan Channing shook her head.

"*Forget it, okay?*"

It was a moment of truth Guchi could've done without. He winced and retreated, sullen enough for everybody to notice. Bristals rolled his eyes at Susan bitterly.

Emma saved the day by the simple device of making it worse. Boldly, she threw her arm around Guchi's shoulders and hugged him to her.

"I'll be your star, Shira, any time you want! Mud in your eye."

"And yours," he muttered, not without pain, for Susan had clearly hurt his feelings.

Sir Guy must have spotted trouble. He dealt with his fresh cigar swiftly, giving it a mere quick lick, jammed the Cuban weed in his mouth, and with a death-dealing gesture lit it.

Never mind, sweet Shira. It was then, of course, that Emma began with the good doctor, then too that Ms. Gloria Goody tried to steer them back to business.

"Doctor Guchi, there has been rather important news," she announced, tapping her glass for attention, "news that changes the legal situation here, perhaps very considerably!"

"Ah, ah?"

Was he interested, or was he not? Emma fought for his

attention. She clutched the good Doctor's shoulder affectionately and, losing no time, seemed actually in the process of massaging his lower body with her other hand which had disappeared below table level. She held her face up close to his, regarding him fixedly, lustfully.

"Our archaeologist has produced an interim report on the so-called burial site," Ms. Goody announced.

"Oh?"

If it was possible for a Japanese gentleman to blush, this was what Shira Guchi was up to. Of course, nobody saw anything, or heard Emma's heavy breathing.

"After extensive... analysis of bone fragments and arti-facts, sorry condition though they're in," Ms. Goody struggled on, fearing, knowing she was losing, "it's been conclud-ed the bones are mostly animal material and the other things—metal, buttons, mortar, and pottery—are not of Indian origin, more probably from the Russian settlement, which we know existed in that general location."

"Well!" With an obvious effort, Emma turned her head and said, "That really rips it! Where does that leave Lyons-balls and his boys?"

"Nowhere," Gloria said icily. "The whole hullabaloo about defilement of a sacred Indian burial ground was... just that: hullabaloo!"

Ishira Guchi wasn't so sure. But he was grateful for the interruption.

"Fact? Or an opinion of so-called experts?"

"It's as sure as sure can be," Gloria said. "Sure enough to take into a court of law, if that's where we've got to go."

Guchi shook his head and said, "I wouldn't fight on such grounds. It wouldn't be graceful."

"But they don't have a leg to stand on!"

"*Nope.*" One had to credit the good doctor with being decisive, "All-Nippon Prosperoso accepts the place as sacred, and I'm going to have a temple built right there. For Japanese tourists, an Indian burial shrine can be a place for meditation. Especially good for golf players, Sir Guy might say. You get the picture?"

Give Guchi full marks. He was going to be easier for the Indians to deal with than Jasper International. Gloria Goody was furious, though Susan couldn't see why. In a very short time, it wouldn't be any of her business what Guchi did with the place—or did she hope to land a lucrative job representing All-Nippon Prosperoso, this after accusing Susan Channing no more than a half hour before of selling herself to Jasper Gates in return for Greenswards?

Well, it might not be in La Goody's nature to cave in without a fight, but right now she would do better to keep her mouth shut, which she did, clamping her lips fiercely. Just as she should do about Greenswards.

Emma cried out emotionally, "That's beautiful, Shira, to turn it into a shrine. The Indians are going to be so happy!" She thumped at her heart. "God, I feel undone . . . so faint! Quite . . . beside myself."

Her eyes rolled, showing white, and then, unbelievably, for a woman so stalwart, she sagged, tilted, tipped toward Guchi. Her body began to slip, then slide down the smooth leather.

"Emma, for God's sake!" Bristals cried. "Enough!"

"Guy-balls . . . just don't bother me for a moment."

"No, on no account, Emma, no, no, no!"

In a second, she would've been under the table. But with quick pressure to Emma's elbow, Guchi stopped her, not only that, but forced her upright. Emma gaped. He had hurt her, but also returned her to her senses.

With relief, Sir Guy drew untidily on his cigar, spewing smoke, wheezing and not with great pleasure.

"Emma has these spells, sort of mild epileptic attacks. She'll be all right in a moment."

"Will I *not*," Emma snarled.

"Of course," Gloria Goody sniped, trotting along beside Susan, having followed her out of the dining room and upstairs, "all is in abeyance until the arrival of Mr. Blick. He may not wish to go along with the sale to Guchi's group."

"I wouldn't know," Susan said.

She wasn't even going to mention August's Hong Kong Chinese buyer. Let Ms. Goody find out for herself.

"Whatever, Jasper Internats is out of here," Gloria said. "And wouldn't Blick like to have it behind him too?"

"Like I said, I wouldn't know." Going up the stairs, Gloria Goody trailed behind her like a mascot. "What happens to

Jasper International now anyway?'' Susan asked, not that she cared anymore.

"Are you busy?"

"I have to call New York."

"A minute of your time," Gloria requested.

"Come in then."

Once inside, Gloria looked around and said airily, "As to Jasper Internats, the reins have already been passed. How to say it? Big Sea was Mr. Gates's hobby, his *folie*, barely tolerated by the board, as was fresh involvement with his old financial crony."

"AHB."

"Exactly."

"And the cruise ship? The *Freckles*? A hobby too?"

"Oh, no," Gloria said. "The *Freckles* has nothing whatever to do with Mr. Gates's off-the-wall projects, like this place *or* the house in Ireland. If you see what I'm saying? That's why Jasper Internats is so anxious to get the investments liquid again."

Tiredly, Susan sat down. She'd been hoping for a nap.

"Like you said before, I'm not an heiress after all?"

"No offense." Ms. Goody smiled calculatingly. "We're rather hoping AHB will want to get Big Sea off his books too, to clear the decks, in a manner of speaking."

"Well . . . what can I tell you?" Susan said warily. "I don't think he's ever been very comfortable with the investment. And I must say, I don't know why they did this in the first place."

"Property, they adore huge plots of land."

Fuck all that, Nate would've said. No, what Nate actually would have said was take the money, take the property, promise everything, deliver nothing. That was the grandest strategy of all. But not for her.

Susan noticed how Gloria was looking at her. She'd sat down too and stared, nervously twisting her fingers in her lap. But this was not Susan's fault. If Gloria was bothered by something, that was her problem.

"Susan! We all . . . *I* watch *Hindsight* with great attention and admiration."

"Well, thank you!"

This did not, however, sound like the very efficient Ms. Gloria Goody she'd grown to know and dislike.

"You're the most . . . but even more beautiful in person."

Modestly, Susan murmured, "Amazing what a little make-up will do for you."

"No, no, you're *genuine*, Susan! Such adorable, soft skin..."

Ms. Goody raised a trembling hand, as if to caress Susan from the distance. No, an uncomfortable and undesired situation.

"Tell me, Gloria," Susan said briskly, "how did Jasper Gates come to acquire Greenswards from Guy Bristals?"

She knew Jasper's story. Perhaps it was time she heard the official version.

Susan was aware of Gloria's deep breathing. It made her uneasy and it did not stop. Gloria made a heavy sound, almost like a dropped book.

"*Gloria?* I'd like to know how Jasper acquired the property!"

The lady lawyer groaned, then mumbled, "In consideration of a payout on a TV station. Bristals got behind and..." She choked up, gagged. "Susan, please, you are wonderful!"

"And to make good, he had to sign over the Irish land?"

"Yes, yes!"

Gloria was very annoyed with Susan again and didn't hide it. She was a small woman, but looked strong, Susan warned herself, not that this was the first time she'd found herself in such a predicament over the years, and considering the business she was in, not a bad record, and so far she had always managed to protect herself. But, really, Gloria did have gall. They'd barely met and Gloria was practically asking for a date. Even if Susan had been inclined that way, wasn't it a bit sudden, something of a preemptory strike and, moreover, how could Gloria be sure Susan wasn't promised?

"Look, Gloria..."

Susan was hoping the little thing would simply take the hint and leave. But no, Gloria had to burst forth, startling the hell out of the steadily more embarrassed Susan Channing.

"Susan, if you had had any *real honor* as a woman—you'd never have accepted that place from Jasper Gates!"

The Greenswards business seemed to bother Gloria more than any other aspect of poor Jasper's estate.

Susan countered calmly, telling no lie, "Jasper gave me Greenswards as a gift, a mark of his esteem. He'd asked me to marry him."

"You certainly got over it fast enough," Gloria cut. "Spending the night with that Teller!"

"How do *you* know that? And even if you do, so what? It's none of your business."

Gloria's bosom heaved.

"I've been watching, don't worry."

"So, you've been spying on me, *Ms. Goody.*"

"In the interest of Jasper Internats! Only that." Gloria's mascara had begun to run a little; she was losing control. "Jasper Gates gave you Greenswards because you gave *it* to him—and you gave the same thing to Harry Teller last night. And that's what I'll report to Jasper Internats!"

"I think you had better leave, Gloria."

Gloria saw there was no hope. As they said in the legal trade, she threw due process out the window.

"You're a *whore*, Susan Channing, and TV is your pimp."

Susan chilled her voice.

"Thank you very much for your opinion. I shall always treasure it."

The rebuttal sounded like a form letter and did not help Gloria's mood.

"Women like you give women a bad name!" Gloria jumped up and began pawing the carpet with her tiny loafers. "It makes me boil, but since you are *what* you are, our proposition is one that might interest you: you help us with August Blick and we'll overlook the Greenswards matter."

"August Blick is a big boy, Gloria. As to the Irish property, Jasper signed the deed transfer and it's notarized."

Gloria Goody gusted mocking laughter, almost too much for her diminutive body.

"Do you think that matters to us? Don't you know I could tie you up so you'd be begging to kiss *my* ass, not the other way around!"

"That's ugly—and crude."

"Look, *tootsie,*" Gloria hollered scornfully, fully recovered now, very much on top of things again, her muscled little hands made into fists, "Jasper Internats will also want from you a statement removing yourself from any claim on the Gates estate."

"No kidding. We're talking sixes and sevens, aren't we, *sweetheart*? I'll think about it. Was there something else? I do recall Jasper was talking about a piece of the S. S. *Freckles*. I shall have to speak to my lawyer. My father always told me—"

"I do not give a goddamn what your father always told you, Miss Channing."

Susan curled her lip.

"I see, *Ms. Goody*, that we are *not* going to be friends after all."

Gloria snarled bitterly. She flexed her muscles, loosened her shoulders and made as if to bash her right fist into her left palm. Susan collected herself on the couch, setting her feet more firmly in case she had to spring to the defense.

But as they faced each other the doorbell buzzed, maybe saving Susan, maybe not. She would never know, she thought, as she dashed across the room.

Wrapped in a Big Sea robe, his uncorseted body like unbowled jelly, Sir Guy Bristals trundled forward.

"Susan!" He saw Gloria Goody, taken by surprise, still in a semicrouch, prepared for the attack. "Dear ladies!"

Susan said, "Hello . . . Sir Guy."

It occurred to her to continue on, through the door and downstairs, to leave these two to their devices.

Snapping his fingers, Bristals spun around.

"Do you know, darling, I quite forgot to tell Doctor G. the best thing of all about the *Tokyo Express*—in keeping with our sports orientation, we shall be pressing editorially for an opening of American baseball to the Japanese leagues. Think of the investment!"

"Very catchy."

Gloria Goody said, "I'm just going." Head down, she made doggedly for the door, which Susan was still holding open—not necessarily to suggest that Gloria leave, but if Gloria interpreted it that way, okay. Gloria paused for a second to glare up and Susan and snap, "Consider well what I said."

"Good-bye."

Susan closed the door after her and turned, just in time to receive the Bristals onslaught. Face dissolved with concern, Sir Guy rushed at her, then, astonishingly, he dropped to one knee and seized her hands, slobbering over them a moment and finally earnestly asking, "May I?"

"No, Sir Guy."

"I quite understand." Croaking unpleasantly, he looked up

at her again, but not as soulfully. "What I do *not* understand is why you were so aloof this evening, even rude, Susan, if I may say so. The good doctor was quite flummoxed."

"If the good doctor was flummoxed, it wasn't because of me, Sir Guy."

As usual, he didn't hear.

"Money does interest you, doesn't it, old girl?"

"Oh, yes."

"And property?"

Once more, Sir Guy ran his lips across her hand. Next, since she was so unresponsive, he struggled to his feet and, in worse humor yet, flounced across the room. He hurled himself down in the window chair and pulled a metal cigar tube from somewhere within the robe. One leg, chubby, heavily veined, dead white, swiftly lifted and crossed over the other. Thankfully, Sir Guy was wearing black swim trunks.

"I see you've been to the spa," Susan remarked.

"Just going." Spinning words slowly, Bristals said, "Let's be clear on one thing, old darling: *all* you people at NAN are on sufferance. Don't think for a moment that the Bristals London Group accepts that *any* of you are immune from criticism or . . . possibly . . . worse." Not pausing, he went straight to the hard-edged specifics. "You are close to August Blick."

"So?"

"So, I'm very anxious to meet Blick. I bought his holding but have never even seen the man. His arrival makes my stay at this bloody place worthwhile, whatever else happens. A fact, Susan! And a question for you," he finished craftily.

"Which is?"

"Will Susan Channing find it in her heart to become equally close to Guy Bristals . . . to become Sir Guy's valued ally and colleague?"

"That's sort of going to depend on *Sir Guy Bristals,* Sir Guy!"

"Delightful!" He chuckled rapturously. "Artful Dodger unto the end! Do you know, I came to this godforsaken place on the late Jasper Gates's assurance *you* would be here."

"So?"

"Silly girl, silly girl, oh *so* obtuse!" Bristals recrossed his hairless legs. "haven't I told you that I adore your style? Our relationship henceforward will be one of the highest reciprocity, if you take my meaning. *You* will help me and *I* will help you, in all respects.''

''You're very subtle.''

Susan test-fired a minimal bolt of sarcasm. It bounced off his thick hide.

''Reciprocity! The spice of life.''

Bristals eyes sparkled and he played daringly with the cigar tube, as if considering a next move. Just watching him was enough to make her ill. Mr. Moneybags, better *Sir Moneybags,* took it for granted he would have his own way, with her, with NAN. He would recast the network in his own image. Finally, he unscrewed the cap of the tube and withdrew the cigar, thrusting it between his fat lips, gazing at her knowingly, the genuine article, with the viper's eye.

''Must we continue this fencing?''

Susan shook her head. She had it figured out—Bristals expected her to come across, in every way. Let him do his worst. She'd simply run for it and, ironically, it wasn't as if she had nowhere to go. There had been those vague soundings by CBS.

''It's come to my attention,'' Bristals said, ''that Jasper G., for some odd reason, has deeded over to you a *property of value* in Ireland.''

''So?''

''*So,* unfortunately, old dear, Greenswards was not Jasper G.'s to give away.''

Bristals struck a match and lit his cigar, rolling it, as he did so, twisting it in those lips. He gazed at Susan . . . benignly? In a way some people would've called benign, others threatening.

'As it *so* happens,'' Susan declared, ''I'm told Jasper acquired Greenswards as part-payment for a TV station—all legal and proper, Sir Guy.''

Bristals was annoyed, for no good reason. Why wouldn't Susan have known this?

''Oh, yes, of course, there will be a bill of sale, Susan—a silly piece of paper, a mere scrap of paper!''

''Signed, sealed, and delivered.''

''A meaningless document. And I will tell you why. And depend on your good instincts. You see, my dear, when Emma and I agreed to part, my assets were made very vulnerable. As you can well imagine, Emma is a determined person.'' Susan could agree to that, only slightly, but Bristals grimaced appreciatively. ''Therefore, to protect myself in a modest way, I disposed of certain properties for cash and other considerations . . . here and there . . . in order that they wouldn't show on the asset side of the ledger.''

"So, you sold Greenswards to Jasper. I understand. What's the argument?''

"A fictional sale, old dear! Don't you see?''

"Who says?''

"Remember what I said about reciprocity, darling! Take my word for it. I sold Greenswards to Jasper G. but I didn't *really* sell it to him, if you take my meaning.''

Susan did take his meaning. Now that Jasper was dead, Bristals intended to *steal* the property back. And Gloria Goody's plan was the same.

"I'll speak to my lawyer.''

"My word is not good?'' As she had with Ms. Goody, Susan took careful note of the location of the door. You never knew. Even then, a more alarming thought occurred to Sir Guy. "That was for your ears only! To the grave I would deny I ever said it.'' A trembling petulance turned him ugly, even uglier when he drew on the cigar and whined, "I had hoped we'd be better friends.''

"We can be *friends*, Sir Guy, I can handle that.''

He glared at his cigar, as if blaming it for everything, and with reason, for the Marxist-Leninist leaf was burning unevenly and didn't smell very good. Sir Guy dropped it unceremoniously in the ashtray.

"There is a way, of course, to handle Greenswards so it does not grow like a cancer between us. And don't you know how?''

"No.''

"If we deal successfully with Doctor G., Greenswards is yours, old dear, no strings attached.''

"Now wait a minute . . .''

"Susan, Susan! Hear me out! Did you know that Doctor G. has a complete collection of your *Hindsight* shows? No, he wouldn't tell you, but true! He arranges marathon viewing sessions, whole weekends . . . Susan Channing . . . and nothing but Susan Channing.''

She was shaking her head disbelievingly.

"Yes, yes,'' he maintained cunningly, "and not only that! Those most clever Japanese technicians cut and paste together the most *inventive* sequences of you, Susan Channing, getting up to the most outrageous things.''

"And you expect *me* to spend time with this man, to convince *this man* to be your partner in Japan?"

Bristals's triple chin danced the affirmative.

"Absolutely! To be blunt, old dear, the good doctor will agree to anything if he can have his way with you . . . *once*. Just once."

"Oh really?" Susan reminded him again, "I would've thought Lady Emma provided about all that's needed in the way of convincing."

"A most unkind cut, Susan," he responded, affecting piety. "The woman can't help it, believe me." But of course. "Emma's hobby, if we might call it that, has always been most disconcerting, take my word for it."

"I do."

"Causing me great embarrassment, many trying moments, as you can well imagine. When push came to shove came to split, you understand, old thing?" Bristals sat there grinning at her, as if he had victory on his hands, not defeat. "What a team we'll make, my sweet!" He was oblivious of her shock and horror. "You and me. Your fire, my determination. Your passion, my brilliance."

Susan wanted to answer, to put him out of his misery at once, but he wouldn't let her speak.

"You'll discover, old girl, that *reciprocity* will be very much to your advantage. "He patted at his robe, in search of another cigar. "Susan," Bristals went on in unctuous fashion, "I refer to the essence of reciprocity. And in reciprocity, Sir Guy will elevate your status from Star Face to Media Goddess!"

"I don't think so."

Bristals grinned at her blindly, not hearing, not wanting to hear. His eyes seemed to merge over the top of his shiny nose.

"Isn't what I require of you a small price to pay? After all, old girl, it's a mere gesture of good faith."

"Good faith, how?"

She would fool him. If Greenswards was the prize, Susan would simply get rid of it, but not by returning it to Guy Bristals! Rather, give the property to an Irish charity, a home for unwed nuns or something like that.

Bristals was watching her, his little pig-eyes amused. Poor thing, all confused, slowly twisting in the wind, he'd be thinking.

"Have you thought it through, old girl? A caper with the

likes of the good doctor should be of no more significance to a woman like you than water off a duck's back, a yellow dog peeing on your leg. Do you follow me?''

"And what am I, some kind of a goddamned lamppost?''

"My sweet,'' Bristals carried on madly, "you don't seem to understand. Men like Doctor G. adore blondes! The Japanese love all things of a Nordic look or nature. They swill our whiskey and dress in our plaids and roger our blondes. Our obligation is only... to humor them, to cater the snob in the Japanese soul.''

"I do not buy that.''

Wearily, head wobbling, he exclaimed. "Believe me, old thing, *there is not a man alive who doesn't yearn to possess you!*''

So saying, and Susan should have been better prepared for his second serious attempt to get at her, Bristals dropped to the floor and hustled toward her on his hands and knees. If she'd had the presence of mind merely to laugh, he might have stopped. Or she might have been able to run before he rounded the coffee table. But then Bristals was there, at her feet. His fingers were fiddling with her shoes. He was untieing her Reeboks, he was pulling them off, he was slipping her white athletic socks from her feet. And then, nose down, snortling like a truffle-snuffing pig, his swollen lips nuzzled her bare feet, his tongue licking and darting like a snake's between her toes.

He was asking for something, Susan didn't quite understand the words. An old pair of slippers, was that what he was saying?

"Sir Guy, if you please! No more!''

Of course, he wouldn't stop. Abjectly, he licked and kissed and honked, next nipping at the big toe of her very vulnerable right foot. And how to get him up without kicking him in the chops? The campaign to subvert Ishira Guchi had become secondary; maybe it had always been secondary.

But of all the perversions! The sight and sound of the humped-over baronet sucking her toes was the worst.

"Sir Guy, stop groveling!''

That did it. His head bobbed up.

"Grovel? Never! Susan, I was not groveling! Obviously, I have something of a foot fetish,'' Bristals acknowledged bitterly. "Is that so bad? It's a perfectly ordinary hangup.''

"Ordinary *where*?''

"Everywhere, I should think!" Bristals elevated himself enough to grab her knees. There was both plea and bargaining in his eyes. "Susan, cooperate with me, reciprocate . . . and the world is your—"

"Don't say oyster."

"No, no, I was about to say the world will be your private pleasure palace. Think about it, old girl! And let me take you in my arms."

"No."

Grunting churlishly, gripping the arms of Susan's chair, Sir Guy Bristals pushed himself up. and stood tottering. He scowled at her, but not because he was embarrassed. Shame was not in him. After a moment, mumbling unapologetically, he strutted to the window.

Susan knew then as surely as she knew anything that she wasn't going to be able to do business with Sir Guy Bristals, beginning with the trip she was *not* going to make to Osaka with Ishira Guchi. Harry had been right about that. The only thing left was to plan her departure from NAN; the problem was how to do it without causing terminal damage to Arthur Fineman and Jack Godfrey.

"Well, I'm sorry about that, old girl. The old boy couldn't help himself. *Most women*," Sir Guy said, "rather like it, chaps playing on their digits, or ped-gits, whatever you call 'em."

"I grant you," Susan allowed, "it's not a troublesome sort of molestation. But I don't happen—"

He interrupted emotionally, "I quite understand. You're stressed out. It happens to the best of us."

23

Out of a sound, though perplexed, sleep, Susan came awake to an insistant tapping at the outside door.

It was only six, all quiet, save for the restless growling of the ocean—and now this.

After a moment, it came to her: August Hugo Blick! Too early for another visit by Guy Bristals.

Groggily, Susan reached for her long red robe.

Harry, she thought as she got to the door. Could she get so lucky?

"Yes?"

"Darling . . ." Susan recognized the voice, not Harry's. "Darling, it's me!"

"Scott!"

Groaning to herself, for she couldn't not let him in, Susan unlocked the door.

"And what the hell are *you* doing here?" She stepped back. "Where's your grandfather? Did you come with him from New York?"

Scott was limping a little and his face was worn, perhaps

from the overnight flight. But he was young enough to handle a thing like that. Or was he? He looked more than ever like a dissipated thirty-year-old. Just when Susan had settled things with herself, made her peace with the future, this boy, man, whatever, had to show up again.

"They put AHB next door," Scott informed her importantly.

Of course, that figured: straight into Jasper Gates's so recently vacated suite. Well, Jasper wasn't going to mind.

"It's the middle of the goddamn night!"

"No, darling," he corrected her archly, "it's morning. We came into Oakland, Sue . . . hot stuff! The old man rented a *whole* 727! And he *wanted* me to come with him. He insisted! We're getting along like crazy. But, Jesus, darling," he whispered, "I'm exhausted out of my mind."

"Well, goddamn it!" she swore again, for her own weariness was considerable. "Why didn't they give you a room? Why'd they send you to me? Why didn't you go next door?"

"Why? Aren't you glad to see me? I thought you'd be very glad to see me. And what the hell, we're leaving again, practically as soon as we get here. AHB is sending me back to Los Angeles and I don't wanna go to Los Angeles. Darling, please! Talk him into letting me go back to New York . . . please!"

"Stop calling me darling! I told you not to call me that."

"Darling," he cried, deliriously, "please! I've *gotta* go back to New York with you guys. I'm enjoying this! The good life! And I'd miss you . . ."

"Will you cut it out? I want you out of here. Go next door with August."

"AHB told me to sleep on your couch. *Darling, he knows about us!"*

Scott hobbled toward her, his arms outstretched.

"Get away from me!" Her voice was hard. "What are you saying? What do you mean?"

"I mean that AHB knows about us, darling."

"Knows *what*? What did he say?"

Scott regarded her proudly.

"That he knows what's going on and he gives us his blessing. He says it's good experience. . . ."

"For you?" He moved his head in the affirmative, dared to say it was so. "Educational, I suppose?"

"He didn't mention education. Please, darling, give us a kiss!"

"Get away from me, I said!"

Scott backed away, trying to grin and keep up his brave front, but obviously knowing the chances were no better than even that she wouldn't do him great damage.

Humbly, he said, "it's an experience for you too, isn't it? After all, you don't have access to *young* guys, I think you even said so, that if anybody knew about us, autumn and springtime, they'd be shocked out of their socks, but that you didn't care because I'm one in a million and I've got what it takes."

He sat down on the sofa and Susan wanted to smack him. But she stood, quite still, very controlled, so very calmly. If he'd known how calmly, he would've been looking for somewhere to hide.

"Is *that* what I said? I did not say that!"

"Yeah, you really did." He winked enticingly. "And I can tell you that in my book you've got what it takes too! I'm not just blowing smoke. You're the best of all my mistresses. Your moves are dynamite!"

Susan didn't budge.

"Did you have your interview with *Time*?"

Scott made a face and shook his head.

"Yeah. Trouble was the lady interviewer. She had the idea I was just another spoiled little Beverly Hills brat. . . ."

"Really? Where did she ever get an idea like that?"

"Yeah," he agreed, densely, "so the deck was kind of stacked against me. But we got along, or seemed to."

"You're incorrigible. What happened to your leg?"

"That's a long story, Sue."

"And you don't want to tell it, do you?"

Susan turned away, glancing out the window. Day had arrived, or at least its advance guard. The sun rising behind them in the east cast a reddish golden glow across the western sky. It was much too good and beautiful a thing of nature for any of them, herself included.

"Did Sid Wilmer come with you on the plane—and Emily?"

"Yeah." Scott nodded, his eyes half closed. "Darling, I get the feeling AHB envies me being your lover."

"Really?"

Susan yearned to strike, with her fist, a vase, a chair, anything.

"Darling, please don't be mad at me." Scott reached for the bottom of her robe, but Susan moved out of the way. He smiled winningly, so sure the rebuff would be only temporary. "The truth is I don't know if they'll end up doing the profile

or not. It'd be a combo anyway, me and five or six baby-
writers, she calls us. But she got PO'd. Don't ask me why.
Veronica Dante, can you believe the name? I asked her if it
was made up, like mine. V'ron, she likes to be called, made
the connection of Blick to Blake, which wasn't too neat. I
made her promise not to use it.''

"And?"

"She wouldn't promise."

Susan laughed blackly.

"That's trouble!"

"Maybe." But he wasn't worried about it. "Worst is they
changed the title of the book. I was going to cancel, then
decided what the hell!'' He scowled. ''*O Ravaged Youth*,
instead of *O Savage Youth*.''

"Not bad."

"It doesn't have the same ring, darling."

He smirked so cockily, one might have figured everything
was just fine. In fact, Scott looked a mess. His clothes were
wrinkled from more than a plane ride and the way he favored
his leg was a dead giveaway that something else of physical
ill-fate had happened to him. Worse for him, he held no
further attraction for Susan Channing. She was going to
expel him, throw him out in the cold. She had outgrown the
abberation. About time too.

Scott pulled his bad leg up, flexing the knee cautiously,
rubbing the calf tenderly.

"What happened?" Susan demanded. "Who was it this
time, the girl from *Time*?"

He flinched at the suggestion.

"Actually, darling, and I know you won't believe it, I was
attacked and viciously by a lady artist, the one who's designing
the book jacket. Polly... some Italian name, like Pizza or
Lasagne..."

Scott did weave a good story. Too bad he was so self-
destructive. It was a tossup whether he'd survive publication
of *O Savage* or *Ravaged Youth* and his fifteen minutes of fame.

"And *why* did this lady artist attack you so viciously, pray
tell?"

"It's hard... difficult for me to explain, Susan... *Mom*."

"I am *not* your mom."

"Susan, darling! I'm feeling very... I don't know what."

"Ashamed? Guilty? Nauseous?"

"Sue! I'm innocent. We were getting along like... swimmingly, isn't that what your generation says? Up in her studio, we were talking, you know, about the book and stuff.'' He stared at her guilelessly. ''I figured I'd try... you know, a man can but try.''

''And she kicked you in the shin, very hard.''

''No, actually not. She seemed to be very receptive. She knew I'd been around. She said she was going to paint me into the artwork of the book and nobody would ever know...''

''Sure,'' Susan said. *''And?''*

''Then, we left and we were in a cab, I think...''

''You think?''

''I forget,'' he muttered. ''I know we were going to her favorite place for dinner and I said something...''

''Did something...''

''Touched her, okay, you want to know? I think you get a big thrill out of hearing these things.''

''Yeah. Really.''

''Okay, so I'll tell you! So, I touched her tit and what's so bad about that? She pushed me, but I kept trying like anybody would, kissing her and I had my hand right on it. But then, when we got to where we were going, she jumped out of the cab first, and when I stuck out my leg to go after her, she slammed the cab door on it, really hard and I thought she practically cut the goddamn leg off, Susan, but it's just bruised like shit all around....''

He caressed his leg again.

''So then I have to go off to the hospital to have it X-rayed to see if it's broken.''

''They must know you there by now.''

''And here I am.''

''Joy.''

''Sue... darling,'' he whispered.

''What?''

''Can I tell you something? Would you be shocked?''

''Probably.''

''No, you wouldn't, not you! AHB whispered something to me.''

''About what?''

''Well...'' He hesitated, smirking wickedly. ''You know, man to man. I tell him a story; he tells me one. He's a character.''

''About what?''

''Nothing.'' Then he thought better of it. ''Emily...''

"Oh, for God's sake."

"Yeah, that's what I thought. I wouldn't much go for her."

And what else had they talked about, these two Blicks, young Scott and the nasty old ruin, possibly a quiet word or two about Susan Channing? Scott couldn't imagine how negatively Susan was reacting to his little report, or he wouldn't have moved again. He pushed out of the sofa, balanced on his good leg, and limped toward her like Pegleg Pete.

"Darling!"

"Scott . . ."

Her rude tone didn't register for, swiftly, he grabbed her shoulder, sought the curve of her chin with his fingers and thrust his mouth at her, at the same time whipping aside the robe, seeking her flesh with his grubby fingers.

"Back off, buster!"

Direct enough? Again, it didn't sink in. He was already groping her left breast when she retaliated.

Barefooted, but effectively enough, Susan kicked him in the bad leg, not exactly at the spot where the cab door had caught it, a little lower. Even so, the effect was catastrophic. Scott howled and hopped away, face white and suddenly slick with sweat.

"Sue! Hell! Oh . . . oooh! Jesus! Why did you do that? *Bitch!*"

He fell backwards in the sofa, eyes closed, whining and shaking.

"Because you're a lout."

"Darling . . . I'm sorry, I'm sorry." He began to sob, covering his face with his hands. "And now you hate me too."

Scott was so pathetic. He reminded Susan of his father, the loser, Roger Blake, and Scott wasn't even twenty years old.

"You can sleep there, on the couch," she said coolly. "You look horrible."

"I can't help it," he moaned. "I can't help what I look like, can I, or how life cheats on me?"

"Yes, you can. Just start behaving yourself, little man. You really don't know a goddamn thing about women, I don't care what's in your goddamn book!"

"Okay . . ."

He didn't fight it. He slumped sideways on the sofa and painfully drew his legs up.

"I'll get you a blanket."

Taking her time about it, Susan went into the bedroom and

found the extra blanket on a shelf in the closet. Holding it to her like a shield, she stopped in the doorway, He seemed to have calmed. His eyes were closed, the bony face finely outlined in profile against the morning light. Yes, like father, like grandfather, no question about it, but the resemblance was closer to AHB.

Susan came in quietly and spread the blanket over him. But he wasn't asleep. Scott grabbed her hand and held it to his cheek.

"My clothes feel so tight . . . Susan."

"Oh, goddamn it!"

Nothing made even a slight dent in the smooth surface of his blundering self-assurance. You couldn't even call it arrogance. He was too young to be very arrogant.

"Aw . . . Sue!" He held her hand fast, daring to kiss her fingers, daring, even after she'd kicked him, to pull her down beside him. "Sue, no matter what happens, you'll always sit next to me like this, sometimes, won't you?"

Her hip was against his warm body.

"You know something? I think I'm going to get married."

"Married?"

Had she kicked him again? His whimper made it sound so. His eyes bulged with shock. Scott was one hell of an actor. Big, gobby tears ran along his sharp nose.

"Yes, married."

"Darling," he cried out, sobbing, choking, so unreal, so phony. *"Mom!"*

Scott put one arm around Susan's shoulders, pulled her down roughly and jammed his wet face into her bosom. He made all variety of gross noises, then just as aggressively shoved his hand under her robe.

No, Susan was not having any of this.

She had to hit him again, to strike a serious blow for liberty and equality, never mind about fraternity. And he had to holler again, horribly, what real man wouldn't? Real men do holler when they get punched where it hurts. He wept bitterly, calling her names, real pain in his face.

"Oh, ravaged youth," Susan said. "I wonder if August heard?"

24

"Jasper Gates is dead," August Blick said stiffly. "And what now?"

Susan blinked at him.

"Can August Blick expect . . . hope . . . now that Mr. Gates has been removed from the scene that Susan Channing will resume her previous life?"

She had a ready answer.

"You've already thrown me over, August. You've sold me out to Sir Guy Bristals!"

He shook his head violently, with an old man's incoherent rage.

"No, no, that is not yet a done deal! It is to be finalized when we get back to New York . . . as that *fool* Bristals should know!"

"August, what's really in your mind?"

"That I need not sell him my interest, darling," he whispered, like the sly and slippery old fox he was. "But what do I hear from *my own grandson*? That Miss Channing-Osborne has become *the mistress* of this child!"

Susan laughed as loudly as she could, mockingly, stridently, disbelievingly.

"My god! Did Scott tell you that? The boy fictionalizes life itself!"

"So! Not true! Wishful thinking, we have no doubt, and understandable wishful thinking!" But whatever he said, he would believe Scott. He wanted it to be true; he wanted Scott to be just like him. August laid his thin old hands on hers. "I have always been most protective of you, my blonde darling! As regards Jasper Gates. And now, this . . ."

Twerp was the word.

"Rat-faced adolescent."

Susan said mildly, "He can't help boasting and making things up."

AHB stroked her wrist reassuringly.

"Sweetness . . ." August weighed his words. "Were the terrible thing true, well . . . Since it is not, let me say, *darling*, that I've missed you." Brooding deeply, he turned his head to look out the limousine window at the passing scenery, then back at her. "What do you think of Guchi? The *Baron Ishira Guchi*, oh yes, one of the old, old Japanese families. Is he an honorable man, my dear?"

"Very honorable, I suppose," she murmured, "in his own way."

"But of course he is. He *must* be—it is written in the blood! I *can* do business with him, don't you think, darling? Have you talked to him?"

"A little. I can't really judge him. I have no way."

What should she admit, after all, that Guchi had made a fumbled pass at her, said a couple of vile things . . . behaved, in fact, like an AHB, or grandson, or son? Susan could have told AHB about Guchi's reluctance to go partners with Sir Guy Bristals in a Tokyo newspaper, how fearful he was of losing face when Bristals, as he was sure to do, slipped pictures of barebreasted girls onto page three of the *Tokyo Express*.

"The baron will never . . . *never* do business with Bristals," AHB growled.

"You know about Bristals's scheme?"

"Of course." August looked at her reproachfully. "Sooner or later, Bristals would bring down shame on All-Nippon Prosperoso and Baron Ishira Guchi."

Now, the Blick limo eased around the first tight turn which

lifted them off the main coastal road and into the hills, in the direction of Rancho Mondo. At once, it was warmer. August had already complained of the Pacific seaside coolness, so unlike the temperate weather of his private island, Wade's Reef, in the Caribbean. In fact, August had dressed for the day in one of his tropical outfits, a light tan cotton suit, with madras-stripe shirt, and a Panama hat. Susan too had taken more care with costuming, now that AHB was here. She'd put on a light cotton dress, bright red, with gold buttons, and red sandals, a little something of an afternoon ensemble she'd picked up on a spree at Bloomingdale's.

The limo fell back into second, then low gear, creeping around curves so tortuous August wondered if the driver wouldn't have to back and turn again.

"Hairpins," August complained. "Are we safe on this road, darling? What am I doing here? I must be mad! This man Lyons, this maniac, could have come to the hotel."

"People drive it every day, August."

"Are the others behind us?"

"Our convoy." Susan looked out the back window. "Right on our tail."

They hadn't needed the three cars, but August had wanted Susan to himself. She was to tell him all about Dick Lyons before they reached the ranch. Ms. Goody, Guchi, and Bristals—this business had nothing to do with Sir Guy, of course, but he refused to be left behind—were in the second car while the much-subdued Scott Blake was in a third with Sid Wilmer. At least Emily Eliot, compromised old trollop, had remained at the inn.

"It occurred to me on the flight out here, *darling*, that Jasper International may be ripe for the plucking—the cruise line, at least, *darling*, what do *you* think? Could AHB move into the void?"

This was not Susan's thing and why did he try to involve her? It was almost like the old days all over again. What if August began to plead with her to come back, and make everything whole, as life had been... how long ago, two weeks, a month, impossible to remember, it seemed an eternity. *What if?* Why not kick him in the slats too, hurt him as she had his grandson who was aching badly this morning from all his injuries, including the most recent, Susan's left hook to the balls.

No, everything had changed and even August would have

to admit it. She was done with him. But she hadn't the nerve to tell him, outright. To her shame, maybe, but did she owe August a full report? He wouldn't know about Harry; how surprised he'd be to learn she had a ready replacement for Jasper Gates. AHB was going to find out soon enough. Harry would be at Rancho Mondo; it was his story too. And then? God knows. Susan was ready for anything, everything. But not for August Hugo Blick.

"All I know is that Gloria Goody said: the reins have been passed at J.I., whatever that means to you."

"Transition," AHB murmured sweetly. "I do wonder if my new friend, Baron Guchi...did you see how he bowed to me, darling? I might have been the emperor...perhaps the Baron would be interested in a joint flutter? All-Nippon Prosperoso's hotels and resort company is huge, my dear, and they've lately been bidding billions for properties in Paris and London." He clacked his tongue against cheek staccato. "Therefore, *why* this tiny place? There must be more to it than Big Sea. No, our Japanese friend was in the middle of something far bigger with Jasper Gates, *before* his, that is Jasper's, untimely death!"

"How would you and Guchi manage that? What would you do with it, August?"

August's bony nose quivered with merriment.

"Why, *chop it up!*" He made meat-cleaver motions with his hugely knuckled hand. "Sell its parts, *darling,* which are worth more than its sum, make a healthy profit. The cruise ship by itself, biggest in the world, would bring hundreds of millions of dollars!"

The poor old *Freckles.* Susan smiled secretively. No, she would not tell August that the ship might sink on launch. Let him find out the hard way.

"On the other hand," August said dispairingly, "is it worth it for Blick and company to stay in for another hand?"

"With Guchi?"

"Exactly, darling. I could retain my share. J.I. might not like it, but too bad. Or would All-Nippon Prosperoso then proceed to *devour* Blick? Perhaps that would be best. If commerce does not interest the young man, my grandson, *the novelist,*" he murmured snidely, "and, of course, his father, *Blake,* is completely out of it. Why go on, darling? This old man is growing old."

"August...you shouldn't say that."

"And why not? Why not be honest about things, Susan?" The old actor was acting up. Susan was there, conveniently, to hear his soliloquy. But she wouldn't fall for it. Sadly, tragically, August's eyelids drooped. "The end is near, darling," he whispered, "which is why I have so desperately missed your..."

"August..."

But he would not be stopped.

"Your own golden parts, *darling*," AHB confided, "each worth more than the whole: free-fall of breasts, golden undulating treasure, the temple of your loins..."

"August! Stop or I'll call the sheriff."

"Ha, ha, don't be funny, darling." His pasted-on smile gave her the chills. "Speaking of which, I am told the Baron Guchi has promised to build a *temple* for the local Indians!"

"On the site of an old burial ground, yes."

"Unheard of, my dear! Certainly not in Jasper Gates's style at any rate."

"Plus," she said, willing to hurt him, "All-Nippon will guarantee a quota of jobs and medical insurance and a scholarship fund and God knows what all. Jasper Internat's lady lawyer is horrified."

"Small wonder," August snorted. "I will rethink an alliance with All-Nippon Prosperoso, you can be sure."

The unpaved track off the macadam highway was so cracked and dry that the three cars left clouds of dust behind them as they cranked along toward Lyons's low-lying ranchhouse.

"Rancho Mondo," Susan said informatively.

"I know."

"Dick Lyons's wife, Jenny Driver, has just left him."

"Oh? Why was that?"

"It's possible she's fallen in love with somebody else."

"*Possible?*" August honked derisively. "She's an actress! Therefore insane. Of course! Amazing she hadn't deserted him much sooner. Am I not to mention the matter?"

"Nothing like that. Lyons doesn't care. You should also know that Sir Guy Bristals's wife, estranged wife, Emma, lives nearby. She's also a little mad."

"Is she, indeed?" AHB wasn't much interested. "And will Lyons agree to stop making trouble, do you think, Susan?"

"On balance? I'd think if Guchi is ready to make guarantees to the Baskets, Dick Lyons couldn't justly continue the fight."

"Is there any logic to this place, however?" August peered out the window and grumbled, "Rancho Mondo? What a slovenly dump! And here August Blick must bargain for his life? And fortune?"

Laughing, Susan said, "Seems so, AHB."

"The place is deserted," he snarled. "We have an appointment! *Cursed California!* Laid-back fools, bah! Not to be trusted any of them, white, black, red, or brown, they all become one in California—lazy, unreliable, and troublesome!"

"Maybe we're driving into an ambush, August."

"I shouldn't be surprised at that either."

"They'll jump us from behind the barn—lift the men's hair and rape all the women—we should be so lucky. Like the old West. Did you ever make a Western, August?"

His temper flared. Was she making fun of him? Yes. Was that something she'd often dared do? No.

"Of course I never made a Western! I was a leading man. A matinee idol!" Disdain marred his face; that same nasty expression might be remembered from his prewar potboilers. "*Darling*, you're enormously amusing."

Susan went quiet but she didn't stop thinking about it: the forces of financial evil, of merger, takeover, leveraged buyout bushwhacked by fierce Basket tribesmen...tribespersons, Ms. Goody would say.

Circle the limos! Circle the limos!

Ahead of them now, finally, the overweight person of Richard Lyons emerged from the ranchhouse.

He crossed the veranda and came down the steps to stand in the yard, waiting. Then Susan spotted the Custerd twins, Beau at least, in a little circle of people on the shaded bunkhouse porch. Or was it Belmont in the leather suit? It was easy to understand how everybody confused them, although, to make it even more of a puzzle, practically nobody ever saw Belmont and Beaumont together, at the same time, as twins should properly be seen.

Everything was such a mystery and what a weird place it was, the world.

There was no sign of Harry's Mustang.

AHB's limo pulled up next to a bright red pickup truck. Susan got out quickly, hoping she could warn Dick to be good, to be cooperative.

"Good morning, Dick."

"Howyadoin', Suzette?"

"Dick, this is August Blick. You know who he is."

"Do I!" Lyons roared, setting her back on her heels. *"He helped Jasper Gates burn down the rain forests."*

Negative vibes bounced off August like radar signals. But for the world he kept cool, absorbing the frontal attack with aplomb. There could be no question of his contempt for Dick Lyons, though his slight bow was polite. Indeed, Lyons looked rather contemptible, like one of the great unwashed, beard and hair uncombed. Had he slept under a bush? At the very least he was monumentally hung over. A long red gash marked his forehead, a cut festered under his left eye. But if Lyons happened to be embarrassed by his appearance, he didn't give it away.

"Fucking ecological hatchetman!"

August's strategic reserve didn't last long.

"This meeting is not essential, Mr. Lyons," he said, voice as big and cold as an iceberg. "I agreed to attend only as a courtesy to my Japanese friend..."

With his Panama hat, AHB gestured toward Baron Doctor Guchi.

"I know Mr. Guchi."

As for the good baron, if he'd wished, he might have seen before him a disreputable and half-mad American of the ugly variety. What he chose to see was this delightful American eccentric, Richard Lyons.

"Great to see you again!"

"As I was saying..." AHB was sensitive to the important nuances. He took his time about replacing the crisp Panama on his head and again became the very picture of sophisticated West Indies planter he liked to play when they were on Wade's Reef. "... we eagerly anticipate meeting your friends."

"Sure you do. Horseshit!"

Lyons barked back, like a mongrel, but nonetheless August had managed to deflate him just a little. By now, the gaggle of Indians had come up.

"Well, now you're here, Blick, and you, Mr. Guchi, meet my friends...*friends*?" Lyons laughed hoarsely. "These roughneck bastards tried to beat me up last night... horsing around... but they don't look any the better for it either, do they?"

Lyons pointed them out, one by one. There were bruises all

around, except on Beau Custerd's face, he was unmarked. It had all been in good fun, no? Whatever, they seemed jolly good friends now, though all in need of aspirin. Roughly, but quaintly, in a way poignantly, Lyons's primitives, clucking and cawing, like so many roosters, embarrassedly, for they were, after all, very shy creatures, nudged each other with their elbows, slapped Lyons's back, and hugged him so nobody would get the wrong idea.

"A few six-packs with these guys and . . ." Lyons blustered, fending off the hands. "Anyway, this is Beaumont Custerd and he's the *main man* of the outfit. This is Beau's business now. We settled that last night. Beau, it's all yours."

Guchi was quick. He pushed in close, past AHB, his hand out to Beau Custerd, openly, palm up, and there was nothing hidden up the sleeve of his expensive silk sports coat. Plainly, whatever it was he was doing, Baron Doctor Guchi was a master at it.

"My name is Ishira Guchi and you guys call me *Shira*. Beaumont Custerd? Beau?"

"Yeah."

Beaumont's voice was soft, like the rest of him. And obviously he didn't ever talk too much. What was it they said: Beau, with Bel, was a dancer, not a talker, a bedeviled artist, the impressionistic Native American dancer, he and his twin sister, Bel, the Astaires of the Basket Tribe. For sure, Susan told herself morbidly, Beau was, too, touchingly good-natured and she had to wonder how Dick Lyons had ever talked him into this, Beau and the other children of the dwindling Basket Tribe.

Beau was unquestionably handsome; Susan realized that better than she had before. The weird thing was his resemblance to Ishira Guchi or, put another way, Beau looked more like Guchi than he did any of the rest of them. His face was beardless and smooth. Beautifully cut dimples imposed beauty on the lower part of his face, the full lips and firm chin; and his coloration was the healthiest rosy-brown she'd ever seen. The facial features were as well defined as if they'd been drawn on him, as on a piece of paper. Black eyebrows, darting black eyes went to long, jet black hair brushed back and gathered in a ponytail at his neck. He was perfect—physically, at least. The rest of it? That remained to be seen.

"See this?" Lyons was not done with his grievance. He pointed at his forehead. "Drinking a couple of beers, sitting

on my porch and this one, Jackson Wobblybridge," he
gestured at one of Beaumont's gang, "laid into me from the
back, knocked me down the steps on my head."

"Hey, Dick . . . I'm sor-ree!"

The villain in question sang out gleefully, not particularly
serious about his apology.

"Shut up!" Beau ordered shrilly. "Everyone be quiet,
except for me."

Maybe Beau did have some presence. At any rate, he
achieved quiet, a lull that Gloria Goody used to muscle into
the group.

"I want to introduce myself! Mr. Custerd. I represent the
other principal in this negotiation—Jasper International." Beau
nodded warily, glancing at Lyons. "My name is Gloria
Goody—"

"*Good* name," Beau quipped, causing his men to laugh
heartily.

"Is your sister going to be here?"

Beau shook his head no.

"Bel's in the house. My *associates*," Beau remembered,
"Fred Burningbush and the other one is Toby Warpowers . . ."

"So, go ahead, Beau," Lyons ordered brusquely, making a
shooing motion. "The conference table is all set up in the
bunkhouse, guys."

"You are not taking part?" Gloria Goody asked doubtfully.

"No way, I'm out of it." Lyons glared at her. "You were
there, *Miss Goody*. You heard Jasper Gates screaming about
me taking advantage! So, go ahead, but you better get it
right. I won't believe any of this 'til I see the color of your
money!"

Of course! Dick Lyons had removed himself from the
bargaining, but he was right there. He'd have to ratify the
agreement or Beaumont Custerd would never accept it. Because of Dick Lyons no one had ever bothered to ask who it
was, exactly, that Beau Custerd represented, for whom he was
speaking. This must have occurred to Ms. Goody, for her face
flushed and she hung back as Beau, like a sleek sheepdog,
began to nudge them in the direction of the bunkhouse.

"Mr. Lyons," August said severely, "why do you *not*
participate? Better to have you—"

Lyons mocked, "Better to have me inside pissing out than
outside pissing in, right?"

Lest they should forget the razor-sharp legal mind of Ms.

Gloria Goody, she said crossly, "This is getting us nowhere. Doctor Guchi is prepared to agree to *all* the Basket demands—everything, including the so-called burial ground . . ."

Guchi held up his hand, interrupting her impatiently.

"A moment, please." He might have been talking in general but he was addressing Beau Custerd personally and to stress his sincerity, Guchi put his hand on Beau's arm and held it there. "We're gonna work a terrific deal, good for all parties concerned. You guys are gonna be part of our family."

"How beautiful," August murmured, with fading voice.

Susan hadn't thought about the family part of it: like other Japanese companies, did All-Nippon Prosperoso have a company anthem the Baskets could sing every morning whilst going about their Prosperoso calisthenics?

"With great respect, Mr. Blick," Baron-Doctor Guchi said, "it is good business strategy: *What is good for the people is good for Nippon Prosperoso!* Our motto. This place will hum."

August's old eyes widened.

"These promising young youths," Guchi continued cordially, "will become our business partners in the Pacific Basin good neighbor sphere. And I'm predicting right now that within a short period of time we'll have qualified Basket Indian youths studying at universities in Tokyo."

"Really?"

"Exactly, exactly!" Bristals intervened. "A multilingual zone of prosperity!" He went goggle-eyed with the vision. "That rings a bell."

Guchi moved his hand paternally to Beau's leather-clad shoulder, pressing fervently, gazing into Beau's eyes as if taking an oath.

"My friend Jasper Gates used to say, 'You ain't gonna get to first base if you don't behave in an enlightened manner.' "

August nodded sadly, the old fraud.

"Ah, our Jasper! My dear baron, you make the case convincingly."

Smiling tightly, not quite believing what he was hearing, Dick Lyons addressed Gloria Goody.

"I take it you've got a memo of understanding for Beau to initial, saying all these things properly and legally."

"Of course! It's an addendum to the agreement between Doctor Guchi and the J.I.-Blick interests."

"And, Mr. Lyons," the good baron-doctor said further, "we of All-Nippon invite you to serve as trustee!"

"Trustee? Me? What the hell are you talking about?"

Ms. Goody looked peptic.

Guchi said simply, "To ensure this goes very well, Mr. Lyons, we will have a board of trustees to oversee the Indian Island Foundation."

"Foundation?" Lyons had lost him. "First I've heard of a foundation!"

Ms. Goody cried, "Foundation? Since when?"

"Ah, ah." Guchi nodded cleverly. "Jasper's idea, see?" He glanced at Ms. Goody; the message was she'd better not object. "People should give Jasper Gates credit for being ahead of his time."

Lyons exclaimed, "I like your style, Mr. Guchi!"

The good baron-doctor laughed heartily.

"Gentlemen . . . could we?"

Ms. Goody wheeled around and stomped impatiently toward the bunkhouse.

Lyons's look followed her distastefully.

"That's some little number! What did she think? That these guys were going to sign away the farm, just like that?"

"Hey," Guchi said, "have no fear, Dick."

Arm in arm now, the best of chums, Guchi and Beau sauntered after Ms. Goody. Still, August lagged. He was suspicious, Susan could see it in his eyes. Why were Guchi and the lady attorney so anxious to railroad this thing through, that's what he would be asking himself. Oil, he'd be thinking, mineral rights, forestry, there had to be a reason for Baron Guchi's generosity.

"Sidney . . ."

"Right here, Mr. Blick," Sid Wilmer called.

What was August trying to tell him? That if he wasn't back in an hour Sidney should call in the U.S. Cavalry, or an air strike?

"Why don't you guys go have some coffee or something? This is going to take a while. There's beer in the refrigerator. But take it easy, for chrissakes! You hear me, Jackson Wobblybridge?"

"I hear you, Big Dick!"

Though tense, for his coup was not quite accomplished, Lyons watched fondly, actually affectionately, as the Indians tumbled across the yard.

"Jesus, I tell you, these guys can be nuts, I mean really nuts! I'd have second thoughts about getting mixed up with them again, let me tell you."

Like oozing matter, Bristals had come up beside him.

"It sounds to me they think very highly of you, sir."

Lyons studied Sir Guy curiously.

"You're Sir Guy Bristals."

"Precisely." Sir Guy put out his hand. "A pleasure, sir."

"Well . . . I'll be!" Lyons guffawed for effect. "This is that man, the husband of the wife your neighbor has coveted? *I'll be dogged!* So this is what a Sir Guy Bristals looks like!"

Of course, Dick Lyons knew exactly what Bristals looked like. He was playing the fool.

And how was Sir Guy supposed to react to the challenge, rusty old gauntlet thrown in the dust? In character, he drew himself up, conceitedly straightened his silk tie and the lapels of his pinstriped suit, not the handiest costume, Susan might have already noted, for this sort of outing. Lyons didn't give him time to huff or puff. He grabbed Bristals's hand and shook it mightily, causing the portly knight to wince.

"You are aware of course, Mr. Lyons . . ."

"Dick."

". . . that Emma and I are legally separated?"

"She's certainly not kept it a secret," Lyons muttered.

Instantly, he'd lost interest in Bristals. Something was wrong. There was something in his head, dark and deeply buried, which dragged him down. Something about Jenny, Susan didn't doubt, for Lyons's eyes dimmed and he stared at her in that fixed, slightly manic way he had.

Why didn't he tell her what was wrong? Maybe he would have, then and there, had it not been for the racket from over the horizon—not that far away really, more likely from the patch of ancient redwoods up near the main road. Lyons swore grandly and grabbed Susan's shoulder, one of his reflexive and studied gestures. He would shield her from barbaric intruders.

Susan heard a raucous whoop and another. Far away, two people rose out of the hill, on horseback, very much at home on the range.

The Lone Ranger and Tonto?

No, Emma Bristals, with another, less identifiable rider.

"Well, for chrissakes! Small world, Sir Guy!"

But it was Sir Guy who announced her and why not, Emma

being his wife, though legally split. As knowledgeable as Lyons, one would assume, Bristals would recognize her muscled body, the white face, and black hair, though the latter was partially hidden under a riding hat. She was wearing a red coat and leaning well forward in racing posture, taut upper torso jutting over the horse's head. Emma was surely aware that everybody had stopped whatever they were doing to watch her, for she slapped the horse on the flank and whooped again.

"Gad!" Bristals exclaimed, "it's the old girl!"

By the look of it, Emma was on her usual, frothing beast. The difference today was the smart huntcoat and black hat over her unruly hair. Yards behind, also dressed in red, there was another horseman; but, as Emma charged forward, evidently targeted on Dick Lyons's middle, the second rider lagged back and eventually veered up the slope toward the ocean.

Emma came on by herself, still whooping and laughing. Not a moment too soon, she reined in, swore good-naturedly, and jumped down, panting and snorting, in a manner of speaking more like a horse than the horse itself.

"Emma here!" She yelled at the top of her voice, daring anybody to disagree. "Everybody's favorite equestrian. What ho, Guy-balls! Lyons-balls! Sue Channing! How are you, ducks?"

"*Old girl!*" Bristals exploded, spittle flying, "is *this* your hunt? Just the two of you?"

"There you have it, Guy-balls! A tiny hunt indeed, the Petertown Blazers—" she taunted Lyons, "which Lyons-balls calls Petertown Turds! Salacious monster!"

Emma was in a rare mood, intoxicated by the ride, the air, possibly by something else, who could say? She pranced about and stomped and what a sight she was, kicking up her heels, slicing the air with her riding crop and screaming nonsense. With a lift of chin and jarring laugh, she greeted those watching her from the bunkhouse porch.

"What ho, Madame Goody, is it not, and *Chewy* Guchi! Beau the Magnificent!"

Of course, Emma had also seen AHB, the stranger across the crowded prairie, but she didn't let on, quite deliberately avoiding his avid look. Then, with an electric wheeze, Emma noticed Sid Wilmer—no, actually she had seen Scott Blake.

He was still in Wilmer's car, his chin propped against the rolled-down window. Scott was staring dreamily at her, this woman, in so many ways bigger than life.

"Heavens!" Emma yodeled, "who might this young lad be?"

"Scott Blake."

Susan introduced him for the umpteenth time. Finally showing signs of life, Scott dragged himself out of the car.

"Well, young man," Emma trumpeted, "I want you to come straight over here and see to my horse. He's very winded and who wouldn't be..."

Dick Lyons winked at Susan. Not unkindly. He was fond of Emma. Why? Probably, because he liked people with problems, people like himself.

"Scott is from Beverly Hills, California," Susan muttered, stupidly.

"Oh, yes?" Emma cried. "And how old are you, young clerk?"

"Eighteen." He answered bravely, voice as clear as a bell.

"Eighteen, going on fifty."

Emma would approve of that. Her eyes heated up.

"Very good! Of age, are you then?" Emma extended her callused hand and shook Scott's flabby young fingers. "Well, young clerk, will you help Lady Emma with her horse? Do you think you have the stuff to handle a really spirited animal?"

"Just a minute." Lyons pointed up the hill. "Isn't that your lover, *old girl*, skulking around, that low-grade moron Moon Rivers? Why doesn't he come down?"

Peevishly, Emma said, "You know yourself Saladin is very shy, Lyons-balls. He'll never come down if you keep glaring up at him that way."

Emma barely paused. Not making any excuses, such as her horse being thirsty and in need of oats, she wrapped young Scott's arm in her hand and, before anybody could do anything more than gasp or gulp, marched him toward the barn, horse following behind. And notice: Scott didn't resist. Perhaps he didn't dare.

But, just a minute. Hold it! Somebody had to stop her, or try to.

"Oh, my Gawd!" Bristals appealed. "So blatant! Poor woman!"

Emma didn't like that. She whipped around, face stormy.

"Poor woman? Is that what you said, Guy-balls? Are you referring to me?"

"Old thing, no, no," he bleated. "I most desperately want to introduce you to the *young lad's grandfather, August Hugo Blick!*"

"Oh." That gave her pause. "The *famous* August Hugo Blick?"

Emma turned in August's direction and, at once, seeing his chance, and therefore as spryly as a man half his age, August hopped back down the bunkhouse steps.

"Gentlemen . . . Mr. Blick . . . *please!*" Gloria Goody wailed.

AHB ignored her totally and Baron-Doctor Guchi, Beau Custerd, and his assistants, overtaken by curiosity, emerged from the bunkhouse.

"Mr. August Hugo Blick," Bristals declaimed, "permit me to introduce Emma Bristals."

"How do?"

Emma hailed August boldly, as bold as brass, and in a condescending way she must have somehow known would dumbfound him. AHB stopped short. Whatever horrific imaginings had been in his mind must have doubled and tripled. Clumsily, like a schoolboy himself, he removed his Panama hat and put it to his heart. Why the big effort? Was it possible AHB was also aware of the Emma Legends?

"Lady Emma . . ." He dropped his voice to theatrical pitch and ricocheted it off the barn. *"Enchanted!"*

There was more. Glancing briefly at Scott, Emma coyly responded, "And *enchantée* to you too, Mr. Blick! Such a tickle . . ."

August's thin lips parted in a carnal grimace. Yes, Susan thought vengefully, yes!

"This charming boy, your grandson," Emma called out to AHB fragrantly, "is helping me with my horse."

August didn't want to hear about Scott.

"Please, call me August, *or AHB.*"

Susan heard it all. She believed. She didn't believe.

Emma twirled on the toes of her dusty boots like a large ballerina. What was this, heavy-duty *Swan Lake* or maybe *The Corsair*, after Harry's paper? Harry would be very amused—if he ever got there. Emma battered August with her willing, giving, wanting gaze, beneath the red riding coat immodestly fiddling with her disarranged blue shirt, as if she desired nothing so much as to rip it off and offer herself to him on that very spot.

Do feast your eyes for I am yours!

"Ta! Back in minute, all!"

Unceremoniously, she grabbed Scott and continued on.

"Dear boy..." That was Bristals, eyes squeezed with worry. After all, AHB was not going to take kindly to Emma ravaging his grandson and, separated or not, he would blame Guy Bristals for the transgression.

"Emma, *goddammit*," Lyons hollered, "what about Moon?"

It was too late. They were in the barn and nobody was brave enough to follow.

Moon, as one with his horse, snorted and danced, pirouetting against the western horizon.

Perversely, but predictably, for he couldn't resist causing trouble, Lyons picked up a long-handled shovel leaning against the fence of the barnyard enclosure and, waving the blade like a flag, bellowed at Moon.

"Hey, *schmuck*! Come join the human race!"

Lyons's voice carried over the distance and had a profound effect on Moon Rivers. His body went rigid in the saddle. A second later, he struck brutally with his riding crop. The horse bolted forward. Moon was a wildman on a horse, certainly a worthy member of the Petertown Turds. He pulled his slouch hat down over his eyes—he wasn't wearing the official hunt hardhat—and, as Emma had, rode straight at Lyons, but more purposefully, stopping the headlong charge at the very last second. The horse reared back, spun in the air, and came down like thunder.

Lyons held his ground. His voice was nonchalant.

"Welcome, Moon. What's the good word?"

Moon's answer was not delivered in the same good-neighborly fashion.

"Son of a bitch, troublemaker!"

Remember, over the years Dick Lyons had grown accustomed to being cursed and vilified, and by better, more articulate people than Moon Rivers.

"Troublemaker, yeah, story of my life."

But he never took his eyes off Moon.

Impatiently, once again, Ms. Gloria Goody thumped her heels on the porch.

"May I point out we have work to do?" she screamed. "Who is this *man* and why must we be interrupted?"

Moon snarled at her from atop his fidgety horse, "Shut up, *cunt*!"

Ms. Goody went red. Her mouth opened and closed. Fat chance now of getting them back inside. They would have to negotiate another day.

"Moon, Moon, take it slow," Dick Lyons said serenely.

But there was no way to sooth him.

"Lyons, you're trouble around here!" He smashed his riding crop against the pommel of the saddle. "Why'd you ever come to Petertown, anyway?"

"I like the place, Moon, and I like the people."

"Stirring up the goddamn Indians, Lyons, that's what you're doin', and now one of your goddamn Indians killed that man Jasper Gates." Moon aimed the riding crop at Susan. "*You* were with him at the hotel the other day!"

"So?" Susan was almost grateful for the opening. "What's it to you?"

Lyons said, "Listen to me, Moon. Jasper Gates was *not* killed by any Indian. Got that? Repeat, *not*!"

"You son of a bitch, Lyons. I'm sayin' one of your fucking Indians killed Gates."

"And you're full of crap," Lyons shouted, too soon out of patience. "Now, either get down off your horse and behave or get your ass off my property."

Beau Custerd's chums, not the negotiating team but the rest of them who'd gone into the house, finally roused themselves enough to stroll outside carrying their beer cans. One by one, Warpowers, Burningbush, and the Jackson Wobblybridge who'd been jousting with Lyons began to snicker and point at Moon. Which drove him plumb crazy.

"We gonna hang all you bastards!" Moon shrieked.

Did Emma Bristals come rushing out of the barn to quiet him? No. Did Susan expect she would? No.

"You're out of line, Moon," Dick Lyons warned.

Nothing would stop Moon. He screamed infinite frustration; his poor brown horse, hurt each time Moon yanked the reins, snorted and reared, pawing at nothing, and crashed down, hoofs hitting within inches of Lyons's feet.

Still, Dick Lyons did not give.

His defiance or indifference to very real danger sent Moon berserk.

Viciously, he swung the riding crop and the stiff leather caught Lyons across the temple, where he'd been damaged by the amiable roughhousing of the night before. Lyons cried out and staggered; but for the support of the shovel he would've fallen.

The sight of blood, evidence that damage could be done to his enemy, excited Moon even more and, yelling crazily, he raised his arm again.

But unexpectedly, massively, Dick Lyons struck back.

A mighty blow! The flat of the shovel took Moon in the right side beneath his lifted arm and blasted him off the horse.

Arms flailing, legs kicking, Moon came down in the dust; the floppy black outlaw hat went sailing, and the horse skittered out of reach.

For a count of five, Moon lay stunned.

"My ribs, you broke my ribs."

"And that's not all I'm going to break!"

Lyons trundled toward him, prepared to do real damage. Coming to his senses, heeding danger, Moon rolled away and leapt to his feet. Crouching, spitting, he slid away.

"Fuck you, Lyons! I'm gonna kill you. I should kill you. I want to kill you!"

Lyons kept coming.

And Custerd's boys, jeering loudly, crossed the yard, also converging on the unhappy Rivers.

"Hey, Big Dick," the unlovely Wobblybridge shouted, "let's beat the shit out of Moon. C'mere, Moonie, c'mon, Moonie . . ."

But Lyons held up his hand commandingly.

"Just stay back, Wobblybridge!"

J. Wobblybridge's bloodthirsty cry shattered any hope of peace.

"Moon Rivers humps sheep!"

Moon snarled, bared his teeth, indeed the long incisors.

"That's not polite, Jackson," Lyons said, grinning thinly.

Moon dodged away, backing toward the barn, and Dick Lyons tracked him with deliberate, menacing stride.

With good reason, Moon looked desperate. He *was* desperate.

And then, perhaps not surprisingly, he shoved one hand under the skirts of the dusty red huntcoat and hauled out a revolver with barrel so long you wondered where he could have comfortably had it hidden. Moon cocked back the hammer and whilst uttering another filthy curse let off a shot over Wobblybridge's head. Then he pointed the gun at Dick Lyons, no more than a yard or two away from him.

"I'm gonna, Lyons. I finally got you where I want you."

Wobblybridge and the boys yelled, "Watch out, Big Dick! Moon's got a gun!"

One might well have wondered in danger's flow what had happened to the leader of these Merry Men, Beaumont Custerd. Beau stood, as if glued to Ishira Guchi, one foot inside the ranchhouse, one foot on the porch. Guchi was also frozen in place, one hand on Beau, the other hugging his Vuitton briefcase to his chest.

"I see the gun and Moon's not going to do anything with it."

"The fuck I ain't, Lyons!"

Moon waved the revolver at Jackson Wobblybridge, at Bristals, at Susan Channing! So it had come to this: violent and undeserved death. By now truth was struggling out of its egg—it was Moon Rivers who'd taken the shot at Lyons and missed. Moon was also the killer at the bridge to Indian Island.

But did Dick Lyons know it?

With deadly contempt, he said, "You haven't got the guts to kill a man while he's looking you in the eye, you little buzzard!"

"Oh, no, oh no?"

"Now I know who shot that pail of horseshit out of my hand!"

Moon giggled, bobbing his hand slackly, too far gone to back off now.

"Yeah, and I'm sorry I missed. The sun must've been in my eyes."

"Why?"

"Because I hate your goddamn guts, that's why!"

"Savage!" Sir Guy accused Moon loudly.

And a beer can came flying out of nowhere, bounced off Moon's chest, spewing foam. Moon ducked down, Lyons could have struck again, if he was going to, but he did not. Rather, smiling with a kind of condescension, he leaned on the shovel and regarded Rivers as if they were in the middle of a friendly discussion.

Perhaps he'd seen Emma, for just then she appeared in the barn door behind Moon, scowling, her face dark as a cloud and heavy with annoyance.

"What in God's name do you think you're doing, Saladin?"

Moon spun around. And again Lyons could have hit him and, again, did not.

Emma was not a pretty sight, Moon would have noticed. She had obviously been up to no good. Susan's heart sank, then soared: she wasn't child Scott's guardian.

Sir Guy cried out, "Emma, for God's sake! Have you no bloody shame?"

Moon looked Sir Guy's way, murder still on his mind.

"Shut up you! Whoever you are!"

"My husband, Saladin, or I should say, my estranged husband."

"We are legally separated," Sir Guy explained pompously. "And what are you to Lady Emma Bristals, my good man?"

Moon spit repulsively. "I fuck her. Why?"

"My God! Insolent savage!"

"Oh, do shut up, Guy-balls. And for God's sake, Saladin," Emma complained, "what's a person got to do for a little piece in quiet?"

Lyons roared appreciatively. Perhaps there truly was something hilarious about Emma. Susan didn't quite see it.

"This is surreal!" Guy blathered.

Whatever else, Emma was at the moment rather in dishabille. Her blue denim shirt was unbuttoned, and heavy, sportswoman's bra pulled askew. A hugely nippled breast was exposed to the crystal-clear California light, a painter's light and, not at all surprisingly, Susan heard from behind her several new noises, grunts, gasps, a throaty exclamation as real as a death rattle.

Emma's hat was gone, her black hair disheveled and brilliant red lipstick smeared.

Shakily, Moon pointed at the barn. Was someone lurking there, partially hidden in the shadow—but not out of the reach of Moon Rivers's sharp eyes?

"Who is that son of a bitch?"

"Nobody."

"Nobody?" Moon screamed. "I can see *somebody*!"

"That'll do, Saladin."

"You were in there bangin' somebody!"

"You're mad. I was watering my horse."

"With your tits out? Oh, no!" Moon's feral face was bleachy white, he was sweating from every pore. He croaked, "You been in there with somebody's prick in your mouth."

"Saladin! *Enough!* You're being uncouth!" Emma's gypsy

eyes flashed. "Enough, I say. First of all, it's none of your
bloody business, and second, that's no way for a member of
the Petertown Blazers to speak!"

But Moon simply flung his head back and howled. You
couldn't blame him. He had arrived at a time and place of no
exit. If somebody lied to you so outrageously and you knew
what they said wasn't true, and nevertheless they went right
on lying, it was not a magic sort of moment, was it?

"Come forward, young Scott Blake!" Emma called.

What baldfaced, unperishable nerve, no, insolence, arrogance! Thankfully, Scott at least had the wit to look sheepish,
enough so people wouldn't think him an absolute moron for
getting caught with his pants down. Look around! How many
people were watching? Like a couple of dozen before you
finished counting.

Scott limped out of the barn, dragging one foot, his hands
deep in his trousers pockets. He was holding himself there, as
if in some discomfort.

Moon sucked air so loudly he sounded like a pump, but he
was merely hyperventilating. Dulled as he was, Scott realized
at once that Moon was pointing a gun at his guts. His sharp,
not overly strong, jaw began to tremble.

Emma didn't notice. She stood between them, her bared
chest heaving passionately.

"Saladin, meet young Scott Blake."

"I don't want to meet any kind of fucking Scott Blake!"

Emma stared at him witheringly.

"Saladin, I want you to put that gun away."

"Oh no!"

Moving like a ferret, Moon ducked behind Scott. He
locked his hand through Scott's arm and jammed the barrel of
the revolver in his ribs.

Scott whimpered. His eyes rolled with fright.

"I'm getting out of here!" Rivers grated. "And you can
take a last look at this little daisy, Emma!"

"Saladin!"

Moon whacked the gun at Scott's spine, making him cry
out.

"Back off, *lady*! Get out of my way!"

Moon Rivers had flipped out, it had to be faced. Scott was
done for. Moon would take him into the woods and blow his
brains out. In a way, you couldn't blame him. After all, he
would be a very territorial sort and Scott had invaded his

territory. They might never even find the body, unless Moon was forced to tell and by then Scott's remains would have been devoured, bones scattered by packs of wolves or hyenas or the like.

No, they'd never take Moon Rivers alive; *face it,* he was a desperate man. He'd already confessed to shooting at Dick Lyons. He'd been threatening the assembly here with a loaded firearm. And it was only a matter of time before the sheriff tumbled to the fact Moon had killed Jasper Gates. So, when you came to think about it, Moon Rivers hadn't much to lose whatever he did next.

Scott was terrified and he had every right to be. After all, he'd been no more than an innocent bystander. It hadn't been his idea to go with Emma. He was young, too easily seduced, and Moon should take that into account. And, think! What a chapter this would make in a new novel.

There didn't appear to be much realistic hope, however, that young Scott would ever write another novel.

Moon pushed and shoved him toward the red pickup, into the passenger side, and slammed the door. Waving the gun threateningly, he scooted around the truck.

Susan found her voice.

"You killed Jasper Gates!"

It was as if Moon had run into a wall. He stopped dead, dazed. The words triggered him: confession, as damning as it was, spilled out. Everybody, even the noisy Indians, was silent, out of embarrassment really. They *were* embarrassed for him.

"Yeah," he screeched, obviously unbalanced, "I did it, but it was an accident. I was trying for Lyons."

Thereby was Moon reminded that he still hadn't killed Dick Lyons.

He crouched, braced his hand on the hood of the pickup, and aimed. And again, Dick Lyons faced him with such little concern that he might as well have walked straight at Moon, baring his breast to accept the bullet.

A second beer car arrived, better pitched than the first, and not an empty can, which came down, thumped, and bounced off Moon's head, knocking him sideways.

Moon's hand jerked, the revolver fired, but away from Lyons.

The front windshield of the pickup shattered.

Scott Blake cried out.

Blood spurted.

The gun fell out of Moon's hand and he was down, on his hands and knees, shaking his head groggily when Jackson Wobblybridge hit him. A blur, catlike, Wobblybridge leapt, it seemed from yards away, and came down on Moon's back, crushing him into the dust.

Moon gasped hoarsely, gagged and choked as he lost his air. For all Susan could tell, J. Wobblybridge might have broken his back. But that wasn't enough. Grunting and squealing, Wobblybridge grabbed handfuls of Moon's greasy hair and slammed his face into the ground.

"Shoot my pickup, you bastard!" Wham! "This Native American boy is gonna beat the shit outta you, Moon Rivers!"

Within the glass-strewn pickup, Scott Blake lifted his hands to his head and saw his blood and loosed an animal scream of anguish.

Dick Lyons rushed forward.

"Gimme some handkerchiefs!" He yanked open the pick-up door. "C'mon, kid, lemme look at that!"

"Scott! My grandson! My beloved grandson!"

What? August? Susan had never heard him like that. Mignon's death had aroused no more than a raised eyebrow of grief. AHB's knees buckled.

Emma Bristals leapt forward, caught him in her arms. August hung on her shoulders, down her front like a sack.

"Here, here . . ." Emma was strong enough to manage him. "Lean on me, old chap!"

Lyons yelled in Scott's face, "Can you hear me?"

"Scott, my beloved grandson!"

"I can hear you, for chrissakes! Stop yelling. *I can't see!*"

"Take your hand out of the way. Lemme look!" Lyons pushed Scott's hand aside. "You've got your hands in front of your eyes and blood in your eyes, no wonder you can't see. It's a scratch, a crease. Missed your eye by a mile. Shit, I think you just caught a piece of glass." Lyons laid a handkerchief against the wound. "Sue," he bellowed, "it nicked him is all. Tell the old man. He's okay!"

"He's bleeding like a pig," she whispered.

"Head wounds always bleed. The head bleeds hard!"

"Here, let me do this."

Blood didn't bother her, did it? Susan was used to blood. She should be, she'd seen enough of it.

"For chrissakes, Sue, you'll get it all over you," Lyons cried. "He's okay, nothing to worry about."

"Just go get some bandages, Dick."

Her hands were busy, with the blood-soaked handkerchief, holding Scott's head against her bosom, wiping blood away from his eyes, his mouth, onto her shirt-top and skirt.

"Sue, *for chrissakes*, take it easy!"

Then Moon howled, like a wolf in a trap.

"Wobblybridge," Lyons ordered at the top of his voice, "stop pounding his head!" Then he whispered to Susan, "He'd like to kill Moon for making a pass at Bel Custerd."

"At Bel?"

"A few years ago, when they were all in high school. Wobblybridge is secretly in love with Bel . . . not so secretly."

It was a numbing scene. Scott's head hurt and he was still scared. Susan mopped blood; her hands were stained with it to the wrists. Slowly, though, the bleeding ebbed, slowly Scott calmed. Susan had been so *sure* this was the end of him, and nothing had happened beyond a superficial scratch that would become a scar of more importance, something he could boast about for the rest of his life.

Lucky little . . . whatever. Swine?

And Lyons? He had always been lucky. People had been trying to kill Dick Lyons for years and hadn't yet succeeded.

"In another age," Lyons muttered, hanging over them, "Jackson would've already taken his scalp. Moon's lucky. Hey, Wobblybridge! That's enough. Leave something for the sheriff, okay?"

"Yeah, okay, Dick." Wobblybridge had tired himself out. "We tie him up, eh, Dick?"

"Tie his hands and feet and rope him to something, and somebody go inside and call the law."

"And a doctor," Scott moaned. "Jesus! How about a doctor? Huh?"

Suddenly, it was all business again. Though Emma Bristals had gotten AHB most of the way to the ranchhouse steps and tried to restrain him now, assuring him bossily that everything was fine, August dragged her back to the pickup. Keeping clear, so as not to soil his suit, August frowned at Scott, at the wound and blood-stained clothes.

"Well, boy? Are you all right?"

"I'm sorry to worry you, AHB."

"Brave lad," Emma exclaimed huskily.

August whipped off his Panama hat and waved it angrily in his grandson's face. A nervous tic shook the fold of skin at the corner of his left eye.

"*Susan!* Take care of this boy! *Wilmer!*" August clamored, in quavering voice. "Wilmer!"

Wilmer was responsible for this, of course—but where was Sidney Wilmer?

"Good God, man," Sir Guy Bristals wheezed, grabbing August's arm. "Take hold of yourself. It's all over. The boy is fine."

"Let go of me."

"Of course. So sorry." Bristals yanked away his hand as if AHB had burst into flames. "Emma, old thing . . . well, at last you two have met," he murmured uncertainly.

Sir Guy saw how it was.

And so did Susan.

Sir Guy Bristals, of course, would have sold his own mother to a man of the wealth and stature of August Hugo Blick. In Emma Bristals's case, this would not be necessary. Fate had stepped in. For every woman, said Fate, there was a man and for Emma Bristals that man was August Hugo Blick. Fate's will be done. The course of coincidence had been carefully plotted; or was it really just a cockeyed jumble of events that had finalized in the assassination of Jasper Gates and AHB's first trip to California in forty years or more, and even then not back to the Hollywood of his youth, but to the northland and collision with the unlikely person of Emma Bristals, of London, England.

No, fortunately, Fate was not well-organized, nor as all-powerful, or as whimsical, as different sorts of people supposed. Win some . . . lose some. No, Fate was not as sure a force as gravity, for instance.

Once again, Bristals tried to catch AHB's attention.

"I had hoped, sir," he spouted, "you and I, as you're aware, *AHB*, are doing a certain piece of business together. Finally, we meet! But we must talk!"

Emma pushed him away, hectoring, "*Now,* Guy-balls? At a time like *this*?"

"Surely, Sir Guy, surely we are meeting in New York City . . ."

"Well, yes, but . . ."

August jacked his eyebrows impatiently, but then he remembered without so much as a glance at Nurse Susan that

he would, after all, want to conclude his business with
Bristals.

"Why not fly back with me tonight in my chartered
aircraft? If we are *ever* to finish our work in this awful
place."

"Well!" Bristals brightened. "Very kind. Thanks much!
Certainly, my own purpose here has"—Unhappily, Bristals
peered toward the bunkhouse where Baron-Doctor Guchi and
Beau Custerd were again earnestly talking, Ms. Goody chaf-
ing, pacing back and forth across the veranda, remembering
too, it was to be hoped, what Moon Rivers had called
her—"so long as the good doctor is occupied with these
bloody savages!"

AHB's face buckled with the force of his next inspiration.

"And *you,* m'lady?"

Emma's eyes were alive, like black bugs crawling on
AHB's face.

"And I?"

"Do you fly or stay?"

"But I live here, August. Across the hill. I'd love for you
to see my spread."

And? Here sat Nurse Susan, all covered in blood.

25

Then, not a moment too soon, relief was in sight. Harry's flashy red Mustang, a quarter or half mile down the road, outrunning a cloud of dust, and within seconds, or hours, whichever was longest, rounded the final curve past a lone eucalyptus tree, cut into the yard and stopped. Hair attractively windblown. Harry waved, cut the motor, and climbed out. He reached in the back for a cotton jacket and slung it over his shoulder.

He was, Susan observed, wearing an open pink shirt and desert boots and mirrored sunglasses and looked altogether most desirable.

Harry.

With all her might, Susan restrained herself from leaping off the veranda and hurling herself upon him. She waited, mugging like a wanton, she knew it, but unable to stop, unwilling to try to stop.

Harry ambled toward them, holding what must have been a copy of this weeks's newspaper.

The Corsair!

Yes, he was.

"So! I hear you caught a perpetrator."

"Yeah, Teller," Dick Lyons said, "and you really missed the boat this time. Excitement's all over. Tell 'im, Suzette."

"A little *hairy*, Harry." She smiled bravely, telling him with the smile, *Better late than never, big boy*. But, scared, yes. She was still feeling the shock of two days ago, and now this. "I thought you'd never get here," Susan added with relief.

"My beloved car..."

"Broke down? No!"

"Flat." He tossed the jacket on the other shoulder. "Sorry. But you can fill me in." He offered the *Corsair* to Lyons. "All the news that fits, Dick. So it was our Moon Rivers the whole while, was it?"

Harry looked around. What he saw was a bedraggled group. After the fact, anticlimactic lethargy had set in, on top of a warm, listless afternoon. With all her might, Ms. Goody had finally managed to get her parties into the bunkhouse—out of necessity, if AHB intended to fly away at the close of the business day.

Emma roused herself to look keenly at Harry. If she hadn't, Susan would have doubted her own good judgment about him.

"And *whom* might this be?"

"Harry Teller," Harry said. "We've never met. But I know you're Emma Bristals..."

"My estranged wife," Bristals piped up, adding spitefully, "Bad show, Harry! Should'a been here hours ago, old boy!"

Harry just grinned and looked at Susan, as if to say, *See?*

Lady Emma growled, "Do shut up, Guy-balls. Haven't you caused enough trouble already?"

"Trouble?" he sputtered, "what have *I* done, old girl?"

"Provoking that poor boy into shooting, isn't that enough?"

Emma did not seem to be as indifferent as one might have forecast to Saladin's humiliation and impending arrest. One could say, of course, that she had been momentarily diverted from depression by August Blick's barely veiled invitation to fly off with him and then very pleased by his fervently expressed wish, yes, to see her spread—her ranch—before he left for New York in the evening. Once they had gotten young Scott into the ranchhouse to rest on the lumpy sofa until medical assistance arrived, and AHB had finally gone off to

the bunkhouse to negotiate the Big Sea Treaty, Lady Emma
had proceeded straight to the drinks, a large pink gin in
particular, which she knocked off at once and then replenished,
bringing it outside to her present space on the steps from
whence she had an uninterrupted view of the bunkhouse door.

If Fate had constructed the scenario, Emma was not about
to allow any rewriting.

"Lady Emma has no imagination, you see." Bristals pouted
with all his jowls. "And such a red-letter day indeed for Sir
Guy Bristals of London, England. Never been through the
eye of the storm before."

"For a minute, I thought you might not make it when
Moon started waving his artillery around," Lyons lauded
him.

"Exactly! A close-run thing, Harry, *what*!"

Sir Guy sipped preciously from a water glass of brandy. For
once, the swilling baronet had not demanded champagne.
Perhaps because he sensed Lyons didn't have any or, if he
did, was not about to open it for him.

"I'm looking forward to telling *Her Majesty* all about this
adventure!"

Emma deigned to look at her estranged husband.

"Guy-balls, I'm sure *Her Majesty* will listen with bated
breath. *My God!*"

"You can be sure *She* is going to read all about it in the
London Final at the very least!"

"Guy-balls, *Her Majesty* does *not* read your filthy scandal
sheet!"

"*Au contraire,* Lady Emma, I have it on the best authority—"

"Bugger your best authority, Guy-balls!"

"Ah . . ." Bristals eyeballed her reprovingly. "You really
are out of sorts. And we do know why, old thing! No mind! I
say, Dick . . . Isn't our Doctor Guchi a real go-getter, American style? Indeed, he's so like his mentor, our dear, departed
Jasper Gates, indeed a Jasper Gates himself of the slant-eyed
variety! The good doctor will make a *superlative* partner for
Bristals London Group, take my word."

But Susan didn't think he should count on it. Everybody
was aware of the Japanese national strategy: let a project run
out of steam on its own rather than deliver it a straight-
forward coup de grace.

"He seems like a good guy."

"He's giving you everything you wanted, Dick," Susan pointed out.

"And more," Lyons said. "So much I'm suspicious. You think he might be a little bit too good to be true? Or too true to be good?"

"I'm *proud* to be associated with him," Bristals said stoutly.

Again, Susan let him blather. Be politic about it, *old girl*, at least for the next few weeks, until it was decided, one way or the other, just what lay in the future.

"These savages couldn't get a better deal . . . *what!*"

Shaking his head sadly, Lyons mused. "Paternalism, Japanese style. They'd never buy it from Washington and now they are, from Japan. The mind boggles!"

"You should be proud, Dick," Susan said. "It's all your doing."

"You mean I ain't completely lost it, Suzette?" He raised his damaged eyebrow. "Okay, but kind of discouraging, isn't it, that they can't get a good deal from their own countrymen— we *are* their countrymen, Sue. Teller will agree with that, won't you, Teller?"

"On this, we agree, Dick."

"But not on all else, right?" Lyons demanded.

"That's right."

Harry removed his sunglasses, looked at Lyons, and put them on again.

"I know what you're thinking, Teller. And to this day, I'm not sorry I went to the North. A lot of people won't ever stop hating me for it but I can't help that."

"I don't hate you," Harry said.

"Well, what then?"

"I don't know."

"What the hell do you mean you don't know? You must know."

Harry wasn't going to answer impulsively or thoughtlessly. He took off the glasses again and looked Dick Lyons in the eye. Easy to say, yes, I do hate your guts for consorting with the enemy, as misguided or whatever our side might have been about tearing up Indochina, my country right or wrong, and all that.

"I'll tell you," Harry said slowly, "what I've always wanted to tell you. Maybe I'm absolutely wrong but I've always figured it wasn't so much a mistake as it was a *selfish* thing to do. You were indulging yourself, playing God. Maybe looking for the publicity. I'm telling you the truth—I respect your right to go, but not you for going. How's that?''

"Okay," Lyons muttered doggedly, "and I'll admit it was partly a publicity stunt. *How's that?*''

"All right. So?"

"So, now you'll have to admit, Harry Teller, that being the kind of horse's ass I am, I could do no other."

Harry laughed grudgingly.

"I'm sure that's true."

Lyons turned to Susan, frowning dispiritedly.

"That's just about all I'm going to get out of this son of a bitch!"

"I think so," she said.

"Right." Lyons sighed grimly. "So I'm not sorry I went to Hanoi. I'm just sorry about *everything*. About being a horse's ass—and a loser."

"Come now, Dick."

"Jenny could never stand a loser," Lyons muttered.

"I don't think anybody ever called you a loser, Dick," Harry backed her up.

And Bristals whooped, "Loser? My dear man, you're living the dream of modern man. Back to nature!" Eyes round with insincerity, he spewed nonsense. "Absolutely, totally idyllic. The life of the noble savage! Orgasmic!"

"I never heard a lifestyle described as orgasmic, chum."

"Nor I, Guy-balls," Lady Emma said, spitting manfully into the dust. "Kindly shut your trap."

And, yeah, yeah, Lyons went on, it was Bear Jay, in his most insidious bedside manner, who'd convinced Jenny that if Lyons, her husband, had not been so resentful of the world, he'd have been a *winner*, not a loser.

It was all Jay's doing, this latest rupture of the Lyons household.

"I think," Lyons brooded, "I'll just go ahead and move up with the Custerds in their trailer. Join the old man. Baldy Custerd. He watches TV all day long—he's a fan of yours too, Suzette. You've got fans in the strangest places. . . ."

"Lyons-balls," Emma said unkindly, "why don't you just sit down here next to me and drink your drinkie and stop the drivel?"

"You see?" Lyons demanded, waving his arm. "Everybody wants me to shut up and be good! And, naturally, the reason

I've always done fine is that I *am* resentful and I *won't* shut up and be good! I take it personally that crooks cheat and politicians lie! Are you with me on this, Teller?''

"Sure I am, Dick. Trouble is, what are you going to do about it? The great American public doesn't appear to care anymore. . . .''

"They're use to fraud and deceit!'' Lyons said loudly. "They expect it of their elected officials! Jesus Christ! They're so numb, they think it's written into the Constitution. They *love* being lied to and cheated out of their money. Agree, Harry?''

"Yeah, by and large,'' Harry said.

"I want to get back to Washington. And fight 'em! Like I used to.''

"Dick,'' Susan encouraged him, "You *should* get out of here. Why *don't* you go back to Washington?''

"Yeah, sure, but would Nader have me?''

"Or one of the think tanks, Dick. You don't have any money, do you?''

No question could've pleased him more.

"Susan, this boy doesn't have a pot to piss in.''

"So what?''

"You're right! Who needs it? You don't need money to raise hell and that's why, see, Bear Jay is such an asshole! If I ever admitted that I'm mad at the world for some dumb psychiatric reason—it'd be all over for me. I know it! Right, Harry?''

"Right.''

Emma kicked at Lyons.

"Really, what in bloody hell *are* you talking about?''

"History, Emma.''

"Anarchists, Em,'' Bristals snarled. "Just as dear Jasper warned us, remember, my dear Susan?''

"No.''

Scowling, Emma told him to shut the hell up and turned belligerently on Harry. "You might want to ask me, Mr. Scribbler, how I'm bearing up, and I'll tell you it does tend to deflate one when one's lover is accused of murder and mayhem and other such things. Not only accused but, evidently,'' she added, "guilty! Guilty of trying to kill Lyons-balls out of sheer jealousy. *Crime Passionel*, one might say, out of passion for none other than Yours So Very Truly!''

Sir Guy stopped rocking, his leather heels clacked on the floor.

"Am I hearing a'right? Do I hear, Dick, that you also rogered Emma, my estranged wife?" He wasn't especially unhappy about it. There was in his voice a resigned sort of pleasure in welcoming Lyons to the fraternity of the innumerable. "Did *you* know this, Brother Teller? Doesn't *The Corsair* keep its ear to the ground for local gossip?"

"No," Harry replied succinctly.

"Why, on the *Final* we have a daily column absolutely devoted to such stuff: Between the Sheets, as in sheets of newsprint, you see—"

"Oh, for God's sake, Guy-balls! Do shut up!"

"I deny everything," Lyons said in cavalier manner.

"I too," Emma yelled, "and make the most of it, Guy-balls. I'm . . . thinking of going back to New York City now the fun is over here."

"Over?" Lyons echoed. "Who says it's over?"

"I do."

"You're off the expenses now, old thing!"

"We're only estranged, Guy-balls, remember.'

Bristals smiled biliously.

"Put in a good word for me with *the old boy*," he said insinuatingly. What a sport he was. "You know, old thing, there's still a possibility we shall reconcile!"

"Not bloody likely, Guy-balls!" Emma cried derisively.

The next thing they heard was the familiar but always disquieting sound of a chopper.

At the same time one of Wobblybridge's crew shouted, "Bandit! Off the port bow."

Red and white designer-decorated in the colors of the Hispaniola County sheriff's department, the helicopter swept toward them, racketing a few feet above the Rancho Mondo road, and settled down to a landing, the ugly thing, on a flat spot off to the side of the bunkhouse.

Motor cut, blades sweeping in diminishing, slowing circles, the monster opened its side door and a pair of uniformed deputies hopped down, followed by two other people, most unexpected arrivals. Or maybe not so unexpected, given how Lyons had been going on about Jenny and Bertram Jay.

Lyons sighed again, very loudly to be heard over the noise of the flying machine.

"Jenny," he said to Susan, "and her fuckin' shrink! They've come to close the books, deliver my obituary, Suzette. It's the end. I am defeated!"

"Never, Dick," Susan assured him, winking at Harry. "Never! You're God's very own angry man!"

"Sorry I'm late. I didn't mean to be."

Harry's arm had found its way around her waist. He pressed, intimately. You recognized that, when it happened, once or twice in a lifetime.

"No problem—now that you're here."

"When can we bug out? What's happening?"

"Bad," Susan murmured. "Blick's going ahead with Bristals on the NAN deal. They're flying to New York tonight. I've got to get back too, Harry." He made a disappointed sound. "I'm sorry. I've got to. It's life and death."

"I thought . . . I was hoping . . ."

"I know, but don't worry. I promised Fineman and Jack."

"You're going to save them," he said flatly. "Fat chance. Okay, you've got to do what you've got to do. I know."

"Do you, Harry, please?"

"Yep."

Then Jenny was trotting in their direction, Lyons's direction, actually, leaving Bear Jay behind. She slowed to a walk when she neared Lyons.

"Dick!"

"For it is I," he said solemnly.

"I thought for sure it was you who got shot!"

"Sorry, no."

"Ass!" she exclaimed angrily. "I hate you! You're always in a jam!"

She put her arms around his circumference and hugged.

This was very touching to watch. Especially, as the today-Jenny was far younger than the careworn creature Susan had seen a week or two ago. She'd had a facial or two in the meantime, her dark hair had been trimmed, conditioned, and sleekly braided; she was wearing a helpful bit of makeup around the eyes and a city-slicker outfit—pleated white cotton slacks over sparkling white tennies and a blue silk shirt with pearl buttons. Even the silver loops of earrings had been polished and she'd toned down the turquoise display to one mammoth ring on her left hand.

"Hey," Dick said gruffly, "I'm all in one piece."

Lyons, this roustabout of a man, wasn't such a dunce, was he, that he didn't realize why she'd come back? To read him his obit? No way. But he was so clumsy. He should've grabbed beauteous Jenny in his arms and smothered her in embrace but he didn't and all of a sudden there were the two lawmen in front of him, and roly-poly Bear Jay.

"The victim is in the house," Lyons said. "And what're you doing here, Bear?"

"He's an M.D., don't forget," Jenny said.

"I'll look at him," Bear said.

"Do that!"

Bert "Bear" Jay was not at all happy. Hangdog, he kept glancing at Jenny, as if she'd let him down in the worst way, and perhaps she had. Jenny looked concerned but not for long. With one scorching look, she put Bear on ice. He uttered a sound much like a sob and broke away, trudging toward the house, his heavy shoulders sloped in defeat.

"Hi, Susan. Harry," Jenny said nonchalantly.

"Hello, Jenny."

"That *shit*," Lyons said gruffly. "No more Mr. Nice Guy, me!"

Jenny gazed at him critically.

"Look at your face, Dick!"

Lyons shrugged, like a trouper.

"The show must go on," he said.

Then she kissed him.

"I'm glad you're all right."

"Well, if you were worried, you could've called! Moon tried to kill me and you didn't even call, never mind about the flowers."

"I didn't know until today."

"Well, ain't *that* fine and dandy!"

With a frosty nod and grimace, Jenny finally acknowledged Emma who burst out, "Where the hell have you been? Lyons-balls has been very worried."

"San Francisco."

"San Francisco!" Emma yelled. "What you mean is with poncey Bertram Jay."

"No, I mean what I said, Emma! San Francisco."

"What the hell do you . . ."

Lyons began to rant, but the senior of the deputies finally got up the nerve to butt in and stop him.

"Well, Mr. Lyons, we're back again."

"Yeah. Sorry. It's such a pain in the ass, all this." He nodded toward the pickup. "Moon's over there. The boys tied him up."

Lyons managed a self-conscious grin, aimed mainly at his beautiful wife, Jenny Driver, the actress. It was an astonishing thing to see. Out of that drudge, that beat-up pioneer woman ready to die for her land, had come this...what? Actress, sophisticated enough for any stage. A princess from a frog. A woman of many faces, playing God knows what new role.

Jenny was watching Dick bemusedly. She shook her head as if to ask, Had there ever been such a reckless boy, or excuse for such a fool?

And Dick Lyons? He was so smitten it was enough to make you sick. He put his big hand on Jenny's shoulder and gazed at her limpidly, only after a minute forcing himself back to the deputies.

"Well, guys..." He drew a deep breath. "Everybody heard Moon admit he was the guy who killed Gates. Like a dozen witnesses, Charlie. And also that he took the shot at me. Remember, Teller?"

Pensively, Harry chuckled. "Remember? How could I forget? It's all in the paper, Dick."

"What do you mean?"

"In *The Corsair*. We smoked him out, didn't we?"

"Yeah," Lyons said uncertainly, "I guess we did."

"You see," Harry explained, "I figured the sniper who shot at Dick was probably the same character who killed Jasper Gates. We don't usually have two madmen running around at once, do we, Charlie? I think that kind of rattled old Moon."

"Harry is brilliant," Susan elaborated, without thinking. "Didn't I tell you that, Jenny?"

"I don't remember the exact words."

"Brilliant is close enough," Harry said.

The distinctive Bristals sound found its way to them.

"Not brilliant today, Mr. Teller! *Today* you missed the party. Were I proprietor of *The Corsair* I would discharge you!"

Harry half turned, grinned crookedly.

"But I'm the proprietor. And I don't work for you, you fat fart!"

"Good-O!" Emma cheered.

And that was not going to make things any easier.

"Insufferable bore! Backwoods hack! Consider canceled my offer to buy your rag!"

Sir Guy resumed rocking, his face wreathed in ill humor.

"That's okay, Guy, I'm selling out to Time-Warner."

"Clown!"

"Okay," said the number-one deputy uncomfortably, "we'll take down all you folks' names."

"And there's another group in the bunkhouse," Lyons said, "working out a deal to sell Big Sea, taking care of Jackson Wobblybridge's best interests, so he'll never have to work another day in his life."

From the porch, Wobblybridge hooted. "If only it was so, Big Dick. Greetings, Jenny..."

"Hello, Jackson."

"First," Lyons said, "you'll want to get Moon loaded up."

His arm around Jenny, Lyons moseyed toward Wobblybridge's pickup and the unlucky Moon Rivers.

Harry held Susan back. He looked concerned.

"You've got blood all over you."

"From Blick's grandson. He got a head wound—"

"Your hands."

"I didn't wash them yet."

"All over your dress, Susie," he said, looking at her worriedly. "It looks like you *soaked* yourself in the kid's blood."

"No! I was trying to stop the bleeding, that's all."

"Susie," Harry said charily, "the time has come. It's years ago now. You've paid and you never even had a gun in your hand." She understood and she didn't try to stop him. "The time has come to cut it out!"

"Harry, never mind! Finally, everything is under terrific control."

Lyons let out a yell.

"The son of a bitch has got away!"

The deputies looked at each other. And Harry looked at her, nodding and calmly smiling.

"*Not* under terrific control, it seems. The perpetrator is loose again."

"This rope's been cut," the senior deputy diagnosed. "Are you telling us, Mr. Lyons, that you had Moon Rivers tied up here and he cut the rope and got away?"

"Yeah."

Jackson Wobblybridge leapt off the porch. When he wanted to, he moved very fast.

"It *has* been cut," he confirmed, "by a *very* sharp knife."

"Agreed," the junior of the deputies said, "and where's he got to, then?"

"That is beyond me," Wobblybridge said. "I tied him up and when I tie them up, they stay tied up. Moon Rivers has disappeared into proverbial thin air! And I cannot explain it." But to some of them he gave it away by his quick glance toward the house. "Somehow...he got a knife, cut his bonds, and slipped away."

"In broad daylight?"

"Yes," Wobblybridge said, "in the blaze of high noon, Moon Rivers has escaped. I wonder, had Moon an accomplice in the neighborhood?"

Lyons snorted. "Nobody liked Moon. Who would be his accomplice?"

"Just a thought," Jackson W. murmured. "Should we fan out, officer?"

Preoccupied, perhaps speculating about the destiny of her erstwhile lover, Emma Bristals studied the distant horizon. Actually, Emma was the prime candidate for accomplice. But she had not once budged since bringing her pink gin outside and sitting down on the steps.

"Well," said the senior deputy complacently, "he won't get far. We shall radio an all-points-bulletin."

"Wobblybridge," Lyons suggested, "why don't your well-trained trackers run in every direction and see what...they see."

"They could do that, Big Dick."

Cautioning calm, the lead deputy invited them to consider various options. It was decided, quickly enough, that one of Wobblybridge's men should go back to the crossroads as lookout; the others could sort of search the adjacent fields and ditches for Moon's trail, a *spoor*, Wobblybridge called it, even as he acknowledged they should have been more vigilant, for Moon Rivers was a well-known slimeball.

Emma might have had a comeback on that slur, but she said nothing, her thoughts clearly elsewhere.

"At least," Wobblybridge said, "he's no longer armed and that is some consolation."

Beau Custerd was extremely irked that Moon had given them the slip. But first things first: after he'd finished stomping the bunkhouse porch and berating Jackson Wobblybridge, Beau led Guchi, AHB, Ms. Goody, and the others back inside, announcing that very shortly they were going to cross t's and dot i's and smoke a peace pipe to put the final okay on the agreement.

But it was also Jackson Wobblybridge's moment. For no good reason, except perhaps to have a leak, he sauntered inside the ranchhouse and was gone three or four minutes. Looking extremely worried, he returned, easing up to Lyons and whispering some bit of information in his ear. Lyons's cheeks fired up and he and Wobblybridge rushed back into the house.

Whatever had been troubling them was confirmed as Trouble. Bel Custerd had also gone missing.

"Madness," Jenny said sharply. "If I hadn't given up smoking, I'd have a cigarette. You know, Sue, Eugene O'Neill is Mickey Mouse compared to this gang of maniacs."

Never mind, though, Jenny was not in a bad humor, oh no. Dick made life interesting, unlike *some other* people she might name, and all told she was happy she'd returned to the Great Buffoon.

Privately, so Emma Bristals could neither read her lips nor overhear, Jenny confided, "I still love him . . . and I don't. I don't love him . . . and I do. He's like a child who won't let you get on with your life."

"And Bear?" Susan whispered, hesitantly.

Jenny shrugged. Could she be so cruel? Kill or cure, she said, feast or famine.

She replied, "I'm ready to go back to work," as if that explained everything.

No time to hear any more, for Lyons of the Apes was there, throwing an arm around Jenny, leaning on her, hanging on her.

With an eye on the helicopter, whence the deputies were exchanging spirited roger's and over-and-out's with headquarters in Rio Tinto, Dick whispered melodramatically, "It seems Bel has known Moon a long time."

"Seems?" Jenny repeated acidly. "Biblically, you mean? *Seems?* It *seems* Princess Belmont was not as taken with you as you thought . . . Big Dick."

"Jenny!" Lyons went red in the face again, for all the world like Falstaff caught in the act. Then, he caved in. "Yeah. Okay. Point taken."

"Well taken!"

"Yeah," Lyons agreed. "I can't say I'm surprised, honey.

Bel was always in some kind of mood. And now we have to worry about Wobblybridge. He's suicidal.''

The Wobblybridge in question was stretched across the porch floor, on his back like a corpse, with his hands crossed over his eyes. He must have heard what Lyons said for he spoke in a hollow, haunted, entranced sort of voice.

"And I thought she was reading poetry or meditating. But in fact, she was sneaking out the back door to rendezvous with Moon, and even now around through the forest with her scout knife to cut the rope and let Moon escape, not only that, but to flee with him, God knows where. . . .''

"Easy, Jackson.''

"And I said . . . I told you, Big Dick, that Bel would never love a white guy.'' Wobblybridge's friends chimed in with mutters and murmurs of such condolence as: Yo, Yeah, and Fuckin'-A. Then J. Wobblybridge extended one arm, indicating a teeny measurement between thumb and forefinger. "Then I remember from long ago, when we were all in school, that Moon has got that much . . . a smidgeon . . . of Basket blood, dating back to a great-grandfather who also happened to be—'' his voice broke, "a Russian. Does *that* explain it?''

Emma Bristals finally reacted to this new insult to her womanhood.

"The Indian girl, you say . . .''

Bristals ceased rocking again.

"Shush, Em . . . you're out of it. Leave well enough alone.''

"You are saying the Indian girl loved Moon?''

It was conceivable Emma was deeply wounded. Whatever, her discomfort was sure to please, even delight, her estranged husband.

"And Moon loved the Indian girl, old thing!''

She turned on him ferociously.

"What? What are you saying, you fool?''

"That all this time, old thing, this ruffian loved the lady called Bel!'' Bristals shook with laughter, holding his sides, wiping tears from his eyes. "Ah, ha, Em, ah ha! It seems our lad Moon had more than one arrow in his quiver.''

Emma snorted noisily enough to make him go silent. Then she stomped up on the porch, kicking at J. Wobblybridge as she passed. For a moment, it was a definite possibility she'd retaliate against Sir Guy in a physical way, making one wonder whether the Bristals's separation had resulted from his understandable antipathy to husband-beating. Fearfully, Bristals looked the other way, concentrating on his rocking, and the spindly chair creaked in complaint of his bulging occupancy. Emma kept going into the house, grumbling that she was overdue for another drink.

But she had pursued the logic of the situation to its even more disturbing conclusion: that Moon's hatred of Dick Lyons stemmed not from Lyons's camaraderie with the Lady Emma but his fondness for Belmont Custerd? This was important. It made all the difference: between romantic tragedy and mere sociology.

Lyons lowered his voice to a whisper.

"Rough on Jackson. He didn't have any idea about . . . that Bel was so promiscuous." He raised his voice. "Sir Guy, here's a Noble Savage who's not feeling very orgasmic right now."

Jackson Wobblybridge rolled over, whining, "In no way whatsoever very orgasmic right now, Big Dick."

"Wobblybridge . . ." Appealingly, Lyons took his time with the tongue-twister name. "Wobblybridge, I want you to pay close attention. More than anybody in the world, I, Richard Lyons, know how sick and transitory glory can be. I who have been up and down and up again and down again! There are many battles to be fought, Wobblybridge, much hair to be lifted, and many girls to be loved. So many causes to champion, so many people to be saved. I recommend that you return to the purity, honesty, simplicity of the mountains. Wobblybridge, and to your first love, the works of Baudelaire. . . ."

Jackson Wobblybridge began to weep.

"Perhaps you're right, Big Dick."

Jenny had been listening to this unlikely exchange very patiently, but now she spoke up, making no pretense she was at all interested in such local doings.

"I'm going East, Dick. *I'm ready now.* I've heard from Sidney—" she paused, "my director, and he's ready too. I can't delay it any longer."

"Oh, hell, honey! Where?"

"To Jonestown, Maine. I've got an appointment with *The Iceman*. And I am ready!" she repeated.

"I suppose Bear has got you in a properly neurotic state of mind?"

"And then some," Jenny admitted ruefully. "I guess this isn't what you expected, Susan, coming to see us again."

"Your shrink!" Lyons scoffed. "The road to hell is paved... Harry?"

"Yeah, I pretty much agree."

"That goddamn Bear Jay and all his Freudian garbage." Jenny looked at him adoringly. "You don't think Jenny's such a dope to fall for all that! Besides, she's learned everything she'll ever want to know about family hangups from O'Neill."

"It's got nothing to do with that," Jenny said.

"Jay's hold over you?"

"He doesn't have any kind of hold over *me,* Dick. Maybe the reverse."

Jenny colored slightly and, in the circumstances, that shouldn't be surprising. What was this all about anyway? Susan glanced at Harry. Did he have any idea? True, there was a bit of the Svengali about Bert Jay, Susan had deduced that, remembering how he and Jenny had behaved in the car, for God's sake, literally right in front of Susan, and Jenny couldn't deny it'd happened. Her trust in Susan's discretion must be boundless; Susan could've betrayed her so easily. Of course, the way they were acting, it was questionable Dick Lyons would've listened or believed.

You might justifiably assume he already knew, accepted, approved. Yes, the show must go on.

Carefully, Susan asked, "Are we allowed to wonder if Bear Jay is competent?"

"Competent? He's a goddamn charlatan," Lyons said. "What the hell did he do for Jenny? Besides make her feel guilty... and crazy?"

"He did do that," Jenny said.

"Like he did that wife of his," Lyons said nastily. "After you cut through all the bullshit, you discover he was sort of *exiled* out here by his headshrinker pals."

Susan didn't quite follow.

"You know that to be true? How do you know?"

Smiling cagily, Lyons said, "I made it my business. That New York school, ha! They decided chubby Bertram was playing fast and loose with his Freud. Dangerous revisionism! Primal hedonism, for God's sake, sexual atavism-therapy, as practiced in the caves. As opposed to dream analysis, even worse! Don't *ask* how I know, Suzette! I'm a bit of a shrink myself. I've read the books. I was a fan of Ayn Rand, you

bet! In fact, well . . ." He glanced at Jenny. "Anyway, after
the thing with his wife, he had kind of a personal and
professional breakdown and, to get him out of town, they
cooked up this big research project in faraway California to
examine the psychiatric effects of overindulgence in grass.
Etcetera." He grinned. "I think Jay has been smoking too
much of his laboratory materials."

"Doctor, cure thyself," Jenny murmured supportively. "He
just got worse."

"Well, then . . ." Susan had to ask, "If Bear's such a
charlatan, why did you consult him?"

"Good question."

Jenny flashed Susan a significant look. Yes, she knew that
Susan knew. But that part of it was not going to be discussed.
The question did not arise.

"Could I ever blow the whistle!" Lyons chortled.

But who wanted trouble with the New York school?

"Quiet," Jenny warned, "here he comes."

Scott had appeared in the ranchhouse doorway. Bear Jay
and silent Sidney Wilmer were behind him. There was a
swath of bandage around Scott's head, just a mite whiter than
his ghostly face. He looked like he'd bled away three-quarters
of his blood.

"Well! Are you okay now, bub?" Lyons asked.

Scott smiled effetely, holding on to the doorframe.

"The *experience* keeps turning . . . over . . . and over in my
head," he said, voice near a whisper, "like a slow-motion
headache, you know what I mean? And then . . . I think, *Hey*,
what great raw material for my second book!"

Laughing meanly, Emma barged past him, holding her
latest drink.

"Second book! Did we know you wrote a first one? Don't
assume, lad," Emma cautioned him outrageously, "that plenty of other chaps haven't had that experience. This may be the
first time for you—" she turned and smirked beguilingly,
"but it's commonplace, I can tell you. Women might not
generally admit it . . ."

"*Em*," Sir Guy said agonizingly, "he's talking about
getting a gun stuck in his ribs and shot at, not—"

"Oh, for God's sake!" she exploded, "do you mind? I
know perfectly well what he's talking about, Bristals-balls!
Give me a break!"

Lyons was staring hostilely at poor Bear Jay.

"Well?"

"He's all right," Bear reported glumly. *"He's lost some blood but the wound is superficial."*

"Well?"

"He should have a tetanus shot, soon as possible. Mr. Wilmer here is going to drive him to town right away."

"Well?" Lyons demanded a third time.

Bear gazed back at him lengthily, silently, almost menacingly, and finally said, "You're a paranoid schizophrenic with delusions of grandeur."

"Well, I know that, for crissakes!" Lyons's look was withering. *"And?"*

"And nothing. That's it. You're clinically insane. And Jenny knows it. She's going away with me... at least she was. Now, I don't know..."

Bear Jay looked so bewildered, entirely lost, as if his compass was missing its needle. The halo of hair, once thought to be so enchanting, was more disarranged than usual. He looked the mad physicist, if it wasn't sufficient that he be a mad psychiatrist.

"Bear," Jenny said quietly. "Dick and I are going East, are we not, Dick?"

"Yeah."

"I..." Bear looked at Susan and Harry, then at Jenny. "I... Ted and I are going East, too, back to Boston, when he starts school."

"Wonderful, maybe we can have lunch," Jenny said, in complete possession of all her faculties, supreme, the eyes of her audience upon her, what more could she want? She turned gracefully to Susan and suggested, "You know, darling, about this interview of ours? Wouldn't it be amusing to do it in Maine?"

"Could be." Might as well agree, Susan thought, even though she wasn't sure she'd be working for *Hindsight* or NAN by then. "If you'll have the time."

"We'll make time!"

Poor Bear. He stood rooted, speechless, his face destroyed. He didn't understand any better than Susan what was happening, what *had* happened. Poor Ted. What would happen to them? No sooner asking herself the question, Susan could answer it: Nothing would happen to them that hadn't already.

And did she finally, at last, begin to appreciate the dynamic of the Driver-Lyons alliance? The fact was this had happened before: at another time and in another place and with different characters, before a different audience! But it had most certainly happened!

Jenny Driver and Dick Lyons had played out the whole charade *before*.

As if to put Paid to it, the rockers on Bristals's chair suddenly cracked loudly and split. He hit the porch floor with a grunt and thump and hiss, like a punctured balloon.

26

The last time Susan Channing ever saw August Hugo Blick
was at his place on Park Avenue, the evening before she
moved out, this in keeping with Clause One of her Personal
Declaration of Independence and for the sake of propriety, to
a fashionable sublet on Fifth Avenue, ironically, the location
she'd have preferred in the first place. Park Avenue had
always seemed to Susan, even at the best of times, a barren
and characterless sort of boulevard.

Her new situation on Fifth between Sixtieth and Seventieth,
and Susan was divulg ing the precise address to no one, was
airy and open, facing the park. And across the greenery was
the West Side where you never went, people had used to say,
unless you were catching a boat for Europe. That her new
place had once upon a time, in recent years, been a high-class
brothel bothered her not at all. That was the way of things in
the Big City.

To be perfectly honest about it, moving out was the only
thing she could do. Emma Bristals had become August's
"houseguest" and the odds were the arrangement would be

permanent. Did it seem unlikely that Emma so willingly had given up her rough-and-ready Western existence, a shovel's throw from her horses and the wide-open range? It was easy to accept that Emma might wish for a more engaging mate than Sir Guy Bristals, but at the same time one was entitled to expect the replacement would be more like Teddy Roosevelt than old August Hugo Blick.

Still, as they said, everybody to their own taste-thrill. And, as all this was the work of surehanded Fate, not Fate's fickle finger, who was to argue? Emma and August suited each other for good reason and for reason that was better than the purely physical. Emma liked August's money and the prospect of lots more of it when August, finally, went where Emma had just come from: West. From August's point of view, Emma was perfect: she didn't have a career to nourish and only the one horse, which she rode in the park once a week. Emma had nothing else to do but be available.

And it went without saying that Susan was not half Emma's match in the demanding task of courtesanship. Emma would make very enjoyable the last years of the tenth richest man in America, perhaps ninth now that Jasper Gates was dead.

And, of course, Susan didn't have to remind herself, as she walked beneath the Bohemian crystal chandeliers toward seven-oh-oh, there was the matter of her very definite sort of arrangement with Harry Teller.

"Hello, Konrad."

For the last time.

"Hello, Miss Channing, Mr. Blick is in his usual place." Konrad swung back one side of the wide salon door. "Miss Susan, Mr. Blick."

"Ah . . ."

Oh, yes, she wouldn't forget the Ah. Every time she went to the doctor with a strep throat she'd remember Ah. *Say Ah!*

"Hello, August."

"Please sit down and Konnie will bring you a drink. The usual? A vodka over ice? Yes?"

Susan studied the new August. His face had more color, his hair fuller, more modern styling, and he was wearing a red velvet smoking jacket above his black floorwalker trousers. The stiff collar and black tie had been replaced by a soft silk scarlet foulard.

"You look smashing, August. And *where* is Emma?"

August thumped his knee with his fist.

"Due back any moment. So! You are leaving us?"

"I thought it best, August. Matters are in such flux, as you can imagine—*as you know*, now that Sir Guy is in the picture."

He didn't care. Why *should* he care? It was no skin off his nose that Bristals had arrived at the NAN building like a whole rampaging army, or one dark angel.

"And how are you getting on?"

How indeed? Not well. Susan had already had her private conference with the Great Man, had heard his heroic lecture: for Bristals London Group and God and Country! Bristals had taken over Simon Hayford's corner layout; his plans were even more grandiose. Breath sweet and hot and intimidating, he'd boasted about being Mister Media, or in his case Sir Media, Sir Guy Media, and even—knowing what he must about her and Harry—invited her to become Lady Media, Mister and Missus Media, Sir Guy and Lady Media, the most powerful media-bonded couple in all Christendom.

How did one say it? Closed for the holidays. Out to lunch. No trespassing!

Now that Jasper is dead, Remember Greenswards...

Which she did, constantly: her beloved Irish estate!

He tended to astonish, oh yes, he yearned to crush her to him, to worship her, to run his hands over her body...

To fondle her shoes, slippers, pumps, ski boots!

He adored her icy reserve...

She was frigid.

No, a torrid and eager and expansive and expressive lover...

And how did one say no in a few dozen languages?

"We'll survive, August."

There was no point in saying anything else. It was too late.

"I'm happy you've come before Emma returns. She's attending a cocktail party at the United Nations."

"Without you?"

August knew she was needling him.

"I could not accompany Lady Emma, for I was waiting for an important phone call." His eyelids came down, appropriately, like blinds. "From none other than Baron Guchi. Does that surprise you?"

"Not at all."

"It seems, my dear, that the baron and I are going to do things with Jasper International after all."

"Great."

Whatever... Susan didn't care. AHB's machinations had ceased to interest her. And as for Ishira Guchi, who could say what he was up to? According to the latest rumors from California, Guchi had carried Beaumont Custerd off to Japan with him, for schooling in the ways and wiles of international finance.

If you believe that, you'd believe anything.

Beaumont or Belmont?

Aha, a fascinating speculation. There was a vague indication out of the West that somehow or other Beau and Bel Custerd had switched identities on that fateful day. Why they would do this, nobody, including the brilliant Harry Teller, could say.

"Yes, we seem to be on the verge of acquiring all of Jasper International." August's mouth moved, in a sort of mime of mastication. "Shipping, land, oil, food processing, a steel mill or two, the cruise business, which was the apple of Jasper Gates's eye."

"That's depressing, August," she said, thinking of Jasper again, as she did, more and more affectionately every day, remembering his enthusiasm, the vibrancy, the dedication, and not least his affection for her. "What'll happen to the SS *Freckles*?" "All-Nippon will take *Freckles*. And also retain chosen pieces of J.I. The rest of it?" He shrugged brutally, avariciously. "*Chop-chop!* We'll sell it off, down to the last desk and typewriter and pencil. My guiding strategy: the *parts* are worth more than the whole."

"Yes," Susan said, "I remember. And the people?"

"People?"

"The employees, the people who've worked for J.I. all these years."

August shrugged again. Jasper certainly had good reason if he was rolling in his grave.

"Labor is a commodity like all others. If you do not need something, you sell it or throw it out. Employees? Open the gates and let them go. Besides," AHB said, "*people* tend to be expensive to maintain. Give me a piece of machinery anytime! Prosperoso will take care of many of them; it is the Japanese paternalistic style. Flocks and herds of people singing Prosperoso's song, roaming the world in unruly and barbaric groups, a new Japanese army as bloodthirsty as the old." He snickered cynically. "Not the style of AHB. People are too expensive," he repeated. "Automation is better. And investment finance is better than automation: no people, no machines. Only paper: money.''

"Very neat, August," Susan murmured, more depressed than before, at the same time so thankful she was moving out and away.

"But we are not here to talk *religion,* my dear!" August said slyly. "I *am* pleased for us to have a few moments alone. . . ." He waited while Konrad came and went. "I did not mean to mention this but, as Sir Guy Bristals, a ridiculous man, by the way, as you know, and Emma certainly does not disagree . . . well, my dear, it was your choice to go off with Jasper Gates and break my heart!"

Susan shook her head.

"Oh, no, August. If your heart was ever broken, it isn't any longer, as anybody can plainly see. Anyway, it's better this way."

August smiled begrudgingly, looking more than ever, speaking of tribes, like a cigar-store Indian.

"Well, I admit that the Lady Emma is a goddess! Should I tell you that?"

"You just did, August."

"Black-haired vixen!" he cried. "Gypsy princess! Her maiden name was Smith."

"And that's a while ago," Susan said dryly, "I mean since she was a maiden."

"Smith is the most common of gypsy family names." August groaned erotically. "Her body is textured like ancient ivory, as if from a pharaoh's tomb, or like Goya's *Maja* on canvas, those mesmerizing shadows and hidden places, blood-red apertures, moist orifices, those dusky recesses . . ."

"August . . ."

"You know my fondness for . . . my predilection . . . my artistry? I am an artist, in my own style."

"Yes!"

August wagged his long, high-priest's head.

"But you cannot know what drives Emma, can you?"

"Yes, I can. She told me."

"Oh?" That wouldn't please him. "So . . ."

"August," Susan said impatiently, "everyone is saying . . . the whole world knows it. You and Emma are perfectly matched."

"Who knows? Who says?" he demanded angrily. Then he

smiled with one side of his mouth. "Why not? Yes, we are matched, like two spoons! Or the figures Six and Nine!"

August sighed and wheezed with merriment.

"That just goes to show you," Susan said, "God's in his heaven and all's right with the world."

"Yes, my dear," he said. "So, surely, you must see my other reason for selling my NAN interests to Sir Guy Bristals. *Quid pro quo*. I take his wife, he takes control of NAN."

"And Emma knows that?"

"Of course! She understands, there can be no trouble with Sir Guy Bristals at the divorce. My name must *never* be mentioned."

"Did Bristals threaten? Blackmail! I'm not surprised. He's an awful man!"

"Not especially awful," AHB said mildly. "He makes the most of his opportunities."

No, on the contrary, emphatically, Bristals *was* an awful man. Susan had more or less decided she wouldn't fight him for Greenswards. She wasn't ready to make the sort of deal Sir Guy demanded in order to hang on to it; nor was she ready for an expensive four or five years in court defending her title to the place.

"You'll marry Emma? Congratulations. I wish you a happy marriage, August, and a . . . long one."

"A long one, amen!" She had pleased him. "You did say, Susan, that AHB will outlive us all. I do sincerely believe that."

"I hope you do. It would only be just."

The remark was not intended to be kind and he took it as meant, with a scornful chuckle.

"You'll hang on me the curse of everlasting life? I am amused, my dear, but it would not be amusing to be the man who could not die."

Susan didn't bother to answer. She was ready to leave. Was there anything else he had wanted to tell her, or give her, such as money or advice, and now couldn't remember?

She was saved from further damage by a big noise at the front door. Emma Bristals had returned.

"What ho! Konnie! Here! Take care of my sable!"

A sable in July? Why not? Emma plunged into the drawing room, whirling a crocodile-skin handbag that matched her brown croc shoes. Life in New York City suited her; Emma looked fabulous! Her stalwart self, and Emma was what the brassiere ads called a full-figured woman, was swathed in a knee-length silky-woolly striped sheath, the rust-red shade of which was no less than striking, even dramatic, against her jet-black hair and the ivory skin tone August had mentioned. Gold dangled from her wrists and diamonds from her neck.

"Susan! Hello, ducks!"

"Yes, hello, Emma. My word, I have to say—"

"Say, Susan, say!"

"You look wonderful," Susan said generously.

She didn't dislike Emma. Why should she?

Emma was a very different person than the one who'd never dressed in anything but smelly jeans and sweat-stained denim shirts, but the energy level was just as elevated. She swooped across the room and dropped on her knees beside August, grabbing his hands and mouthing them hungrily.

"Hello, darling!"

"Treasure . . ."

Emma popped back up on her feet, smiling brilliantly.

"You'll be interested to know what happened to our poor, misguided friend."

"Which one of them?"

Emma snorted. "Quite so! No, I mean the hapless Saladin Rivers, ducks!"

"Oh, yes."

"Saladin has been arrested in San Francisco,"

Susan felt the weight of August's curiosity. How much would he knew about the Lady Emma and Moon Rivers?

"Saladin was preparing to board a freighter for Valparaiso."

"And they got him? Bad luck."

"He was with Belmont Custerd," Emma stated, not angrily, not happily.

August broke in, "The twin of that boy Beaumont, our cosignatory, the boy who's become the baron's protégé?"

Yes, so it seemed. Or did it? Emma was not inclined to go into detail about the Custerds, one way or the other, at least not in front of August. She batted her heavy eyelashes.

"Keeping AHB company then, are we, Susan? Did your phone call come through, darling? Baron Guchi was to call . . . He did! *Wunderbar,* darling, as we used to say in Berlin, *what*! How are you anyway, Susan, and I can't think why we haven't seen more of you, living next door as you do." Emma spun around as she talked, and spun again, from Susan to August and back, underlining every other word for emphasis. "And too soon, moving on, I understand, but just as well, I always say, time waits for no man and all that rot."

"Emma, Emma!" August spouted wondrously. "Susan, dear, remember Wade's Reef? Isn't Emma for all the world like a tropical storm, so passionate, so vital...so alive! *Hurricane Emma*, you overwhelm us!"

"I *was* named for Lord Nelson's mistress!"

Bawling for Konrad to bring her a pink gin, Emma hurled herself down again, facing August. Immodestly, she crossed her long, sleek legs, knee over knee, showing herself to him all the way up to black panties.

August gloated. He didn't try to hide it.

"And, my darling...how was the cocktail?"

"It was marvelous, my darling! You know," looking at Susan, "I cannot think how or why I hid myself at that goddamned ranch! I must have been insane." Emma extended her hand toward August. "Darling, the *drinky* was wonderful! I met the most *fascinating* Russian, from their delegation. He said he had known Lenin, or was it Stalin?"

"Stalin, I would imagine," AHB said, looking just a little worried. "But I don't like it when Lady Emma meets Russian spies."

"I am counterspy!" she cried.

Konrad hustled in with Emma's drink. He'd learned, it seemed, that she didn't like to be kept waiting.

"Chin-chin!"

In tentative fashion, August said, "Young Scott Blake will be coming back to New York soon."

So? No, Susan hadn't known that and she didn't care. Scott Blake was yesterday's news.

"I've grown very fond of the boy," Emma murmured.

"And he of you, darling," said AHB. Then, with a giveaway look, he said to Susan, "And he'd like to see you too while he's here, as you can imagine."

"Me?"

August nodded. "Why, the boy was hysterically in love with you!"

"With me?" Susan laughed a denial. "I don't think so."

"Besides," August remarked, shaking his head despairingly, "no sooner had he left me..."

Emma sneered. "That boy is absolutely accident-prone!"

'Again? What now?"

"As you know," August said, "we put the boy on an

airplane for Los Angeles, sending him back to his father, or so we thought. En route, he fell into the clutches of an ambitious movie starlet.'' August paused for a boost of brandy-soda. ''I can tell you from personal experience that there is nothing worse that can happen to a young man of Scott's age and inexperience, and to think it would happen to a grandson of mine!'' he slurred angrily. ''I would have expected that my own hellish experiences would have brought my family immunity from such grief!''

''Darling,'' Emma yelled irritably, *''the point . . .''*

''The point: This ruthless young thing convinced the gullible boy that his *novel*, this trash, was perfect for the silver screen and she perfect for a starring role. And so, etcetera, etcetera: Money, money, money. Well, Susan,'' the old man related in fevered tone, ''they proceeded south of the border where, in due course, they were picked up for passing bad checks in the Zona Rosa in Mexico City, and deported at *considerable* cost to AHB. Do you *begin* to understand?''

''But . . .'' The big question: ''Did she do him any physical harm?''

Emma glanced at August.

''With a hairdryer . . .''

''Suffice it to say,'' August grumbled, ''that the boy was damned lucky he wasn't electrocuted. The reason I'm telling you this, Susan, is that I feel you are the only person with any sort of influence over that boy. I would wish—''

''Oh, no! Oh no! Not me!''

''Please hear me out! It is obviously much too risky for the family—primarily myself, AHB, for the boy to be on his own, prey to unscrupulous forces and ruthless women. He's coming back to New York where I can keep him under observation until he gets to Princeton. I cannot *afford* the financial risk of his roaming loose. *Do you see?*''

''I follow your reasoning,'' she said. ''You make him sound like some kind of a nut-case, which he's not. He's not even very neurotic. Reckless, yes, unthinking. He'll be fine when he gets to school, don't you think so, Emma?''

''I'm sure August in his youth would've made the lad look like Little Lord Fauntleroy.''

But August refused to be reassured. He rubbed his face and blinked anxiously, as if facing disaster, eyeball to eyeball.

''I am worried sick. Don't you see? If something catastrophic were to happen, either accidental or planned, thieves and con men would beat a path to August Blick's door, demanding pounds and pounds of flesh. Once it was established that this reckless, wayward, foolish boy is my grandson, farewell peace and quiet, forever!''

Emma roused herself and yelled again for Konrad.

''Ducks, what AHB is getting around to in his lugubrious way is he'd like to buy your flat. That way, we can keep the lad next door with Sidney Wilmer, under lock and key. . . .''

''For a minute, I was afraid you were going to ask *me* to watch him.''

''Nothing so awful as that, ducks! Your flat is for sale, is it not?''

''Oh, yes.''

''That's what you wanted of Susan, darling! Remember? *Poor* darling *is* becoming forgetful.''

''Not,'' AHB muttered scathingly.

But if he was, no wonder! Emma was wearing him down, depleting his resources faster than ever he had the Amazon and Congo basins, stripping from the old boy stockpiles of minerals and vitamins. Poor darling? August was nobody's *poor* darling. But say it often enough and pretty soon he wouldn't even be able to walk, let alone think straight.

Astonishingly, for a man like August, he was falling for it. Long gone were the days he'd lorded it over Mignon, or Susan Channing for that matter.

Stricken, he cried, ''Did I forget? No, yes, Susan, I forget, yes, I do forget, I admit it, what you paid for the place?''

''A million,'' she said quickly.

''A million-*two* then?''

''August, it's on the market for. . .'' Think fast. ''. . . two and a half.''

''Two-five!'' August jerked and cried out as if she'd put a knife in him. ''Then . . . two million!''

''Two and a quarter and it's yours,'' Susan said recklessly. *''Done!''*

But it was Emma who said so.

She smiled sweetly at Susan, but not all that sweetly either.

Outmaneuvered, August fumed. His mouth trembled, his hands shook so much he clasped them between his knees. He was a mere shadow of his former swashbuckling self. Then, using both hands, needing both hands, he reached for his brandy-soda and hoisted it to his mouth and drank punishingly.

Fortunately, Konrad was just coming.

"Same again, Konnie!"

Susan had never thought to see August Hugo Blick so far gone.

"The lad gets here over the weekend and we'll move him in then," Emma said efficiently. "Just you leave it to Emma and Sid Wilmer. We'll enforce a certain curfew and sensible rules. *And*," she pledged, "we'll put him to work right away on his next book—that'll use up his energy as much as any good sedative. He won't have piss or vinegar for any more adventures, you can count on that. We'll *whip* him into shape, ducks! Such talent must not be squandered. Ain't I right, AHB? *AHB?*"

What! August dropping off to sleep?

"August!"

"What? Yes ... yes."

"Another drink, Sue?" Emma asked her.

"No, thanks no, Emma. Must be off." Susan got up quickly. Now, came the hard part. "August, good-bye. Thanks for everything, across the years. I'm grateful. . . ."

And so should he be. Susan had probably treated him a good deal better than Emma was going to.

"Susan, my dear . . ."

"Don't get up."

Were those tears in the bleary eyes? Perhaps senility had also come to live with August Hugo Blick.

Susan stooped and kissed his cheek.

And before he could say anything that she would be bound to answer, Susan left the room, Emma following close behind. When Susan turned to say good-bye, Emma was waiting.

"Take care, ducks." Emma even kissed Susan's right cheek. "I think you got a good price for the flat. Considering it was on the market for a million and a half."

"Yes, quite a good price, thank you. I'll have the agent get in touch."

Emma guffawed, like her frontier self, and slapped Susan briskly on the back.

"My feeling is you deserve the extra million, Sue. You earned it, the old-fashioned way."

27

Susan still felt it, the sting of Emma Bristals's parting shot, even into the next day when she left the Park Avenue place for the last time and headed downtown.

Ms. O'Rourke, Meriam, her daily helper, had packed all the clothes and labeled the boxes; Susan had decided which bits of furniture, mainly the antique pieces, she'd take with her to the new flat, which were to be stored, and which given away. It was not a bad thing to have a periodic housecleaning—of possessions, of people. It might have seemed insensitive, but Susan was able to do it with no regret, not a wayward tear, simply pick up her pocketbook and leave.

That night, after dinner with Jack Godfrey, she'd be starting life anew on Fifth Avenue, not bad when you came to think about it.

Jack would be up from Washington that morning for the most crucial discussions since they'd started *Hindsight;* times, they were a'changing, Jack said, Guy Bristals or no Guy Bristals.

Emma's last words made her wince, but Emma had a

certain point: Susan *had* earned the profit she'd make on the apartment. It had been work; and it had been play, if you remembered the trips down to Wade's Reef. Eighty percent play and twenty percent work? Fifty-fifty? In retrospect, she didn't think Emma had intended the comment to be really mean; more of a woman-to-woman aside. Emma would know; she wasn't exactly a peaches-and-cream sort of doll herself.

Out of the cab in front of the NAN building, Susan paid, throwing in a five-dollar tip. Thus, declare it her lucky day! Why not? He'd heard from Harry late the night before. She was about to make over a million dollars, reason to talk to her accountant, and agent, Morty Morton, another good reason to forget about Greenswards if it came to a shoving match with Bristals.

Ten A.M.

No rush to get inside. Susan strolled through the five-acre atrium that made the NAN building such a New York landmark. It was laid out like a park, stuffed with greenery, boasted a minor zoo. Exaggerating, people said the place was big enough to land a 747. The whole vast ecology-dome had its own temperate climate, favoring such northern foliage as elms and maples whose leaves fluttered in a man-made summer breeze, two rose gardens, and banks of flowering bushes. Susan passed the Café de la Midtown, shops, the entrance to Hotel-Hotel New York-New York, three hundred rooms on the first five floors above the atrium, thinking she was going to miss all this and who wouldn't?

She laid her *New York Times* on the lip of one of the flower boxes and sat for a moment to watch the rushing, onrushing, mindless tide of people, businessmen, businesswomen, office workers, gawkers, tourists, assorted maniacs. Was she going to miss all this?

Maybe it was not going to be such a grand day after all.

Collecting the newspaper, Susan proceeded, more seriously, waved good-morning to the security man she'd known to greet for the past three or four years, and entered the south elevator bank.

Susan pushed twenty-two, for the executive floor.

All was quiet, deceptively quiet, as the man said. Of course, twenty-two was the holiest of floors; one more stop exposed you to the news operation and twenty-four hours of bedlam per day. Twenty-two was as whispery-silent as a church, as Saint Pat's, a few blocks south. Naturally, the silence itself would heighten one's sense of foreboding, of approaching or impending doom. Do or die! Man the barricades! Fire when ready, Mr. Fineman!

Fineman was in a horrible state. He was feeling Bristals's heat not only as it concerned *Hindsight,* but elsewhere within the NAN news division. The day before, back from his usual lunch at the University Club, Fineman had been exhibiting un-Fineman-like symptoms of nihilism and abandon. According to his number one secretary, Maybelle, and who more anxious in times of crisis than Maybelle, Fineman had darted into his office and swept everything off the desk and into the wastepaper basket, babbling: Have a Nice Day! Drunk? No, far from it, cold sober. Indeed, Fineman had always been reliable that way, a winner of the Sobriety Medal year after year. Susan had found him there at three-thirty talking to himself and laughing very loudly about nothing.

Nothing! And wasn't that funny?

Whatever happened, they had to go forward, press on, as if there were no Bristals. Assignments must be penciled-in and prepped and produced: the piece on Atlantic City; interviews on the proposition of statehood for the District of Columbia; a Florida-Iran-contra-dope story. The editing was still to be done on Susan's oil story, and last arrangements made for her trip to Canada and then to Europe re: the European community of ninety-two, and Moscow for Gorby. . .

Arthur! Just to mention a few!

What *was* Bristals's plan, Fineman kept asking. *Was* there a plan?

A notorious bottom-liner, first indications were that Bristals was going to go heavier on sports, movie reruns and game shows. There were fifteen rumors around that Bristals was going to demand massive budget cuts in the news department— and didn't the Limey *schmuck* realize that news was the cheapest form of entertainment to produce? Yes, and more: Bristals London Group didn't believe in the star system.

And maybe, Fineman just might allow, Bristals had a point there; take a look at Jack Godfrey, the star system in person.

For more formal functions such as answering mail, Susan had a fairly sizable cubicle within the deeply carpeted *Hindsight* suite and another upstairs within sight and sound of the newsroom. Susan always said she preferred twenty-three; she was, after all, one of the troops.

"May. . .hi."

"Hello, Sue."

Fineman's secretary was acting very solemn. Susan made herself a cup of coffee, waiting, but Maybelle didn't give.

"Well, what's up, May? Is Arthur inside?"

"He doesn't want to be disturbed."

"May, the place is like a morgue."

"Maybe it is a morgue."

"We are meeting with His Mightiness?"

"At eleven-thirty."

"It's a quarter of. I guess I'll go inside and have a nap."

"You had a call, Sue."

"Oh. . ." Now she tells me. "Let's see."

May handed her a telephone-message slip.

It read, Teller called.

"He's up early, it's not even eight A.M. in California."

"Anybody I know?"

"No, you don't know him."

Casting May a smile-frown, Susan went on into her office, leaving the door open, and sat down, swiveling the desk chair. Her window was a little dirty, but it looked south, toward the needly Chrysler Building, the Empire State and, faraway in the morning haze, the twinned World Trade Center. Nothing much of interest had happened to the New York skyline in the last few years, people said. True? Was this a tipoff to a city in decline? Of a city and country going broke? But why build to suit the tastes of Ishira Guchi and All-Nippon Prosperoso Limited who'd probably own the whole place within a few more years? Twenty-first century architecture? Put in all that work. . .and Wham! It'd be sold off to the Japanese, just like Big Sea, on a smaller scale.

The Medicis of Florence. The Ishira Guchis of Osaka and Tokyo.

Still, as the man said, good, hard work was its own justification.

Perhaps inventive America would figure a way to get all the money back.

As a matter of fact, this precise topic was the basis for an impending story. Question: What happens to the rest of the world if the American consumer stops consuming?

* * *

Jack Godfrey was leaning against her door.

"Are you in pain, sweetheart?"

He flashed his white teeth, uncrossed his arms and walked to her desk. His thinning sandy hair was brushed back perfectly, not a strand out of place. Everything about him was neatly pressed and crisp. Susan, as usual, was stunned and envious of his even tan.

"Jack! Here you are!"

Though she hadn't asked how he was, the answer came anyway, "Terrific," and he backed away for a second to slam the door. "Come to me, my beauty!"

Jack held out his arms. Susan jumped up and hugged him, kissed him warmly, very emotionally, on both cheeks, then the lips. He tightened his arms and grinned, making a pleased sound.

The kiss made her remember Harry who had called again and that she must tell Jack about Harry.

"How was California . . . again?" Jack asked.

"Eventful, to say the least."

"Jasper Gates getting offed," he murmured, sympathetically, "and right before your eyes, something else! That piece of film was *fantastic*, Suse."

"I know." Yes, Susan thought, what about that? Where was her bonus? No, those days were gone forever. "Sit, Jack. Take a seat on my casting couch."

Careful of his trouser creases, Jack let himself down in the corduroy-covered cushions, dung-brown and white striped to go with her pictures, desert shots, seaweed studies, driftwood portraits. There was a tall, dead cactus stuck in a pot of sand in the corner. He ran his hand across the fabric.

"We made it once on this couch, remember?"

"I had it recovered."

He didn't hear, instead said absently, "I've got something to tell you, Suse."

"If it's bad, I don't want to hear it, Jack."

"It's not bad. At least, *I* don't think it's bad. I . . . well, as we know, Bristals is on my case. Right?" If Jack cared, he didn't show it. "Anyway, look, Suse, I'm not hanging around for it. I'm making my best deal and getting out of here."

"Without a fight?" she cried. "I figured we'd at least make it tough on him."

"It's not worth the trouble. He's not either."

"I've already served him notice that if you go, I go too!"

"I don't want that, Suse! I'm going anyway, no matter what." Jack smiled at her, a bit shyly for Jack Godfrey, slyly too, which was more like him. "The thing is, sweetheart, I better tell you straight-out and I don't want you to weep and wail. Your ole pal is getting married. Her name is Lily Tiger, like tiger-lily spelled backwards. I'm retiring, Suse, and the hell with it!"

"Retiring? You wouldn't dare!"

"Yep, to Palm Beach."

"*Palm Beach!* Palm Beach, Florida? The graveyard of lost hulks?"

"Now, Suse," Jack cautioned, very happily, it seemed, "you know there're golf courses galore down there and you know I'm a golfer. I could've been a champ if I'd stuck to it instead of getting into goddamn broadcasting."

"Jack . . . Jack . . ."

"I know, I know, it's hard, sweetheart, but so the world turns."

"I'm jealous, Jack, very jealous."

"You're going to meet her tonight. You'll like her. She's smart and she's very . . . she owns a rather large house down there."

"She's rich."

"She's reasonably well-off, yes."

"Jack . . . sleek pussycat, you got the canary! Don't tell me—she doesn't want you to work anymore."

"She wants to play lots of golf and I can't see anything wrong with that." Jack leaned forward. "I'll miss *you*, but little else, Suse."

"Jack . . ."

Susan's vision blurred. She was on the verge of telling him about Harry, but something made her stop. Bad luck, she thought, it might be bad luck to talk about it. Don't count your chickens.

"What're you going to tell *me*, Suse?"

"I'll tell you later."

Eyes intent, very honest, he said, "I feel like a kind of punk, running out on you and Artie."

"Jack. Don't be silly."

They went in for Arthur Fineman at eleven-fifteen, in plenty of time to get down the long corridor to the former Simon Hayford boardroom where Bristals had been operating since coming on the scene, any normal-sized office not being large enough for his overweight ego.

Fineman looked worse than he had the day before, ashen-faced, drawn, very jumpy. His suffering was beyond anything Susan was willing to accept, certainly beyond anything Jack could feel. Such betrayal, and the consequent invasion of the forces of sleaze was too much for the critically attuned Fineman intellect to bear.

Nevertheless, Jack asked the usual, opening question: "So, what's new, Arthur?"

"What do you think?" Fineman mumbled the ritual reply as if his fire had been put out. "The same old shit, except deeper."

"Come on, Arthur, lighten up," Godfrey said. "They're not going to line us up against the wall as far as I know."

"No? Might as well—" Fineman coughed violently, holding his chest, miserably enough to make Susan and Jack exchange looks. "We know this London *prick* got the board to make him interim CEO, the reason being they couldn't outvote him and rather than fight, they joined. Simon is gone, out on his ass, as you know. And we're twisting in the wind." He shrugged. "You know the story."

"So what?" Jack demanded. "What the hell do you care, Artie? You can walk out of here to any of the networks. Just like Suse!"

Fineman grimaced.

"She's promised to CBS. Me? I'll wind up in some piss-assed station in central Arkansas."

"Don't be ridiculous!"

"Well, I am. I'm gonna be entirely ridiculous until this is done with. I intend to exhibit classic symptoms."

Roughly, tenderly, Jack yanked Fineman to his feet.

"I've got something to tell you, buddy-boy. You don't have to worry about going to bat for me. I told Suse already. I'm pulling out. I'll have my handshake, please, and I'm on my way."

Fineman's eyes narrowed, then widened.

"What're you, crazy?" he screamed. "Quitter! You're doing this to torture me."

"Nope," Jack said. "Look, Bristals is going to be gunning for me. I tell him to shove it and that takes the heat off you guys. He'll have drawn his blood. Sated. Quiet. He'll go back to sleep."

"You son of a bitch! You *cannot* be serious!"

"Artie, I'm gone. I'm getting married—"

"Married? Again?"

"Yes. In love again. Can't help it. Romantic fool."

Outraged, insulted, Fineman turned away and kicked at his desk. It was abundantly scarred and marked, as one could imagine.

"Goddamn you, Godfrey! He'll shitcan the show for sure."

"No, no, Artie! Jesus, where *is* your strategic mind? That's what'll save the show! He'd be stupid to cancel it. Anyway, he's on record he wants Susan Channing to go it alone." Fineman sat down again, shaking his head, rubbing his belly, feeling his pulse. "Arthur, he's determined to get me because of what I said about his shitty paper." Jack shrugged, so joyfully, so logically. "It's a matter of principle. *His* principle. I'm making it easy for him. Suse doesn't have to throw an ultimatum. You can reorganize the show. Look like a hero."

"Wrong, Jack!" Fineman groaned. "I've been listening to the tom-toms. He's putting Channing on the *Evening News*."

"Like hell he is!"

Fineman turned on her angrily, "No? Ask him yourself."

He got up again, anger and bitterness having revived him to some degree, adrenalin supplying the rest of it. Shoulders swinging belligerently, head slung down like a bulldog's, Arthur Fineman strode forth, out of the office and into the long corridor.

Simon Hayford's former conference room was located in the corner, wall-to-wall windows looking south and east. In the morning, the blinds had to be drawn against the sun.

Facing in, toward the door, Sir Guy Bristals was seated behind a large, square, leather-covered table, designed in centuries past to be a partners' desk: two-sided, with room for chair and legs under each side. Thus had sat loving, trusting partners, facing each other: Partner One couldn't pick his nose or scratch his ass without Partner Two seeing.

Bristals, of course, was alone at the desk. He looked up and smiled at them in that purse-mouthed smirky way he had, gushing words, continually rewetting pink lips with his pointed, probing tongue.

"Aha, aha! And here we are, my *star turn*. Please do sit."

Some managerial genius had arranged three straight-backed chairs in a row facing the desk, windows, and plump baronet. Fineman took the right-hand chair, Godfrey the left; that put

Susan in the middle. As they settled, Sir Guy regarded them benevolently, with amusement, patience, sprinkle of suspicion, dash of disapproval, just like the jolly and loving parent he might aspire to be.

"So then," he finally said with a sigh, and predictably, "what *are* we to do with *Hindsight*?"

Susan expected Fineman to start firing, but he didn't. He sat tensely, silently perspiring, his hands white-knuckled on his knees, probably the smartest response to a man like Bristals. Let the viper lead.

"Susan..." Bristals lipped her name. "So nice to see you again."

She didn't say anything either, merely nodded. Maybe, just maybe, they could outplay him. Doubtful, of course: Sir Guy held the cards. As if in no hurry, he tacked, looked away, running his hand along the edge of the desk.

"I had this beauty flown in from London. Do you like it?"

"It's a partners' desk," Susan said.

"Quite so."

Blithely, Godfrey murmured, "But you don't have a partner to share it with, Sir Guy."

What a subtle, damaging jab! Bristals's eyes came up, blinded. He didn't know what to say. What new and terrible thing was Jack Godfrey implying? That nobody trusted Bristals enough to be his partner; or that Sir Guy Bristals was so peculiar he couldn't work with a partner? Or what? He launched a truly malignant look at Godfrey. His eyeballs must weigh a ton apiece; you wondered the sockets were strong enough to contain them.

"For the moment, no," he said icily. "For the moment, Sir Guy Bristals sails alone, Mr. Godfrey...May I call you Jack?"

"Certainly."

"Well, *Jack*...I'm here to tell you..." He interrupted himself. "Aha, aha!" My noontime libation, excuse me a moment."

Perhaps Susan should not have been shocked or surprised to see Jasper Gates's man, Mr. Dudley, but she was. Carrying a laden silver tray, Dudley slipped into the room. Upon the tray, of course, was a split of champagne, crystal flute, and tin of caviar, with toast and the usual furnishings.

A spiteful smile passed Bristals's face.

"I'd offer you something to drink as well..." He shook

his head at Mr. Dudley. "... but we shan't be here that long. I've a luncheon date at 'Twenty-one' with the president of ... oh, no matter!"

"Mr. Dudley!" Susan couldn't resist. "How nice to see you."

"Miss Channing."

Dudley gave nothing away. What else was new? He was a mercenary, prepared to follow any master if the price was right.

"Yes," Bristals confirmed, "I persuaded Dudley to come *butle* for me. After all ..." He shrugged, then went on busily, "I'm having a kitchen and dining room built in the adjoining offices there." He pointed at the north wall of the room. "One can direct a whole editorial conference from behind a bowl of soup. Time-saving device, *what!*" Bristals lifted his champagne to them. "Cheers!"

They were not to be offered any caviar either. Ignoring them, much to Jack's amusement—and Bristals should have seen his eyes—Sir Guy chose a piece of toast, piled it with black seed, and messily squeezed a quarter of lemon. His fat lips accepted the gift and he munched contentedly, his hot eyes flicking, from Fineman to Susan to Godfrey and then back, as if he were deciding not so much about *Hindsight* as whether or not *they* would be allowed to live.

Pressing a white napkin against the lips, Bristals cleared his mouth with more champagne, and then, at long last, returned to what he had been preparing to say to Jack Godfrey.

"Yes, Jack. I was about to tell you that, unfortunately ..."

Bristals's eyes shone. He was going to enjoy this. No, he wasn't, for Jack was about to finesse him.

"Before you go on, Sir Guy," Jack interrupted elegantly, his timing, as always, perfect, "I want to tell you. I'll be leaving the network. Mind is made up. Don't try to talk me out of it. Leave as soon as possible. My contractual obligation ends with the end of this month. Enormous amount of unused vacation time." He held up his arm and looked at his watch. "Be gone *at five o'clock tonight* ..."

Bristals butted the desk with his belly, forgetting champagne and all.

"Just one moment! By whose leave ..." Furiously, Bristals shook his finger at Arthur Fineman. "And the program? where does this leave *Hindsight?*"

"In the shit," Fineman muttered, holding his stomach.

Sir Guy also looked ill. How dare Jack Godfrey quit just as he was about to fire him? Bristals's cheeks puffed and blew, like a whale.

"Well! This is certainly a fine show of loyalty! I did not expect *this* when I bought into NAN. And now what do I hear? That the finest team in American television is breaking up! My God, my God!"

Enjoying it immensely, Jack sang, "Now, now, Sir Guy, Susan can handle *Hindsight* on her own and, if necessary, you can always find a replacement for me. Dime a dozen!"

"Jack!" Susan cried, "without you, I'm *zilch*. I may as well cash in too."

In this also there was an element of great satisfaction.

Bristals slapped the desk with the flat of his hand.

"You will do no such thing!"

"I'm tired too . . . and I'm fed up with all the intrigue."

"Intrigue? *What intrigue?*" Bristals exploded with insult. "No such thing! You impugn my management style!" He was livid, face red, jowls shaking; again he banged the desk with his palm, then grabbed it, shaking it with pain. "You people should not *ever* forget who I am!" He pushed back his chair, tipping it over behind him. On his feet, he braced his shoulders and thrust out his chest. "I am one of *Her Majesty's* faithful servants, a knight of the realm, not merely some jumped-up Fleet Street upstart."

Bitingly, Susan said, "Maybe you're not receiving good intelligence, Guy. The news department is a shambles."

"What! What?" Bristals turned on Fineman again. "You reported no such thing."

"I did. You weren't listening."

"Dastardly!" Bristals put his hand to his forehead. "And what will it be with all the talent quitting, Fineman? All right, all right," he mumbled, "one thing at a time. What I was about to say to you, Jack, is that in light of Bristals London Group's new venture in the Orient, we will need a Pacific Rim spokesman and who better than you, silver-tongued Cato."

"Cato?"

"A Latin spellbinder!"

Jack knew better. He shook his head insincerely.

"Wonderful of you to think of me but I'm afraid not."

"But man, *why*?" Bristals marched out from behind his desk. "You cannot merely turn your back and walk away."

Jack looked at his watch again and stood up. He was taller, slimmer, and stronger than Bristals.

"I'm through, in just a little over five hours."

It was quite impressive to consider the things Jack might have said and didn't. He was a gentleman, after all. Bristals must have realized Jack was being extra nice and that he shouldn't do or say anything to provoke him. Angrily, he turned on his heel, returned to his desk, righted the chair and sat down.

"This meeting is concluded!" he said. "We will talk of this later, Mr. Fineman. And *we* have things to discuss as well, Susan."

Susan endeavored a tight little nod.

Then they were outside again, heading back down the hall, and Artie Fineman looked at Jack Godfrey solemnly.

"Okay, Jack, you did it. And how are you going to get out of it this time?"

"I *am* leaving, Artie, get it through your head."

"You're not, you cannot be. How could you? You'll change your mind. *Schmuck!*"

Hunched over, more miserable than before, and there was no reason for that, Fineman stopped in front of Maybelle's desk.

"Anybody call?"

"Your barber."

"That's a big help," Fineman yapped. Bitterly, he looked at Jack. "Is she that rich?"

"She doesn't have to work for a living, Artie."

"That's disgusting."

Fineman offered the assessment as Maybelle informed Susan that that friend of hers, Teller, had called again.

Susan began to think about going in and calling Harry back, which was the moment Fineman chose to begin making alarming noises.

With a sudden intake of air, he staggered to the side and, without shame, began to collapse. His eyes faded shut and he gasped, grabbed at his upper left arm and chest.

Jack caught him before he hit the floor.

"Oh, goddammit! I knew it. May..."

Maybelle was already picking up the phone.

"Help me a little, Suse," Jack grunted. "Get him inside."

Jack slung Fineman's right arm over his shoulder and,

holding him around the waist, half dragged, half carried him back inside his office.

"Shut the door, Suse."

Jack let Arthur down on the couch, heisted his legs up, and, as Fineman was breathing very hoarsely, gobbling for air and panting, quickly loosened his tie and collar.

"Put something under his feet, Suse. Take his shoes off. Is there a blanket anywhere around this place? Suse, see if you can find a blanket."

Once upon a time, as Susan remembered, there had been a rough-wool serape-type blanket in a closet in Arthur's executive washroom. It was still there. Jack wrapped Arthur in the rough thing as Maybelle stuck her head in the door. Help was on the way. There were big tears of fright in Maybelle's eyes; this was even worse than Sir Guy Bristals's threat to all that was holy.

"Take it easy now, Artie . . ."

Hearing Jack, the Fineman eyes reopened behind his shiny spectacles. But he did not look very frisky.

"Arthur, do not move a muscle. Are you comfortable?"

Fineman whispered, "Who the fuck are *you*, Doctor Kildare?"

"Ah, good, Artie, good!"

Jack looked up at Susan. His face was so dismal, so tragic, like this was the end of the world or at least of civilization as they knew it. Fineman had had a slight heart attack—it happened every day. Yes, okay, it didn't happen every day. The three of them went back a long way, the alliance of Jack and Artie a lot further.

"I'm an expert at this, Artie," Jack said. "It's always happening on the golf course."

Especially in Florida, he might have said.

Godfrey crouched there with Fineman's hand in his until the paramedics rushed in with their folded stretcher and toolbox of medicine and needles. Fineman was sedated and ready to roll in about thirty seconds. Maybelle jotted down the details of where he'd be taken and they tried to think who should be told. Didn't he have a wife? No, he was married to NAN.

"Please," Maybelle said, "I'll go along, is that all right?"

Well, okay, the medics thought, since there wasn't anybody else.

Then, bad luck, just as they were rolling Fineman into

the elevator, Sir Guy Bristals, wearing a black bowler hat, rounded the corner into the reception area. He skidded to a stop.

"What's happening here?"

Harshly, angrily, bitterly, the only way she could just then, Susan replied, "Arthur has had a . . . an attack."

Bristals eyes clouded with annoyance.

"*Serious?*"

Artie stared up at him owlishly, far out of it, but Jack frowned at Bristals distastefully. It was the only time his real feelings had surfaced that morning.

"No."

"*God, what a bore!* Now, what are we to do?" Bristals hesitated, then pulled himself together. "Well, no matter! I'm off to luncheon!"

Just then, Susan thought, might have been a good time for Jack to deck the self-absorbed baronet. As it was, Jack's look should've burned the chalk-stripes right off Bristals's suit. But the elevator arrived and the medics pushed Arthur Fineman aboard. Maybelle was right behind and Jack moved to join them.

"C'mon, Suse."

This was definitely not an invitation to Bristals. He hung back anyway, waiting for the next car, not wanting to be with them. The door whooshed across his pout. He would be thinking they didn't like him. And he would be right.

Through the indifferent lunchtime crowd, the medics wheeled Arthur Fineman. People looked away, at the phony atrium sky, into the shops; such sights embarrassed people, as did muggings, subway suicides, and murders. Onto the sidewalk and to the waiting ambulance, the medics maneuvered their cargo and efficiently loaded it. Maybelle climbed in behind.

"Should we?"

"No, Suse, let May, it'll give her something to do. She's always loved the four-eyed madman. Hey, May! We'll . . . uh . . . we'll get a drink and see you when you get back. Take care of him?"

"Okay, Jack."

Jack squeezed Susan's arm. They readied Fineman for the trip. One of the medics got in the back with Maybelle.

"Suse, look," Jack muttered.

Sir Guy Bristals had given himself an extra few minutes in

order to avoid them. Only now did he emerge from the building and, obviously having seen the ambulance, cut obliquely toward the uptown corner. Bowler crushed down tightly on his round head, he progressed in a tipped-forward fashion, as if bucking a strong wind.

"On his way to 'Twenty-One' or 'Chico Paley's.'" Jack chuckled. "Want to follow the fatman?"

"God, no!"

The back door of the ambulance slammed. The driver revved the engine and the vehicle moved forward.

Bristals had reached the corner.

Head down, eyes on the sidewalk, he ploughed to the curb, heeding nobody, immune to good manners.

Then, what happened?

The rendezvous might have been plotted, rehearsed, timed.

Susan and Jack watched, bemused, mesmerized, as the grand accident unfolded.

They *knew* what was coming, perhaps could have stopped it, perhaps not. No, they could not have intervened. Fate, once again, was at her indiscriminate best.

As the ambulance bearing Fineman's stress-wracked body picked up speed to take advantage of the green light at the corner, just then, at that very specific needlepoint of time, Sir Guy Bristals made the terrible mistake committed by a few, not many, but more than several careless Britishers, not least of whom had been Winston Churchill many years before.

Sir Guy, forgetting for that instant that he was not in London, city of backward-flowing traffic, looked in the wrong direction and stepped off the curb, directly in front of the accelerating ambulance.

It was an impressive, if heart-thumping, -stopping, sight. The hefty Brit went spinning, arms and legs doing unseemly semaphors, black bowler jarred loose by the force of the collision and falling, tumbling, rolling into the gutter.

"For... I'll ... son of a ... holy..."

Jack tried to get out an appropriate epithet. Nothing was big enough for the occasion.

"Sue!"

"Yes."

"Pretend you didn't see."

* * *

Lunch at Orsini's, which had been billed by Jack as his farewell blast, turned out more of a wake, in that sense long and liquid. Jack's feeling was that they should linger long enough for the dust, and Sir Guy Bristals, to settle.

Finally, when they summoned courage to return to the office, half-convinced Bristals would be at the elevator door waiting, having bounced back up to twenty-two, like the two innocents, See-Nothing and Hear-Nothing, Maybelle was very much involved with the telephone and they realized it was very serious indeed. Maybelle looked at the ceiling and heaven, and managed a limp smile which could only mean that Arthur Fineman was okay.

But not Sir Guy Bristals.

It was awful, disgusting, revolting, to think in terms of poetic justice, of chickens-come-home-to-roost. But Jack had always been good at that; he was ungenerous and vengeful, and proud of it, he claimed, leaving it to Susan to be consumed by guilt for getting a secret charge out of a man being hit by a truck. A man? The *thing* tossed off the horns of the ambulance had looked more like a ragdoll. And, what the hell, as Jack had assured her over his third scotch, Bristals was blubbery enough to bounce off most hard objects. If they hadn't known better, they could even have been convinced he had made a one-point landing on his bowler.

Hey, don't worry! Nothing ever happens to the bad guys. It's the good that . . . never mind.

"Suse, did you hear that?"

Yes.

"Yes, yes, Mr. Dwyer," Maybelle was babbling, "I realize Sir Guy Bristals stood you up. I'm authorized to tell you that Sir Guy didn't make lunch *because he's dead*!"

Susan looked at Jack. Jack looked at Susan. No joke. Susan sat down on the couch, feeling sick, the vodka burning her stomach.

"I don't believe it! Do you, Suse?"

Behind Jack's gentlemanly exterior lived a barbarian, satisfied only by blood comeuppance.

"Mr. Dwyer," Maybelle was bleating, "I don't know if Sir Guy was carrying documents with him. No, I don't know if he had a contract in his pocket. . . ."

Susan lifted her head. She looked at Jack and Jack looked at her, thinking the same thing: Dwyer? Of the opposition?

"Mr. Dwyer," Maybelle said, "I've been authorized to

say. . ." She lifted a piece of paper and read from it. ". . . that
a special board of directors meeting has been called. Yes, we
are in touch with Simon Hayford. Yes, Mr. Dwyer, this can
be used in your evening newscast. Yes . . . we're very sorry
too about lunch."

Susan laughed bitterly. Was she hearing right? Sir Guy
Bristals regrets he didn't make lunch on account of he's dead.

Jack said, "The bastard was going to hire Dwyer, Suse. He
was lying. Dwyer was going to take my place."

"You don't know, Jack."

"What do *you* think?"

"Anarchy," she murmured, remembering Jasper Gates.

Once off the phone, Maybelle spun around. She was dazed,
without her prepared statement well nigh speechless.

"We hit him," she said. "He stepped out in front of the
ambulance. The boys said he never knew what happened.
I . . . they plucked him up and put him in beside Art . . . Mr.
Fineman. And I had to get up front and away we went, sirens
blasting."

"Did we hear sirens?"

"Did we? No, Jack, we didn't hear sirens."

"May? Goddamn it! How's Artie?"

She blushed happily.

"Oh . . . fine, Jack. They let me see him before I left. He
was singing to himself . . . humming. I never heard him sing
before."

"Maybe guardian angels, May."

"It was mild . . . a warning shot, the doctor said."

Shuddering, whispering, Susan asked, "And now?"

Jack tried for a measure of gravity. After all, this was a
serious situation.

"May, did you say Simon's been contacted?"

Maybelle nodded happily. Crisis, crisis, but she loved it.
And God knows what sweet nothings Fineman had whispered
on his way to the hospital.

"Cecily Zimmerman . . ." This was Simon Hayford's long-
time secretary, by Bristals's surprise demise also rescued from
the skids. ". . . Cecily has been command-posting for the last
hour. Cecily just caught him—Mr. Hayford was leaving in the
morning on his round-the-world yacht trip. They were at the
dock, loading supplies."

Jack nodded admiringly.

"Did you ever notice, Suse? They get the ax and the next

minute they're doing what they always wanted to do and never had the time to do—that is, sail around the world with a couple of trusted buddies, or learn ancient Greek and Mandarin. Simon must be feeling like Lazarus out of his grave.''

''I don't think he had any comment,'' Maybelle said.

Susan knew what Jack was thinking and it was going to depress everybody very much if he tried to make the case that in a certain tangential way Arthur Fineman was responsible for Sir Guy's death. If Arthur hadn't had his attack, Jack would argue, there'd have been no ambulance in that exact spot at that precise time. Or? On the other hand, if Sir Guy's good-bye had been predestined, he'd have been struck down by one of the other deadly instruments at Fate's disposal.

How poetic. How perfect in a generally imperfect world.

Once more, fortunately, Maybelle was in a position to intercept nauseating speculation.

''That friend of yours called again.''

''Harry Teller? That's the third call, May!''

''Or fourth.''

28

Little knowing, Harry would be wondering. He'd be thinking, well, wasn't she ever going to call back, little knowing what had happened, and back to square one with Miss Susie.

"I've got to go make that phone call, Jack."

"I'm on my way, Suse."

O callous warrior, he'd already forgotten about Sir Guy Bristals.

"Lily was going to Bergdorf's and Tiffany's. To buy me some cufflinks. God knows why. Suse? About seven? At the hotel? Do you mind? We'll go on from there?"

All confused, Susan stood with him in front of Maybelle's desk, wishing him gone, wanting him to stay. She was going to miss Jack, practically as much as she'd miss Harry if it was in the cards she wouldn't ever see him again. Why *was* he calling? To tell her it was over between them? No, he wouldn't keep calling if that's what he wanted to say. Nevertheless, she was almost afraid to go in and make the call. What if she left with Jack, pretended she'd never gotten the message, waited for a better day?

434

In a way, it was unfair. Jack had asked her more than once, playfully, to marry him and she'd just laughed. And maybe it had not been a laughing matter. The proof of that was Jack getting married to a woman called Lily Tiger.

"I'm going to miss you, Jack."

"Me too, Suse. And Maybelle, gonna miss you too." Already swollen, Maybelle's lips trembled. "I'm gonna go see Artie tomorrow. Will they let me in?"

"Call ahead. And no flowers. Art . . . Mr. Fineman detests flowers."

"What an unsentimental and hardhearted swine he is."

With that, Jack Godfrey exited, slipped away, so smoothly, so sleekly, to the elevators, center stage.

Susan trudged the fifty yards of quicksand carpet to her office, banged open the door, and stepped inside.

Somebody was sitting in her chair, chair turned, back and head silhouetted against the afternoon sky. She'd have recognized him at twice the distance; she's have smelled him, sensed his presence.

This man sitting in her chair was Harry Teller. He swiveled the chair around and faced her.

"Hello, Miss Susie."

But it would seem he had just called from California.

"Harry, you're here."

"Yes, I am."

Naturally, he was grinning at her and Susan was trying to catch her breath, feeling awkward and stupid and girlish and tongue-tied and embarrassed.

"You called four times. I was just coming to . . ."

"I did call. But not from California."

"You were here all the time." His teeth were as white as Jack's, but he didn't attend to his tan. "What're you doing here, Harry?"

"Well, Susan, I came to see you and, like I said, everybody's got to be someplace. I thought I'd better get on a plane and get down here. I figured . . ."

"Yes, Harry?"

Finally, she was able to move forward. Susan approached, facing him, spreading her fingers in octaves across the edge of the desk.

"Well, you knew I was coming to New York."

"I didn't know when."

"Too soon?"

"Oh, no!"

"I thought you might like to see me, Susie."

"I would."

Harry stared at her, sort of implacably, from *her* chair, across *her* desk. He was sitting very erectly, his eyes fixed on her intently, intensely.

"I've missed you, Susie, a lot."

Susan marched her fingers across the desk, reaching one of his hands.

"Harry, I'm glad you're here."

Keep it simple, somebody had said, otherwise you'll just sound clumsy and childish and stupid. There must be a better way to say important things. Too bad she couldn't sing; she'd sing him something. Why didn't she simply announce that she loved him and see how he reacted? That seemed too easy.

"Did Maybelle tell you what happened?"

"Yes." He nodded grimly. "Quite a morning you've had. I'm sorry. I suppose I *should* say I'm sorry. I'm sorry about Fineman. I gather he's going to be okay."

"Jack's quitting. Maybelle told you?"

"No. Not good for your show, I guess."

"The show's finished."

"Trying times."

He stroked her knuckles.

"Harry, the desk is coming between us."

"Symbolism, Miss Susie . . ."

"Miss Susie?"

"Oh, sorry." He laughed softly. *"Susan . . ."*

"I don't care. You can call me Miss Susie if you want to. In fact, I sort of like it. So please do . . ."

"Symbolic of your career, Miss Susie. Will career be allowed to separate these two brave young people?"

"No! The answer is no, Harry!" This was the split second of choice, the crossroads. "Career will not separate these two brave, beautiful, brilliant young people! And what about *your* career, Harry?"

"My career? *The Corsair*? I'm out of it, Susie."

"What do you mean you're out of it?"

"I'm handing the paper over to Ralph, if he wants it."

"Ralph is not a journalist, Harry!"

"He doesn't have to be. All he's got to be is an ad salesman. He's got Ella Salmon, I told you about her, we'll give her twenty percent. Ella's the editor anyway, for all practical purposes. To hell with it, Susie," he said, "my mind is made up, my conscience is clear. I don't need it. You were right. I'm fed up with Rio Tinto and all the Tinto-ettes. Fighting country editor throws in his cards, disillusioned with hicktown America? *Believe it!*"

"You take my breath away. What're we going to do?"

Harry came around the desk then, finally, her desk, yes, part of the furniture of her ambition and success, and so what? He let go of her hand, taking her shoulders gently, kissing her cleanly on the cheek.

"What do you say we drop out for a while, Susie? Can you? What about your contract?"

"I'll break it. Let 'em sue." Such a daring move for Susan Channing who'd sacrificed everything for career. "Could we do it, Harry? Could we get away with it?"

Could she trust him?

"I don't see why not."

"What'll we do?"

"We'll go on a trip. Where do you want to go that you haven't been?"

"Iceland, I've never been to Iceland."

"Okay, we'll go to Iceland."

Susan kissed him back, on his dimpled chin, then the soft lips, for a second, thinking to herself a month, a couple of months, a year, what were they going to do, line her up against a wall and shoot her?"

Greenswards, she thought, no problem about that now.

"I've never been to Venice, Harry."

"Hard to believe you've never been to Venice, Miss Susie."

"And then? After that, what'll we do?"

"I dunno. After we finish doing that, whatever we do, we'll just go ahead and do something else . . . whatever it is."

"Kind of open-ended, Harry."

"We owe it to ourselves, Miss Susie. The world is a very open-ended kind of place and I'm an open-ended kind of guy."

"Okay then." She put her arms around him, thinking she did trust him, thinking she had no choice about trusting him and that, anyway, the time had come. "Why don't we do that, Harry, *whatever it is.* . . ."

"Right. And then later we'll do something else."

ABOUT THE AUTHOR

BARNEY LEASON is a former newspaper and magazine editor, and the author of such bestselling novels as RODEO DRIVE, PASSIONS, SCANDALS, NORTH RODEO DRIVE, and RICH AND RECKLESS. He lives with his wife, Jody Jacobs, author and former society columnist for the *Los Angeles Times,* in Mendocino, California.

Now there are two great ways to catch up with your favorite thrillers